DARK IMPERIUM
PLAGUE WAR

More Ultramarines from Black Library

• DARK IMPERIUM •
Guy Haley
Book 1: DARK IMPERIUM
Book 2: PLAGUE WAR

BLOOD OF IAX
A Primaris Space Marines novel
Robbie MacNiven

OF HONOUR AND IRON
A Space Marine Conquests novel
Ian St. Martin

BLADES OF DAMOCLES
A Space Marine Battles novel
Phil Kelly

THE PLAGUES OF ORATH
A Space Marine Battles novel
Steve Lyons, Cavan Scott & Graeme Lyon

DAMNOS
A Space Marine Battles novel
Nick Kyme

DAMOCLES
A Space Marine Battles novel
Phil Kelly, Guy Haley, Ben Counter & Josh Reynolds

ULTRAMARINES
A Legends of the Dark Millennium anthology
Various authors

• THE CHRONICLES OF URIEL VENTRIS •
A six-volume series of novels by
Graham McNeill

NIGHTBRINGER
WARRIORS OF ULTRAMAR
DEAD SKY, BLACK SUN
THE KILLING GROUND
COURAGE AND HONOUR
THE CHAPTER'S DUE

WARHAMMER 40,000

DARK IMPERIUM
PLAGUE WAR

GUY HALEY

BLACK LIBRARY

A BLACK LIBRARY PUBLICATION

First published in 2018.
This edition published in Great Britain in 2019 by
Black Library,
Games Workshop Ltd.,
Willow Road,
Nottingham, NG7 2WS, UK.

10 9 8 7 6 5 4 3 2 1

Produced by Games Workshop in Nottingham.
Cover illustration by Igor Sid.

Dark Imperium: Plague War © Copyright Games Workshop Limited 2018. Dark Imperium: Plague War, GW, Games Workshop, Black Library, The Horus Heresy, The Horus Heresy Eye logo, Space Marine, 40K, Warhammer, Warhammer 40,000, the 'Aquila' Double-headed Eagle logo, and all associated logos, illustrations, images, names, creatures, races, vehicles, locations, weapons, characters, and the distinctive likenesses thereof, are either ® or TM, and/or © Games Workshop Limited, variably registered around the world.
All Rights Reserved.

A CIP record for this book is available from the British Library.

ISBN 13: 978 1 78496 910 3

No part of this publication may be reproduced, stored in a retrieval system, or transmitted in any form or by any means, electronic, mechanical, photocopying, recording or otherwise, without the prior permission of the publishers.

This is a work of fiction. All the characters and events portrayed in this book are fictional, and any resemblance to real people or incidents is purely coincidental.

See Black Library on the internet at
blacklibrary.com

Find out more about Games Workshop
and the world of Warhammer 40,000 at
games-workshop.com

Printed and bound by CPI Group (UK) Ltd, Croydon, CR0 4YY

It is the 41st millennium. For more than a hundred centuries the Emperor has sat immobile on the Golden Throne of Earth. He is the Master of Mankind by the will of the gods, and master of a million worlds by the might of His inexhaustible armies. He is a rotting carcass writhing invisibly with power from the Dark Age of Technology. He is the Carrion Lord of the Imperium for whom a thousand souls are sacrificed every day, so that He may never truly die.

Yet even in His deathless state, the Emperor continues His eternal vigilance. Mighty battlefleets cross the daemon-infested miasma of the warp, the only route between distant stars, their way lit by the Astronomican, the psychic manifestation of the Emperor's will. Vast armies give battle in His name on uncounted worlds. Greatest amongst His soldiers are the Adeptus Astartes, the Space Marines, bioengineered super-warriors. Their comrades in arms are legion: the Astra Militarum and countless planetary defence forces, the ever-vigilant Inquisition and the tech-priests of the Adeptus Mechanicus to name only a few. But for all their multitudes, they are barely enough to hold off the ever-present threat from aliens, heretics, mutants – and worse.

To be a man in such times is to be one amongst untold billions. It is to live in the cruellest and most bloody regime imaginable. These are the tales of those times. Forget the power of technology and science, for so much has been forgotten, never to be re-learned. Forget the promise of progress and understanding, for in the grim dark future there is only war. There is no peace amongst the stars, only an eternity of carnage and slaughter, and the laughter of thirsting gods.

CHAPTER ONE

CHRONICUS NOVAE IMPERIA

Weak light bobbed through pitchy black, casting a pale round that grew and shrank upon polished blue marble quarried on a world long ago laid waste. The hum of a grav motor sawed at the quiet of the abandoned hall, though not loudly enough to banish the peace of ages that lay upon it. The lamp was dim as candlelight, and greatly obscured by the iron lantern framing it. The angles of the servo-skull that bore the lantern further cut the glow, but even in the feeble luminance the stone gleamed with flecks of gold. The floor awoke for brief moments at its caress, glinting with a nebula's richness, before the servo-skull moved on and the paving's glory was lost to the dark again.

The lonely figure of a man walked at the edge of the light, sometimes embraced by it completely, more often reduced to a collection of shadows and mellow highlights at its edge. The hood of his rough homespun robe was pulled over his head. Sandals woven of cord chased the light at a steady pace. The circle of light was small, but the echo of the man's footsteps revealed the space it traversed as vast. Less could be discerned about the man, were there anyone there to see him. He was a priest. Little else could be said besides that. It would certainly not be obvious to a casual observer he was militant-apostolic to the Lord Commander. He did not dress as men of his office ordinarily would, in brocade and jewels. He did not seem exalted. He certainly did not feel so. To himself, and to those poor souls he offered the succour of the Emperor's blessing, he was simply Mathieu.

Mathieu was a man of faith, and to him the Space Marines seemed faithless, ignorant of the true majesty of the Emperor's divinity, but the Mortuis Ad Monumentum had the air of sanctity nevertheless.

Mathieu liked it for that reason.

Beyond the slap of the priest's shoes and the whine of the skull, the silence in the Mortuis Ad Monumentum was so total, the sense of isolation so complete, that not even the background thrum of the giant engines pushing the *Macragge's Honour* through the warp intruded. The rest of the ship vibrated, sometimes violently, sometimes softly, the growl of the systems always there. Not where the priest walked. The stillness of the ancient hall would not allow it. Within its confines time itself held its breath.

Mathieu had spent his quieter days exploring the hall. Its most singular features were the statues thronging the margins. They were not just in ones or twos, effigies given space to be walked around and admired, nor were they ensconced in alcoves to decorate or commemorate. No, there were crowds of stone men, in places forty deep, all Adeptus Astartes in ancient marks of armour. It may be that they were placed with care once, but no longer, and further into the hall, the more jumbled their arrangements became. The hall had been breached in days gone by, and the statues destroyed. Untidy heaps of limbs were bulldozed carelessly aside and ugly patching marked wounds from ancient times.

The warriors remembered by the statues had died ten thousand years before Mathieu's birth. Perhaps they had even fallen in the Emperor's wars to create the Imperium itself. Such an incredible length of years, hard to comprehend, and yet now the being who had led these self-same dead men commanded the ship again.

It dizzied Mathieu that he served a son of the Emperor. He could not quite believe it, even after all that had happened, all that he had seen.

Mathieu stopped in the dark where a group of statues huddled together. White stone glowed grey in the gloom. He had the terrifying notion that they had come alive and gathered to block his path, a phalanx of ghosts angered by profanity. He put aside the thought. He ignored the cold hand of fear creeping up his back. He had come off course, nothing more. It was easy enough to get lost in a hall half a mile wide and almost as long.

His servo-skull bore a large HV upon its forehead. By the letter V alone he called it. He could not bring himself to refer to it by her name.

'V,' he said. His voice was pure and strong. It cut the shadows and frightened back the dark. Mathieu was an unimposing man, young, slight, but his voice was remarkable; a weapon greater than the worn laspistol he carried on his left hip, or the chainsword he bore into battle. Loud and commanding before his congregations, it seemed tiny in the face of the dead past, but like a silver bell chiming deep in winter-stilled woods, it was clear and bright and lovely.

V emitted a flat, static-laced melody of acknowledgement.

'Ascend five feet. Elevate lamp, pan left to right.'

The skull's motors pulsed. It rose up into the high voids of the monumentum. The light abandoned Mathieu, angling instead for the still figures surrounding him. Stone faces leapt from the dark, as if snatching the chance to be remembered, quickly drowning again in the black as V turned away. For a moment Mathieu's fear came back. He did not recognise where he was, until V's pale lamplight washed over a Space Marine captain of some unremembered era, the right arm held so proudly aloft broken off at the elbow. This warrior he recognised.

Mathieu breathed in relief. 'Descend to original height. Rotate lantern downwards to light my way. Proceed.'

V voiced its fractured compliance. There were pretensions to musicality in the signal, but the limited vox-unit was fifth hand at least, scavenged like all V's other fittings, and overuse had blunted its harmonies.

'Proceed to the hermitage, quickly now. My time for this duty is running out.'

V banked around and swept onwards. Mathieu picked up his pace to keep up.

The Adeptus Astartes pretended to disdain worship. It was well known among the Adeptus Ministorum that they did not regard the Emperor as a god. Mathieu had known this all through his calling. The truth had proved to be not so simple. On the ship there were many shrines, decorated lovingly with images of death, and containing the bones of heroes in reliquaries that rivalled those of the most lauded saint in their ostentation. The Ultramarines' cult was strong, though they did not worship. In chapels that denied religion their skull-masked priests protested loudly about the human nature of the Emperor and the primarchs while venerating them as gods in all but name. Their practice of honour, duty and obedience was conducted with a fanatical devotion.

There was an element of wilful blindness to their practices, thought Mathieu.

The way the Adeptus Astartes reacted to Roboute Guilliman bordered on awe. From the beginning Guilliman had warned Mathieu himself not to be worshipful, that he was not the son of a god. The priest had witnessed how irritated the primarch became with those who did not heed his words. And yet, these godless sons of his looked upon him, and they could barely hide their fervour.

Mathieu did as he had been told. He affected to see the man Guilliman wished to be, but his familiarity with the primarch was largely an act. Mathieu did revere the primarch, sincerely and deeply.

Previous militant-apostolics had carved themselves out a little realm in Guilliman's palace spire atop the giant battle-ship. The position came with appropriately luxurious quarters. Some time before Mathieu's tenure the largest room had been converted into a chapel of the Imperial Cult. It was gaudy, too concerned with expressions of wealth and influence and not faith. Mathieu had done his best to make it more austere. He removed some of the more vulgar fixtures, replaced statues of ancient cardinals with those of his favourite saints. There had been a sculpture of the Emperor in Glory standing proudly, sword in hand, upon the altar. Mathieu had replaced that with an effigy of the Emperor in Service; a grimacing corpse bound to the

Golden Throne. Mathieu had always preferred that representation for it honoured the great sacrifice the Emperor made for His species. The Emperor's service to mankind was so much more important than His aspects as a warrior, ruler, scientist or seer. Mathieu always tried to follow the example of the Emperor in Service, giving up what little comfort he had to aid the suffering mass of humanity.

The chapel was tainted by the dishonesties of holy men. He preferred to lead worship with the ship's bonded crew in their oily churches. He maintained the private chapel only because the display was expected of him. He rarely prayed there.

For his private devotions he came down to this deserted cult monument of irreligious men.

At the back of the hall was a small charnel house, where the stacked skulls of fallen heroes were cemented in grim patterns. The dust lay thick on all its decoration when Mathieu had discovered it. Nobody had been there for a long time.

Beneath the eyeless stares of transhuman skulls, he had set up a plain wooden altar, this also bearing an effigy of the Emperor in Service. Arrayed around it were lesser statues of the nine loyal primarchs, as could be found in any holy place. That representing Roboute Guilliman was three times the size of the others. Mathieu genuflected to both Emperor and His Avenging Son, though the real Guilliman might well shoot him for doing so.

He knelt awhile and prayed to the statues, the Emperor first, His sons and then finally to Guilliman. He stood and took from a large ammunition box thirty-six candles which he added to the racks of hundreds around the periphery of the room. When the candles were in place upon their spikes, he ignited a small promethium flame, and from it lit the wicks one by one, whispering solemnly over each.

'Emperor watch over you,' he said. 'Emperor watch over you.'

Each candle represented the wish for a prayer from a menial somewhere, those ordinary folk who made up the majority of the Imperial citizenry yet otherwise had no voice. When someone asked him for the blessing of light, Mathieu never refused, no matter how high or low, but promised to burn a candle for every request. There were so many pleas, so many in pain, even within the small world of a starship, that he could not possibly hope to keep his vow. In the end he had taken on aid, as his deacons insisted he should. Having always denied himself servants or servitors he was troubled by how easily he had got used to them. He never wanted to become like other high churchmen, with bloated households thousands strong, and feared this was but the first step on that road.

When he found himself taking the servants for granted, he had taken penance, straining the capacity of his auto-flagellator to punish himself. After his scourging he had prepared this hermitage for himself, clearing it out with his bare hands, washing the floors, crafting the objects of worship. When he had done, he had reverently set up an identical rack of candles to show his sincerity, so now every lost soul had two candles to burn for them; one above lit by his servants, and one below lit by himself. His hermitage was dark when he arrived. He doused the candles when he left and he relit them every single time he went within, until they burned down to stumps. There were always more to replace them.

'The Lord Guilliman chose me for my humility,' he said to himself. With one unwavering hand he touched the promethium torch to every stick of wax. His other hand was clenched so tightly in his robes his knuckles glowed white in the candlelight. His auto-flagellator ran at a setting of mild agony. He let the pain thrill his body, purifying him of his selfish thoughts. 'O Emperor, do not let me lose myself in this office. Do not let me damn myself by forgetting Your grace and Your purpose for me. Let me be free of pride. Let me be pure of purpose. Let me help Lord Guilliman to see the truth of Your light. Help me, O Master of Mankind.'

After an hour, he was finished. He took out a sanctus-astrogator from his robes and let it find the likely position of Terra for him. Whether it truly worked in the warp he did not know, yet he followed its suggestion, and genuflected in the direction of man's ancestral home, where the Emperor dwelled in majestic pain.

That done, he went to his desk.

He lit six large candles lodged into the open tops of a pair of skulls. They had belonged to the faithful dead, martyred in anonymity by the marauders of Chaos. He thanked each of them for providing him light in the dark. Then he sat down and opened the leather tome he had upon the desk. The paper was smooth and creamy, far better than any he had used before. There were some benefits to being the primarch's tool. The book fell open at the title page, displaying the legend *The Great Plague War*. Mathieu turned the pages, looking upon those chapters he had already finished but whose illuminations remained rough sketches. Before committing his thoughts to this history, he worked and reworked them in chapbooks, until he deemed them ready for this first drafting. Today was a momentous day. The next part of his testament was finished and could be laid down for posterity.

Guilliman required so little of him. Mathieu's assessment of the position of militant-apostolic as a mouthpiece was accurate. He was called upon from time to time to advise the primarch on how to handle the church, or to deliver oratory to one gathering or another. Often, Guilliman rewrote his sermons.

Mathieu filled his time with service to the Emperor as he understood it. As he had gone among the poor and sick on the worlds of Ultramar, now he went among the Chapter and vessel serfs that served aboard the *Macragge's Honour*, dispensing alms or medical aid, and bringing spiritual comfort. In the dingy chapels of the lower decks he spoke of the Emperor's mercy. Baseline humans in the fleet were discouraged from religious demonstrations, for the Ultramarines found open worship distasteful, but they were not forbidden their beliefs either. Mathieu gave them what comfort he could. Their lives were hard. He pitied them.

At other times he wrote. Partly he wrote in slavish imitation of the sainted primarch, whose every spare moment was spent in his scriptorium. Mainly it was because he believed the deeds of Roboute Guilliman should be recorded by one of the faithful for the faithful, and not only preserved in the obscurity of the Ultramarines librarium.

Mathieu turned to the next blank page and opened his inkwell. He looked away from the book, his fingers spread on the paper, and took a moment to steady himself, clear his mind and make his soul ready for the sacred task. Only then did he take up his quill, dip the nib into black ink and meticulously write an ornate title.

The Sainted Guilliman's triumph upon Espandor against the horrors of the unclean powers.

He drew the letters slowly, filling the bubbles of each with decorative flourishes. Later, should the writing still stand up to his critical eye, he would expand these efforts at illumination, illustrating the document with fine pictures. For now, he sketched in a few ideas, only lightly so he might easily scrape them out. Once done, he thought a moment on whether to name himself as the author of the chapter. He wavered, then decided he would, and wrote quickly before he could change his mind.

As related by Militant-Apostolic Frater Mathieu of the Acronite Mendicants, third line postulant, who was present personally during the campaign.

He regretted his vanity as soon as he finished the sentences. Before commencing each instalment he had the same fruitless inner battle. Knowing only too well how fragmented documents could become over time, he had put his name under every chapter heading. Although he had been there on Espandor, and intended to refer to sights he had seen with his own eyes, there was little need to attribute the writing, less still to point out who he was and who he had been. His story was not the point, the primarch's was, and yet he yearned to be recognised as its author. There was twofold pride in that sentence, in stating his exalted rank, and in insisting his humble origins so that all would know how high he had risen.

He meditated a moment, asking the Emperor for forgiveness. He resolved to write the entire account of the war, then remove his name. That was the way. He would continue with his ritual debate until the end, then purge himself from the account.

Breathing evenly so as not to disturb his penmanship, he started his story.

Upon Espandor, the Sainted Guilliman did drive back the forces of the dread primarch Mortarion, may he forever be condemned to suffering the Emperor's punishments for his treachery. With great force and intelligence, the Imperial Regent Guilliman, the last and most faithful of the sons of the living God-Emperor, did set his forces against those of the unspeakable ones, and so remove them from the world and its attendant subject planets. And in the star systems close by he attacked with such aggressive certainty of victory that the fell voidcraft of the enemy were pushed out, and the blockade lifted, so Espandor was brought relief. The cities were retaken, and in them all the Sainted Guilliman wept to see the temples of his father profaned, and the servants of Terra much reduced by sickness and by war, so that only a tenth of the peoples of Espandor who had been before living remained in the Sainted Guilliman's service, and that of Ultramar, and of He who rules from Terra.

For fifteen days the primarch did battle across Espandor, overthrowing the hegemony of daemons and Heretic Astartes alike. By cunning strategy, he drove them before himself, breaking their might and annihilating them piecemeal with his fury. With lightning strike and surprise assault, he divided the enemy and so overcame them. At the Spires of Priandor he cast down the rusting daemon-golems of the fallen Legio Onerus. The river of Gangatellium ran black with daemonic ichor so deep that to purify its waters required the prayers of twenty-two high cardinals. In the provinces of Berenica, Ebora and Iorscira the enemy were routed and slain. So swift and terrible was the primarch's advance that all went to disarray before him, whether daemon, mortal, or undying legionary. At every clash the primarch led, the sword of his father flamed bright in his grasp. About the Sainted Guilliman the protection of His angels and His saints burned bright in a terrible nimbus that lit the souls of the faithful with great strength, and smote the servants of the enemy wheresoever it did shine upon them. The minions of the Plague Lord, who feed upon despair and hopelessness, knew despair themselves. Yea! And their skin did smoke at the light's touch, and their wargear faileth, and the machine things that should not be fell into steaming parts, and were sent out of this realm forever.

Seven battles the primarch waged in defiance of the Plague Lord's unholy number, for seven brings the Plague Lord power. The seventh battle was the greatest of all.

At the commencement of every fight, Guilliman strode forth out before his armies and spake these words for all to hear.

'I am the Primarch Roboute Guilliman, fury of the Emperor! These worlds are under my protection. You will be driven out, and cast down, and all your number slain. There shall be no mercy for you who have turned your back on the holy light of Terra, and defied the divine grace of the Emperor. I call to you, and say, present unto me the arch-traitor Mortarion, my brother, fallen primarch and high daemon, and I shall take him, and slay him, and your multitudes will know the mercy of a swift death.'

I, Militant-Apostolic Mathieu, know these to be true accounts, for I was there at the Sainted Guilliman's side, and fought in the Emperor's name in the primarch's sight.

Naturally, Guilliman had not phrased his challenges quite like that, and there was maybe a little bit of flourish around the displays of the primarch's power. But Mathieu was convinced that the Emperor fought alongside His son. He could practically see Him. One day Guilliman would believe the truth of his father's nature, and thank Mathieu for showing him the path to faith. What he wrote might not be strictly accurate, but it was truthful, he was sure of that.

These minor additions bothered him not in the least, but another part did cause him disquiet.

His shameful pride had resurfaced. He chewed his lip in anguish, rereading the lines where he mentioned himself. He had fought there. The Emperor's name was ever on his lips. That, more than the bolts of light his holy gun had fired, had brought many fell beings to ruin. He was, however, far from unique. Many other faithful warriors of the Imperium had lent prayer and las-blast to the charge. Their names were not recorded, why should his be? But then, was it so very wrong to recount his own, modest part in these struggles? In many hagiographies the narrator regaled the reader with their own deeds at the sides of the saints. On the other hand, how many other accounts had he read where there seemed to be no connection between teller and tale because the writer had let modesty win out, when their own deeds had been greater even than Mathieu's, so as to better honour their subject?

Mathieu's neck flushed. He was tempted to scratch the

last sentence out. He had not intended to include it. Pride moved his hand.

His pen hovered over the offending line. Another memory stopped him. Guilliman had said to him after the battle of the Cooling Spire on Espandor's scorching equator that he had fought well. The approval of the primarch had been bestowed upon him. Had he not won the right to celebrate himself, if only a little?

He set aside the question for the time being. He was due on the lower decks soon, and he wished to finish before he went. A swift jolt from his auto-flagellator refocused his mind. Once the pain faded, he recommenced his work. The scratching of the pen cast its spell, and he fell into the story-teller's rhythm.

The power of the enemy was broken by degree. No final glorious struggle was fought upon Espandor, for the enemy was craven and would not be brought to battle, preferring instead the quiet ways of disease and despair. By many hundreds of desperate skirmishes were they finally rooted out. Dirty and hard the struggle was, and seemingly without end. Sickness and maladies of the soul took their toll on all but the most faithful of the Emperor's servants. But by His mercy the forces of evil are not infinite in their number, and so in this way was Espandor retaken piece by piece, until but small groups of the enemy remained upon its sacred earth, and these were ringed about by the siege lines of the avenging hosts, and marked by them for cleansing violence in due course.

Unto his lieutenants the primarch gave the final tasks of Espandor. War raged across the firmament, yea, from Talasa unto Iax and all places between those systems. In this, wise Lord Guilliman spake to his generals.

'A single man cannot in every place be, but he might move swiftly, and bring the full force of his might to bear upon the weakest places, and so with pressure crack the walls of the enemy, and shatter his line of supply. Thusly shall we triumph, and make Ultramar clean again.'

So speaking, he took his leave, and with him went fully eighty-nine point three per cent of his armies. From the blighted forests of Espandor did the Lord Primarch Roboute Guilliman set out with mighty host in train, driving his course towards Parmenio where the forces of dread Chaos gathered in great multitude.

This was better, Mathieu thought. More honest.

The warp was in awful tempest as the sainted primarch travelled, and the great vessel Adarnaton *was lost with all hands, and others scattered far. The light of the Astronomican did flicker dimly, and be obscured for a space of time, and the fleet was sundered. Lo! And the holy fields of Geller did break, and daemons run amok amid the ships of the Emperor's servants, and the primarch fought alongside his sons and with the lesser men, and did drive the warp spawn from his ship, and by his example did inspire other men to do the same.*

The faithful raised shouted prayer to their Emperor as they fought, and the light of the beacon burned true again, and the warp calmeth, and what daemons did remain were burned by the hymns of the faithful, so that soon no unclean creature remained, and those men struck by unnatural sicknesses were miraculously made well, and those close to death rose up and were become hale!

I saw this. I was there.

* * *

He grimaced. He had done it again. This time, he upped the output of his pain device so much that he cried out at its activation.

The expanses of the empyrean thereafter calmed to perfect smoothness, for the Emperor of all Mankind commanded it to be so, and in good time the primarch's fleet made translation at the Tuesen System, which lies not far from the Parmenio System, and there regathered with much relief, for ships thought lost were brought home into the fold, and losses made good.

Sundry undertakings were ordered to make the fleet fit once more, and a layover of three Terran weeks decreed.

On the ninth day there was a great rejoicing when the sky was rent and from out of the warp came one hundred and one ships in the service of the God-Emperor. Many loyal children of men journeyed from across the Imperium, seeming as if by chance, and Guilliman's warhost was greatly fortified by this good fortune. Taking his opportunity, Guilliman bade all his astropaths sing out a message without fear, for the warp was at rest, and he told them to summon what other aid they could to Ultramar, for many men under arms and war machines had come already at his command, but more he would have.

And then did he retreat to his strategium awhile, and set himself into thought.

He emerged ten hours later, and lo! was there the promise of victory upon his face, and a light did shine about his head. 'Tell my finest astropaths to speak with their brothers upon the star fortress Galatan, and bring it hence to orbit around the prime world of Parmenio, and rain its fire down upon the unbelievers and the faithless, for in this way am I sure to destroy my brother, and undo the works of the unspeakable Plague God.'

Immaterial breach was made without incident, and in fine

array the ships sailed again upon the seas of the empyrean where the light of the Emperor may be witnessed, and His eye is upon all.

From Tuesen, Parmenio was but two weeks' journey, and the beacon light in the empyrean blazed strongly, and the soul seas between were much becalmed, so that the Navigator of the Macragge's Honour, Guilliman's great conveyance, did come down from his navigatorium to speak in wonder and in faith of the sights he had seen upon the currents of that Other Place. Of angels, and of saints, and walls of gold that held back the tides of evil that would drown us all, and take out our souls from our bodies.

By the grace of the Emperor, messages passed between the fleet and the fortress of Galatan, whose power was commanded that day by Chapter Master Bardan Dovaro of the Novamarines. Dovaro promised fealty, and immediate obedience, but delivered his utmost apologies. The star fortress, stationed then at Drohl, was slow in its hugeness, and so was delayed by dint of its own might, for verily it mounted many guns and carried a great host of the Emperor's warriors, and much labour was needed to bring it out of Drohl thence to Parmenio. The Avenging Son would not wait, but told Dovaro to come as fast as he might, and upon arrival deploy the ancient power of Galatan in the Imperium's favour.

Guilliman was resolved to make haste to the prime world of the Parmenio System with the greater part of his armies, where the enemy gathered all but exclusively, and there to save those of the good people of the Imperium that he might from painful death and the soul oblivion. Victory was assured by His decree, for the Emperor protects, as all faithful men and women know.

CHAPTER TWO

ROGUE TRADER

Mathieu laid aside his pen. He had kept matters concise. He had not told too much of his own efforts on Espandor or the worlds close by. He did not write of the prayers he had shouted that had unravelled daemons. He did not speak of the miraculous shot, taken from fifty metres, that had drilled out a plaguebearer's sole eye and saved a Sister of Silence from death, nor of the benedictions and comforts he had given to the dying. He did not speak of walking into the poison fogs of the Death Guard, or bearing the toxins of their weapons without sickness.

In any other circumstances his own actions would have been noteworthy. In comparison to the deeds of the primarch they were nothing. He was glad to live in such heroic times.

'Perhaps I have not been too vain,' he said, though he did not believe it completely.

He was late. He had spent too long indulging himself. He had duties to perform. Hurriedly he sanded his final words with pounce, let the ink dry, and closed his book.

Sirens warbled all over the ship, signalling five minutes until watch change for the thousands of mortal crew. He left the book where it was. Nobody ever came down there, and he had nothing to hide by anyone reading it.

Did he in fact want someone to read it? He dithered, thinking perhaps he should hide it. Was it prideful to leave the book out to be found? Was it yet more vanity to suppose it so important it must be hidden?

He tapped the cover thoughtfully and let it be. He would atone for his pride with prayer and mortification. Next time he came to the Mortuis Ad Monumentum he would light a hundred more candles to display his piety.

Decision made, he was about to go, when a small noise made him turn around.

The midnight face of Yassilli Sulymanya leaned out of the dark of an empty alcove.

'How long have you been sat there?' he asked. He was furious. He felt naked, violated to be so observed without consent. Sulymanya was of the worst sort of person, a mortal human who did not believe in the Emperor's divinity, a heretic, and so he did not hide his scorn.

'I got here ten minutes before you did,' she said. In contrast to Mathieu's anger, she was all soft words and smiles. She climbed down from the alcove and stretched out her back, then leant against the empty plinth. All was done with an unfussy nimbleness. Sulymanya had an economic way of movement. She was tall and sparely muscled, so much that her head seemed slightly too large for her body and her neck too long, but her gracefulness made these features assets. She was a switch of a thing, a young tree bending, enjoying the wind.

Now she had revealed herself, Sulymanya activated her electoos. The design flickering over her face included blocks of text proclaiming her as a scion of the Sulymanyan Rogue Trader house, but her uniform was that of Logos Historica Verita, Guilliman's cadre of snoops. Supposedly historitors, their attentions strayed to matters that Mathieu regarded as being a long way beyond the remit of simple history.

'What are you doing down here?' he said. 'This is my sanctum. This is an invasion of my privacy.'

'This is the Lord Guilliman's ship, not yours,' she replied. 'You have quarters in the command spire. Why come down here? I understand you have a writing station in your chambers.'

'So you've been poking around my business there too.'

'Poking around?' she laughed. House Sulymanyan's planetary holdings were on a hot world bathed often in the effusions of its parent star. The ever-flexible human genome called upon the heritage of equatorial Terrans from ages past to protect itself. Consequently Sulymanya's skin was a velvety black, so dark it appeared blue in gentler lighting. Her thick hair, currently tamed into a complex braid at the side of her head, stood up around her head like a dark matter star when unbound. Sulymanya was a very beautiful woman. Mathieu was a holy man, and his concerns had progressed beyond the needs of the flesh. Still he noticed her physical attributes, and he thought she knew he did. When clarity was upon him he wondered if the attraction he felt to her were not the source of his antipathy.

'I read your book, Mathieu,' she said. 'I am a historitor.

I am interested in what you are writing. I have to say that it's a little over the top for my tastes. I prefer history to histrionics.' She laughed at her own joke, her smile a perfect crescent moon in the dim chamber.

'I am telling the truth of the matter. Someone must make a proper religious history of this war, or how are the faithful to be illuminated?' he said tetchily.

Around Sulymanya's wrist was a small creature. Eight limbs clamped around her arm. There were no identifiable features beyond the limbs and soft grey fur that contrasted with the deep blue of her uniform. If it had a head, Mathieu could not tell at which end it was; both tapered into identical, prehensile cones that occasionally lifted up to twitch at the air.

'Religion isn't the truth, Mathieu, it's the biggest lie there is. Your work will go down very well in the scholams, but it has no complexity, and that's among a lot of other things it lacks,' she added. She tickled the creature affectionately. It purred and wriggled. 'My pet here knows absolutely nothing about the Emperor, or the dark gods, and worships neither, but he is at the mercy of them all. Faith is meaningless in his world. Is that fair?'

'Fairness does not come into it. Just because he knows no better doesn't mean that faith should not be part of your life,' said Mathieu. He got up from his chair to face Sulymanya, resting against the edge of his desk, but he found it hard to look her in the eye. She had a lively face, and her eyes sparkled with intelligence that teased and tested him. 'You are sentient, it is not. You can apprehend the majesty of the divine.'

'I can understand that the universe is troubled by beings of stupendous power. It doesn't make any of them gods.'

'You deny the Emperor's power as well as His divinity?'

'I never said that, did I?' she said. She held up her wrist, transferring the creature to her shoulder where it nestled into her epaulette. 'In fact, if you think really carefully about what I did say, I said exactly the opposite. Power is easy to judge. My order delves into secrets beyond the history of our species. The older races understood what you call the divine far better than we ever have. There have been powerful beings before. I don't think they were really gods either.'

'The aeldari have so-called gods,' said Mathieu.

'You know, I speak a couple of aeldari dialects,' she said, 'as well as any human can. Their word for god is not the same as our word for god. It means god, but it also means about a dozen other things besides. You can't call their gods so-called and yours real, then cite their mysticism as support for your case. You're having it both ways.'

'I am not. The Emperor is the one true God.'

'That was my point,' she said.

'The divine infuses us all as the highest pinnacle of evolution. Even the Space Marines have a sense of the holy, though they deny it. This hall is enormous. Though for much of the last ten thousand years I'm sure there were never enough Ultramarines aboard this vessel to fill it, there have been recently. This fleet was stuffed to bursting with warriors when I came aboard, and yet they never did anything with this space. It hasn't been properly repaired. Why do you think that is?'

'I expect you will tell me,' she said.

'Reverence. Piety. Remembrance of the dead. They have their cults. We are all holy, and the Emperor is the holiest of us all.'

Sulymanya ran a long finger down the heavy brow of a transhuman skull embedded in the wall. 'If He is a god, He's surrounded by a lot of other things with similar attributes. Just because something exhibits all the characteristics of a divine being, does not mean it is a god, nor that it should be worshipped as such. If that were true, we'd all be bending the knee to the Ruinous Powers.'

'Blasphemy!' spat Mathieu. 'You are a heretic. Unworthy.'

'By your terms, I am. By mine, you're insane. Good luck finding anyone who'll burn me as a heretic on this ship, priest,' she said. 'I don't deny that the Emperor is powerful, nor that He watches over us, but it's all simply a manifestation of extra-material physics. The psychic realm can be understood as a science, it doesn't need your obtuse mumblings. Not that science is well favoured in this age,' she added mildly.

'Faith is more powerful than rationality.'

'Tens of thousands of years of human stupidity tells us that is so. It doesn't mean faith is right,' she said. 'You should listen to the primarch some time. He has taught me so much. You will be happy to hear I was going to be executed for what I believe. Even my own family couldn't stop it from happening. Guilliman did, and he saved me for the reasons people like you would condemn me. Don't you think that's a little ironic?'

'Has he sent you to spy on me?'

Sulymanya's eyes widened in mock surprise. 'Now why would he do a thing like that?'

Plenty of reasons, thought Mathieu.

'Then you come here to bait and tempt me because you feel you are free to do so. You don't understand, Sulymanya. I wouldn't burn you, I would try to save you.'

'You'd probably do that by burning me,' she said. 'What am I supposed to be tempting you with?' She gave him a look that made him feel deeply uncomfortable. He fought away a blush.

'Abandoning my faith for reason,' he said, though that was not the principal temptation. He could still not meet her eyes. 'You must hate me. You want to see me destroyed.'

She laughed at him. His bashfulness soured to anger which melted back to embarrassment again when she came up to him and laid a delicate hand on his shoulder. The roughness of his robe's material came to sensuous life under her touch.

'I like you, Mathieu. I want to understand you, truly. You are a good man, but your efforts are misdirected.'

'Have you finished?' he said brusquely. 'The watch change sounded minutes ago and I will be late for my ministrations. Those coming off shift will be exhausted and eager for the benedictions of the Emperor before their sleep cycle. More conflicts await us, but I place attending to the spiritual needs of the menials aboard this ship far above the glory of battle. There is a larger war to be won than that which the primarch fights, one waged in the hearts of every man, woman and child. You forget this vessel was held by the enemy for some time. Their taint may linger. We must be vigilant. In this theatre of war I am the general, the soldier, the armour and the voidships. I must not shirk my duties.'

'Watching the primarch's spiritual back?' said Sulymanya. 'That's a high opinion you have of yourself.'

'That's why he employed me.'

'Is it?'

'Ask the Imperial Regent if you think my efforts worthless.' He remained calm in the face of her impudence.

'I never said they were,' she said. 'I'm sure he doesn't think so either. They're only misdirected,' she repeated.

The klaxon blared again, three short blasts signifying the turning of the watch. A subtle vibration spread through the ship as tens of thousands of men and women left a day of pitiless work for four brief hours of rest and others took their places.

'I have to go,' he said. 'V. Activate.' He moved away from Sulymanya and busied himself gathering his effects.

The dormant servo-skull bleeped and jerked to life. With a whirr of powering repulsors it lifted unsteadily into the air.

'I always thought it was morbid, having the skulls of your mentors following you around like that,' she said, her eyes following the skull.

This was too much for Mathieu, and he struggled with his temper. 'There is nothing wrong with it! It honours the servants of the Emperor. It honours all she gave up for me.'

Sulymanya tilted her head in interest. 'She?'

Mathieu had given too much of himself away. He turned his back on the historitor and departed, V buzzing along behind him.

Sulymanya watched the militant-apostolic until he vanished into the dark.

'She,' she said, drumming her fingers against the wall. She had probed a nerve there, though not any she had intended to touch. She sat in thought a moment, then stood up suddenly. She touched a brass pip at her shoulder, activating the vox-bead within. A channel opened to Logos headquarters a hundred decks above her. 'Please inform Lord Guilliman that I wish to speak with him soon. I will be departing after we break warp.'

Without waiting for a reply, she shut off the link. Mathieu had not extinguished his candles, and they wafted slightly in the wake of her departure, turning the dour skulls cemented into the walls into brief, jerky facsimiles of life.

CHAPTER THREE

NOVAMARINE

The galaxy was littered with the relics of enterprise and war. Across the cosmos gargantuan structures swung about stars, in some cases all that remained of the people who had built them. Artificial platform worlds, hollow spheres large enough to accommodate planets of a hundred thousand Terra-mass, rings that bracketed suns in metal, and in instances where such constructions had died, glittering metal belts of artificial asteroids. Many were made for peaceful purposes, but outnumbering them a hundred times over were those made for war.

Galatan was the greatest of the Ultramarian star fortresses. It was a hundred kilometres across. Its population ran into the millions. Its manufactoria rivalled the shipyards of Luna. Its weaponry was the equal of an Imperial sector fleet. Large enough to raise its own regiments for the Ultramarian Auxilia, it maintained a garrison of specialised void troops tens of thousands strong, supplemented since the days the Plague Wars began with hundreds of Space Marines and other, more secretive, operatives.

Galatan was a world unto itself, with the power to destroy a planet. Mightier by far than the other five void bastions that had guarded the space lanes of Guilliman's realm, it had proved too daunting a target even for the pride of Typhus, whose lamentable speciality of late had been the reduction of Ultramar's stellar castles.

It was to Galatan, and the Novamarines who guarded it for the primarch, that Justinian Parris, Primaris Space Marine, was sent.

'These are the Peaks of the Titans. Here we commemorate the heroes of our Chapter. This is Honourum, this is our home. These are the Peaks of the Titans. Honour the statues of the heroes, for they are brothers as we are your brothers.' A soothing voice played over a highland scene unlike any other.

Justinian stood upon the flat summit of a mountain. Hundreds of statues fifty metres tall had been laboriously carved from the rock, leaving them rooted by the feet to the stone while the rest of the peak had been chipped away around them. They were Space Marines, tall and proud. The most ancient ringed the edge of the plateau, so old the sharpness had eroded from the edges of their armour plates and their faces were lost. The newest were towards the centre, though these too had suffered the effects of the weather. By the look of them the mountain had been carved a long time in the past, the sculptors moving on to the next summit when all the space was used up. Then on to the next, then the next.

Every mountain in the range, as far as Justinian could see,

was carved this way. Horizontal rain lashed the statues in a freezing wind.

Under each statue squatted a human youth, many of them resting against their spears. They were shapes in the shadows of glory. Lightning lit them up, then cast them back into dimness again. They watched other youths guarding other statues with murderous eyes.

'Here, the tribes of Honourum prove their worth,' said the voice in Justinian's head. 'They watch and guard the heroes of the past. This is one path to the Trial. If one among them should falter in his self-appointed duty of wakeful watch, then he will be challenged, and in this way a potential aspirant might come to guard a hero of greater rank. Rank is determined by age. Rank is determined by valour. Serve long, serve well, and you shall have high rank. You too shall be so commemorated. These are the Peaks of the Titans. This is Honourum, this is our home. Honour the dead.'

The youths did not see Justinian. They were data ghosts, conjured by cogitator and data crystal for his instruction. Or was he the phantom? He was entranced by technology. The effect was disturbingly real, like nothing he had experienced before in a hypnomat. The ersatz memories implanted by other machines in his long life had felt real in retrospect, so real he could rarely tell them from genuine recollection, but the experiences they recalled were never directly undergone, only remembered, and by careful examination their falseness might be discerned. This was different. He felt like he was upon the home world of the Novamarines and not in an isolation tank. He had been told that as time went by he would not need the tank or the hypnomat, but would learn to enter this state at will, and commune with the dead of Honourum in something the Chaplains called the 'Shadow Novum'.

It sounded dangerously like witchcraft, and he had said so. He had been assured it was but a mental exercise made possible by a Space Marine's gifts and careful meditation.

His mind wandered. His own memories fought with those of the machine. In his suggestible state, he experienced them afresh, images and sounds overlaid on the soothing lector voice. Flashes of the evening of the Triumph of Raukos, when the Indomitus Crusade was dissolved and all of his brothers from the Unnumbered Sons awaited their orders. Most prominent was poor Bjarni's face at the moment he found out that he and the other sons of Russ remaining in the crusade were to form the core of a new Chapter to guard the Pit. Bjarni was not to go home to Fenris after all. All his fears had been realised.

Justinian was not to return home either, or at least, not for long. He had hoped that he would be chosen for the founding Chapter. He had wanted the honour of serving in Ultramarines blue. He had unrolled the order scrip from the capsule with shaking hands. The details were sparse, but clear: he was to join the Novamarines, a storied primogenitor Chapter of Guilliman's line, founded by a great hero.

But they were not the Ultramarines.

Justinian was of Ultramar. The culture of the Ultramarines was his own. That of the Novamarines was alien to him, bizarrely mystical, the ways of Ultramar taken, changed, and twisted about, like a familiar tune played on an alien instrument.

The hypnomat tapes were for neophytes chosen to reinforce the Novamarines' roving companies. As much as the Chapter tried to source all of its members from their cold, barren home world, it was a mobile brotherhood, and fragmented. Their battle forces could be away from the fortress monastery for centuries, and so the Chapter often recruited from wherever it found itself.

The image wavered. Justinian was losing the machine's false reality. He had been told to concentrate – ordered to, in fact – and he was not. Cursing, he fought his way back into the phantasmal world.

When he opened his mind's eye again to the hypno-mat's lies, he found himself stopped dead at the foot of a mountain carved all around with a single relief depicting the Novamarines in battle. The story proceeded as a ribbon spiralling all the way to the peak, where a Chapter Master from times past held aloft a broken sword, his other fist raised in victory.

'Let us see the glory in full, for this is Honourum, and it is the most beautiful of worlds,' said the voice.

With a lurch more sickening than the roughest combat drop, Justinian's consciousness was cast high upwards. The Peaks of the Titans shrank, becoming part of the massive Heavenward Mountains that divided Honourum's sole continent of Honourius in two. From the inhabited part of the Fortress Novum at the centre of the massif, statuary spread out in all directions. All but the furthest reaches of the range had been refashioned into enormous statues. Gigantic aquilae opened screaming beaks at the stars, the individual feathers as large as voidcraft and visible from space. One entire sub-range had been carved into busts of the Novamarine's Chapter Masters. The most modest was that of Lucretius Corvo, their founder. It had probably all started there, an honour that became a tradition, inflated by repetition into obsession. Beneath the surface it was the same. Honourum's mountains were riddled with chambers plunging into the deep heats of the world. The mountains *were* the fortress-monastery. The Chapter had been adding to its home since its inception. They could have housed a hundred Chapters in there.

It seemed like a ridiculous waste of time to Justinian.

Honourius clamped itself to the western hemisphere of the planet as if afraid it would fall off. Honourum was a world of grey, black and white. A grim, monochrome lithograph of a place. The tops of the mountain statues were crusted in snow. Much of the rest of the land was inhospitable highland; brown moors riven with dark valleys, or plateaus of cracked stone pavement. Giant storms, born over the huge ocean, rolled in relentless succession to batter the continent. Wetter, colder, bleaker; it was even more like Macragge than Macragge. Macragge Ultra, he thought. The Chapter must have selected it on purpose for its similarities. A pious choice, part of their need to retain their home culture at the breaking of the Legion. It had not worked. The Novamarines had drifted and drifted from their roots until they had become a parody of the Ultramarines.

'This is the Rounding Sea, our ocean. It is customary for our new initiates to prove themselves in the deep hunt under its surface.'

The ocean was flinty black. Only on the continental shelf was the sea a different colour, peat brown with the run-off from a million small rivers that tore away what little fertility the land had. The waves upon the Rounding Sea were inconceivably huge, and it was cold, he could feel it in his bones. There is something about cold water that gives it a frigidity worse than the void. A magos would say it was because of the thermal conductivity of water, whereas vacuum is a perfect insulator. That was trite. Justinian's uneasy reaction to the ocean was a primal thing; an ancestral mistrust, born of mankind's terror of Terra's long-lost seas.

Thick white caps clustered round the poles. Icebergs, as monumental as everything on the unfriendly planet, sailed in armadas from the ever-fracturing pack ice.

'This is Honourum, this is our home. This is your home. We shall go to view the...'

Poor Bjarni, thought Justinian. He had taken his assignment as badly as only a son of Russ could. Physically. Ferociously.

The *Rudense* barracks needed a new refectory after he had finally calmed down.

Can I honestly say I am doing any better? he thought.

He could not take any more.

'Enough!' he said, though his words were a silent tourbillon in water. Justinian tore away the bulky headset that engulfed his head. He felt a rush of faintness from magnetic induction fields stimulating the wrong parts of his brain as the equipment shifted around his skull.

He was afloat in a saline tank, his multilung breathing brine oxygenated by a stream of bubbles. A tocsin blared. Outside, disapproving machines complained about what he had done to their brother device.

The two Space Marines on the other side of the glass looked barely more pleased.

The water rushed out of a grille in the floor of the chamber, leaving him dripping wet and cold, as if Honourum's frigidity had followed him from the machine-vision. Was this what it meant to be a Novamarine? To carry that coldness within him forever?

Mentally numb, Justinian clambered up the ladder and out of the hatch. There were a dozen tanks in a line with his, each one playing host to one of the Primaris Marines assigned with him to the Chapter. Many of them were now his squad, his brothers, though he had known none of them well before. One tank had its lid open. He was not the only one struggling to assimilate.

He wondered who it was.

'Brother-Sergeant Parris, come down.' Captain Orestinio called to him. He and Chaplain Vul Direz were in full armour. Orestinio was bareheaded. Lines of tattooed images crept up over his neck softseal to the very top of his throat, curling up round the line of his jaw to touch the corners of his lips. Vul Direz's features were hidden by his skull mask. As in some other Chapters, the Chaplains did not reveal their faces to anyone below a certain rank. Justinian could feel Direz's disapproval nonetheless.

He clambered down to face them. His bare feet rested on deckplating that vibrated hard. The star fortress Galatan was many times more powerful than any warship, and the working of its reactor arrays conveyed that fact through every bit of its structure. He welcomed it after Honourum's graveyard quiet. The peace of the frigid, marmoreal world was not one he wanted any part of.

Captain Orestinio looked dolefully up at him – Justinian was a head taller than he. The captain was born Honourian. You could tell by the expression. It was the kind of face that woke up every day to rain.

'It is not working,' said Justinian, somewhat petulantly,

and the slip in his manners made him angrier. He waved away a pair of serfs in Novamarines' quartered heraldry who approached bearing towels. He wanted the water to drip away from him, so he could be free of the memory of that black ocean. The ridiculous idea dogged him that if he dried the water off too quickly the black sea would be angered and plague his dreams.

His skin quivered a hard, canid's shudder.

'You fight it, brother,' said Vul Direz. His voice was as miserable as Orestinio's face, made more so by his vox-mask. 'You should not. You must learn of your new home. You must become one of us.'

'I am sorry,' said Justinian. 'Maybe it is my age. Maybe my brain is too developed to accept the machines.'

'The Novum hypnomat works as well on any brain,' said Direz. 'These machines are used by our full brothers as well as our neophytes.'

'And is it calibrated for Primaris Marines?'

'It is,' said Orestinio. 'To Belisarius Cawl's specifications.'

'Cawl?'

'We asked, he answered, brother,' said Orestinio.

Justinian let his anger get the better of him. 'It is not working. It is…'

'My brother,' interrupted the captain gently. 'I understand. What you have been through is hard. It is no easy thing to undergo the breaking of a brotherhood.'

Justinian looked from the impassive bone-white helm of the Chaplain to Orestinio. He should hold his tongue, he thought. He could not.

'How could you understand? You are Honourian, born a Novamarine.' His tone was sharp.

'You would do well to moderate your words, brother,'

said the Chaplain. 'You address your superior. It is you that is at fault here, not we.'

'Please, Brother-Chaplain,' said Orestinio. He held up his hand without looking at the warrior-priest. The fingers curled into a loose fist, but not aggressively. It was a grasp not a bludgeon, meaning to cradle something delicate. 'Listen to me, Justinian Parris. I do understand,' said Orestinio. 'We have a home, Honourum, and our hearts are there. But we are an itinerant Chapter. This is why we place such importance on Honourum, and on commemorating the deeds of the dead. These things bind us together when we are apart. We are often distant from one another.'

'How is this similar to what I experienced?' said Justinian.

Orestinio tilted his head in admonishment. He was not angry. Justinian had the impression he felt sorry for him. 'I have not finished, brother. We may fight together for as long as you and the other Unnumbered Sons did. Sometimes longer. We may come to the Chapter, and grow to some age within a single group. The bonds between us go deep. But we must go where duty commands. When we finally return home our brotherhoods are broken up according to the demands of war. We may never see our comrades again. Does this sound familiar to you now?'

I will never see my brothers again, thought Justinian.

Orestinio gripped Justinian's shoulder. 'There is always another brotherhood, brother. Always. You have done many great things in your life already. I have read your combat record.'

Justinian gave a hesitant nod.

'Come with us. We shall perform a remembrancing. You will receive tattoos of your past glories, as we all bear.' He tugged the edge of his neck softseal down, revealing the exquisitely inked rendition of a dying aeldari.

'So that the Emperor might judge the worth of our deeds when we fall,' said the Chaplain.

'Ordinarily, we require corroboration of autosenses and brothers from within the Chapter,' said Orestinio, 'so we know the act is true. We shall trust you to inform us correctly of your worth. It will help your sense of belonging. You should do it now, before we go into action at Parmenio.'

'Another time,' said Justinian. He looked away, no longer able to bear the captain's sincere eyes. 'That was my old life. This is my new. I shall record the deeds I do in this Chapter's service in this Chapter's manner. My old deeds belong in the past.'

'Very well,' said Orestinio. He was disappointed, but did not insist. 'As you desire.'

Direz seemed to glare at this rebuffing of the Chapter's traditions. Justinian felt it through the skull mask's black eye lenses.

'If I may, I would like to go,' said Justinian. 'My squad's duty rotation is not for another two hours. I wish to train. There will be little opportunity once we reach Parmenio.'

'War is our calling. Go with my blessing,' said Orestinio.

Chaplain Vul Direz did not offer his.

CHAPTER FOUR

KU'GATH SUMMONED

'More slops! More gore! More rot! More! More!' bellowed Septicus Seven, the Seventh Lord of the Seventh Manse, Great Unclean One of Nurgle, and most fortunate servant of Ku'gath Plaguefather, third in Nurgle's favour.

Or so Septicus styled himself. Today was not a fortunate day. Ku'gath – glorious, flatulent, exalted Ku'gath – although never cheerful, was especially disappointed. His mood was turning ugly.

'More eyes and livers, guts and gore. More despair! More pain! More sorrow! Now, now, now!' Septicus shouted with a huckster's melodrama at the labourers in the plague mill. *'See how sorrowful our lord has become. Do not let him feel such misery!'* Septicus raised his flabby arm to point. *'Oh, see how he weeps!'*

It was a somewhat disingenuous call to action. Ku'gath Plaguefather was always sorrowful. He glowered at his lieutenant from on high. With a sour expression, he pushed his giant wooden paddle around Nurgle's Cauldron, peered inside dolefully, and sat back on his haunches with a sad tutting. Sickly green lit his rotting face, picking out his sores and tusks at their worst angle and making him appear especially hideous, but even that couldn't cheer him. He hunched with misery, his peeling shoulders brushing against the broken edges of the medicae facility roof the legion had commandeered for its plague mill. Rain pounded from the sky, running over his greasy flesh in torrents. In his current guise he was so huge his minions sheltered beneath him, the mighty Septicus included.

To his eternal chagrin, Ku'gath's surly moods could never dent the spirits of his daemonic host. Misery loves company, and he had none. The din of gleeful industry filled the plague mill to the brim. Daemonic jollity stuffed every ear with maddening titters. Nurglings giggled as they worked. Cohorts of plaguebearers droned out counts of daemon mites, mortal germs, fresh diseases, supernatural maladies, flies, parasites and whatever else their blind, roving eyes alighted upon. They were irksomely devoted to their work.

Little trace of the facility the plague mill had supplanted remained. The floors were smashed through down to the lowest sub-basement. The roof was open to the poisoned sky. Once-white walls wept black slime. Crumbling rockcrete played host to a dripping array of mosses, fungi and yellowed weeds. In the rank foliage were the rusted cages of hospital beds. Glass cupboards peeked out through slimy leaves with huge window eyes. Bones gleamed in the boggy mulch carpeting the floor. These remnants were all that was left of the medicae facility's equipment and patients. All else had been subsumed by Chaos. On Iax, the Garden of Nurgle had spilled out of the warp and made of the world a living hell. Beyond the walls of the hospital, the Hythean wetlands were transformed into a stinking morass where unnatural creatures swam. Already, past their watery margins, the taint was spreading further with every day, sickening the globe, bringing its populace the heady delights of Nurgle's maladies.

Soon after arrival the daemons had broken the hospital, polluting and corrupting it to their own design, turning it from a place of healing to a manufactorum of disease. Nurgle's Cauldron dominated the shell of the facility. The cauldron was not tied to the physical universe in any meaningful sense, and it had swelled in size since the plague host had arrived.

Most of the internal walls had been torn out to accommodate its potbellied bulk. An enormous breach had been gnawed through the exterior shell to allow it to be dragged within. A fire of soaking logs ripped from the dying vegetation of Iax gave slow, spluttering flames to heat the cauldron. Noxious vapours lifted lazily out of it day and night. Lacking the energy to rise higher, they gave up and streamed down the side in smoky falls that poured out of the hospital. Outside, the smoke and steam added to the rank mists slowly choking the life from the world.

Ku'gath had swelled in size to match the cauldron, nourished by winds of Chaos blowing into the mortal realm until he was the size of a hill. Septicus came to his knee. The nurglings were like fleas to him. He was an impossibility, too huge for the anatomy of mortal creatures to support, but there was nothing of possibility about Ku'gath. On Iax, at that time when sorcery waxed and physics waned, he wore whichever shape pleased him best.

The Plaguefather's plans as much as his size necessitated many of the changes to the medicae facility. The edges of certain of the floors had been left in place and cleared of internal divisions to serve as work benches. What had been wards housed bubbling alembics of filthy glass. Offices were handy spots to house rotting wooden boxes containing his supplies. Pinches of the choicest ingredients of decay drawn from dozens of realities rested in moss-covered personnel lockers tipped on their backs.

No effort was spared in making this giant's laboratory. There was no need for one of Mortarion's alchemical clocks to spread the network of decay on Iax. The cauldron was Nurgle's own artefact, a piece of himself, and therefore the epicentre of all of the Plague God's efforts within Ultramar. It was the lynchpin of Mortarion's and Ku'gath's scheme. From its bubbling depths, Chaos' foulness spilled out into the network of warp fissures generated by Mortarion's infernal devices and spread all across Ultramar.

Legions of daemons toiled in the plague mill to ensure the plan's success. Around the cauldron a spiralled walkway of rotting wood wound, allowing a multitude of nurglings to hike to the brim and tip filth inside. To carry their sloshing loads they used all manner of ephemera taken from the mortal realm. They bore bedpans and bottles, empty skulls and stolen cribs, gourds, cups, bowls, rusting bathtubs, helmets, canteens, ration tins, empty food containers, halved tyres and broken plates of armour. All were rusted, rotted, caked in filth so thick many objects' origins could only be guessed at. Drip by drip, slop by slop, slime by slime, the nurglings poured disgusting matter into the cauldron. Quite a few pitched themselves after in their enthusiasm for the work, to the hilarity of their fellows.

Septicus glanced up nervously at his lord. *'Quicker now, you rotting wretches, fill the cauldron! You impede the great work with your sluggardiness!'*

'It won't do, it won't do!' grumbled Ku'gath. Before his rheumy eyes, a green vortex gurgled. Its glassy shaft reached past the confines of the blighted garden world into other times and places entirely. Ku'gath saw himself in some of them, and smiled fondly at the decay he unleashed there.

'But not here!' he snarled. 'No! Never here!' He trembled with frustration. Sheets of rotting skin unpeeled from his antlers and fell into the pot, bearing tribes of screaming nurglings to their doom.

'I... I... I will whip them harder!' said Septicus, forcing himself to remain cheerful. *'I will command the horde to head out into the swamp and fetch more sickness. We will bring more mortals to incubate Nurgle's diseases. Let your servants heed the word of I, Septicus. Do not trouble yourself, dear lord. Let Septicus set all to rights for you!'*

'No, no, it won't help,' said Ku'gath miserably.

'Perhaps, then, a tune will jolly them along!' Septicus declaimed, and sliced reality open in order to pull out the bag of guts and wind that made his plague pipes.

'No piping!' roared Ku'gath. His anger was so tempestuous that the sickened sky belched yellow lightning and rumbled dyspeptic pain. The nurglings ceased their giggling, and blinked in shock at their master, shuffling

backwards to avoid attracting his attention. The plague-bearers' droning enumeration came to a mumbling stop.

'Certainly no piping. No music. None of that. No, no, no, no!' Ku'gath said. *'Let me have some peace! Let me have some quiet!'* He turned his attention to the cauldron's heart. The noise returned, quietly to begin with, but the tittering of the nurglings was irrepressible, and the groans of the plaguebearers as they realised they must start their count anew was louder still.

'Your efforts are for nothing, Septicus. This cauldron is a loan from the Grandfather himself. It is a great honour to be given its use! It has an infinite capacity for slime, guts and all other manner of vileness. It will never fill. You can tip in a universe of filth, and the mixture will never overtop. Truly, it is a marvel. My birthplace, my pain.'

A nurgling crawled from one of Ku'gath's boils and stood upon a scab as commanding as an outcrop on the cliff of his cheek. Unlike his capering fellows, the nurgling was a sombre imp, who looked into the cauldron with the air of a disappointed connoisseur.

'He knows.' Ku'gath tickled the wobbling chins of the imp with a gargantuan black fingernail. *'He knows what it is to be so mired in sadness.'* He smiled affectionately. *'Care not, little one. I will not make the same mistake Grandfather made with me.'* He plucked the nurgling from his face and into his mouth, popping it between tombstone teeth. *'It is a terrible thing to bring a being into this world only to suffer, a terrible thing,'* he said. He looked morosely into the cauldron, and pushed his paddle around. *'Maybe one day it can be done, this disease to end all others, a malady to slay a primarch, and bind all this realm of Ultramar into the bounteous garden forever.*

But– Oh, bother.' Ku'gath sighed mightily and looked at his clawed foot. *'It begins with the itch and the burn! The creeping tightness of fungal infection. Oh!'*

'Sounds delightful,' said Septicus.

'It is not! It is not!' moaned Ku'gath. *'It is the troublesome itch of the Mycota Profundis. Lord Mortarion is calling to me.'* Creeping mycelia ran up over Ku'gath's foot, rushing in criss-crossing tendrils up his leg, into his groin, up over his belly, where they multiplied in size and thickness, and continued their race towards his face.

The first veins reached his lips. One burst up his face and plunged into his eye, turning it milky, then black.

'Bother it all! Septicus, stir this for me a moment. I shall not be long.'

'My lord?' said Septicus.

Ku'gath went rigid. His giant mouth flopped open. Septicus held his foetid breath as Ku'gath's massive bulk swayed on the brink of fleshy avalanche.

The Plaguefather slumped into himself, and remained upright.

Letting out a sigh of relief, Septicus made for the foot of the ramp and hauled himself hand over hand up its creaking timbers.

'Out of my way!' he boomed. *'You heard him, I must stir! The mixture must not stiffen!'*

Ku'gath found himself recreated in miniature as a living bust supported upon a toadstool stalk. The sorcery recreated his head and shoulders in every detail, including the pulsing inner parts ordinarily obscured from view, which were revealed in cross section by the projection. A daemon lacks the sense of the body a mortal has, being eternal and impermanent of form, but though Ku'gath had been many things in many shapes throughout his immeasurable existence, he found the sensations bestowed by the Mycota Profundis a little strange. In truth he welcomed it. Eternal life offered few new sensations.

The Mycota Profundis was employed solely within Mortarion's horarium, and though the physical location of the room of clocks varied – it was often within the Black Manse upon the Plague Planet, in the corrupt hives of Rottgrave, or housed in a wing of Nurgle's own mansion in the warp – for the last decade it had resided upon the *Endurance*, the daemon primarch's flagship from his days in the Emperor's service. Hateful, unsullied, mortal stars shone through the gaps rotted in the wall. Ku'gath could smell the void beyond, clean and untouched by Nurgle's corruption.

Mortarion was not ten feet from Ku'gath's manifestation and covered up to the neck by the black mycelia that allowed their communion. The grand clock at the centre of the chamber was still. Silence, Mortarion's battle scythe, served as the clock's pendulum, but currently the weapon was in the primarch's unmoving hand. From the bell jar atop the apparatus, the alien ghost of Mortarion's adoptive father looked on.

'O great and most potently pestilential Mortarion!' declaimed the daemon into the clashing of the clocks that crammed the room. *'What service might I provide for you? You call upon Ku'gath Plaguefather, and he answers!'* The irony that Ku'gath had to play the cheerful servant to Mortarion much as Septicus did to him was not lost on the Great Unclean One. It annoyed him enormously.

Mortarion's mouth was hidden behind his ugly rebreather.

Despite this his voice was clear and sepulchral, deep as midnight bells in drowned cathedrals tolling for the damned.

'My brother approaches. He will arrive in the Parmenio System within a few days. This I have foreseen. Our plans change. I require your help.'

'But this is part of the plan!' said Ku'gath. *'You goaded him to come to Parmenio. He treads the seven-step path to ruin as you desired.'*

'He runs the path too quickly. He uncovered the secrets of my warp-clocks far faster than I would wish. He banished Qaramar, guardian of the final days, to the warp. The rootling network joining world to world is vulnerable without Qaramar's ceaseless watch.'

'I sensed his passing. He is fifth in Nurgle's favour. The storm his return to the garden whipped up blows winds all can smell.'

'You are phlegmatic about his banishment,' said Mortarion.

'My humours are well balanced. I am not a scion of the Blood God to see rage everywhere, or of the infinitely cursed changer who anticipates schemes and plots, and writhes with dissatisfaction. I see what there is. It is well within the power of Roboute Guilliman to end the likes of Qaramar forever. The sword he bears...' Ku'gath shuddered.

'Are you afraid of him, third favoured of Nurgle?'

'I am,' said Ku'gath, deciding the course of honesty was best. *'The sword he bears burns with the wounding fires of the Anathema. The death it carries allows no rebirth, only an end. The sword is the creation of the being I will not name. It is a weapon that could kill me. It could kill you.'*

'Nothing can kill me.'

'Ah, Lord Mortarion, do not be so sure,' said Ku'gath

with exaggerated sagacity. *'Qaramar was lucky. He is present at the end, he always has been, and therefore always will be. Fate grants him protection neither you nor I can claim. We must be cautious.'*

'Then it is of the highest importance that our plan works correctly. Guilliman moves too fast.' Mortarion's blind white eyes looked at Ku'gath piercingly.

'We can accommodate these shocks. We will prevail.'

'Is your phage ready?'

Ku'gath pulled a face. *'Need you ask?'*

'If the answer is no, then he does indeed move too fast!' Mortarion rebuked. *'If he comes to Parmenio, I must snatch him away to Iax. When he dies there, his realm will become mine in the materium and the warp. But he comes too soon. I am not ready. The rootlings have not finished their growth from clock to clock.'*

'Can he not be slowed, O harbinger of ruin? Perhaps you might employ your mastery to upset the warp?'

'I have tried,' said Mortarion guardedly. *'Etheric storms fail. The first daemonic legions I commanded against him were defeated. Those sent after again frittered to nothing before they could draw close to his ships. My attempts to force him from his course come to naught.'*

'Troublesome,' said Ku'gath.

'More than troublesome,' said Mortarion. *'I fear that he is under the protection of the thrice-cursed Emperor.'*

Ku'gath winced at open voicing of the forbidden name.

'I said I would not name Him, why must you?' the daemon wailed.

'The warp is smoothed, and though Guilliman is too unimaginative to see that this is the case, hateful light quells the storms before his ship. My father's work, perhaps.'

'Who else could it be?'

'My brother Magnus. He too is my rival.'

'Better it is the red cyclops! If your so-called father is again moving His will in so coordinated a way we have much to fear!' said Ku'gath in dismay. *'Not only the sword, but the Anathema Himself? It cannot be! We cannot face that sort of foe and live.'*

'Calm yourself, Plaguefather.' Mortarion took a phlegmy, rattling breath. Yellow vapour puffed from the vents of his rebreather. *'My cursed sire's influence in this realm has long been weak. If He were gathering more power to Himself, we would know. It could be that the misplaced faith of the mortals eases Guilliman's passage. Guilliman surrounds himself with sorcerers, priests and psykers in his hypocrisy. Perhaps it is their doing. Or maybe it is simply ill luck. Or perhaps my father does not remain a worthless corpse and is active again. I cannot see. The numbers are not clear. My divinations tell me nothing.'*

'I am not so optimistic,' said Ku'gath.

'When are you optimistic, Plaguefather?'

Ku'gath's antlers quivered bashfully. *'I tend to pessimism, I agree, but this is too much. A primarch walks the stars for a century, and saints of the Anathema and His unliving legion are abroad. These are all signs that He-of-Terra is gathering strength again.'*

'That may be,' said Mortarion. *'If so, He is ten thousand years too late. The plans of our master and his warring brothers are too far progressed. Extinction awaits humanity. Chaos shall pull this galaxy entire into the depths of the warp, and the Great Powers shall glut themselves upon the souls of every species. We must gather what lands we can before they are snatched from our grasp and become

the kingdoms of other beings. Ultramar will be ours, if you help me now.'

'I am busy,' said Ku'gath. *'The plan demands my attention on Iax.'*

'Plans change. You must come to Parmenio with your Plague Guard. My warriors require the support of Nurgle's glorious Neverborn.'

'What of my great work? If I leave now, there is a danger it will not be finished and all we have done will have been for nothing.'

'There will be no great work if my priggish brother is not there to receive it as a gift. As in all things, Ku'gath, material effort must conjoin with the ephemeral to result in effect. Parmenio is the house of the sixth plague. The Pestiliax Godblight cannot be the sixth plague, it must be the seventh, for if it is not the seventh, it cannot be the Godblight. Iax-that-will-be-Pestiliax is the house of the seventh plague. It is ordained. Number is all, timing is all. The plan must progress to the order of the sacred order of three and seven. Seven Hundred Worlds in Ultramar and beyond can be ours, or none shall be.'

Ku'gath grumbled deep in his gut.

'Something ails you?' said Mortarion. *'Perhaps you do not agree,'* he said with a dangerous glare.

'No, no, sacred numbers of Nurgle need the proper care and attention. A touch of blessed wind, that is all.' He forced a hiss of foetid gas from a perforation in his exposed guts.

Mortarion was not fooled. *'I know you, Ku'gath. You do not agree with me. Let me put it another way. Guilliman has brought many men and ships from beyond Ultramar to his cause. This realm of his has become a rallying point for the Imperium. You may not care very much for the doings of mortals and the world of flesh beyond a playground for your pestilences, but what happens in this mortal sphere will affect you. The great victory of Nurgle will be delayed. Perhaps our gains could be reversed. You will be forced to start again. How many times have you failed now to pay back the Grandfather for your life and recreate his greatest sickness, the one your greedy former self devoured? It could be remade soon. It will not be if my brother pushes his advantage.'*

Ku'gath looked aside, embarrassed by this reference to the manner of his birth. He was unworthy, a pest made mighty by chance. Mortarion plucked mercilessly at the strings of his insecurities.

'I require reinforcement,' said Mortarion. *'At the least I must blunt Guilliman's attack, force him to take time to recover his strength so that the transformation of Iax to Pestiliax will be complete, and a new Scourge Star shall shine with baleful light at the heart of Ultramar.'*

'You have a more ambitious plan?'

'To take him alive. Snatch him from his armies. If we are fortunate, and bold, we can capture him, and imprison him, and then you might work your great skill upon his body at your leisure.'

'That would be most welcome.'

Mortarion nodded. *'Yes,'* he said. *'But he must die on Iax whether we catch him or not. Only then can the clocks chime in dolorous harmony, and the rootway that binds them tick to tock drag this pathetic realm into Grandfather's garden. The Lord of Rot will be pleased. If you choose not to help, Guilliman will drive us from Parmenio, and push back our gains across his kingdom, and then will*

Lord Nurgle be happy? Will he laugh and indulge us if a trillion trillion trillion baccillae are purged from existence?'

'He shall not,' said Ku'gath stoically. *'What of Typhus? Can he not aid you? The last I recall from looking into the wider war, he leads a substantial part of your Legion. Summon him.'*

Mortarion's scarred face wrinkled with anger. *'My son will not heed me. He uses his disagreement with our change in priorities to vie with me for Nurgle's favour. He does not see that ravaging Ultramar with plague and sword is not enough. He cannot see the greater prize. Typhus never had vision beyond his own aggrandisement. The primarch must die when and where we say, and to plague. His realm must be offered to Nurgle under our stewardship, or another of the four shall take it. It is we two who must push forward this plan. Three would be better. Two will have to suffice.'*

A sigh rattled its way up from Ku'gath's diseased lungs. He did not want to leave his work. *'Very well,'* he said. *'The Plague Guard will join with you. If you will give me a few days to prepare a path through the garden from my place to yours. The way is winding, and not lightly traversed, I–'*

Mortarion lifted up one hand with difficulty. The strands of the Mycota Profundis prevented easy movement, but his gesture was clear. Silence.

'All is prepared. Your passage here will be easy. Pestiliax is a viable anchor, there is no need for you to walk the wending ways of Grandfather's garth. A cabal of pest-witches begin their summoning ritual. They make much of their abilities. I shall allow them to prove what little worth they have, vile magicians that they are.' He sneered when he spoke of the sorcerers. He was steeped

in magic, yet he still attempted to deny the truth of his being.

'Very polite of you to inform me before tearing me away from my business,' said Ku'gath. He half meant it. A summoning could be abrupt, and unpleasant. Ku'gath was unkind to mortals who dared to interrupt his experiments with foolish requests and demands for power.

'Though I know you resent me, I truly do not wish your endeavour to go awry for it is my endeavour also,' said Mortarion in conciliatory tones. *'Roboute Guilliman must die by plague, and he must die on Iax. If any being in any realm can accomplish that, it is you, Plaguefather. You shall redeem yourself, and I shall win Nurgle's eternal favour. Your presence is required here on Parmenio Prime, to ensure the road is laid for my brother to Iax, by one way, or by another. I cannot do it without you.'*

'I almost believe you flatter me.'

'I do,' said Mortarion. Without warning he burst from the stringy fungal strands cocooning him. A sweep of Silence cut the stalk bearing Ku'gath's manifestation through. It toppled, and the miniature head burst on the floor into a mound of rancid meat, sending Ku'gath back to his body.

'Hmph,' said Ku'gath, opening his eyes. His corpulent body shivered, bursting the mat of mycelia clinging to him. The strands shrivelled back even quicker than they had grown. In no time at all Ku'gath was covered in little more than a smear of black slime. Septicus stepped back quickly from the edge of the cauldron, relinquishing the paddle to its owner. He walked down the spiral gangplank, crushing nurglings as he went, and took up his station by Ku'gath's knee.

The Plaguefather looked down at Septicus. His doleful mien was a marked contrast to the jollity of his servants.

'What did the Lord of Death want from you, my most noisome benefactor?'

'A lot of this, and a lot of that,' said Ku'gath. *'For one so enamoured of silence, he talks a great deal. What he did not voice is his misgiving.'*

'How so?' said Septicus.

'Mortarion frets that I cannot do as I promised!' Ku'gath said indignantly. He took up the paddle and forced it through the slurry in the cauldron. *'I, the brewer of the finest maladies in the universe. He had the insolence to lecture me on the importance of the proper use of the sacred numbers!'* he added. *'Not that it matters. The plague will be efficacious no matter where it is deployed, and in what order of whatever sequence the fallen Mortarion deems important. Pah!'* He snorted hard, blowing out ropes of snot and showers of maggots from his nose. *'Seven this and three that, he's obsessed! As if numbers excuse him of his connection to the warp. Numbers! The lengths Mortarion goes to distance himself from sorcery are laughable. The primarchs were creatures of our world before any of them fell, and he is now an arch-sorcerer. He is a liar, and, and, he insults me! I am an artist!'* Ku'gath looked sadly at Septicus. His stirring slowed as his mood lowered.

'You are, my lord. You are a most talented artist!' said Septicus.

Ku'gath sniffed. *'If Mortarion wants a plague to kill one of the Anathema's get, then he will have one. Eventually.'* He looked dolefully into the cauldron. *'Mortarion is a troubled being. He keeps his jealousies to himself, but mark my words, Septicus, and mark them well, I suspect this entire campaign is the result of him wishing to prove his fortitude over that of his brother, and nothing more than that. Seven times, probably,'* he grumbled.

'A fine way of showing his devotion to our Grandfather, who is the lord of endurance among his many dominions,' said Septicus, attempting to soothe Ku'gath. *'Now is your chance to prove yourself to Nurgle, and create the most potent disease ever devised!'* As soon as he said it, Ku'gath's glower showed his efforts had gone awry. Septicus' smile of relief slipped as Ku'gath growled.

'Or, perchance, to fail again.'

'Never, my lord!' said Septicus. He waddled forward and placed a solicitous hand on Ku'gath's obese thigh.

'Oh yes. Again. Every time I try, I fail! If I may confide in you, dear Septicus.'

'You may!'

Ku'gath's voice dropped to a hissing whisper. *'I fear I shall never recreate Grandfather's greatest plague.'* His stirring slowed to a stop. His head drooped. *'Rotigus waits to replace me in Grandfather's affections. He would be third, or perhaps even higher! I cannot fail now, or I shall be exiled from my place at Grandfather's right hand.'*

'You need but a little time, your grotesqueness.'

Ku'gath breathed out heavily. His nurglings looked up at him in concern, their games forgotten. *'What do I know? Mortarion is right, of course. I am but a humble concoctor of disease. Mortarion is a general born. For now, we must defer to his leadership. If he says the spawn of the great destroyer must be delayed, then we should take him at his word. Septicus,'* Ku'gath said.

'Your most verminous?'

'Pack up your abominable pipes, summon the Plague

Guard to our side. Call back half our legions from the cities of Iax-that-will-be-Pestiliax, gather up my palanquin bearers from the sumps and cesspits. We have a new world to infect.' Ku'gath returned to pushing the wooden paddle around the sea of goo. *'This will have to wait, although mayhap all is not lost, for fresh ingredients might be procured to enliven the mixture.'* He nodded to himself. *'Yes. We will not be long!'*

'I will see it done, my lord!' said Septicus. With a flourish, he plucked up a handful of nurglings from the floor. Their giggles turned to shrieks as he pounded them flat, spat on them, and threw the mess into the air. While falling messily, the crushed bodies flowed together, distended and inflated with a wet pop, becoming the still-living stomach sac of a gargantuan beast. Septicus caught the rubbery mass, and with an affectionate squeeze forced three spines of bone from the top, pop, pop, pop! Lastly, he reached into the roomy pouch behind a flap of skin upon his breast and pulled out an ivory mouthpiece. He licked the sticky juices from it, then took up the tract dangling from the stomach bag and plugged its ragged end with the mouthpiece. He tucked the bag under his arm and gave an experimental squeeze. The most repellent noise honked from the bone pipes, making nurglings burst. With a gleeful smile playing upon his blistered lips, Septicus set the mouthpiece between his teeth and took a deep breath.

The suddenness of Ku'gath's movement took the whole plague mill by surprise. His bulk brushed against wood, breaking it and sending part of the walkway crashing down. The Plaguefather glared down at Septicus so hard his loose eye fell out and hung upon his cheek.

'If you start playing those miserable pipes where I can hear them, Septicus Seven of the Seventh Manse, I'll rip out your filthy guts and eat them in front of you.'

Septicus performed a squelchy bow. *'My lord,'* he said. With admirable decorum he let the mouthpiece drop and departed, shouting for the remainder of Ku'gath's six bodyguards to join him.

Nurglings squealed with laughter. The plaguebearers went into a frenzy trying to count each breath of mirth.

'And you can all shut up as well!' rumbled Ku'gath. He swung his massive head around, his glare silencing all it touched upon. His minions fell into fearful quiet. Even the plaguebearers took to counting in their heads.

Ku'gath gave out a profoundly grateful sigh, allowing his irritation to condense into droplets of phlegm and rain into the stew. He approved. A little skin-crawling annoyance never hurt a good disease. He licked his eye to lubricate it and pushed it back into its socket.

Stirring took his mind off his woes. He enjoyed a short moment of this peace, before Septicus' pipes set up their squawking beyond the plague mill's walls. The nurglings burst out laughing again, and plaguebearers, startled from their fear, recommenced their count. Hammers banged as the walkway was repaired.

Ku'gath shook his weary head and hunkered down over the cauldron, wishing in his rotten black heart that they would all just go away.

CHAPTER FIVE

TYROS BESIEGED

Major Devorus of the Ninety-Ninth Calth brought the magnoculars away from his face and leaned against the sandbags of the forward observation post, as if the extra few centi-metres would give him a clearer view into the mist cloaking the shore of Hecatone. Dark waters slapped against rockcrete pilings near his position. The wharf edge was a hard line of pale grey against the sea. Not far away enough, the enemy came, piling up their rocks.

The wind was fresh and coming up from Keleton on the far side of the River Sea. Devorus risked the air with the hood of his suit pulled back and mask dangling from its straps. Every movement squirted his warm stink up out of his suit as he moved. The smell coming off his own body was almost as bad as that hanging over the blighted marshes to the east, and being trapped beneath the mask with it was far, far worse, so he took his chances. Besides, he could see better without scratched plastek between him and the world.

Grime-ringed eyes blinked in a face hollowed out by lack of sleep. He squinted, trying to see what he could without the magnoculars' aid. There was a trade-off, greater magnification with the device against a wider field of vision without.

Both views told him the same thing: Tyros was doomed.

The port city was a proud place. Its people were independent minded, islanders raised eight hundred metres from the shore. Near enough to spit on the mainland, if the wind was right. 'Part of Hecatone, but forever apart.' The Tyreans pronounced the old saying often, especially when outsiders were within earshot.

Never had the sentiment been more correct. Tyros was free of disease and unnatural influence. The wide plains of Hecatone between the city and the mountains, invisible in the yellow mists, were infested by both. Hecaton, the mountain city and Tyros' not so good-natured rival, was a pit of filth.

The Death Guard had taken what they wanted in Hecatone and despoiled the rest. But although they had overrun Tyros' mainland port facilities days after the invasion, months had gone by and they had yet to take Tyros itself. While Tyros stood, the enemy could not cross the River Sea at the city's back. The River Sea was a wet nothing, fifty kilometres across at its widest. But on the Keletonian side, sanity prevailed so long as Tyros held.

Thanks to Tyrean effort, half of Parmenio remained unsullied. *While Tyros stands*, Devorus reminded himself. He glanced back at the damage wrought by the war's opening bombardment upon his birthplace. City walls soared high behind the main defence line. They had suffered a major breach before the orbital defences of Keleton had driven back the plague fleet. A huge gap, big enough for a parade to sing its way through, gaped behind his command bunker a hundred metres away.

Typical of Keleton, thought Devorus. Never there when you need them right away, but they come good in the end.

Late to start their retaliatory fire, the defence laser batteries on the far side of the River Sea had not rested since the attack. Nothing flew close to the city in the atmosphere or in orbit. Nothing could. Tyros was defiant.

The sons of Mortarion were working to rectify that situation. At the shore's edge they had begun the construction of a creeping mole. Day by day, their shovel-fronted vehicles pushed thousands of tonnes of rock into the water, inching out slowly across the channel. The distance had reduced by three-quarters already, and the giant tracked mantlets the Death Guard used to protect their engineers were moving closer. They were currently two hundred metres away, and that really was close enough to spit on.

When the Death Guard got across the water, that would be that. The breach was an open road with a feeble doorstop of defence lines and bunkers in the way.

Decorative, thought Devorus, to show we're making the effort.

He wasn't stupid. The enemy would have an easy time of getting into the city.

As the Death Guard extended their reach to the Imperial lines, so the Ultramarians had sought to do the same, digging up the flat wharves at the wall's base to build out their trenches and redoubts to the water's edge. At the beginning, Imperial guns had the range on the Death Guard, but not any longer. That was another thing that had changed. He had to be more vigilant. He was well within the range of a boltgun.

Devorus glanced at his chronograph. He wore it over the rubberised environmental suit that he had ceased to think of as clothing and come to regard as somewhere between a second skin and a prison.

'Should be about now,' said Devorus. He held up his magnoculars one-handed.

Sure enough, the work had stopped. The end of the mole was deserted. The mantlets loomed ominously out of the fog.

'Same time, every damn day, like the Heretic Astartes want us to know.'

He leaned back from the wall of sandbags and shouted as loudly as he could at his command squad, although they were only paces away.

'They're starting up again! Everybody into cover! Now! Chem and bio hazard protocols in force!'

Vox-Operator Bacculus pumped the dynamo handle bolted to the master vox-unit. The enemy's method of war wreaked as much havoc on their equipment as it did upon their bodies, and they'd run through a year's worth of replacement parts for the vox-system in four weeks. They weren't beaten yet, but they had been forced to be creative with repairs. Devorus watched Bacculus relaying the order down the line, and muttered quiet thanks to Enginseer 4-9 Solum for his ingenuity in repairing their kit.

From the contravallation on the far side of the harbour channel, dozens of tank-mounted mortars coughed out deadly loads. Thick smoke wafted from the armaments, breaking up the mist. Sound chased vision, dull thumps arriving seconds late, soft as flour sacks hitting a mill floor. By then the shells had already reached the apex of their climb.

As the rising fall of the raid sirens started its second round, the shells were howling out of the sky.

The rigours of survival had beaten many lessons into Devorus' officers, observation being at the top of the list. Most of them would have been watching the Death Guard lines like hawks, and they were already shouting at their men to take cover and get their environmental gear into place before the voxed orders reached them.

Thirty metres over the line of bunkers and trenches, the shells burst open, filling the yellowed sky with expanding clouds of brown gas. Like powder paint ejected from paper bags smacked open by clapping hands, the smoke rolled out in bulbous roils. Gravity dragged them in streaky lines towards the ground.

'Bacculus, get out!' he said. 'The rest of you, out! Out! Gas, gas, gas!' He waved his arms at his men, shooing them from the observation post.

His command squad grabbed up folders of orders, maps and other important documents by the armful and moved out quickly and calmly. Devorus felt a flush of pride. He was last to go, staying to watch the brown trails of tumbling powder reach long, deathly fingers for the trenches. They caught upon a striation of the atmosphere, were pulled sideways and stirred into a deadly fume by the wind. Not hard enough, he noted, to blow the gas away. The gas was heavy stuff, unnaturally dense. He pulled his suit in tight, as automatically as a man tying his laces. Catch fabric sealed his gloves shut. Zips and buttons closed up the front. He glanced at the puttees laced against his legs. The seals were either good or they weren't. There was no good fussing over them now.

He waited for the last possible moment before drawing up the hood, setting the respirator over his mouth and nose and fastening the press studs shut on the rubberised straps, confining himself in a sauna of old sweat, bad breath and fear.

By the time he was moving out of the forward post, the chemsmoke drifted freely through the trenches, thick enough in places to obscure the walls of Tyros. He jogged on up the spur trench towards the main line in front of the breach. The squeaking of crank handles winding armaplas panes up to seal firing slits cut eerily through the gas. Sometimes the Death Guard lobbed a few explosive shells over to catch men hurrying for cover, but for the time being they were content to let their gas do the work. It could be viral, it could be purely chemical. Sometimes it was both. The plague warriors liked to keep the defenders guessing. He'd ask 4-9 Solum for a report afterwards. The results would join the rest in his log, adding to the columns of minute notations recording the many deaths the enemy flung at them.

He reached the end of the spur and joined the main trenchline. Somewhere in front, the wall stood, an invisible yet palpable presence in the fog. The gas was thickening. Cries came out of the murk. He turned to find the source, his breath loud in his mask. His foot snagged on a soft obstruction. He nearly fell.

A body. He stopped to check for life. Pointlessly, he knew, but Devorus was a man with a kind heart, and he did not want to let the war diminish him.

Hands clumsy in his gloves, he rolled the soldier over.

The mask came free. Acid in the gas had perished the straps. Poison had done the rest. Dead white eyes stared out from a blistered face.

Devorus didn't recognise the man; his face was too badly disfigured. He snagged the soldier's ident tags and stuffed them in a large external pocket. Once decontaminated, he'd pass them to the regimental Adeptus Munitorum attaches in the city. The soldier's name would be put in a book somewhere and promptly forgotten, but that was procedure.

'Pity,' said Devorus.

The safety catch on his laspistol caught on his leather holster. He really needed to get that fixed.

He put a single las-pulse through the soldier's eye, cooking his brain to jelly. Steam curled up from his ruined eye socket. They'd not had an outbreak of the walking pox for a few weeks but it had to be done.

Procedure.

The catch snagged on his holster as he replaced his gun.

He followed the short-lived whooshes of venting units purging bunkers of gas. Cleaner air perturbed the smoke in excitable bursts. Soon after he was at the dull plasteel door of his command post near the wall breach. He ducked through into the tepid gush of the decontamination shower, then out the far airlock door, reborn a dripping rubber man into the snug interior.

He pulled his mask off and swapped his own breath for the combined fug of five others. Antiseptics, sweat and chemical counter agents scented with an incongruous dash of floral soap pricked tears from his eyes, yet he breathed the stale recycled air with the relief of a drowning man breaching the surface.

'Where did you get to?' said Bacculus.

All the command squad were there, huddled on ammo boxes, leaning on their lasguns like sitting beggars hugging their crutches.

'Sir,' said Devorus. He busied himself checking and rechecking his seals.

'Screw you, sir,' said Bacculus. 'What happened?' He was on edge, worried for his commander.

'I stayed to watch,' said Devorus.

'You take too many risks,' said Bacculus. 'Sir,' he added. 'I mean, we quite like you. I don't want you to die mostly for that, but mostly because you're the last ranking officer in this detachment, and if you go, then we get Commissar Trenk in charge.'

'I'm touched by your concern,' said Devorus.

'I can imagine what Trenk would say about bodies staying out "to watch",' Bacculus said archly. He too was going over his seals. Pat pat, tug tug, stretch stretch; Astra Militarum procedure was somewhat enthusiastically inculcated into the Imperium's soldiers, but the most brutal drill sergeant could not teach as fast as the myriad ways to die the Death Guard had for them. No seals, no life. A simple equation every soldier knew the answer to. Pat pat, tug tug, stretch stretch.

'I imagine that he'd probably shoot the man,' said Devorus. 'Because he shoots people readily, including for not calling their superiors "sir", Bacculus, so you best hope nothing happens to me.' Devorus patted his seals again. He recognised it as borderline obsessive. He was lucky his mind had begun only to fray and not break like so many others had.

'That's what I am trying to do,' said Bacculus.

'Alright, alright,' said Devorus irritably. 'I'm fine.'

Bacculus scraped mud off the vox-set. 'Yes, *sir*,' he said.

The others said nothing. They watched the exchange with haunted eyes.

Devorus sat on an upended ammo crate. The power packs it had conveyed to the front line were long used up. They should have lasted through a decade of recharging cycles, but entropy danced to the Death Guard's tune on Parmenio, and the packs were worked out in months. He leaned the back of his head against the plascrete wall. Gas bombardment rumbled on outside, the erratic heartbeat of a dying giant.

He was so tired. Sleep had become a luxury to be jealously guarded. Every moment of rest, every moment, he'd shoot a man for stealing. Every moment should be...

Devorus' head jerked back upright. He blinked grittily. His men were staring at the floor, a still life of misery. They were already dead, remembered only as a painting on a museum wall.

He blinked again. And again. His eyes wouldn't stay open. Periods of dark outlasted light. He didn't mean to fall asleep. A jumble of memories crowded his imagination, desperate for attention before they followed the waking world into black.

A shattering roar punched him from the crown of his head to the soles of his feet, hurling him sideways into the wall. He rolled over, coughing pulverised rockcrete. Microparticles hazed the air in a floury blizzard that obscured all.

A murderous hail of explosive ordnance pounded down, shells expertly dropped onto the line of bunkers and redoubts. The bastards had herded them into cover.

A burning stench chased down the thought. There was a breach in the wall. A snake of brown smoke eased itself inside. Venom preceded the smoke invisibly; a rough catch in Devorus' nostrils, a heat gathering in his pharynx, readying itself to spring upwards and burn out his brain.

'Gas! Gas! Gas!' His eyes streamed. Chemical heat tickled his lungs. His panic was swallowed by a greater pandemonium of screams and explosions. His dust-white hand skated through debris on the floor, feeling for his mask, finding slicks of blood beneath the grit instead. His throat was closing. Men were screaming, on and on, until splutters silenced them, and death drew out their breath.

Bacculus had been obliterated. An arm and a leg garnished a spread of guts next to his vox-set, which was absurdly intact. Etpin lay on the floor, his hood pushed into a hole in the back of his head like a conjurer's handkerchief partway thrust into a fist. Jacov clawed at his face, his fingers raking through a mess of snot and blood clots coughing out of his mouth. Devorus' other two men had been sitting exactly where the shell had hit. A bunker penetrator, the explosion directed forwards in a thin cone to shatter defences. Explosive force, targeting and delivery had been expertly calibrated. By rights, the explosion's shockwave should have destroyed the occupants. The Death Guard had made sure it did not deliberately. They had a disdain for quick deaths.

Devorus gulped for air. His throat was closing. The gas was pure chemical weapon. No disease load. Suffocation was his lot. It could have been worse.

Coloured spots swarmed his vision, busy as bacteria in

a sample dish. This was it. Death had come. Twenty-nine years of life, over.

Bombs shivered the earth. Devorus coughed. Hot glass raked his throat. No air came.

A metal hand grabbed his hair, another jabbed into his armpit, levering his nerveless arm away from his side, and dragged him roughly up. A mask was placed over his face. Hard fingers yanked the straps closed and probed the seals. Another hand yanked back the collar of his uniform. A cold nozzle pressed into his neck and fizzed a stinging kiss into his skin.

Suddenly, Devorus could breathe again. He half-leapt up, drawing in great lungfuls of filtered air.

The hard metal hand pressed him back against the wall. A female voice spoke, melodious despite the harshening of her voxmitter.

'Calm, let the antidote do its work. You'll be needed to fight soon enough, servant of the Emperor.'

The helmet of Sister Superior Iolanth hovered over him, her red armour brighter than the blood soaking into the plascrete dust. Behind her a white-armoured Sister Hospitaller was reloading her medicae gauntlet with fresh phials of antidote.

'He's fine, move on. Treat as many as you can.'

'Yes, Sister Superior,' said the hospitaller, and left the bunker. Incredibly, the rear part of the command post was intact and powered. The cleansing lock opened smoothly. The nozzles still jetted water when the Sister passed through to the outside. The smashed-in bunker front looked like it belonged in another place.

Iolanth shoved a lasgun at him. It wasn't his.

'Get up, you're needed. They're launching an assault.'

'They targeted me deliberately.'

'It looks that way, but by the grace of the Emperor, you live. Come.'

He followed her out of the command post. Her immaculate wargear was a beacon of rich crimson, leading him on into a world stripped of vibrancy; mixed clouds of brown gas, white dust, grey smoke.

'This way,' she said. Iolanth's squad were blots of life, hurrying down the defence line in strict formation that no explosion, rubble or threat disrupted. Iolanth looked skywards. Her voxmitter clicked as she switched to a private comms channel.

'They're coming in now,' she said to Devorus. 'Look to the sky and ask for salvation. I have something to show you, something miraculous. Pray you witness it before you die.'

The west wind blew stronger, caressing Devorus' hood and chilling the rubber unpleasantly against his skin. Even through the breathing mask a stink reached him, a watery reek redolent of stagnant meres and pits clogged with the blackened flesh of trapped corpses.

A buzzing monstrosity drifted through a gap in the brume, and then a second, as tall and bulky as a groundcar tilted onto its nose.

They were machine abominations of flesh and metal, made with diabolical arts, repellent in every way. They called them engines, but the appurtenances of a machine – the glaring glass oculus, the armour and throaty engine block – could not disguise their origins in the warp. They were a hideous melding of the material and immaterial. Pulsing flesh sagged against greened brass hoops in the armoured shell, too loosely held in place, like the whole lot would slip free and slop out onto the ground. Each was a diseased crustacean of a thing.

Iolanth held up her hand. Her squad halted instantly, and Devorus ran into the power pack sitting on her back. She didn't move. He bounced off. 'Wait,' she said.

The daemon engines flew by, ducted fans chopping thickly through the battle smog. They vanished.

Devorus' men opened fire. The thinning clouds of gas lit up with red. Light bursts stabbed into the side of the machines, bringing showers of yellow sparks from rusting armour. The thick column of a lascannon's discharge stabbed into the side of one. Black smoke corkscrewed from the bloated flesh, and its palpitations quickened. The engine stopped in the air, the collection of pipes hanging from its rank underbelly snaking around beneath it. The slightest tilt of its triple engines had it lazily turn on the spot.

From the brazen nozzles of its weapons, the droning engine vomited.

The defences offered little protection. The slop found its way through the smallest crack, corroding and infecting those it touched in the same instant. Shouts clotted into gurgles. Boils swelled with supernatural speed on skin that was already melting. Devorus looked on helplessly, praying that none of the fluid would touch him. The noisome smell was an assault in itself.

'Move!' Iolanth snapped. She shoved him forward. The strength imparted to her by her battle armour sent him on his way.

More screams greeted the toxin's hiss as the second engine opened its valves. Iolanth's Sisterhood paused and opened fire with their boltguns, driving the nearest of the great machines off in a storm of micro explosions.

'This way!' Iolanth shouted. She broke into a run. Extra power hummed into her limbs. Devorus struggled to keep pace. They ran as another barrage fell among the lines, dodging explosions with nothing but luck to preserve them.

They barrelled into an empty gun emplacement. Iolanth came to a stop, her domed helm sweeping back and forth across the mess in search of something. 'Where is she?' she shouted.

A poorly ranged shell slammed into the harbour and blew, sending up a spout of water a hundred feet tall. The boom of the explosion and rush of the short rain deafened Devorus. He flinched. His ears rang. The Sisters stood firm.

When his hearing had recovered they were shouting excitedly.

'–on! She's alive!'

'Up there!' One of the women pointed to the top of a pile of rubble that had been a bunker last time Devorus had seen it.

A girl in a white shift dress climbed the wreck, floating serenely rather than walking, it seemed, with the underwater slowness of a person bewitched.

'What's she doing? Get her back down here!' said Devorus. 'What by the Sainted Throne is that girl doing in the port?'

'Wait!' Iolanth shouted. The women watched, rapt.

'Throne!' Devorus swore at the Sisters' inaction. By then he was already moving, racing out of the empty emplacement and up the heap of broken rockcrete. Iolanth's footsteps clashed on the false stone close behind him.

The girl stared unblinkingly, her eyes fixed on the sky as she clambered up chunks of bunker wall. Her feet dislodged the rhomboid shards of broken armourglass.

Her bare feet.

Devorus looked her up and down. She was young, maybe sixteen or seventeen standard years. So unlikely was the situation, he only truly saw then that the dress was all she wore. No stockings, no shoes or gloves, no helmet. Nothing to shield her from the enemy's diseases. The dress wouldn't have protected her from a cold spring day. She was out in the poison murk unharmed.

He reached his hands out to her unsurely.

She looked back at him, walking forward now without looking where her feet were placed. Serenity surrounded her.

Devorus reached for her trailing shift. Iolanth caught his arm in a robot's grip, halting it instantly.

He looked into glaring eye lenses.

'Wait, and see what happens,' she said.

'You're condemning her to death!' he shouted.

Iolanth squeezed his arm. Her hands were small, even in her battleplate, but the force she exerted was crushing.

'Stop,' she commanded.

'Alright! You've made your point,' he said, trying to shake her off. He couldn't.

'I know your heart, Devorus. If I let you go you will try to save her. I cannot let you go.'

He looked helplessly at the child.

'Watch,' said Iolanth. 'Watch! She's the one I told you about, the girl that cleansed the well.'

'Was that true?' asked Devorus. 'Did it happen?'

Iolanth did not answer his question but said, 'Prepare to witness a miracle.'

When she was upon the edge of the shattered bunker the girl caught the daemon engines' attention. They shut off their plague torrents and turned around in stately contempt of the men firing at them, descending through snapping intersections of lasgun beams to hover over her, their ducted fans humming insect songs.

Organic liquors dribbled from orifices. The daemon machines stank like a thousand years of rot.

The girl stood fearless before them. Her shift was purest white, impossible in the dire state of the siege. Her skin was pure and clean.

'Before decay stands purity,' said Iolanth, her voice awed behind the roughness of the voxmitter.

Astounding sights were commonplace in that age. Devorus had seen things he could not explain and did not want to. This was something new.

The daemons' ruby lenses gleamed silent hatred at the girl. Venom gathered in the tips of the vast hypodermics protruding from their foreparts.

The girl held up her hand.

From the machines came the thump and whine of pumps building tempo. Vessels set behind their nozzles gurgled with pressure. They released their deadly torrent together.

They were all caught in it: girl, Battle Sisters and the major.

Devorus screamed as the wash of liquid hit him. He continued screaming as it ran over his face, and infiltrated the seal around his hood. He screamed as it filled his nostrils and seeped through his lips.

He was screaming still as he tasted it. His brain froze.

The liquid in his mouth was nothing but water; pure water, cleaner than any he had drunk for months. He blinked, and looked up in confusion to the engines.

Filth left the nozzles. Water hit the people.

Something shielded the girl. Before the slime hit her,

it changed and a sphere of water splashed and sprayed from an invisible barrier. Devorus, naturally, assumed an energy field of the sort carried by fortunate priests and the highest officers – all dead now, he thought. The fields hadn't helped them. But no, it could not be. She wore a white shift. She carried no kit nor any form of device.

'How?' he said, holding his hands into the sweet water deflected from the girl's shield so he might see better.

'The Emperor,' said Iolanth rapturously.

Wonders grew into greater wonders. Bright yellow light sprang from the girl's eyes, spearing the machines in their single, unblinking glass oculi.

'*Begone,*' she said. The voice wasn't hers. It sounded like… It sounded…

Devorus could not recall what it sounded like, even immediately after hearing it. But it wasn't the voice of a girl, and it scared him to the core.

Grinding fan blades seized. The machines fell from the sky all of a sudden, first one, then the other, like hanging victims with their nooses cut. Smoking armour plates crashed off the rubble, empty, their fleshy contents gone. The poison fog blew back from the girl, and the sun blazed around her head until… No, Devorus saw he was mistaken again. The light came from no sun but the girl, shining around her head in a complex halo.

She turned to look at him, only at him, and all the fear Devorus had felt in the last nine months was trivial to the terror he felt in that moment.

'*Keep faith, Devorus,*' she said. Light blazed from her mouth as it did from her eyes, so brightly he could not bear to look into it. Her voice possessed an ancient power that pushed inside him, rearranging the clockworks of his soul.

'Through faith you shall be saved. Belief is the path to victory.' Fog swirled, afraid. *'Believe, and live.'* She looked skywards, through the dissipating gas towards the sickly heavens. *'The primarch is coming.'* Thunder rumbled a single peal, silencing the thumping barks of the Death Guard mortars. A sudden wind blew outwards from her, tugging at the Sisters' cloaks and whipping the girl's hair around her face.

The wind hurried the gas away from the line. The fog went with it. For the first time in days, Devorus could see beyond the broken curtain walls of Tyros into the city.

The girl held her hand up to her face, tottered, and collapsed with a moan.

'A miracle,' said Iolanth. 'A miracle,' she said to Devorus. She finally let his arm go. It had gone completely numb, and sparkled with the pains of returning blood. He barely registered it as he scrambled up the mound to where the girl lay.

The light extinguished, she was frail, young. He took her up in his arms. She weighed nothing, nothing at all. He shook her gently. Consciousness remained resolutely elusive.

'I told you that you should have come with me this morning,' said Iolanth. Her wargear glistened with droplets of pure water. Some of the Sisters were setting aside their bolters and uncorking tiny glass philtres, capturing the drops reverently as they ran from their armour plates. 'The Emperor turns His face towards Parmenio at last. We shall be saved.'

Her Sisters were moving up to Devorus. They took the girl from him.

He looked down the line. There were figures at the edge of the mole, but they would not come out of the mist, and they retreated with it.

'A miracle,' said Iolanth reverently. She rested her hand on Devorus' shoulder, and this time the touch was soft. 'A saint.'

CHAPTER SIX

TYPHUS CHALLENGED

Focused light cut through the smog preceding Typhus' advance into the kill zone. Hundreds of collimated beams sliced the air in rapid pulses. Too fast for the eye to see, only on extended bursts did they become visible as stuttering lines boring through the smoke.

The Death Guard advanced into the teeth of it, droning their miserable hymns. They fired as they walked, their boltguns rusting but deadly functional, smashing apart bodies and robbing lives in time with their ponderous steps. Typhus regretted the waste of flesh. Bullet and blade were effective tools in the prosecution of the Long War, but his preference was for pestilence. Little despair was generated by explosion's swift dismemberment, only a flicker of shock. Typhus did so enjoy their despair. His psychic ability was greater than it had ever been. Through witch's eyes he watched the souls of the lost flee their bodies into the uncertainty of the warp regrettably quickly.

Despair was exquisite. The utter loss of hope was Typhus' favourite wine, only exceeded in piquancy by the emergence of those few mortals with the resilience to survive, see the truth, and turn to the worship of Grandfather Nurgle. But there was a battle to be won. He must indulge himself another time. Lingering death was prevented. He resented the loss of possible converts; he could taste the enemies' wavering resolve in the face of his sclerotic majesty. Some at least would have turned. They all had to die.

The last defence regiments of the Ultramarian Auxiliaries gathered in the secondary operations halls around the orbital starport's command hub. There were a few Adeptus Astartes scattered among them. The Great Plague Wars stretched Ultramar's defences to the limit, and there had not been many Space Marines loyal to the corpse god on the world of Odyssean anyway. They had all ascended to the station. In tedious fashion the Space Marines attacked and retreated, attempting to lure the Death Guard into traps and killing grounds as per Guilliman's predictable combat doctrine. Typhus and his warriors marched right into them, trusting to their resilience to keep them safe. A few had fallen, but that was the Death Guard way; indomitable assault, stoic in the face of losses. A little blood spilled sharpened the satisfaction of killing the sons of the lapdog primarch.

Typhus fought from the front. It was no good if Nurgle's chief worshipper hung back. The mortals had to see the power granted him by his god, to witness how little regard their false deity had for them. They had to see his glory; only then might they relinquish hope and loyalty and throw themselves upon Nurgle's mercies.

Typhus handled his war scythe gently. The slow grace

of his movements was magnified by the length of the shaft, becoming the unstoppable blur of the blade. It hissed through the air chased by blue sparks. Anything it met was obliterated with the almighty bang of disruptor fields. He kept the edge sharp, but mostly the manreaper did not so much cut as smash. With a deft flick he brought the blade round in a loop, cutting into a defence line of welded plates. It broke plasteel as easily as flesh. Makeshift defences fell in two. He kicked his way through the barricade. Another sweep. Three men exploded. Las-bolts slammed into the energy shield around his Cataphractii plate. His gaze locked with that of a terrified soldier, whose eyes were wide behind his breath-misted gas mask visor. Typhus saw the wavering of resolve in the man's aura.

'Lay down your arms!' he said to the man. 'Forget your merciless god. Join with us. An eternity of death and rebirth awaits! Father Nurgle is generous – he has many gifts for the faithful. There is a place for you all in the fields of his garden, where blessed suffering may be endured without hurt or harm, and the joyful may live forever in holy filth!'

The man responded with a lasgun shot to Typhus' face. The beam snapped past the power field, scoring a black line across Typhus' white helmet. Daemonic ichor wept from the wound. The armour had bonded to Typhus' body long aeons ago, and he felt the blow as a hot needle of pain.

With a grunt of annoyance, Typhus held up his hand and crushed the man's head with psychic force.

The mortals would not listen. It saddened him. They were so foolish; all they saw were monsters garlanded in rot. They did not apprehend the favour the Death Guard's mutations were, nor see their maladies for blessings. Typhus tasted the mortals' horror. If they could but see past these things they regarded as disfigurements, they would spy salvation and see Nurgle's gifts as beautiful. It was their loss.

He would take their souls by violence instead.

As the last of the men fell in half around the blade of his manreaper a volley of boltgun shells exploded across his energy field. A couple made it through to the armour plate beneath, detonating on Typhus' ceramite hide. He lumbered around, seeking his assailants.

The approach to the command centre was guarded by a wide killing ground. A pair of projecting bastions flanked the outer gateway. Strongpoints had been laid to guard the approach. It had been done skilfully, probably by one of Dorn's sons, thought Typhus. Of course, any who manned these bastions of sheet metal and fresh rockcrete blocks would die, but the defenders knew they would all perish. They were selling themselves as dearly as possible. The last of the Adeptus Astartes were advancing into the Death Guard, seeking to break up their advance and pin them in place so that they might be at least delayed. It was a hopeless last stand. Typhus' army was the full first company of a Space Marine Legion, a force that outnumbered a Chapter of Space Marines many times over, and there had only been half that – five hundred – present at the spaceport to begin with.

The Space Marines were of many liveries, a composite force assembled by Guilliman from the small groups sent to Ultramar by distant Chapters. Though many were the sons of Guilliman, they had no bond beyond this brotherhood, and they fought without the coordinated finesse of the XIII Legion of old. It was laughable. Fear had compelled Guilliman to break up the Legions after Horus fell, emasculating them in the process. Typhus felt nothing but contempt for the primarch and these diminished warriors.

Five of them were shooting at him, ignoring nearer threats in an attempt to bring down the general of their foes. It was what Typhus would have done in their place.

Death lurked in the toxic miasma surrounding Typhus and his men. With a thought he drew in the vapours, weaving them into questing arms, and sent them spearing towards the Space Marines. They arrowed towards the weak points of their armour, attacking their breathing masks and the softer insides of their elbow and knee joints. The warriors carried on firing for a second, until their seals dissolved and the disease-laden air infiltrated their war suits. They collapsed, clawing at their throats, blood fountaining out of breathing grilles.

The battle was coming to a close. The spaceport itself was sickening. Cogitator phages ripped through its operating systems, destroying the cables and data relays along with the machine code. Defence turrets went limp, their weapons tumbling from corroded bearings. The lumens were going out. Ventilation and recyc systems tried to purge the atmosphere of the First Company's poisons, only to be destroyed. Fires were catching in the walls where insulation peeled back from infected wiring. Clotted oils and lubricants ran from dead devices. The infection of machines was almost as fine an act of worship as the mortification of living flesh. Nurgle would be pleased. As the humans died, their psychic resistance to Nurgle's powers weakened. A tide of corruption ripped across the fabric of the Odyssean port, enacting a thousand years of decay in an instant.

A dying klaxon attempted to announce the activation of the port reactor's self-destruction mechanisms. It repeated its mechanical warning before perishing in a bubble of static. Typhus tensed, awaiting the change in vibration that would indicate the governors had been taken offline and the core ejection mechanisms disabled.

The reactor throbbed, shaking the ground with a fever's palsy. It was sick, but that was Typhus' doing. Whatever attempts had been made to immolate the Death Guard along with the station had been thwarted again by the daemonic scrap code and semi-organic dataphages running rampant through the orbital's innards.

A tri-lobe of blight haulers melta-gunned their way through the wall of the leftmost tower guarding the command block gate. A torrent of filth projected by alchemical weapons through the breach ended all resistance from the bastion. The right-hand tower enjoyed a similar fate moments later. A foul blightspawn moved in on the gate while the plasteel of the bastions was still hissing, directing his diseased mortal servants to flick congealed filth all over the main gates. Jagged lines of corrosion crept out from each dot of the mixture, joining together in a web of decay. Where gobbets of the slurry landed, the metal oxidised rapidly, great plates of rust falling from it quickly. Adamantium was supposedly immune to such effects, but the ferric blight was a disease of the warp. To it, the laws of the mortal realm were nothing.

Gurgling with pleasure at the infection, the blightspawn retreated, his misshapen followers hobbling after him. A

Plague Marine squad took his place. Even they avoided touching the worst of the diseased metal as they clamped their krak grenades to the gates, primed the cores and took several steps backwards.

The rattling bang of contained implosions boomed across the chamber. The detonations were loud enough to incapacitate mortal men. The audio suppressors of the Death Guard had long ceased functioning, but they chortled as their eardrums thrummed, revelling in their immunity to pain.

Before the last drifts of rust had pattered to the floor, the Death Guard were moving through, firing in a beat to match their steady pace. Las-bolts and cones of shotter pellets blasted out from the clouds of smoke. The las-bolts flickered, losing their potency as their photons dissipated into the metal-laden air, but even so they could barely miss the bloated shapes forcing the gate. The dented surfaces of ceramite glowed with fresh damage. Las-fire hissed into soft, diseased flesh. It did no harm to the sons of Mortarion. Typhus laughed blackly to see his men take wounds that would incapacitate a loyal Space Marine. What was a cauterised hole in the skin of a warrior whose liver hung from his side?

The first wave spread out into the command centre with the fluidity of ten thousand years' practice. Once past the gateway, they came into the fire arcs of the block's automated gun defences. Now the Death Guard did suffer. Autocannon shells pounded into one warrior like bullets into clay, and with seemingly the same amount of effect. But the fifteenth proved the fatal blow, and the warrior fell with a disappointed moan. A second was blasted into steaming pieces by concerted heavy bolter fire. A lascannon lanced another through. He continued to walk, until he finally decided he was dead, and fell down.

'Target their defences!' ordered Typhus. He pushed his way forward, using his immense bulk to shoulder aside his warriors, and entered the block himself. 'Take out the emplaced weapons!'

He need not have given the order. His warriors had fought the Long War since the hated False Emperor had walked and breathed as a living being. Blight launchers were already coughing, sending their canister shells towards the turrets. Meltagunners ran forward under the covering fire of their verminous brothers. Well trained and better disciplined, few could stand against the Death Guard.

They had costly work ahead of them. Every orbital was different, the product of their builders' individual tastes, experience and idiosyncrasies. This layout was a credit to its architect. The control desks were raised six feet above the level of the floor. The operators sat facing outwards, and the outer faces of their stations were armoured as well as any defence line. Every grouping was a small bastion, and they were arranged in such a way that they covered each other and the paths between. From positions of relative safety the command crew and their protectors poured fire down onto the Plague Marines. Their weapons were ordinarily inconsequential things, deadly to mortal men but not the chosen of Nurgle, except when employed in such large numbers. Then, they could harm.

More pressing were the retractable defence turrets turning the ways into lanes of fire. The roof was low, as well armoured as the exterior walls, preventing the engagement of jump packs. Everything was smooth, without adornment, the bracing set against the wall angled and moulded in such a way that it provided the absolute minimum of cover to the invaders. Further defence points were built into the wall, bunkers in every fourth bulkhead, gimballed weapon mounts protecting them. The command and control systems for the weapons must have been independent from the outer datanet, for they tracked and fired with none of the ill effects of the phage code evident. The hazy air was alive with solid rounds and energy streams.

Plague Marines were falling in some numbers. Still they poured in. Someone with sense and authority must have seen Typhus, for all of a sudden he was weathering a disproportionate amount of fire again. What made its way through his energy shield bounced off his armour. What penetrated his armour thudded into unfeeling flesh. The First Captain pushed forward, heading directly down the central alley, ignoring the autocannon rounds screaming off his Cataphractii plate.

A heavy bolter emplacement exploded, its ammunition cooking off in a series of small, hatefully clean, yellow explosions. Green vapours polluted the honest smoke of battle, an undertone of decay sliding into the fresh, bracing scent of fyceline and hot plasteel, but the malodour was too diffuse to harm the crew. Typhus suspected they wore high-grade protection. Mortarion's assaults on Ultramar had been ongoing for over a century, and the subjects of Guilliman had adapted. He lumbered on, heading for the first bastion.

Under Typhus' influence, the vapours thickened. They probed their way up the sides of the bastions like live things. From the other side came screams that ended in retching, and the fire from within ceased. Next, Typhus turned his attention to the autocannon blasting away at him. He raised a hand and sent a bolt of green warp energy cracking down the alleyway into the weapon. By his will alone it was destroyed, crumpled in on itself as if smote by Nurgle's own fist.

His warriors exploited the opening. Seven of them arrayed themselves before the next bunker and unhooked their blight grenades from their sides. The grenades were as varied in appearance as their owners, from steel canisters venting curls of gas to the still-living heads of past victims, their orifices sewn tightly closed to contain the diseases infesting them.

With slow, overarm throws, the Death Guard lobbed their grenades into one of the armoured control stations. They landed with a dull clatter and exploded with underwhelming force. The effect, however, was immediate. The gunfire ceased. A wall of mustard yellow gas, potent with a mephitic stench, rolled over the lip of the wall. A man stood up violently from where he sheltered, clawing at his throat as his environmental suit dissolved and his face crawled off his skull.

The Death Guard laughed and moved on to the next bastion.

Typhus joined his psychic might into the assault. The Destroyer Hive buzzed inside his skull for release, but he pushed it back. He would show these mortals their finest castles could be overcome without the use of his most potent weapon.

His warriors were bringing the situation under control. Machines squealed and died. Men screamed from within the bunkers as the nozzles of plague spewers were jammed through firing slits and discharged.

The commander of the port and his bodyguard fought

to the last upon the central platform. How noble, thought Typhus. In his younger days he would have surged forward to take the honour of killing the commander himself, but ten thousand years of war and the deaths of hundreds of millions had jaded him. He let his warriors take their pleasure. The Destroyer Hive whined in its myriad insect voices, yearning to indulge itself. Typhus gained a sense of savage satisfaction at denying it. The joy of possessing, and being possessed, by such a weapon was the power to decide when to unleash it, and when to cage it. He had that choice. He was no will-less daemon.

Two of Typhus' Plague Marines dragged a man through the wash of blood filling the walkways between the command posts. He struggled uselessly in the grip of transhuman monsters gifted with the power of Chaos. He could not resist. Never mind that the two who pulled him were the picture of ill health. One hacked and coughed with every step, the other was blinded by warty tumours covering his face, visible through the empty lens mounts in his broken helmet. He wore no breathing mask either. He could not. His mouth was a long snout rimmed with vicious teeth, while the first possessed a frill of tentacles around his neck guard, growing from blended flesh, plastek and ceramite. Such gifts were common in the Legion. They made their bearers all the mightier.

The Plague Marines dumped the man before Typhus, forced him to his knees and tore off the respirator mask he wore. Immediately upon taking a breath of the foul air, the man began to gag.

'The port master,' hissed the blind Plague Marine with the crocodilian mouth.

'The rest?' asked Typhus.

'Dead, my lord,' said the other.

'Fitting offerings to our Grandfather. Withdraw from the command centre. Scour the corridors and the bastions of the near modules, then rig the port for demolition. Drop it on the world below. Never again will it be turned against the servants of the Plague God.'

The port master was a brave man, 'You may destroy my command and take my life, but you shall never beat us, traitor.' He spat bloody phlegm. Only a century ago, men like him were terrified by the very sight of the Death Guard. Frequent exposure had dulled their fear. Typhus thought that a pity. 'Our Lord Guilliman walks among us again, and has returned to Ultramar to cast you out.' The port master's eyes were reddening. He would be dead soon.

'I am aware of this fact,' said Typhus drily. 'Do you have any tidings that might be of interest to me?'

The Plague Marines chuckled. They enjoyed Typhus' bullying of the weak.

'The only tidings I convey to you are of death. You will fall, traitor, and the Emperor will see your soul condemned.' He stared unflinchingly up at Typhus' glowing eye lenses. 'Look at you, corrupt and weeping filth. I cannot believe you were once a Space Marine.'

'I still am, only I now have a truer master than you. You follow a corpse,' said Typhus. 'I follow the Lord of Life.'

'You will die. You will be struck down.'

'No,' said Typhus. 'I think not.' He shook his monoceral helmet, and rested his armoured hand upon the man's head. He had in mind to give him Nurgle's blessing. He was too cynical to expect the commander to convert as the gift took him, but he anticipated his suffering nevertheless.

Something beat him to it. Drops of sweat stood out on the port master's bald head. The skin around his input ports reddened. The whites of his eyes turned deep yellow while Typhus looked on. He removed his hand from the man's head.

'Interesting,' he said. In Typhus' uncanny senses the room took on a polychromatic sheen. Arcs of psychic energy pulsed inwards towards the station master.

'What have you done to me?' shouted the man. Panic finally broke through his Ultramarian discipline. Spittle foamed at the corners of his mouth, flew from his lips and spotted his environment suit.

'Done? I have not done anything,' said Typhus. 'This is not one of my ailments. But someone is doing something to you. I wonder who?'

The port master retched. The Death Guard stepped back from him as he went onto all fours and vomited up black clots of blood.

'Damn you all,' he choked.

'It's a little too late to threaten us with that,' said Typhus.

The port master's teeth locked and he grunted in agony. He fell to the floor, convulsing. His arms moved in uncontrollable spasms, throwing themselves into angular poses Typhus found amusing. His feet jiggled, his knees knocked. He threw back his head, shaking and moaning piteously, until a great seizure had him arching his back so hard his spine snapped with a loud, wet crack. His thighs shattered. Shards of pink, wet bone pushed themselves out of his garments. Pearls of yellow fat dribbled to the floor.

Bloody pus pouring from his choking throat, the port master twitched. He was still alive and moaning as his body folded itself almost perfectly in half. Under normal circumstances, he would have died, but Grandfather Nurgle is kind, and wishes all those who are afflicted by his gifts to fully enjoy the experience, and so the man's soul remained confined within his body. His eyes rolled madly even as they bloomed with cataracts and sank in upon themselves. His lips split, and his tongue turned black and fell from his mouth to writhe away like a salt-bathed slug. Stinking slurry pooled around him. His bowels leaked, his bladder inflated and burst. Still the man lived.

A spectacle of rapid decay played out before Typhus' eyes, and he watched fascinated while the sounds of fighting drew away from the command block, down the access ways to the hangars where the last few areas of resistance lingered. A greasy slick of sorcery clung to the officer. The sheer variety of death Nurgle meted out was a glory in itself, and this was the finest Typhus had witnessed in some time.

The port master's skin yellowed and sank into itself. His ripening gut distended with the gasses of rot and split. Like rapidly inflated balloons his intestines wormed themselves out from under his shirt, where they remained purple and full a moment, beautiful in their translucency. Then they deflated into black twists of hard matter, leaving the port master's skin as a wrinkled, leaking sack. Black and purple bloomed across his face and hands. His body became a glorious sunset of lividity. His environment suit, so prettily presented only moments ago, was stained black with corpse leakage, furred with mould, and split along the seams. In a minute, the man looked to have been dead a week. In two minutes, a month. And yet he still lived.

Typhus clumped a step closer to him, the bony vents of his armour puking thick gasses. The buzz of the Destroyer Hive sawed loudly at the movement, demanding to be set free, but still Typhus disregarded its pleas. The First Captain of the Death Guard leaned on his manreaper and peered down at the dead-yet-living man as well as his Terminator plate and vast bulk would permit, his curiosity fully engaged.

'You are truly blessed by Nurgle! Such fecundity in decay, such colour. Such fertile ground for life you have become. Know this, little man, few of your kind experience such exquisite extinctions, and fewer still are permitted to see the cornucopia of rebirth your mortal shells permit. You are favoured!'

The corpse's jaw clicked open and shut upon tendons dried hard.

'You have fortitude too. You wish to speak? Then speak with the Father of Life and Death in the eternal garden. You have impressed me, his living herald. Tell him Typhus finds you worthy. Perhaps it is not over for you.'

A whispering scratched out of the man's knotted throat, his soul speaking to Typhus' witch senses when his body could no longer. 'K... kill me,' he managed. 'Mercy.'

'You have had your allotment of mercy for today.' Typhus stood tall again. 'Perhaps you are not worthy after all.'

A movement in the stomach of the dead man drew Typhus' attention. The outlines of spread horns pressed into the rubberised cloth of the port master's environment suit, piercing the mouldering fabric and allowing a boiling swell of finger-length maggots to escape.

'My, my,' Typhus said. 'The day grows more interesting.'

The horns emerged into the dying light of the command

block, followed by the bald, scabrous head of a daemon imp, dripping with rotten blood and other foetid liquids of decomposition.

The imp spoke. 'I have words for you, Lord Typhus. Words from the manse.'

'Is that so?' said Typhus.

'A moment,' said the nurgling. 'This form is unbefitting.' Starveling-thin arms tore apart the last of the uniform, and the creature began to frantically stuff its mouth with anything it could get its hands upon. Scraps of gut, writhing maggots, strips of cloth. All went into its capacious maw and was shredded on needle-sharp teeth. The man moaned a tomb gate's scraping. Still he would not die.

The nurgling grew fatter and fatter. As it ate more of the port master, mouths appeared in its flanks. A huge one opened across its belly. Scraps rolled towards it from the dead bridge crew, globules of blood at first, then gobbets of flesh, until limbs and finally entire corpses were drawn towards it. The creature continued to stuff itself, but the larger remains would not fit, and so they softened like wax in a fire, turning the same green as the nurgling's skin, and ran up and onto the imp's body where they joined with it directly.

The nurgling belched loudly. 'Excuse me,' it said, and split open like an overripe fruit.

In the mess rubbery bones formed. Feet first, then femurs, knees and a pelvis hoisted up like the frame of a primitive house under construction. Vertebrae rolled up and stacked themselves one atop the other, threading themselves onto a whipping spinal cord. As ribs sprouted from the backbone, exposed muscle crept up to cover the hardening skeleton, and by the time shoulders branched like tree boughs, skin was laying itself down over the legs. Arms burst out of the mass. Hands budded, and finally, when the gory construction was almost complete, a skull, soft at first, heaved itself out of the chest cavity, inflated, hardened, and set itself firmly upon the neck.

The manifestation of the daemon went from birth to death with no life in between. Its skin hung loose in slimy drapes. Guts unravelled and dropped to the floor from its ragged belly as quickly as they were made. When the vessel was complete, the nurgling who began it all peeped out from the pulsing organs within the open gut and winked at Typhus.

The head rose. A single eye slid open. A set of asymmetric horns sprouted like a crown around its scalp, the greatest thrust forward at the front like a spear.

Typhus bowed his head. He knew this being. At other times, when the warp was weak, Typhus had commanded it. In these circumstances, with the Great Rift open and reality aflame, their positions were reversed. It demanded respect. He would not, however, kneel.

'As Mortal Herald of Nurgle,' said Typhus, giving the title the Plague God's favour granted him, 'I greet you, Lord Mollucos, Exalted Plaguebearer, Immortal Herald of Nurgle, three hundred and forty-third favoured of the great Grandfather.'

Mollucos' single eye narrowed. *'You neglect the hierarchy's blessed fluidity. Your intelligence is out of date. I am three hundredth favoured. The order of decay is ever in flux, epidemics flare and wane, daemons rise, daemons fall.'*

'You have gained a sacred number of rare worth,' said Typhus. 'Three times one hundred.'

'All numbers are sacred to my kind,' said the herald.

'Whether first captain, or fourteenth primarch, the cohorts of the plaguebearers count everything, for everything counts.'

'A daemon of your rank, Lord Mollucos, can be relied upon to speak riddles,' said Typhus, 'though your purpose is clear enough. You have come to speak with me about my gene-father. I trust my concerns about his course of action are to be addressed?'

'Concerns are leaves on dying trees, they fall away in ignorance of the trunk's rotting,' gurgled Mollucos. *'The wardens of the manse speak with the stewards of decay. The stewards of decay gossip with the chamberlains of entropy, who pass to them the words of the Great Unclean Ones. The uncleanly know the mind of the great Grandfather, for they are one and the same. From Grandfather, to the uncleanly, to the chamberlains, to the stewards, to the wardens of the manse these words came, through three times three times three mouths, then delivered to my attention, so I might deliver them to you.'* Mollucos' tongue pushed out past rotted teeth. It waved around in the air with a will of its own, snapped the miniature mouth at the tip and drew back into the exalted plaguebearer's rancid gullet. *'Your concerns are nothing. You will listen. You will obey.'*

'What does the god of blessed rebirth command?' asked Typhus. 'I warn you I will not aid my gene-father. He is sentimental. He yearns for the comforts of old pains, rather than seeking out new suffering. This petulant war against his brother, his creation of the plague planet and his plans to turn every world he finds into a mirror of Barbarus, they reveal his weakness for the past. His will to persist excludes the potential of Chaos. He desires rotting stability. He is blind to the glories of endless rebirth.'

'There is truth in what you say,' said Mollucos.

'Nevertheless, Grandfather commands that you cease now your rivalry with the daemon primarch Mortarion. At the command of the most high, you are to marshal your fleet and sail the aseptic seas of this realm's void to Parmenio. There you will attack the weapon called Galatan, and bring it into the service of our master. Turn the guns of the mortals upon themselves, aid Mortarion in his conquest of that world, and know divine favour for seven years.'

The herald's message angered Typhus. It was he who had brought the Death Guard into Nurgle's service; it was his plans that should be followed, not Mortarion's. After all this time, it still rankled. He was wise enough not to say so directly.

'So. Our god has changed his mind,' he said coldly. 'Our plan was to ravage Ultramar, despoil it, sicken it, pervert it. The victory was to sow the seeds of despair in the king of the Five Hundred, not to give him mercy through death. The misery of a primarch would have been a delicious draught. His death means nothing. It was agreed.'

'It is unagreed. You speak the words of the believer, yet you too suffer an attachment to continuity. Chaos is change. Continuance is in variety. Permanence is death. The schemes of Mortarion are selfish, but laudable. You will aid him to achieve the stealing of Ultramar into the garden, whether you agree with them or not. You will add to Nurgle's domains.'

'Then my lord Mortarion is failing to bring Roboute Guilliman to heel. I will not serve him.'

'Be not foolish, mortal. You overstep your rank. You guess the will of the Plague God. He is unknowable. You cannot second guess a force such as he. Serve him as you pledged to, or suffer the consequences. He is your master. Obey.'

'And if I choose not to?' said Typhus.

Lord Mollucos smiled unpleasantly. *'Among all mortals, perhaps you are arrogant enough to defy a god. Very well, should you take the road away from the garden, you shall know an eternity of divine displeasure.'* The Immortal Herald leered. *'Why do you resist? Already you have clawed three of Guilliman's star manses from this wretched firmament. Breaking another bauble of the Anathema's get will prove no challenge for you. Unless you fear to try the ramparts of ancient, mighty Galatan? Are you a coward as well as unfaithful?'*

'I am neither!' growled Typhus. He vowed to himself that one day, when he had his just rewards and was elevated to daemonhood, he would destroy the essence of this being. The temptation to crush its soul and cast it back into the warp as a foretaste of his vengeance was almost too great to resist.

'Seven years' favour, or forever in anguish. Choose well, Typhus who was Typhon.'

The herald's single eye closed. He let out a pained groan, and his body fell apart into a splash of reeking liquid. The nurgling tumbled free of its deliquescing torso, and plopped down onto the floor. It stuck out its tongue and scrabbled its way back within the remains of the port master's innards, tenting the rags of uniform and skin with its horns. Stumpy legs waggled around its buttocks as it burrowed inside, then its fat little shape sank away. The psychosphere of the command block shifted. Magic dispersed. The way to the warp closed. The herald was gone.

Finally, the port master, reduced to little more than a shrivelled upper torso, was permitted to die. He let out his death rattle, and passed on to the horrors of the warp. The last pieces of his body bubbled and dissolved into violently green slime.

Typhus stared at the mess for a while. Galatan. He had avoided tackling the greatest of the Ultramarian star fortresses. It was vast and powerful, and guarded by more than simple Space Marines. But it was a challenge to overcome, a chance to prove his fortitude again.

'Very well,' he said. 'I shall take Galatan, and I shall make Mortarion choke on the glories of my victory, and have him thank me for it.'

He turned on his heel, already ordering his men to regroup and depart the Odyssean orbital port.

CHAPTER SEVEN

A NIGHT ABOARD THE MACRAGGE'S HONOUR

Yassilli Sulymanya was permitted to see the primarch before they reached Parmenio. She doubted she would have seen him at all if she'd been forced to wait for the drop out of warp. Her ship was ready to depart the fleet as soon as they were free of the empyrean. It would not survive the war Guilliman was rushing towards.

Guilliman called for her while she was sleeping. It was late in the sixth watch, a time designated loosely as night. She rose immediately from sleep, rinsed out her mouth with tepid, metallic ship's water, and picked up the slender stasis box she had for the primarch. Meetings with Guilliman were precious, and she left the room before she had her uniform on properly. She jogged down the corridor doing up her buttons. Time dribbled away from her slowly but unstoppably. The fear of wasting a second of her audience with the primarch nibbled at her composure.

The *Macragge's Honour* grumbled over ripples in the warp. It shook twice, very gently, the twitch of an animal shaking off a flea. The voyage was the calmest Sulymanya had experienced in some time.

She joined Roboute Guilliman in an out of the way transit conduit. He was a blue shadow in the gloom, more apparent by the noise he made than by sight. He paced with a machine's patience, heading towards the distant prow. In his armour he looked like a robot warrior of the Cybernetica Legions. He matched their height and their heft. If his head were hidden with their metallic dome, he could have been a machine, but his face was uncovered – a human component nested in ceramite, a proud face, a fierce face. He was a giant, a mechanical marvel, a post-human demigod.

Guilliman was human in spite of everything about him that was not. She instinctively knew that they were kin. Care for his fellow man had scribed the lines into his face. Upon his shoulders rested the fates of them all.

That is why she did not fear him.

For all the whine and purr of his battleplate and the clank of his boots on the metal decking, and despite her soft-footed approach, the primarch heard her coming. He could not simply look over the massive shoulders of his warsuit, so he shouted out directly forward, loudly enough that she would hear.

'Yassilli Sulymanya, how goes the search for the truth?'

She ran to catch him. He did not slow his stride, which, though seeming ponderous from behind, was swift. As she spoke, she had to jog to keep up.

'Slowly, my lord,' she said. She clutched the stasis box to her chest. 'I've finally finished collating all the information my agents gathered during our last expedition. I apologise it took so long, but my lateness is a sign of our success.'

'I look forward to seeing what you have.'

'It was a good haul, my lord. I will have the materials transferred to your private library as soon as first watch is called. I have the catalogue here for you.' She pulled out a compact data slate from its leather case at her belt and held it out for him. He took it without reading it.

'I am sorry for the nature of this venue,' he said, gesturing at the tight confines of the conduit. 'I must make full use of all my time. I find the walk to the prow focuses my thoughts, and I like to arrive at places without fanfare some-times.'

'I would say it keeps the crew engaged with their work.'

'There is that,' he said. His orator's voice imbued the simplest statement with the force of a passionate declamation, though he spoke measuredly and without drama. 'Mostly it is for my own sanity. Too many trumpets. Too many men in uncomfortable uniforms saluting like their life depended on it. The people need their rituals, but I do not need priests screeching out my titles every time I open a door. Frankly, it is an annoyance.'

She didn't really know what to say to that.

'You will be ready to depart when we break warp, I assume.'

'My crew are prepared. We're ready,' she said proudly.

'I won't ask if you understand the gravity of what I am asking you to do,' he said, still pacing, still facing forward. 'You are too intelligent not to know.'

'It's a risk, a big risk. But my House earned its charter by taking risks, and made its fortune by taking more. I don't want to let my ancestors down by shying away from a challenge, do I? Running Nachmund sounds like fun, in a borderline suicidal kind of way.'

'Fun is a form of justification for action that never worked for me.' He smiled as he said it. 'But your enthusiasm pleases me, even if it does not entirely mask your trepidation.'

'You said I'm intelligent. I like to think so too, but I'd be a medically certifiable idiot if I wasn't a bit scared.' She clutched the stasis box closer to her. It had taken many lives and much effort to get it to the primarch. She had to wait for the perfect moment to hand it over, otherwise it would not seem right. She looked up at his face, trying to read his statue's expression. 'But in case you're feeling worried about me, or even a little bit guilty about sending me to my certain death, it's an honour.'

'I have killed many people with honour in the past,' he said solemnly.

'I'll be fine,' she said. 'I am enjoying this journey. It is incredibly smooth. Every trip I make my ship bounces around like a bug in a sample jar.'

'Nachmund will readjust your parameters for "smooth".' Guilliman smiled grimly. 'Travelling the warp was even easier than this in the days the Emperor walked the stars with us,' he said. 'Then, the warp seemed a calm pond to the raging sea it is in this benighted age.'

'Roboute,' said Yassilli suddenly. He glanced sidelong at her use of his given name.

The liberty had been taken only once before, and recently, and though he had not rebuked her for speaking this way it took him by surprise, she could tell.

'What?' she said, mischief lifting the corners of her mouth. 'It is your name, isn't it?'

'It is,' he agreed, his voice no less stentorian. 'Although I'd half come to believe my name is "my lord" or "the Imperial Regent" or "blessed primarch". A term I find particularly irksome.'

'Do you find my use of your first name impertinent?'

'Absolutely,' he said wryly. A little of the demigod's tone slipped from his voice, a little warmth took its place.

Yassilli was hardly abashed. 'Then I apologise, my lord Guilliman.'

Guilliman stopped his walking and looked down at the woman. 'I said it was impertinent, I did not say I disapproved, Yassilli.' His voice softened further, becoming yet more human, and his heroic expression did not change exactly, but he somehow became more relatable. 'I find your familiarity refreshing. It is good to be reminded that I am a person as well as a primarch. And I do have a sense of humour, despite what you might have heard.'

'I haven't heard anything about that, my lord.'

He laughed. 'Don't lie to me.'

She shrugged. 'I try not to.'

'You really have no fear of me, do you?' he asked. 'I find that amazing, as well as saddening. Everyone is frightened of me now.'

She flashed her brilliant smile at him. 'I suppose I should be frightened of you, but no, I'm not. There's plenty to be afraid of in this galaxy. Why be afraid of the one who is trying to save us?'

He loomed over her, his eyebrows drawn together, two disapproving thunderheads shadowing his eyes. 'I am Roboute Guilliman, primarch, gene-engineered son of the Emperor of Mankind. I am the Avenging Son, the Victorious, the Blade of Unity, the Master of Ultramar.

I am the Imperial Regent. Empires tremble before me. I was made one hundred centuries before your birth, millennia before your House rose to prominence. I have fought daemons and defied beings that call themselves gods. Species have died at my hand. Now, tell me again, do you not fear me?'

She stared up at him. Her smile was a little less cocky, but she was still wearing it, proud as a badge. 'When you put it like that, maybe I do a little bit.'

Guilliman returned her smile tenfold. Some faces are transformed by smiles; Guilliman's was not one of those faces. Warm though his expression was, he retained the look of an image carved from marble to grace a cenotaph.

'More impudence,' he said, though his tone was kind. He resumed his walking. 'You may call me Roboute, if you wish. I miss such signs of common feeling.'

'I thank you, Robu,' she said.

'Now you overstep the limit,' he said.

'I am sorry, my lord.'

'Somehow, I doubt your sincerity,' he said, still smiling. 'I assume you have business you wish to discuss, and have not come simply to test the limits of my indulgence.'

'Yes, yes, I have. About Nachmund. I'll need everything there is to know about the passage through the gap. I've already approached your Navigators, but you know how close-mouthed they are. They won't speak with mine. Likewise your astrogators. In fact, pretty much everyone won't tell me anything.'

'Nachmund is of particular sensitivity,' Guilliman said. 'You have my seal. It will open any door. If it does not, send the denier to me and we shall see whose orders are obeyed.'

'I do have it,' she said. 'I don't like to flash it around the fleet when you're a few kilometres away from whoever I'm flashing it at. It seems... tactless. Like I'm showing off.'

'I understand. That is diplomatic. Every time we speak my choice of you for the Logos is validated again.'

'Are you praising me or yourself?' she said.

He gave her an amused look. 'I shall have the necessary information released. The message I wish you to convey to the warden of Imperium Nihilus is ready. It will be sent to your ship an hour before you depart.'

'That's very precise.'

'Precision is what I was made for. The contents of the message are to remain secret. Although they are encrypted, and sealed within an annihilation casque, there are always ways that secrets can be let free.'

'An annihilation casque?' She was shocked by that. 'I better make it through then,' she said.

'You will thank me for a clean death if your ship is overtaken,' he said.

She couldn't argue with that.

'And now to the matter I desire to speak of. Tell me about Mathieu. You went to see him as I asked?'

'In a way,' she said carefully.

'Please define "in a way", Yassilli. You haven't antagonised him, I hope.'

'Maybe,' she said. 'He's got this little hidey hole down in the bowels of the ship.'

'I know of it, in the Mortuis Ad Monumentum,' said Guilliman.

'Isn't that place sacred?' asked Yassilli.

'Sacred is not a word I am comfortable with. It was a memorial to the honoured dead, once, a long time ago.'

'Don't you mind him lurking down there though?'

'He is a man of a certain temperament. As long as I know where he is, I do not mind him having a space of his own. He is devout, a deep thinker. I would rather he had somewhere to put his mind in order than seethe under watch. I suppose he finds the monument holy. What did you think?'

'I do not think he means you any harm.'

'And what is his motivation in serving me?'

'Since I rejoined you at Tuesen, I've had several conversations with him. I've read what I can about him, interviewed his associates. I believe his only motivation in serving you is to serve the Emperor and the Imperium. Some of the things he said made me think he wants to convert you, but he means no more harm than that.'

Guilliman nodded. 'They all want to convert me, these priests. In that there is a risk. If I am too dismissive of his beliefs there is a danger he may turn on me.'

'Really?'

'It would not be the first religion to tear down its so-called saviour.'

'May I ask something? Something impertinent?'

'I have already granted you permission to be impertinent, Yassilli. Speak.'

'Why him?' she asked. 'Why not someone more pliable?'

'I need some way of reaching out to the common folk, speaking with them in a way they understand,' said Guilliman. 'My last militant-apostolic was too much a creature of the establishment. Mathieu is fresher, more honest, and he understands the suffering of ordinary men. He is not apart from them. I also know he is that way because he is more devout and fanatical. I understand the risk.'

'Won't people transfer their religious devotion to him rather than you, my lord?'

'That is what I want. I dislike being venerated. I tread a very delicate path. I cannot deny the Emperor's divinity, it is too far embedded into the rotting edifice the Imperium has become. To deny it would provoke war. Individuals with your views are few and far between.'

'Mostly because we are burned alive,' she said, as indeed was due to be her fate, until Guilliman's agents had saved her.

'I am unfortunately aware of that,' he said.

'You could just play along.'

'In a sense I do, but to openly embrace worship would make me a hypocrite.'

'There are worse crimes than hypocrisy, my lord,' said Yassilli.

'There are, but to assume control of the church as its figurehead would have the same extreme consequences as denial – factionalisation followed by religious war. I understand there have been plenty of those during my absence. At the very least I would become enchained by their organisation.'

He stopped suddenly, catching Yassilli by surprise.

'I will never be beholden to anyone, human or otherwise,' he said firmly. 'I have been imprisoned by too many beings, and used by more. I must be free to forge my own path or humanity is doomed. The strategy I use with the Ecclesiarchy is a bitter cup containing many unpalatable things, but it must be supped from for the alternatives are worse. I have to be free.'

'You're going to say you'd rather die?'

'Second guessing me is another impertinence, Yassilli,

but yes, I rather would die. I cannot allow myself to be subordinate to anything except the survival of the human race, not even an idea, and certainly not a belief. If I were to become dominated by one faction or another, then I would serve their ends, and not those of humanity. My mission must be pure, as pure as the Great Crusade.'

'Can it be done?'

He gave her a harder smile. 'I will tell you something. This armour.' He spread his hand across his chest. Tongues of pale flame shone on his fingers where the scrollwork caught the ship's lumens. 'I was told it kept me alive. I was warned by the aeldari who aided Archmagos Cawl in awakening me never to take it off.'

'I've seen you without it,' she said. She shrugged. 'I don't see the aeldari as naturally deceitful like most do, but a lie for them is not the same as a lie for us. It pays to be careful with the eldar.'

'It does. I am. Yvraine was not lying. She believed what she said to be true. The aeldari never do anything that does not aid their race directly. They did not resurrect me for the sake of humanity, but for their own species. They see me as another piece in their game against extinction. I cannot be their pawn, just as I cannot become the weapon of the Imperial Cult. She told me what she did because she wants me alive.'

'You took it off anyway,' Sulymanya said. She thought a moment. 'You took it off to defy them?'

'I never have only one reason for doing anything,' he said to her. 'Defying Yvraine was part of it. I do not like to be told what is and is not possible. But the driving reason was that I cannot be in thrall to the aeldari. If I allowed myself to be dependent on it, what happens if the armour malfunctioned, or they turned it off? Cawl built it, but I doubt he understands the fullness of its workings, so much was dictated to him. To avoid alerting them, I conducted the research on the Armour of Fate myself. Do not think there are none of the aeldari's agents abroad in this fleet,' he said, forestalling Sulymanya's next question. 'I do not have the technical skills of some of my dead brothers. The armour is complex, but I was able to determine the majority of its processes and what exactly it was doing to keep me alive. It is esoteric, warp tech. The aeldari make no difference between the material universe and the immaterium, not in the same way we do. I also determined that if I took it off, I might survive. Theoretically.

'I waited for a moment of peace, that being relative. I told no one what I was about to do. I took with me seven armoury servitors, nothing and nobody sentient. Removing the armour was painful and difficult, especially as I did not wish to damage it for it is an exemplary piece of wargear. Furthermore, although my convictions were firm, I wished to leave the option to myself of replacing it should I begin to perish.

'When the Armour of Fate was removed I felt justified in my actions, and when the pain came my belief that I was doing the right thing did not leave me. Not when the strength left my body and the wound my brother inflicted upon me at Thessala opened itself and wept blood scented with immortal poison. I fell, my body aflame with agony. My mind was ablaze, but I held one thought – *I cannot die*. Not that it is impossible, but that I would not allow it. When Fulgrim beat me in combat, I had the same thought. I feared no one would be able to hold the Imperium together were I to die. That fear has been borne out a million times. The stakes are so much higher now than they were in the past. Maybe this gave me strength.' He touched his hand to the breastplate. 'Into realms of thought and terror I passed, and experienced many things there that I can barely recall. But I awoke. I earned my scar.' He ran an armoured finger across his neck, where the ropy mark of Fulgrim's wound peeped out from his softseal collar. 'I was weak, but the worst had passed. I put the armour back on, and went about my duties. That week, I had it removed every night, and each time it became more bearable, until I could go abroad without it in tolerable condition.'

'You are in pain when you do not wear it?'

'Some. Not as much as I was. It is important I am seen without it. The Imperial Regent should show no weakness, nor any reliance on a xenos race.'

Humanity fled him as he said those words, spoken with an intensity a mortal man could not match.

'It could be that my body had recovered enough that it could finish the job of healing itself,' said Guilliman, 'and that the venom in my veins was but a residue it could overcome. Whether or not those things are true, I will tell you one that is. I will not let myself die. The Imperium needs me whole and free of the influence of others.'

'Then you have nothing to fear from Mathieu,' she said.

'Maybe that is true. For now. I do, however, fear the church.'

'In these times, lord, I would take whatever help I can get,' said Yassilli.

He shook his head and began to walk again. 'I think back to Nikaea, so long ago. There was dissension among my brother primarchs about the wisdom of using warp-born powers within our Legions. The Emperor decreed that we abandon the practice. We broke that ban when warpcraft proved to be one of the most effective weapons against the forces of Chaos. Perhaps admitting faith into my armoury is no more extreme than entertaining witchcraft as a weapon of war.' He paused.

'Sometimes I do not know what to think. I can see the strategic value, in fact the necessity, of the Imperial Cult, but I do not understand it. I do not think I ever will. Of all my brothers, only Lorgar had a genuine sense of the spiritual. He had faith in my father once, much like Mathieu does. He was censured for that belief, and now a version of his religion is an indispensable part of the apparatus of state. The irony of that is so black I can only laugh at it. It was Lorgar who fell first, not Horus. Did you know that?'

'The Horus Heresy was a long time ago, my lord. It is a legend to most. Even I, privileged enough to read the materials I collect for your histories, know next to nothing about it.'

'It is not accurately remembered. You know that Lorgar was the root of the Imperial Cult?'

'Yes,' she said. A thread of misgiving wound itself around her guts and pulled tight. 'I... I... didn't before Talsimar.' Did he know what she had in her possession?

'You know also that should this information become widespread, it would cause untold upheaval?'

'Yes,' she said. Her hand tightened on the stasis box. How peculiar he should bring this up now. She did feel a little afraid of him, right then.

'I shall tell you something none now know. The Emperor ordered that Lorgar, who was called Aurelian, desist in his worship of Him. He did not, so my father had me teach him a lesson. Lorgar had raised a city in praise of the Emperor. They called it the perfect city. My Legion destroyed it. I took no pleasure in the act. Though I suspect the roots of corruption were planted long before the Emperor took Lorgar to His side, it was my Legion's humbling of Aurelian that helped push him into the embrace of Chaos.'

Sulymanya's eyes widened in shock. 'You blame yourself for the war? You couldn't have known what would happen!'

'It was my job to know,' he said. 'I was made to plan. Each of my brothers was given a set of talents, derived from the Emperor Himself. Individually our talents overlapped – redundancy, I suppose, as should be incorporated into any system. Lord Rogal Dorn and I, for example, both inherited His capacity for strategy and contingency planning. But in combination our talents were unique. Dorn was a greater builder than I ever was, and I a far better administrator. Neither of us saw this coming. Nor did Sanguinius, who had powers of foresight second only to the Emperor Himself. Of us all, I think perhaps only poor Konrad knew, for he too had the power to see the future.'

'The Night Haunter?' Sulymanya whispered.

Guilliman nodded.

'Was he as gifted as they say the Great Angel was?'

'He was,' said Guilliman. 'He was also insane. Maybe if he had not been, this all could have been avoided, assuming of course the Emperor hadn't intended this to happen all along.'

'Do you really think that?'

Guilliman sighed. He seemed tired. 'Yassilli, do you think you can truly comprehend the workings of my mind?'

'No!' she said. 'Of course not! It's impossible. I've got

a pretty high opinion of myself, but you are far more than human.'

'Then you can understand by extrapolation. I merely suppose, for I am as able to understand the Emperor's mind as you are able to understand mine.'

She pulled a face.

'Has something I said given you cause to worry?' he asked.

'It's funny, and I don't mean in an amusing way, that you bring up your brother Lorgar with me today.'

Guilliman raised an eyebrow. 'How so?'

'Can you read minds?' she asked frankly. 'I don't think you can, but you are, well, you are what you are.'

Guilliman might have laughed again were it not for her deadly serious air. 'The Emperor did not invest me with any appreciable psychic ability.'

Now she was nervous. Quickly, she unhooked the stasis box from her belt and held it up to him, before she could change her mind.

'I brought you this. Once I knew what it was I was pretty anxious to keep it hidden away from the others. Only I and Scopanji have seen it. Danton did too, but he's dead.'

'You do not trust your colleagues.'

'I don't trust anyone,' she said quietly. 'Apart from myself, and you.' She held up the stasis box. 'It's in here. I thought you might want to see this immediately, and I thought it had better be me that gave it to you. I'd be careful with it, it's very fragile. I suppose it would be, being ten thousand years old or so.'

He looked at the box.

'Do you believe in coincidences?' she asked, reaching up to key the cypher into the lock pad on the side.

'Once I did not, but given sufficient evidence now, I will entertain any idea.'

The box lid folded into itself. Soft blue stasis light lit Guilliman's face. The device hummed with the effort of holding time at bay. It was a hollow noise, with a silent centre. The eerie hush of changelessness rose from the middle of the containment field. There can be no noise where time does not flow.

Guilliman looked into the box. His eyes went hard.

'Where did you get this?' he asked softly.

'Talsimar,' she said quietly. She looked at the book inside. She hated it.

'Your report said you were opposed,' he said. 'The Inquisition.'

Regret at the deaths incurred as the price of retrieval clouded Yassilli's eyes.

'I do not want the Logos Historica Verita to war with the Inquisition,' he said.

'Whether that happens or not is out of your hands,' she said, barely louder than a whisper. 'Our mission is to reveal, theirs is to obscure. We are opposed in our natures. Conflict between us is inevitable.' She paused before she spoke again, not wanting to add to the concerns of this weary being. 'So much talent wasted. We are all supposed to be on the same side.' She searched his eyes. 'I hope you think it was worth it.'

Guilliman looked at the item inside for a long moment before closing the box.

'I learned long ago that governance as much as war is a balance sheet whose figures are scribed in blood,' he said.

CHAPTER EIGHT

THE NATURE OF NIGHTMARES

Schola Mistress Valeria is stern, but she is beautiful in her sternness. Mathieu watches her as she paces the long files of desks in the freezing scholam hall. She is one, the children are many, but they obey her without question. Not one of them speaks, not one of them daydreams. They hunch over their tablets, styli ploughing through the wax like the prows of silent boats on a voyage in search of knowledge.

Partly they obey her from fear of her cane, whose sting they dread. Her temper is only marginally duller than the switch, and as quick to rouse and strike. It goes like this – first her eyes widen, then her nostrils flare, then her shoulders set, as if all the impulses that stem from anger spill from the top of her head and cascade down her body, like a flow of lava, or an avalanche in the mountains, rushing down her arms to her hands where, with nowhere else to go, her anger travels out along the cane and thence, with a flash of movement, into the body of a wayward pupil. The first stroke is initially painless, a numb line that heats pleasantly before it sears. After the first, they all hurt.

But the children also obey her from love as much as fear. They are fortunate, they know. The scholam offers them a future different to their parents' miserable lives. To be gifted enough to be worthy of a Ministorum education is a badge of honour, but to pass the exams… Well, pass the exams, Mathieu's father says, in those short minutes when they are both at home in the barracks and neither of them are asleep, pass the exams and high service awaits. Perhaps, he says, if Mathieu works hard enough, he might one day have his own room to think in, and food that comes from the ground and not the nutrient plant.

There are other schools. There are higher schools. There are more vaunted forms of service. The existence of these other institutions cannot dampen Mathieu's ambitions. To be a priest and serve the God-Emperor is his highest desire. Mathieu does not want to let his father down. Mathieu sees the exhaustion peeling away his father's youth. He sees the dirt in the lines of his father's face that he is too tired to clean off. He watches his father lose weight as the rations dwindle and the work doubles. Mathieu doesn't want that kind of service. His service must mean something. He cannot be a forgotten number in mankind's teeming trillions. That would be a waste.

This is pride. Pride in oneself is an affront to the Emperor. Pride in service is acceptable, but Mathieu's pride is not the virtuous kind. He hates the blows of Valeria's cane that come after his confessions, but he confesses to his sin often.

He fears sharing his father's fate more than he fears Valeria's wrath. It is this fear, not that of the cane, that makes him work so hard. He loves Valeria for the route to a different life that she offers. And he loves her for her cane, because the pain makes him work harder.

Service, pride and fear shape the clay of his soul.

But there is one more sculptor at work. Mathieu has a secret that he will not share with the other children. Partly because he fears they will laugh, partly because he suspects he is not the only one and he could not bear that. Mathieu thinks Valeria is beautiful. Her physical allure is faded. Though she is not yet old she is not young either. Her face is lined, her eyes sunken, her hair dry; these are the wages of endless toil. Premature age afflicts everyone that Mathieu has ever known. Inside her, he perceives a light. He sees past her pinched expression, he sees the care she has for them, her desire for them to succeed and ascend the path education offers. She has faith, she loves the Emperor, and she loves them because they will serve Him. His young heart skips when she looks at him and gives the short, sharp nod of approval she reserves for success. He yearns for more.

'The Emperor protects,' she tells him, as he learns the naming of the xenos, and the hatreds reserved for each kind.

The Emperor does protect Mathieu. He remains while others fail and are taken away, to fates the children dare not discuss.

The years pass. His desk seems to become smaller, though in truth it is he who is growing. His handwriting becomes surer. With every erasure of the wax, he scrapes away a little bit of himself. Childhood years are overwritten with the story of manhood. He takes and he passes the tests. The number of children dwindles as the first stage of childhood passes. It dwindles again as they approach puberty, and then again as they become youths.

Five years, six years, seven, then ten. Mathieu knows the *catechism minoris* by heart before all the others. He advances onto the verses majoris before he is fourteen years old. By the time he is sixteen, he knows hundreds of blessings and psalms, his understanding of the histories of the church is deep and considered, and his reading of the tarot is bettered by only three of his classmates. Soon he will be seventeen. Mistress Valeria is older, just as he is older, but he finds her more heavenly than ever. When he thinks of her odd thoughts trouble him, and he retreats to the scriptorium where he may lose himself in illuminating the books the older children are tasked with copying until the thoughts go away.

Four weeks before he is seventeen. There are twenty-three members of the class left. The rest fell by the wayside into other forms of service. Inevitably in some cases, surprisingly in others. Twenty-three men and women remaining from two hundred boys and girls. They are to be priests. Mathieu is joyous, he is proud. This new pride is of the acceptable sort. He has always been faithful. He has duties now, assisting in the cathedra, singing the plainsong that raises acts of worship from duty to elation, but of them all he most anticipates visiting the poorest members of society to hand out alms. Not because it amuses him – it is not amusing, it is gruelling, and humbling, and altogether awful. Very few people are wealthy, or even comfortable, in the Imperium. Most endure levels of poverty that would shock men from the least enlightened of prior ages. The plight of those rejected by this brutal system is terrible indeed. Mathieu finds a profound satisfaction in helping them, even if only slightly, even if it makes his own life harder. He gives away as much food as he can spare, though he has little to begin with. He gives away the cloth he is allocated to make his robes from. He becomes ragged. He gives away his sandals several times. Every time after the second occasion, he is whipped. The pain is validation of his actions. The recipients of his charity are suffering, so he too will suffer.

Mathieu has found his calling.

Fire alters his path. Fire is a rapid oxidisation. Fire changes materials from one state to another. Wood and bone are made into gas and ash by fire. But fire changes subtler things too. Fire can change fate. Fire can change a soul. Fire transmutes lives.

Fire comes from the sky. Fire and death and blood. No world is free of strife. No life is free of pain. No human being is free from change.

He is out on the agrifarms seeing to the bonded workers. He helps their bodies with gifts of food, he soothes their minds with beautiful words, and their souls are refreshed by his faith.

The first he knows of the attack is the unnatural thunder of attack craft speeding down from orbit. They are quick and precise, knocking out air defences and communications hubs before they land their ground troops to deal with the pitiful opposition.

They are Heretic Astartes armoured in blue and green. Their pauldrons bear the device of a many-headed serpent. Few in number, maybe twenty, they are more than enough to kill the company of soldiers guarding Mathieu's town five times over. They butcher the garrison with contemptuous ease. They make a show of it, Mathieu thinks later. They linger. After they are done with the soldiers, they turn their attentions to the priests.

They make for the scholam purposefully, and do unspeakable things there.

Mathieu lives because the poor hide him. When he begins to run down the muddy, unpaved road, they tackle him to the ground. They restrain him. They drag him away and bundle him into a grain silo and they will not let him out until it is all over.

It is brave, what they do, and would earn them a painful death if the enemy did not depart, their mission done, leaving all unharmed but the priests and the soldiers. They set fire to the Adeptus Administratum offices, and execute the chief official there, but leave the scribes. They make a speech. They are making a point.

In the evening, the bondsmen release Mathieu. The first thing he sees is the column of grey smoke piled up on itself, its eastern side golden with the setting sun. It is so thick it seems solid and therefore impossible. The narrow base should not support such a rippled mass. He runs towards it.

This time, the bonded workers do not stop him.

There is confusion in the town. People are shocked, but they are grateful to be alive. Help has not yet come from other towns, and Mathieu wonders dimly if similar acts have been committed elsewhere on the planet.

That is a concern for later. First, he must see what has become of his fellows.

He must see what has become of Valeria.

He hurries up the hill, along streets whose river of

cobbles make cart wheels roar. He goes into the great quadrangle of the seminary, and passes through the portal into its scholam. The doors have been ripped off their hinges.

The smell of smoke and meat mingle. Mathieu is hungry and his mouth responds automatically with a flood of saliva. He is ashamed.

The roof has fallen in. The first stars are coming out where frescos of the Emperor were. The timbers of the scholam still give out a little heat.

The younger pupils have been spared. They are variously hiding, or roaming around in shock, or weeping outside, but the older ones, those into the first years of manhood and womanhood, are all among the slaughtered. Mathieu's classmates are dead. They have been butchered imaginatively. The enemy were cruel, but they saved their most fiendish inventiveness for the mistress of the house, she who had turned empty vessels like Mathieu into priests, filling them up with the Emperor's love.

His precious Valeria is in the middle of the corpses of her students, nailed to a chair painted a gaudy yellow. Her body has been opened from crotch to neck, the organs removed, so she looks like a bag with a red lining tastelessly made in a woman's semblance, rather than herself. Upon her forehead is carved, in a shockingly neat hand, 'Deus Imperator'.

When he sees this, Mathieu falls to his knees in the mixed ash and blood, and he weeps.

'Look at me,' says a voice.

Mathieu does not look up. He is too caught up in anguish. Valeria is dead. His love, his inspiration.

'Look at me,' the voice commands.

This time Mathieu cannot help but obey. He has no choice. He turns slowly.

There is a figure behind him in the scholam portal. Golden and bright, it turns ash into treasure and the ruin into a palace. The figure is out of place in this memory. An aura of perfect light burns from it so dazzlingly Mathieu cannot discern any detail. Nevertheless, he thinks he knows who it is. His heart almost stops.

'Behold me, and pay heed, priest,' says the being. His voice is sweet thunder. His words are blissful pain. *'Through the agony of your memories and the sting of your dreams I speak to you. Mark this well. On Parmenio, I am. Find me, use me, and victory shall be assured.'*

Before the figure vanishes, or before Mathieu wakes up – he is not sure which of those things happen, if either of them – he catches a glimpse of someone else. A young girl, not a child, but barely a woman. He can look at her clearly. He can see her, though the hurtful light burns from her eyes as hot as a plasma forge.

'Find her, find me,' says the girl.

Then Mathieu awakes in his chambers, and the past has become the past once again.

It is in the nature of nightmares to disrupt a man's mind. Mathieu could not rest after the dream. He prayed awhile, and subjected himself to the cleansing pain of auto-flagellation for his remembered longing for Valeria. None of it helped. Finally, when the sixth watch klaxon rang, he scooped up Valeria's skull without engaging its mechanisms, and headed for the one place where he would not be disturbed.

* * *

'They have breached the hull. They are here.'

They were Sicarius' last words. After he had spoken those two, short sentences, his world had changed, and he had changed with it. He was no longer who he had been. He wore the same face, and carried the same name, but he was a different man.

He was a man who still heard the screams.

It did not used to be that way. His had always been a world of screams. Screeching xenos, wailing heretics, shrieking monsters to defy the imagination of mankind in the breadth of their horror and the heights of their malice. Dead or dying at his will, at his order, by his hand. Ruptured into extinction by the application of bolt, boot and sword. Deaths, endless and innumerable deaths, they soaked his soul through and through in blood and pain.

Sicarius never remembered the screams of those who died before the rift. He was righteous in their making. They did not trouble him. Those deaths were just.

But the screams of his men – those he could not forget, and they troubled him deeply.

Bitter saliva leaked from his Betcher's Gland. He swallowed the slow issue of his own poisons. The screams rang in his head. The high screaming of Space Marines in the red claws of agony. He expected normal men without the benefits of Adeptus Astartes gifts to shrill so keenly when faced with death, but his brothers?

He closed his eyes, bowed his head. He enumerated the dead, remembering those lost in the warp, and asked, foolishly perhaps, for the Emperor's forgiveness.

A deep trance enveloped him. He remembered his brothers' faces and forced himself to live their individual deaths again as he fired and fell back, helpless to aid them.

Immersed in past horrors, he only heard the priest at the last moment, and only when he coughed quietly to alert Sicarius he was no longer alone on the observation deck.

Sicarius looked up sharply with red-rimmed eyes.

Mathieu was a slender man, deceptively feeble in build, appearing almost a youth. He had the earnestness of a man yet to reach his thirtieth year, with the blend of hope and despair that marked out those who wanted to change the galaxy, but who could never coax the uncaring stars to move. Sicarius had seen him fight, and knew the strength concealed beneath Mathieu's patched robe. He had seen him speak. Mathieu was a rare man the stars might heed.

Sicarius twitched the fancy away as unworthy. Mathieu was a man, Sicarius a Space Marine, and yet…

Mathieu's hair was shaved around the sides of his head, long and greased tall on top. This flopped over into Mathieu's face, obscuring one of his eyes without diminishing his gaze. Mathieu had an uncomfortable gaze. It implied no judgment, but left Sicarius feeling wanting. Mathieu was cradling his servo-skull. Had it been active Sicarius would have assuredly heard the priest approach, but he carried it carefully in his hands, its systems powered down. The long fingers of one of Mathieu's hands wrapped around ivory bone. The others idly traced the HV engraved into the forehead. The fingers too looked weak, the fingers of an aesthete, suitable for moving abacus beads and determining the fates of men he would never meet with the stroke of a pen. Many men had fingers like that. They were a destroyer's fingers, but not a warrior's. Another misapprehension. Mathieu looked like a bureaucrat, unless one paid a little more attention to the marks on his skin. There, another story could be read.

There were the calluses on his right-hand thumb and forefinger exacted by his chainsword in return for battle skill, and the notch on his left forefinger carved by the repetitive squeezing of a laspistol's trigger. Upon the back of his right hand was a crossed scar, an older and a newer wound joined together. At the base of his left, where wrist met hand to arm, a thicker line hinted at a horrific injury long healed.

Sicarius was well versed in judging threat. The priest was anything but weak.

'Captain Sicarius, isn't it?' said Mathieu pleasantly. The two had been present in the same room on many occasions. Until that moment, they had yet to speak with one another. 'Captain of the Lord Regent's Victrix Guard?'

'Yes,' said Sicarius. He examined his situation. He wanted to stay there, on his own. He did not want to share the space. He had assumed, not unreasonably, that an observation gallery would be the perfect place to be alone while the ship was in the warp, though there were other reasons for his choice. The shutters were closed. There was nothing to see. They were dangerously close to the edge. Who would want to go there? Theoretical, he thought, Mathieu seeks the same solitude as I. But how much of the same? Simply solitude, or more? He constructed a number of practicals to extricate himself from the situation. Irksomely, he did not wish to appear rude. If it were not for that, he would have simply walked away.

So deeply ingrained was the theoretical-practical model of dialectics into his habit that he utilised it without thinking. There had been times that the mode had fallen out of fashion within the Ultramarines, but it had never completely gone away, and Guilliman's return had seen its resurgence.

'It's terrifyingly close, isn't it?' said Mathieu. 'The warp, I mean.' The priest looked up at the plasteel shutters.

Then he wants the same as I, thought Sicarius. More than solitude.

'On the other side of that metal, outside the flimsy bubble of the Geller field, are the depths of the empyrean, where the possible is but one among many, and the impossible is true,' said Mathieu.

Sicarius glanced at the shutters as if he had not noticed them, although he had been staring at them unblinkingly for two hours and three minutes before he had shut his eyes.

'There is only hell on the other side of that shutter,' he said.

'Oh, but there isn't!' said Mathieu with a nervous smile. 'There's so much more. You say a hell, but there is holiness there as well. Out there, the light of the Astronomican burns with a pure light that no evil thing can block. Evil flooded the galaxy, and it could not extinguish the light nor touch its source.' He smiled again. 'Don't you think that's amazing?'

'You have come here to be closer to your god,' stated Sicarius.

'I have,' said Mathieu. He closed his eyes and arched his neck, basking in the light of the Emperor as if it were flooding through the screened-off oculus.

Sicarius' lip curled. He almost walked out then. Outrage rooted him to the spot, outrage that this god-talker would come here and interrupt his meditation on the screams, and speak of glorious light where there was only horror.

'How have the Space Marines managed to avoid the truth of the Imperial Cult for so long, in the face of all the evidence?' asked Mathieu, suddenly looking at him again.

'What?' said Sicarius, wrong-footed.

'There are so many miracles in the galaxy at this time. Why do you not see the Emperor's hand? You do not see him working for us, on all our behalf. I am genuinely curious.'

'We are taught to be circumspect about miracles,' said Sicarius gruffly. 'They are rarely what they seem.'

'We have seen many in this campaign alone.' Mathieu's nervous smile was welcoming, the kind of smile that invited conversation and fellow feeling. Sicarius glowered at him, but the priest was not dissuaded. 'You yourself have seen the Damned Legion fight. You have been in the presence of the blessed Saint Celestine. These phenomena are given us by the Emperor.'

'I have seen what you might call miracles. You will not convince me, militant-apostolic, that what I have seen during my service are inexplicable and, therefore, divine. Hundreds of times, I have seen my brothers of the Librarius cast destruction at our enemies using the power of their minds. If I were to follow your reasoning, I would call them wizards and cower at their might, ascribing a divine origin for powers that are a part of the fact of this universe. The things they do are strange, uncanny by human measure, but there are many things in the material realm also that are bizarre. Are they all the work of gods? All works of artifice and sorcery are but the doings of sentient minds. If what you say is true, and the Emperor is a god, then so in a small way are Brother Tigurius and his ilk.'

'You are attempting to explain the inexplicable, a mistake made by philosophers and technologists alike throughout the ages. The warp cannot be explained,' said Mathieu. 'It is a realm unlike this, where dark powers clash with our most holy Emperor. It is the stage for the performance of gods.'

'None of it is divine. There are things that call themselves gods. They are not. I have fought them. The Emperor fought them. The Emperor is a man. My lord Guilliman has told me so himself.'

Mathieu closed his eyes against the radiance of his Emperor again, and laughed a little. 'Do you know Yassilli Sulymanya?'

'The Rogue Trader that serves Lord Guilliman's Logos? I have met her. I do not know her well. Why?'

Mathieu smiled and opened his eyes. 'She would agree with you.'

'The primarch brings those of like mind to serve him,' said Sicarius.

'He brought me into his service,' Mathieu pointed out.

'You are a necessary exception,' Sicarius said.

'An unwelcome one?'

The way Sicarius moved his head made his opinion clear.

'You find my faith objectionable, and that is understandable. But I am not guileless. The Lord Regent says he elevated me because the less exalted members of his crusade find me inspiring,' said Mathieu. 'The common soldiers, the lowest deck hand. I am glad. It is my vocation to serve the meek. But that is not the reason. The real reason is that having me in the role removes him from the influence of the high church.'

'He is the primarch, he is not influenced by anyone.'

'If only life were that simple,' said Mathieu. 'I do not think you are guileless either. You know life isn't that simple, I can tell.' Again, Mathieu abruptly changed the subject. 'Why are you here, in this viewing gallery without a view?'

'Not for the same reasons that you are here,' he said.

'You were lost in the warp for a while, were you not?'

Sicarius gave him a sharp look. 'You are well informed. Too well informed. That knowledge is not widely shared.'

'I have the trust of high men. What was it like?' asked Mathieu.

Sicarius shook his head. 'I cannot explain, and I do not care to try. I came back through secret ways to Macragge and returned to the service of my primarch. That is all you need to know.'

Mathieu hugged his servo-skull close to his body. 'This is an infernal age. We all have nightmares to contend with. You are not alone.'

'I am alone in what I saw. You ask why I come here? Very well, I will tell you. I come to show I am not afraid, and that I will have my vengeance on the things that killed my men. If it takes me ten thousand years, it will be so.'

'Is that why you come here unarmoured, in your robes, to show contempt?'

Sicarius had had enough. 'You pry too much, priest. My Lord Guilliman might indulge you, but I am not so inclined. Goodnight.'

'They are right to fear you! You are right to show them contempt!' Mathieu called softly after him. His voice shushed to one end of the gallery and back again. 'Be not afraid, captain, be joyful! The Emperor protects!'

Sicarius strode from the gallery. The Emperor had not protected his brothers, and no priest's words would ever silence their screams.

CHAPTER NINE

GALATAN MOVES

Justinian worked in the arena alone. There were dozens of training facilities on Galatan, ranging from small gymnasia to full simulation combat environments and cavernous eco-halls where alien worlds were remade. But with the garrison on high alert the warriors stationed on the star fortress took as many additional training sessions as they could, and most were crowded. Justinian picked the facility he had because it was far from most barracks, and therefore little used.

He wanted to be left in peace.

The disrobing rooms were clean, and the lumens bright, but it had the feeling of benign abandonment. There were rows of lockers, all empty. He always took the same one. He pulled his name slide from his bag and pushed it into the bracket on the door. 'Parris, J. Sgt. V Co., 6th Aux. Sq.,' it read, plain bone within dark blue. On impulse he ran his fingers over it. He had been assigned to lead an Intercessor squad. The Primaris Marines were tacked on to the Fifth Company. They were, for the time being, outside both the normal strictures of the Codex and the organisation they had enjoyed in the Unnumbered Sons. It only added to his alienation. He and his men were outsiders in every possible way.

He removed his robes, then his body glove, exposing a massively muscled body studded with neural interface ports. His black carapace showed as darker patches of skin, ridging his flesh where it ended at the base of his back, at the tops of his arms and on his legs. Under his skin moved his sinew coils, a network of supplementary muscles unique to the Primaris Marines. This was one of three differences between his implants – the Emperor's Gifts, the older Space Marines called them – and those of the original Novamarines.

Most Novamarines were of the older Adeptus Astartes type. They were present in Ultramar at nearly full strength, having kept recruiting the whole time they were engaged in the war. There were only a couple of dozen Primaris Marines in the Chapter at present, but he wondered how long it would be before every Novamarine was a Primaris Marine.

He covered his nakedness with a pair of wide training trousers, leaving his chest bare, and went into the training hall.

A row of tractoris dummies and combat servitors slept in upright glass coffins at the end of the gymnasium. He pressed his thumb to a panel. The coffin lit up. The dummy stood tall. Sensor lights winked behind the blank plastek of its face.

'Tractoris servitor ready for instruction. State needs and training program.'

'Standard martial pattern practice. Minimal violence.'

'Compliance,' said the machine.

The door hissed upwards. The tractoris strode out. Justinian found these dummies eerie. They were unusually smooth for devices of this era, their bodies made up of padded, soft transplasteks, with faceless heads. Strictly speaking, they were an obscure form of servitor. There was a human brain buried somewhere within its chest cavity, but all evidence of the biological was hidden away. These things were designed to take a beating and get back into their coffins without the need for much maintenance.

Tractoris dummies moved in a predictable series of combat routines. They were far less versatile than the true combat servi-tors, but combat servitors were lucky to last a month in the training cages. The tractoris' intended use was for the reinforcement of muscle memory in the Space Marines to hone their abilities, for the practising of combat forms, light contact strikes and take downs, not full combat.

Under most of their modes, fighting a tractoris took barely any mental power; indeed, the warriors were encouraged to think on other matters while they underwent their routines to help further bed their fighting skills into their subconscious – fighting as a physical meditation.

Justinian had no argument with that. Sparring with the tractoris gave him solitary time he badly needed.

'Program selection, pankration. Mode selection, mirror mode.'

'Pankration mirror mode. Compliance,' said the machine voice. It came from the wall, not the unit.

The machine followed him to a padded wrestling square.

Justinian moved in towards the dummy, arms up to protect his face in a posture any pugilist from human history would have recognised.

Pankration was one of several martial arts Justinian had been instructed in. He could not tell reliably if the lessons he remembered were real or if they were the result of hypnomat memory implantation. His life before the Indomitus Crusade was an endless series of short activations for his body and mind to be tested, and lessons that may not have happened anywhere outside of his head. But for a few occasions, he was put back into stasis before he had time to come fully awake. Intellectually, he knew these periods, some no more than ten or twelve minutes long, were separated by hundreds of years. To him they seemed like a series of repetitive days, as if he were constantly trying to focus on something, but was distracted before he could begin by the same questions and the same tests, or as if he had been ill for a very long time, never really sleeping, never truly waking.

That had gone on for eight thousand years. It was a wonder he remained sane.

Justinian was immensely grateful not to be in a box any more.

After his Primaris cohort had been activated and added to a temporary Chapter in the Unnumbered Sons of Guilliman, Justinian had been trained by the older sort of Space Marine. The moves he had been put through were second nature by then, even though he had never physically performed them before.

Justinian went through a series of punches that got faster and faster. As he shadow boxed, his fists made short, sharp noises in the air. He turned his exhalations into matching sounds, little cries that helped him add power to his blows. The machine copied him exactly, helping him pace himself and correct any mistakes. He made few. He was a well-honed fighting machine with millennia of training and a century of combat experience.

But he did not know who he was.

He remembered the day exactly when the men had come to his scholam on Ardium. He had made no attempt to join the Chapter. He had had no intention of doing so, in fact, but the men had come with Imperial writs that all the boys in his class were to be tested. He had no idea why. He had gone into the small, brightly lit medicae bay in the scholam not knowing if he were to be assessed for genetic deviancy, tested for thought crime, turned into a servitor, or prodded at to fulfil some health census for the inscrutable workings of the Adeptus Administratum. Anything was possible.

He had gone in terrified. That day he had stolen a small toy from his brother. He feared he had been found out. In his young imagination, an eternity as a soulless cyborg awaited.

The man who ran the testing was some sort of official. He had teeth so thin they were blue grey. His lips were very pink. Together blue teeth and pink lips made an insincere smile. The man gestured at a chair. Justinian sat down. Another man with metal eyes and a long, white plastek smock with a high collar placed a large device against Justinian's arm. There was a sharp pain and a whir of internal mechanisms.

An age passed before the light on the side illuminated with an audible click: a green light.

That was that. He had gone to the scholam that morning

expecting to go back to his family's cramped quarters in the evening, to ask his father how his day had been in the manu-factoria that filled the lower halves of all Ardium's hives. He would have asked his mother's permission to go into the sky parks where he could play with his brothers and sisters among the trees and look through the armour-glass skin of the hive at the clouds below. Ardium was a hive world, but it was in Ultramar, and the lives of its people had been rewarding. Hard, but good.

He was going to give his brother his toy back.

A green light took all that away.

He never saw his family again. He doubted his parents even knew what happened to him. The Primaris programme had been conducted in absolute secrecy. He wondered what awful lie his mother and father had been told to make his loss easier to bear.

That was eight thousand years ago, a number so shocking he grunted it as he punched.

'Eight. Thousand. Years.'

It was petty to think so with the galaxy going to ruin, but somehow it did not seem fair.

Inner pain made his muscles tense. The tractoris' movements went awry in response. He forced himself to relax. He took a deep breath, turning his sense of dislocation into a steely determination. The machine mimicked him. He stood at ease, so did the machine. He went through the first of the eighty-seven patterns of engagement, working his way up through them to the end, then again, and again, until he had executed them all to perfection.

He had been given great power. It was an honour, he reminded himself. Rather than living an unremarkable life, he had been given the chance at heroism. He would be among the few who would save the many, so that other little boys might go to school, and while away the day dreaming about playing in woods under glass skies.

He had come to terms with that. He had come to terms with the changes that time had wrought on the Imperium, and the war he must fight. If he did not fight it, his species – the whole galaxy – would be lost to Chaos. No man could turn away from that.

What he could not stomach was the loss of brothers for a second time at the behest of those beyond his influence.

He began to kick and punch again, adding twists and grappling moves from other disciplines to create a free-form routine. In a few hours the star fortress would leave the orbit of Drohl and head to Parmenio to support the primarch's battle there. The station was alive with preparation. Its halls shook to the growing power of its reactors. He should have been excited. He enjoyed fighting. It was his purpose.

He remained distracted.

A glorious brotherhood a hundred thousand in number was no more. A future in the Ultramarines had beckoned. It had not come to pass.

Every certainty he ever had was confounded, every time.

He was not the only one to be dissatisfied. He remembered Bjarni, red-faced and angry that he would not return to Fenris. Kalael, close-mouthed as always, had accepted his secondment without revealing it.

Though Felix was a tetrarch now and an Ultramarine, he must have felt the same dislocation, Justinian was sure, when the Unnumbered Sons were divided. They all did, to a lesser or greater degree. Such was the importance of the fraternal bond to a Space Marine. If the bond were not a certainty, or if it were poorly expressed, there was space for doubt. A Space Marine knew no fear, but he was not an emotionless automaton.

His own assignment was a gut punch revelation. Justinian presented a reasonable face to the world. He was liked for it, trusted. Every man hides pain beneath the surface. This was his.

He finished his routine with burning muscles. Sweat ran over his skin in rivulets.

Justinian showered, his allowance of three bursts of scalding hot water blasting his sweat away. Hot air from the same nozzles dried him. He retrieved his body glove and name slide and took a monotrain to his company's arming chambers. Though he had purposefully chosen the training facility for its remoteness, nothing was conveniently placed on vast Galatan. Everything was a journey away.

The Novamarines Fifth Company barracks were temporary – this was an Ultramarines star fortress – but there was plenty of room in the craft to accommodate them. Like most things in this era, it had a massive overcapacity. There was space for the Novamarines, the hundred or so Deathwatch, all thirty thousand of the Ultramarian Auxilia, and all the rest with space to spare.

Who knows how long his barracks had lain empty before it had been given to the Novamarines Fifth Company? It could have been forever. Centuries in stasis had given Justinian a weird sense for neglected spaces, as if he could sense the moribundity beneath vitality. He was attracted to such places. He liked them.

He padded down the central aisle of the company arming hall. There were a few others in their cubicles, quietly working on their weaponry. It was so subdued compared to the raucous chambers of the *Rudense*. He exchanged short greetings with his would-be brothers, and entered his own cubicle. His armour hung on its stand, his weapons on their racks. His workbench was clean and tidy. He had not left it in such good order. The Chapter was well served by its serfs.

The light bone and dark blue quarters of his armour challenged him. A Space Marine could not help but identify with his battleplate. When donned, it moved with him. It became part of him. He saw his brothers armoured more often than he saw their faces. They lived in their armour. Out of it, he was two halves of one being. He briefly felt vulnerable, threatened almost by his own warrior aspect hanging so blunt and brutal on its stand, as if it would reach out and crush him for his weakness.

The feeling fled. He reached out for the armour, and unclicked the right gauntlet.

No imagination could have predicted how his life turned out. He had been many things in a short space of time spread over millennia. Little of it seemed plausible, if he thought about it. But if he did not know who he was, he knew what he was. No matter how awkward he felt, the sense of displacement did not change that.

He was Sergeant Justinian Parris, Primaris Space Marine, a loyal servant of the Emperor.

But he was no Novamarine.

With this sentiment held firmly in his heart, he reached for the buzzer on the wall, and called for the arming serfs.

Galatan was the largest of the star forts of Ultramar. Since before the Horus Heresy it had stood guard over the space lanes of the Five Hundred Worlds. It was a relic of a time before recorded history, when mankind's first galactic empire had risen to heights of technology and power never again attained.

Galatan was no mere battlestation, but a city in space, a hundred kilometres across, as large as the lost orbital plates of Terra. Its weapons bays bristled with machineries of destruction potent enough to see off a fleet of ships. There had been six similar star fortresses in Ultramar. For ages they had been sentinels in deep space. Only during times of the greatest need did they move. During the First Tyrannic War half their number had been redeployed from their strategic points, but that was a rare instance.

That had changed with the coming of the Great Rift, and Nurgle's assault on Guilliman's home. Now they went where they were needed, and they were needed everywhere.

Three had fallen to Typhus' plague fleet. Purposefully targeted and overwhelmed by massive force, their defenders cut down by disease, they had been ravaged and destroyed.

Nobody expected that fate for Galatan. Galatan was the oldest, and the largest. It was equipped with weapons few understood. None could attack it and survive.

The order came to prepare for departure from Drohl early in the first watch, before Justinian had entered the training hall. By the end of the second, when Justinian donned his armour and went on duty, preparations were well underway. The great quadruple reactors at the station's hub were coaxed to full output. Thousands of tech-priests prayed to ensure the task was done with the utmost respect to the venerable machines. All others of the Cult Mechanicus who could suspend their duties did so, wishing to pay their respects as the secret engines of the past were roused so completely.

The fifth watch saw the reactors operating at peak efficiency. Their thumping throb shook the fortress. Shortly after, main motive was engaged. The star fortress was ringed with engines. All along the side closest to Drohl Magna they flared, pushing the giant away from the planet it had been protecting. Such power was required to move its mass, but more was required to feed the integrity fields and structural bracing pistons that kept the station from tearing itself apart.

Drohl Magna trembled. Galatan's movement triggered earthquakes across the southern continent. City buildings, weakened by the war won there by the Novamarines, collapsed. Tsunamis lashed the coasts of Drohl Magna's many islands. Had the population not been so thoroughly reduced by the conflict, millions would have died.

Slowly, ever so slowly, Galatan rumbled away. Its gravity wake displaced the debris of fleet battles. It knocked asteroids from their orbit in the system's belt. For seven days it lumbered outwards, past Drohl Secundus, Ganymedus, Atoli, and the burned-out hulks of the orbital habitats around Dumar. Seven days it took to travel to the inner edge of Drohl's Kuiper belt, and the Mandeville point there.

The point was reached. The star fortress stopped, but there was no time to rest.

Inside the star fortress, a rising scream set up from the hub, penetrating every part of the vessel. The station's huge population took shelter in their quarters. For a day and a half Galatan wailed, until finally it was ready to jump.

With a sucking roar that unnaturally defied the silence of the void, Galatan's warp engines tore a massive hole in the veil between gross reality and the immaterium. Real space plasma engines shot flares of white hot fire, pushing Galatan into the hole, and the star fortress passed from this reality into the warp.

The rift closed with a bang. Comets, perturbed from their static positions in the outer belt by Galatan, drifted sunwards. Otherwise there was no sign the fortress had been there at all.

CHAPTER TEN

THE PLAGUE SHIPS

The Spear of Espandor crusade broke warp and tore without delay towards the centre of the Parmenio System, and the prime world. The fleet was swollen greatly with reinforcements from all over Ultramar. Several were returned taskforces that had completed their missions, driving away splinter forces of the Death Guard and making safe the worlds they had invaded. The rest were reinforcements drawn from across the segmentum. Adeptus Mechanicus formed the main: legions of skitarii, battle robots and three demi-legios of the Oberon, Fortis and Atarus Titan legions. There were dozens of Astra Militarum regiments, convents of the Sisters of Battle, Militarum Tempestus strike groups, and more.

Guilliman had asked for some of this help, but much had come unbidden, to aid the primarch in the saving of his home.

From the command deck of the *Macragge's Honour*

Roboute Guilliman controlled his fleet absolutely. A huge deck of screens was arrayed in a semicircle before the dais where he oversaw everything. His advisers gathered to his right, a horde of functionaries to his left, ready to take his orders wherever they needed to go.

For a full day the ships had burned engines at maximum capacity, attaining speeds close to one tenth that of light, before sailing through the inner bounds and beginning their lengthy deceleration. Vulnerable transport craft flew at the heart of the fleet formation, protected by lines of escorts. The major warships formed a sharp spear blade, the *Macragge's Honour* at the very tip.

Preparations for the attack were constant. Men and women came and went from the primarch's side. Guilliman did not move from his station. He took his meat and drink there but no rest. He monitored every operation, his capacious mind processing all, and making constant adjustments. Ship-master Brahe, tiny in his command throne before the primarch's station, took as little rest as a mortal man could, only leaving when Guilliman ordered him to sleep.

Still slowing, they passed quickly in-system, driving hard past worlds ravaged by plague and war.

'The lesser planets of Parmenio suffer much,' said Tetrarch Felix, Guilliman's erstwhile equerry. His role was to lead the planetfall upon Parmenio, and he was often elsewhere ordering his warriors, but he spared an hour on the command deck when he could to stand at his gene-father's side and learn.

'They will be saved in time,' said Guilliman. 'Parmenio must be liberated first, or we shall find ourselves playing the role of besiegers. We strike fast and strike hard at the heart of corruption. These outlying warbands can be dealt with easily once my brother is dead. We cannot tarry.'

No one disagreed with him. They were all grim-faced. Seeing so many perfect worlds of Ultramar infested with the Plague God's evil saddened them. They had no room in their hearts and minds for anything other than vengeance.

The steady glint of Parmenio grew. First one light among many, soon it outshone the stars and soon after that it was brighter than the globular dots of its sister planets whirling about the sun. Guilliman disregarded his own written strategies and kept the fleet dead on course for the world, sailing along the plane of the ecliptic in defiance of any projectile that might be hurled their way. He wished to send his brother a message by his bold approach: you are not welcome, depart or die.

From glint to dot to ball to globe, Parmenio grew under Guilliman's steady gaze. Three continents graced its surface. Gardamaus was far to the south and alone amid the ocean, while the other two, Hecatone and Keleton, were close to each other and together dominated the northern hemisphere. They were newly split in geological terms, a mere million years apart from each other's embrace. Divided by the narrow River Sea, spurned Hecatone reached yearning headlands towards Keleton's bleak, uncaring hills.

New lights winked into view, curling around the equator from the planet's nightside on a steady orbital track.

'Enemy fleet in sight, my lord,' Shipmaster Brahe announced.

'Give me long-range scans and breakdowns of their capabilities, quickly. I want the main augur array to conduct sweeps on the planet immediately,' ordered Guilliman.

Guilliman discounted the plague fleet; it was a fraction of the size of the Imperial force, with only three capital ships. Still, it had to be dealt with.

The craft were in various stages of decay, more akin to the derelicts one might find caught in gravity wells near the sites of old conflicts than functional ships. But they sailed the void still, rusted and battered though they looked, coasting through the debris fields of Parmenio's shattered orbitals like diseased pelagic predators. Two showed signs of diabolical favour and had been transmuted utterly by Nurgle's whim. The hulls were soft, coated in exuberant growths of flesh. They looked too rotted to be dangerous, but Guilliman knew better. He issued orders that they be targeted as a matter of priority.

'Mortarion's flagship is not here,' said Tribune Maldovar Colquan of the Adeptus Custodes, who alone had not left the primarch's side throughout their approach, but stood by him, brooding in his golden armour. 'He may not be present.'

'His ship does not need to be here,' said Guilliman. 'Mortarion is no longer a primarch. He is empowered by the dark energies of the warp. A daemon requires no vessel to travel the stars, and nor does he. He will be here. He has practically informed me of the fact. Do not be deceived by the strength of his fleet. This is an invitation. See, the fleet he has stationed here are not Legion, but the vessels of lesser renegades.'

'It is a lure,' said Felix.

'It is, but I go willingly to the hook,' said Guilliman.

'The fallen Chapters are more contemptible than the traitors of old,' said Colquan. The Adeptus Custodian simmered in his armour. He rarely spoke but when he did he spat his words, an inch away from anger. He ejected every syllable from his mouth hard, each laden with the energy of a bullet. Colquan was ashamed that his order had done so little before the primarch rose from his slumber. Shame affects all men differently. Colquan's manifested as rage: rage at Guilliman's near usurpation of the Emperor, rage at the state of the galaxy, but mostly rage at himself. He could kill a thousand enemies, and it would not be enough. Every dead foe reminded him of the thousands more his sword would have cleaved had he not been confined to Terra. 'They leapt to their damnation with both feet. They saw clearly what was on offer, and accepted it.'

'Their reasons are their own,' said Guilliman. 'Do not fixate on ranking their degrees of treachery. We need to concentrate on what they are, and how they fight.'

'They are corrupt. Less skilled in combat than the Traitor Legion,' said Colquan.

'They are formidable, nevertheless,' said Guilliman. 'Attack Group Atticus, peel off and assault the plague fleet. Keep them from us as we near the planet.'

Men hurried to relay his orders. The attack group, a fleet in its own right, powered out of formation. Lesser squadrons broke off from elsewhere in the flotilla to form a fighting picket between the main taskforce and Atticus to intercept the plague ships should any break through.

'We have identified a potential source of warp energy, my lord,' Shipmaster Brahe informed him. 'In Hecaton, the capital of the eastern continent.'

'Show me,' commanded Guilliman.

A tacticaria hololith sphere flickered on. Parmenio was presented within as a true-pict graphic. The western continent was untouched, the southern mostly hale looking. These two landmasses were the greens and browns and crystals blues of a healthy, living world, though long dark streaks of smoke tailed off the major cities.

Hecatone was afflicted, covered over with sickly yellow fogs.

'Reveal it,' said the primarch.

'Compensating for atmospheric conditions,' intoned an augury specialist transmechanic.

The image flickered. Arcane technologies stripped the fog away from the holo.

The last time Guilliman had seen the world, Hecatone's fertile plains had been a startling emerald, with circular fields of crops visible from orbit, studded with the brilliant white flashes of marble towns and the grey squares of transit centres. All was gone to filth. On the far eastern side of the mountains dividing the continent in two was nothing but ashen waste, agrilands and urban centres all reduced to dead black ground. On the west, the side nearest to the continent of Keleton, a filthy black marsh had been conjured into being. It swamped the plains of Hecatone right the way to the shores of the River Sea and the port city of Tyros.

'Show me the city of Hecaton,' ordered Guilliman.

The tacticaria rotated until Hecaton was in front of Guilliman's face.

'Close in view,' ordered the Master Augurum.

The holo expanded, sucking the viewers down to near ground level.

Hecaton's famous stepped plazas built into the mountainside were grey with weeds. The channels between its water gardens were dead black lines. Overlays imposed themselves upon the visual feed, bringing forth fresh colours. The effect was similar to heat vision, or dark sight, but this particular filter was gathered by the ship's psy-oculus, an esoteric piece of machinery that allowed the mapping of etheric energies.

With this false witch-sight engaged, Hecaton was replaced by a many-armed vortex rotating over the world. It reached long streamers far out across the planet, and where they touched corruption took root.

'That is certainly where Mortarion's clock is, in Hecaton,' said Guilliman. 'An orbital strike is preferable. We destroy it and break the web he weaves across Ultramar. Determine shielding.'

'Scans indicate the presence of a warp field,' said the Master Augurum. 'No voids.'

'Give me control of the main augur array,' said Guilliman.

'As you command.'

Guilliman's fingers danced over numerous gel pads and brass keyboards. He paused every so often, eyes flicking back and forth over multiple displays. 'Here is the likely source.' A power complex covered over in fleshy veins appeared as a flat pict in a hololithic orb. 'It is defended with a warp field. Prepare psyk-out missiles. Breach the shield. The gap will not last. Unfortunately the power source must be destroyed on the ground. Tetrarch Felix, Captain Sicarius.' Guilliman's voice was carried out to his warriors' dropships by a hovering vox-angel. 'Prepare for immediate deployment.'

A klaxon hooted.

'Loading psyk-out missiles, my lord,' announced the Master Ordinatum.

Guilliman looked to the display where the vanguard of

his fleet and the plague ships tussled as numbered triangles in a vectored sphere.

'Await my order to fire. Brahe, full power towards the planet.'

'We have few of these missiles, my lord,' grumbled Colquan.

'That is why we will not miss,' said Guilliman.

The renegade Space Marine fleet saw the *Macragge's Honour* pulling away from its escort. A squadron of destroyers managed to break the Imperial cordon and move towards the flagship. Brahe ordered his gunners to cast a wall of mass shot in their path. Their death would be several minutes in coming, but they would die.

'Range to planet,' said Guilliman.

'Thirty-two thousand kilometres and closing.'

'Reverse thrusters full,' ordered Brahe.

'My lord, the payload is free and ready for release,' reported the Master Ordinatum.

'Hold fire until two thousand six hundred kilometres,' ordered Guilliman. 'Point defence laser and particle beam turrets stand by to intercept anti-munitions fire.' He looked to Colquan. 'We will not miss.'

The *Macragge's Honour* bulled its way through space, debris meteors from Parmenio's wrecked orbitals igniting a display of localised lightning storms and scintillas of annihilation flare all over the forward void shields. The ship groaned at the twin stresses of deceleration and Parmenio's strengthening gravity. All was quiet. The crew, whether baseline human, servitor or Adeptus Astartes, were absorbed by their tasks.

'Range, two thousand six hundred kilometres,' reported the Master Ordinatum. 'Point defence turrets zeroed and ready.'

'Tetrarch Felix, Captain Sicarius, launch,' commanded the primarch.

A hundred plasma lights shoaled away from the embarkation deck and hangars of the *Macragge's Honour*. Guilliman waited until the attack craft had cleared the fore of the vessel and were speeding towards the planet.

'Release ordnance,' he said.

'Release ordnance,' relayed Brahe.

'Ordnance released,' confirmed the Master Ordinatum.

'We are too far out for an orbital drop,' said Colquan. 'They are vulnerable.'

'Ordinarily, yes,' said Guilliman. 'Hundreds rather than thousands of kilometres is the norm. In this position the *Macragge's Honour* shields them from the attentions of the plague fleet and is ready to respond to any surprises my brother might have for us. Watch and learn, Custodian.'

The *Macragge's Honour* shuddered ever so slightly, a warship's equivalent of a gentle exhalation.

From the plough-blade prow, four massive torpedoes slid free. They were immense, as large as some of the smaller ships in the fleet. Void drives made up the back third. Servitors hardwired into their missile's extensive cogitation suites guided them. They had their own batteries of point defence weapons, jamming suites and decoy launchers, for the warheads they carried were precious indeed.

Carried by each was a cluster of caskets, arranged like the slugs in a stub-revolver's chamber deep inside the missile's layered armour. There were eighteen, in three rows of six capsules, a small payload for such a mighty delivery system, but devastating to the right target.

Within the capsules were the refined remains of pariahs, individuals who, like the Sisters of Silence, had a minimal presence in the warp and whose very existence was anathema to the creatures and energies of that realm. It was heretical weaponry according to some, and vanishingly rare.

Guilliman had no qualms about its use.

The missiles moved slowly at first relative to the flagship, but their engines accelerated them away towards the planet. A cloud of reflective chaff surrounded them, replenished by the missile's onboard launchers every thirty seconds, leaving a glittering trail behind them in space.

Nothing shot at the missiles until they came near to the planet. Defensive fire twinkled on the blighted portion of Parmenio. The torpedoes' own systems retaliated against those munitions moving slow enough to target. Swift missiles were peppered with hyper-velocity ball shot. Micro lasers burned out shell heads. Enemy las-fire dispersed in the chaff field, beam coherency scattered.

'Three minutes to impact,' announced the Master Ordinatum.

'Taskforce approaching planetary envelope.'

The missiles outpaced Felix's invasion vanguard. Orange flared around their blunt noses. Heat shields shrugged aside the burn of re-entry.

The *Macragge's Honour*'s own guns were rumbling, hurling modest munitions at the world below. Their aim was not to destroy the enemy – Guilliman feared for Parmenio too much to do that from orbit – but to cripple the aerial defence network shielding the complex.

A glaring flash blinked through the oculus, slow to die: an enemy ship exploding unnoticed. All eyes were on the psyk-out missiles.

Guilliman leaned forward suddenly as one of the missiles

drew a hail of fire and detonated, spilling anti-psychic fallout into the stratosphere.

Half a minute later, the surviving torpedoes impacted on the target. On the tacticaria display the psychic maelstrom shrank back like paper catching fire. It wavered on the edge of dissipation, then slowly began to creep back.

'My lord, the warp shield is inactive,' reported the Master Augurum. 'Psy-oculus indicates building etheric activity. The shield will be back on line within ten minutes, maximum projection. Minimum estimate of five minutes.'

Guilliman nodded. Even at the worst estimate, Felix would perform his landing without fear of hitting the warp shield. He surveyed the swirling eye of corruption blighting Hecaton. Soon it would close for good.

He opened fleet wide vox. 'Attacking this facility will be dangerous and unpleasant. I do not commit you to this task lightly, but there is no other way. Mortarion's warp network rots the fabric of the materium throughout our realm. It brings his warriors strength. It feeds his daemonic allies with the black energies needed to sustain their essences. It speeds the spread of his unnatural plagues. With the warp clock of Parmenio smashed, victory here will be all the easier. This fight, this initial fight, will be among the hardest performed for this world. So I say to you, go forward in the name of the Emperor. He expects the utmost of you. He demands the greatest of efforts, for you are gifted by Him with strength to be mightier than other warriors, in order that you might watch over lesser men and protect them, and deliver them from these evils that beset our galaxy. As you fight, I shall watch over you.' He paused. 'And my father shall watch over you also.'

He looked to the watch commander. 'Order second

invasion wave drop pods to prepare. Send messages to all troop transports and Titan drop-ships to ready themselves for immediate deployment the moment the warp clock is gone. Brahe, bring us into stable high orbit. Choose a firing position, target the cathedral of Hecaton. Maintain suppressive bombardment upon enemy air defences.'

The crew responded with a chorus of affirmatives. The *Macragge's Honour* slowed and turned about to hold stationary anchor over the city. Its lance batteries charged, and in the decks housing its macrocannons, the gun crews laboured to load the weapons with destructive magma shells.

'Second wave commanders reporting readiness, my lord,' the Master of the Watch said.

'Launch,' Guilliman said.

At the primarch's order the launch tubes of a dozen ships belched fire, and the Space Marines of Ultramar raced across the void past the dying remains of the plague fleet, towards the diseased planet.

CHAPTER ELEVEN

MORTARION'S FANE

A bang, a rumble of jets. Acceleration pushed at Felix's body within his armour. His retinal displays flickered with competing strands of information. Warning chimes and aural notifications drowned out vox reports from the strike force. Databursts unravelled themselves as text, graphics and figures displayed only long enough to notice before the next pushed its predecessor aside.

There was a time of stillness where physics ceased tormenting his flesh, acceleration stopped, and he floated serenely, weight forgotten for several minutes. It was all too brief. Parmenio snatched at the craft and yanked them down through the sky. Time passed now to the roar of atmospheric friction and bow compression.

'Four minutes, forty-two seconds until warp shield reengagement.' There was an edge to the Master Augurum's voice. Felix appreciated his fear. Heading towards probable death with bland commentary in his ears seemed unfitting.

'Fire engines. Accelerate to maximum speed,' Felix voxed to the shoal of attack craft. The orders were obeyed without question, though their execution pushed the torpedoes to the limits of destruction.

They had to get into the facility before the shields recovered, and that had to be fast. Warp shields were a sorcerous variant on void shields, using dark magic to perform the role taken by technology on Imperial ships. Consequently, they were unpredictable. Speed was of the essence. Gunships and even drop pods were too slow. Only boarding torpedoes, designed to be hurled into the hull of another ship and deliver warriors safely within, were strong enough to survive the mad dash for Parmenio's surface and the impact that would ensue without losing valuable seconds to deceleration.

Theoretically. The proof was in the practical, Felix reminded himself. This manoeuvre was rarely attempted because it was so risky.

As an aggressive tool of boarding, the torpedoes could reach very high speeds. What they weren't really designed for was to head directly into a gravity well at full burn. The impact was going to be something, if the little ships did not burn up in the atmosphere first. Boarding torpedoes had ceramite thermal shielding, but it was designed to protect the front end of the vessel from its meltacutters, not the deadly compressive heating of re-entry. Provided they kept the prow to the planet, they should arrive alive. Antique spacecraft, *primitive* spacecraft, the machine adepts told him, had operated under this principle in the dim ages of prehistory.

At least, that was the theory, and only one theory. No one in the fleet had experience with such backward technologies. They might, admitted the adepts, all die.

Felix concentrated on the coming action. A toxic environment awaited him, guarded by warriors who had fought for Mortarion since the birth of the Imperium. The descent was the least of his concerns.

The torpedoes jumped as they passed into the lower reaches of the atmosphere. The familiar shaking of re-entry jounced his bones. He cleared his retinal display of all but two chronometers, one counting down the estimated time until the warp shield burst back into place, the other their arrival time. They were close.

The retinal display Felix's battle suit boasted was superior to the helmplate displays traditionally fitted to Space Marine armour. Felix's head shook violently, but the two chronographs ran down in crystal clarity.

The counters reached the one-minute minus mark. Outside, attack craft would be running over the city, drawing the enemy's fire when not taking out their air defences directly. The torpedoes were coming down on predictable trajectories. Easy targets.

Faster and faster they went, roaring jets powering the torpedoes towards the surface, snubbing gravity for its lack of application.

It was over quickly. Retrojet burn slammed Felix back in the restraint cage, then a tremendous impact tossed him forwards. It was not as hard as he had expected. Ordinarily metal met metal with a ring and boom, shaking those in the tight confines of the torpedoes. Assailing the shield plant was altogether different, akin to a bullet piercing corpse skin than the nail-into-metal insertion of a typical boarding action.

He blacked out for a second. Long enough for his battle-plate machine-spirit to apply a jolt from his pharmacopeia.

The torpedoes knifed through the cancerous hide of the facility. The passage was slicked by internal bleeding, a slippery chute ride instead of the brutal, grinding drill penetration Felix was used to.

At the point where the walls retained their original rockcrete and plasteel structure, the torpedoes juddered slightly, the melta arrays burned more loudly, and needles dropped a little quicker on the dials displaying the limited power source of the vessels. No more notice was given than that. The jump and skip of internal voids encountered in a layered metal structure were not there. Vile growth filled them all, imprisoning mechanisms and men alike in a fleshy hell.

Unlike the drop, the crawl inside the building seemed to take forever.

When Felix felt the journey might never end, chimes registered destination reached, and open air before the prow. Melta arrays cut out and the tracks that had dragged them through whirred into reverse, bringing the torpedoes to a halt.

A slurry of flesh and unspeakable bodily fluids sluiced out around the torpedo into a corridor. Liquid hissed where it ran over hardening slag.

There was a moment's quiet. Cooling metal ticked. Muffled detonations fought their way within the building from the war outside.

Petalled doors burst wide. Felix's squad of five veteran Primaris Reivers deactivated the maglocks holding their feet to the floor. Restraint bars fell loose in the cages and were pushed aside. The two warriors ahead of Felix jumped out into the hellish guts of the building. Being out first was an honourable but dangerous role. Many

Space Marines had died advancing from boarding craft into enemy fire. No one was there to greet them. They took up sentry by the gaping nose of the torpedo, guns raised.

Felix was third to leave the tiny craft. Two more Primaris Marines came out after him. Skull masks, luminous in the dark, bobbed past the sentries to take up point positions twenty metres either direction up the corridor. When they were in place, Sergeant Kaspian emerged, a bulky auspex unit trilling in his fist.

Less than five seconds after the torpedo breached the wall, the six Space Marines were out of the tube and in position.

Pulsing sheets of greenish flesh covered over most signs of man's artifice. In a few rare places bits of the original structure could be seen; junction boxes dripping slime, or lumens obscured by keratinous growths, still shining faintly. There was little other illumination. Stab lights shone from the Space Marines' gun mounts. Where their circles of yellow light touched, waving cilia tipped with black eyes shrank back into the wall as if burned.

The floor gave disgustingly under Felix's boots. There were firmer patches where the grid of floor panels could be felt, but the contrast between flesh and steel heightened his revulsion. A green mist floated at knee height, obscuring the ground. Chittering things giggled in the shadows, running as soon as looked at, and so glimpsed only as fleeting, abominable shapes. Felix advanced carefully, boltstorm gauntlet ready to fire. He reactivated his retinal overlays, and tasked his cogitator to act in concert with Kaspian's auspex to run a full breakdown of the bizarre environment. It was uniformly toxic.

'By the primarch,' said Modrias, one of the veterans. 'Such a stench.'

'Check your helm seals,' Felix said. When he spoke it seemed to dirty him somehow, as if upon leaving his mouth the words left a trail for the power plant's corruption to enter into him. Feeling uneasy, he double checked his Gravis armour's systems. The retinal display assured him his suit was completely sealed, proof against the void and worse, but the meaty reek filled his mouth and nose nevertheless, coating his throat with the bitter smell of rotten flesh tossed onto a fire.

'All troopers' armour is fully sealed against the exterior,' said Kaspian. 'But I can still smell it. Impossible.'

'Impossible under normal circumstances. This is witchcraft,' said Modrias.

'Do not let it distract you,' said Felix. He was running over the deployment of the rest of the force. Several torpedoes had been shot down. One hundred and thirty-eight Space Marines were within the complex. He left the data trickle from his fellows on. He did not speak to them. If any had entered the complex undetected, he wished to keep it that way. Vox was easily traced.

Kaspian was already adjusting his auspex to scan for mass densities and thermal spikes, a sure way to pick up power-armoured foes. 'I get no reading of the enemy. Euphain, Daler. Confirmation of no visual contact.'

'Corridor clear,' voxed Euphain.

'It is as safe as it is going to be, my lord,' said Kaspian.

'Oblivion Knight Voi,' Felix said. 'You may disembark in safety.'

Asheera Voi walked down the tilted ramp of the boarding torpedo. Though small and slight compared to the huge bulk of Felix's warriors, an aura of frightful power clung to her, and she entered the plague ship with a deal less trepidation than the Primaris Marines. She bore a huge sword sheathed on her back, and a small calibre boltgun maglocked at her thigh. Like the Space Marines, she was clad in power armour, though hers was of far more ornate a type. The Vratine armour – the armour of the oath, it was called. Its lesser systems and lighter plating meant she was free of the cumbersome reactor packs the Space Marines wore, and she moved easily. A trade-off for her greater mobility was protection; the Vratine armour lacked the hermetic sealing Adeptus Astartes plate possessed. Her only guard against the toxic environment was the grilled bevoir extending up from her neck over her mouth and nose. This contained a rebreather, but although the way was open between her armour joints to all manner of poison and disease, she showed no fear of contamination. Her head was covered with a high helm that recalled those of the Adeptus Custodes. The effect of helm and mask was to emphasise the face, while denying sight of the mouth. It was a visual reminder of the Oath of Tranquillity the Sisterhood took to forsake speech forever.

Voi signed at Felix as she emerged using her order's ThoughtMark. He read it perfectly, but his suit's machine-spirit blinked electric outlines around her hands anyway, and provided an audio translation.

Your sergeant is correct. This place is steeped in the warp. She continued signing. *The smell is not a physical phenomenon. It is of the Plague God's doing. See.*

She approached Felix. Her psychic null field enfolded him, protecting him from the facility's malevolence. A great weight came off his soul, and the smell receded.

The effect she had on the building itself was spectacular. Flesh-plaques went black as Voi's weird gifts cut dead the life-sustaining energies of the warp. Peels of blubber rolled off the wall, revealing corroded plasteel beneath. Wherever she stepped, the green mist swam and recoiled, and the mat of tissues shivered with pain.

'Impressive,' he said.

I am anathema to this place, she signed. *But you will understand the true meaning of that word once the device is activated. Stay close to me, tetrarch,* she continued, her eye lenses locking with Felix's. *The mortal ailments within these walls can do you little harm, but there are sicknesses of the soul here. Without me, you may succumb.*

'Understood,' said Felix. 'You shall be protected. Do not take any unnecessary risks.'

She nodded, but drew her executioner greatblade anyway. An Oblivion Knight needed no protection. She kept back for their sake, not hers. As their guarantee against the soul-rotting powers of the facility, if she were to die, they would be vulnerable.

Felix flashed a compressed databurst to his men, reminding them of their task. It was information they had been over a hundred times already. Felix thought repetition worthwhile; though they were all veterans of the Indomitus Crusade, and had fought many strange foes, none of them had ever walked the innards of so heavily infested a place before. Few expeditions into the rotting hearts of Nurgle's fanes had returned.

He performed a quick data harvest of other troops. The few Reiver squads were scattered from one end of the building to the other, employing their specialised skills to deliberately ambush the Plague Marines guarding the building. Captain Sicarius and the rest of the force acted as a lure near the entrance of the building. Between them, the Reivers and Victrix Guard should tie down the garrison. Though Felix's team had the true mission, in the Ultramarines' way the other strike forces were meaningful diversions; if Felix failed, the facility might still be destroyed by them.

'Our brothers are engaged in several locations. I do not believe we have been noticed. Bring out the device,' he commanded.

Kaspian worked his auspex again, ushering out from the torpedo the last occupant, a heavily armoured servitor. The upper half of a human body was mounted on the front, like a grotesque cybernetic centaur. Behind was a flatbed enclosed by a rail bearing a black sphere. Modrias and Voi checked the sphere over, ensuring the function lights upon the device displayed the proper patterns. While the checks were completed, Felix took a moment to get his bearings, his powerful gravis cogitator attempting to overlay the actualities on the ground with the ancient plans he had inloaded for this pattern of generatorium. A cartolith shone brightly in his eyes. There was, unsurprisingly, very little correlation between original design and the current layout. Auspex returns displayed a twisted, organic network that had digested and reconfigured the original interior considerably. He found it hard to believe all this change had been effected in a few months.

A large shell hit the planet's surface. The building shook with the impact. A long moan sounded past the Primaris Marines, solid as a physical presence.

'I do not like this place,' said Modrias.

'I do not think it likes you,' said Daler.

Felix examined the options carefully. A major, tubular corridor that looked like an enormous gullet led in the direction of where the reactor chamber should be. He gestured forward with his sword. It was as good a place as any to begin.

'That way,' he said.

CHAPTER TWELVE

THE HEART REACTOR

Felix kept a close eye on the overall battle as they pushed on towards their target. Three other units moving in from different directions were making an obvious run for the reactor to mask Felix's advance. The Reivers raised as much havoc as they could, drawing diseased eyes onto them, before vanishing to attack from elsewhere. Felix's party met so little resistance he suspected the Death Guard to be overly reliant on supernatural senses. Asheera Voi's presence masked them from psychic detection. All the evidence suggested they had not been seen, when a simple augur sweep of the facility would have discovered their torpedo.

As they advanced he thought the building no longer had anything as mundane as machine senses. There were few mechanical parts of the structure left, and though the generatorium was furnished with a profusion of bizarre growths, they seemed to perform no useful function. He reprimanded himself for expecting the growths to follow the logic of biotechnology, which they superficially resembled. They weren't dealing with an artefact crafted in the material universe.

'This is no building,' he reminded himself. 'It is the playground of madness.'

No sooner said, circumstances bore out his words. They turned towards the building's core into a tunnel knee-deep in thick slime that flowed with slow, strong currents. While the party were in its flood, freakish sights greeted them at every turn. Walls of eyes, corridors like the branchings of diseased lungs, and everywhere deformed things skipping through the muck, never seen, only glimpsed.

Felix pulled his boots from the slime. The paint was sloughing off, revealing dull ceramite beneath. Soon it would begin to pit.

'Tetrarch.' Kaspian, his voice tinged with disgust. He was looking into a large machine hall opening up off the corridor. The devices within were covered in pulsing fronds of something halfway between animal and vegetation. But it was the wall that held the sergeant's gaze.

Felix joined him. The threshold of the machine hall was higher than the corridor and he stepped up out of the river. The tetrarch was glad to be free of the slime.

Kaspian played his gun-mounted stab light over the wall. Its beam caught upon rounded organic shapes. Arms, elbows, faces, all human, covered in a thick layer of mucus. At first Felix took it to be a work of art, a frieze depicting a hundred people nestled into one another. He reminded himself of where he was. If it was art, it was not of the conventional kind.

A hundred human bodies were half-melted into the

fabric of the wall. The uniform surface was an illusion generated by a coating of slime. Where the mucus covered less thickly, Kaspian's stab light picked out badges, tools and differing colours of cloth.

'The facility workers,' said Kaspian. He ran the cone of light further up. 'Mortal, servitor and adept.'

Felix looked at it briefly. His attention was on the unfolding battle depicted on his display. They could not hear it down there, but reports blinked into his systems. Casualties were mounting.

'An outrage,' Felix said. 'But we can be thankful they are dead. Move out.'

After the hall, the sagging, slime-filled artery they walked turned by slow degree into something recognisable as a corridor. The cartolith in Felix's datafile suddenly made more sense. The reactor core was not far. The deeper they went into the complex, the more pieces of wrecked technology were visible, and here and there stretches of the plasteel wall were clear of flesh plaques, though all of it was black with corrosion and accreted ooze. Brass plates bearing Nurgle's tri-lobed symbol were embedded in this filth, leaking greenish oxide into the mess.

After twenty minutes of walking, the river slid noiselessly through the floor into a dark void. They had reached their goal. The corridor opened out into the huge cylinder that had once housed the plasma reactor control systems. The reactor was encased in a ferrocrete sphere at the centre of this cylinder. Numerous engineering decks stacked over each other filled the space around the core.

Felix tested the floor of grillwork sections dubiously. The plague lord's attentions had turned the floor into a treacherous landscape, and where the river flowed it had melted away completely. On the far side the plasteel ended at a thick lip of ferrocrete projecting from the reactor core. That looked more or less solid, but the way across to it was rife with peril.

Black veins ran down the walls in rootlike profusion. They covered over the observation galleries, as thick as ivy, obscuring them completely, but on the rotted deck plates they were sparser, a spreading network that endlessly split and rejoined itself before gathering up into ropes and piercing the ferrocrete of the core. They pulsed softly, alive. In the spaces between the veins were gaping holes opening onto falls a thousand feet deep.

'Do you get a reading from the reactor?' asked Felix.

'No,' said Kaspian.

'Voi?'

The Oblivion Knight planted her sword point down. She rested her right hand on the hilt, leaving her left free to speak. *The energy of the warp is strongest there.* She pointed at the reactor sphere. *The ferrocrete shields us as it would have shielded the plasma reactor. Be careful when we approach.* She signed as efficiently with one hand as with two.

'Then our intelligence is correct. Proceed,' said Felix.

'Baskvo, guard the servitor. The rest of you, watch your step,' warned Kaspian. 'Over one at a time. Stick to the line of the beams.'

They walked carefully, following the girders supporting the deck plates. These were visible through the grille of the floor, and were in barely better condition than the metal they supported. They creaked and shook as the Reivers jogged over them. When Asheera Voi ran over, they barely shifted, but when Felix set foot upon one, it moaned dangerously under the weight of his Gravis plate.

'Steady, tetrarch,' said Euphain. 'Maybe you should hold back here. Our armour is lighter.'

'I am aware of the risk,' said Felix. He looked back at where the servitor waited in the corridor mouth. 'The cyborg is about as heavy as I. If I cannot make it, neither will the device.'

'You should wait,' said Modrias.

'No,' said Felix, and strode out. He crossed at a steady pace. The floor bucked and swayed, but he made it across to the ferrocrete casing of the reactor heart without mishap.

The ferrocrete was eaten into strange shapes. The surface of it crumbled to wet powder when stepped upon, but it was firmer footing than the plasteel grid.

'Bring the servitor across,' Felix said, and beckoned.

Kaspian ordered the cyborg to proceed. The servitor's simple brain understood the danger. Tracks jerking with minute course adjustments, it negotiated its way over the unstable deck.

Felix looked down. A succession of similar floors were hidden in the foetid night below. If the servitor fell through, they would not be able to retrieve the device in time, if it was not smashed to pieces by the fall.

The servitor was within three metres of the edge when the beam it was following broke. Deck plating that had seemed solid disintegrated into a blizzard of rust flakes. The cyborg pitched forward into a sudden hole, but did not fall. The front of its tracks were pointing into the yawning black, its chest jammed against the broken edge of the hole. Blood leaked where the jagged metal penetrated its torso.

The servitor bleeped. The light in its augmetic eye

stuttered. The tracks spun, first forwards, then backwards. It shook in place. The floor sagged in. Metal clanged off the floor below.

'Quickly! Shut it off!' commanded Felix. 'Before its attempt to rise results in its fall!'

The tracks spun into reverse. They pulled hard at the deck plates, shredding them with a metallic wrenching. The servitor hauled itself partially out of the hole before the deck around it collapsed further, and it fell through.

'The device!' shouted Felix.

The servitor took a large swathe of broken deck plating with it. Two grapnels hissed out from the Reivers, thunking onto the smooth side of the device. The lines snapped taut. Euphain staggered past Felix. The tetrarch snapped out a hand to grab him, catching Euphain's power pack around a stabilisation nozzle. Euphain skidded to a halt by the edge of the ferrocrete. The weight of the servitor pulled at him and Felix.

'Hold!' ordered Felix, his voice strained. He activated his maglocks. They pulled at the reactor casing, and should have anchored him to the ferric material, but the platform was rotten, and chunks of it were pulled up by his boots. Euphain lurched closer to the edge.

Modrias had the other line. He was leaning back, straining at the grapnel gun with both hands. He was ploughing up a long furrow in the softened ferrocrete as he was dragged forwards, grunting with the effort.

Kaspian let out a shout. 'Disengaging carriage locks!'

Suddenly the pull lessened by more than half. The Space Marines staggered backwards with the change in the weight. The servitor plummeted down into the pit, falling through deck after deck with a tremendous crashing sound.

Felix helped Euphain back to his feet. The two Reivers retracted their lines. Silent motors pulled up the device onto the platform.

Voi and Kaspian went to the sphere to examine it for damage.

The device is functional, my lord tetrarch, signed Voi.

'I have movement coming in from the southern quadrant,' said Kaspian.

'They will have heard that. The time for stealth is done. We must be quick,' said Felix. He deactivated silent running protocols and brought the full capabilities of his armour online.

He broke vox silence. 'This is Tetrarch Felix of Vespator.' He felt strange saying the words. He had yet to go to the world of his new office. 'Attention Strikeforce Purgator, we are in position. Units five, nine and twelve abandon current mission targets and gather on my position. The rest of you, fall back to the rendezvous points and await reinforcement.'

The Reivers raised their weapons. Sighting mechanisms engaged, machine-spirits waking and whining with fresh power. Euphain and Modrias hoisted the sphere up between them. They jettisoned the lines, leaving the magnetic grapnels attached as handles. They lifted the device and toted their bolt carbines in their free hands.

'This way,' said Kaspian. 'The walls of the reactor containment chamber are breached. We can get in. Daler, Baskvo, fall back and provide cover.'

'We march for Macragge,' whispered Daler. He and his brother vanished into the dark, the silent motors of their specialised power armour giving no indication where they were. If it weren't for the unit signifiers flickering on Felix's cartolith, he would have had no knowledge of their position.

'If the wall is open, we can be sure no mortal engine powers the shield, or we would all be dead,' said Felix. 'Proceed cautiously.'

Around the periphery of the reactor core, the control stations and mechanisms used to govern the heat of plasmic reactions were piles of damp detritus. Consoles were reduced to fragile frameworks of corrosion surrounded by shards of brittle plastek, broken glass and wet plates of rust. There was no sign of the thousands of mortals and servitors that ran the machinery. It had the look of an ancient ruin, though Parmenio had been attacked not long ago, and the facility had been as well maintained as any in Ultramar until it had been taken.

They came to the hole in the reactor core. A giant crack ran between the floor and the one above where ferrocrete had crumbled away to nothing, reduced to soggy heaps of rusty waste.

From inside, a ponderous pounding could be heard and a soft unlight issued that threw silver shadows and brought black highlights to the edges of objects.

Kaspian moved to enter first. Felix called him back.

'In this situation, having heavier armour than yours is an advantage,' he said. 'And I also have this.'

A thought impulse activated his iron halo. With a crackle, a skin of blue energy snapped into life around him.

Felix cycled up his boltstorm gauntlet to rapid fire. He held it out in front of himself, fist pointing forward at chest height.

'Await my order. Protect the device at all costs.'

He pushed inside a space no man should be able to

enter. A plasma reactor imprisoned an artificial sun, its raging energies siphoned to power whatever was required. All the titanic needs of the city of Hecaton had been sated by this one crucial location. Once activated, a reactor core could burn forever, provided it was correctly fuelled and cared for.

The star was dead. Felix emerged into the spherical chamber and was confronted with a dreadful sight.

Growing into the empty reactor shell was an immense, five-chambered, black heart. An enormous parasitic cancer that had overtaken its host body, it filled two-thirds of the space. The heart's extremities were close enough for Felix to touch, but the bulk of it was pushed up against the far side, creating a cavity walled with throbbing flesh on one side and decayed technology on the other. Where visible, the ignition spikes that had called forth the fusion reaction were furred with rust. Elsewhere they were buried under drooping folds of rancid skin. Ropes of pale white muscle tethered the pulsing organ. They shivered with every thunderous beat. A sickening, liquid churn filled the space. The drive of each systole sent ripples of force across the heart's veinous surface. Slime dripped from it. Where it flowed most persistently it had eaten through the reaction spikes, adamantium containment flask and the ferrocrete wall behind. For all its appearance the heart was no physical organ. Felix could feel something in the back of his skull, a madness like a caged rat trying to gnaw its way out of imprisonment. A vile aftertaste tainted his mouth. The rest of the building's bizarre changes could almost pass as something natural, but not this. Through the heart's twitching aortas, the power of Chaos pumped. From here the taint ran.

Boltgun fire sounded from the control cylinder.

'We have attracted the attentions of Mortarion's sons,' voxed Kaspian. 'They are here. Two squads, more on the way.'

'Proceed within,' said Felix. He broadcast his helm feed to the rest of his small strike force. 'We must place the device near the heart, but I do not think I can get any closer to it.'

'I'll bring it through,' said Kaspian. 'Modrias and Euphain, support your brothers.'

'Negative,' said Felix. 'Wait a moment while I formulate a theoretical for the placement of the bomb. I shall–'

Swift footsteps came from behind. Felix moved aside at the moment Asheera Voi flashed past and leapt. Her armour powered her across the gap. As she flew, she reversed the grip on her sword so the point was held facing down and forwards.

The silica glass edge whispered through the heart, bringing forth a torrent of blood. Asheera pulled the sword down, opening up the side of the organ from top to bottom as she slid down its black flesh. It spasmed, and a horrible wailing set up from an indeterminate place. The cataract of foul-smelling vitae flooding from the wound filled the reactor chamber as if it were a bowl. She disappeared into it.

Kaspian joined Felix, lugging the sphere.

'Oblivion Knight!' cried Felix.

An area of blood boiled, steaming and shrieking as if it were independently alive. Voi emerged from this turbulence, sheathed her sword and ran on before the rising tide, springing up the dilapidated reaction spikes to regain the edge of the crack. Felix and Kaspian hauled her up, dripping filth.

Throw the device into the wound, she signed.

'Very well.'

Felix and Kaspian had to combine their efforts to toss in the device. It was heavy and awkward, but working together they accomplished the task, heaving it out of the crack and over the six-metre gap. The ball spun around four times as it flew, slapping into the gushing rent Asheera had carved in the heart as it commenced its fifth revolution. The heart quivered from its hurt, the edges of the wound gaped, but it beat still, and swallowed the device without change.

Kaspian consulted his auspex. 'It's active,' he said. 'We have five minutes.' He put away the scanning device and drew a combat knife as long as a mortal's sword.

'We have to keep the enemy back, stop them from deactivating it,' said Felix. He pushed back through the crack in the wall into the control centre. Boltgun fire flared a score of metres away, answered by return shots from one of the corridors. 'Can we survive the bomb's detonation?'

Yes, signed Asheera Voi. *Though it will not be pleasant.*

'Then we make our stand here,' Felix said. He pulsed out a coded communication warning the others to prepare for the device's emissions, along with instructions to their battle-plate to count down from his mark.

The Death Guard were arriving in some numbers, crowding the tunnel several ranks deep. From the safety of the shadows, the four Reivers fired upon them as they arrived, giving no clue from where they would next strike. Felix watched the signifier dots of the warriors shifting position between each burst, and was impressed with their ability to move around so unstable an area whilst keeping up such a high rate of fire. He had fought rarely with the Reivers before. He was a veteran of open war.

'So far they are coming in only from the tunnel opposite the one we used,' said Kaspian. 'They are big, bloated. They do not want to risk treading on this trap of a floor. We can contain them, I am sure. Provided they do not come in to attack from two fronts.'

Felix had been spotted by the foe. The tubercular cough of rusting weapons boomed from the far side of the room. Explosions from bolt rounds impacting Felix's aegis field lit up his armour. The light from the discharge picked him out for the rest, and more bolts followed. Daler felled a traitor with a bolt-round through the head. The Death Guard's relic of a helmet ruptured, and he crashed down onto the deck, making the whole structure shake, but it did not break.

Seeing this, one of the others aimed his bolter at the deck, riddling it. He paused to assess the results. When the plates remained where they were, he stepped out with one cautious foot, the bolt rounds smacking off him ignored. He pushed, once, twice, then stared up at Felix with mad eyes. Chortling maniacally, the Death Guard strode onto the deck. A dozen more followed. Muttering, or singing discordant songs, or laughing like madmen, they spread out across the decking.

They came across the open, ignoring what little cover there was between them and their foe. If easy to hit, they were incredibly difficult to kill. They absorbed a mass of shots which would have slain a Space Marine, but they did not falter. When one did succumb, his fellows stepped over his smoking corpse without care.

Modrias was the first to die. A mortis chime in Felix's helm rang simultaneously as his identification marker blinked out of the thumbnail cartolith. The burning darts of bolt fire coming from his position ceased at the same time.

Felix sprayed the coming Plague Marines with his boltstorm gauntlet, the twin underslung pistols belting out a tremendous rate of fire. Icons warned him that the weapons were overheating and his ammo hopper was nearly empty. By then, it had ceased to matter.

The Plague Marines reached them.

The first Felix slew with a grenade, rolling it under his feet and blasting out the deck grille from beneath him. The Traitor Space Marine fell like a daemon in a mystery play disappearing through a trap door, his insane giggles transformed into a howl of outrage as he plummeted into the obscurity of the lower levels.

Kaspian did the same, tossing a handful of shock grenades first to disorientate the enemy before following up with two krak bombs thrown in quick succession. Bolts exploded all around the Space Marines, blasting massive wet holes in the rotten ferrocrete. The krak bombs detonated, taking out a wide section of the deck, sending three Death Guard down to their long-denied deaths. A fourth grabbed at the floor as he fell, and clung to the edge, the fingers of one hand rumpling the plasteel, a bright pink tentacle wrapped around the girder beneath. His power plant was crowned with a bizarre collection of makeshift, smoke-belching exhausts. His battleplate groaned with the agony of poorly lubricated mechanisms as he hauled his massive bulk out of the hole.

Felix ended his efforts with a volley of bolt shots that tore off his unarmoured tentacle and smashed his helm free along with his head.

Imperial efforts were yielding a satisfying kill ratio. Now they must test themselves hand to hand.

Felix stepped in to intercept a noisome champion, his exalted status marked by his greater bulk and a chattering daemon fly that orbited his head with the regularity of a motorised ornament. Felix ignored the fly, saving his wrath for its master.

The warrior swung a massive power fist of ancient make at the tetrarch. It rebounded from his aegis, but already the Death Guard was following the strike with a trio of bolts from his pistol. All flashed to oblivion against Felix's power field. Felix responded with a hard thrust from his sword. The point punched through the traitor's rotten breastplate. The disruption field flash-cooked his organs. Stinking fluids wept out of the myriad holes in the champion's battleplate. He did not die, but chortled and swung his power fist again at Felix's head.

The blow never connected. A blade flashed behind him, taking off the rusting gauntlet at the man's elbow. Felix was presented with a grim cross-section of flesh and bone bonded unnaturally to armour. The fist, hand still inside, clanged off the floor, and the champion turned with a snarl to face his attacker. The blade emerged through his back, pulsing flame and sparks from the champion's ruined reactor.

The champion fell down, revealing Voi, sword in hand. Shrieking, the fly dived at her, mouthparts clacking, but as soon as it came near, it evaporated into a smear of greasy smoke.

'My thanks,' said Felix. He riddled a warrior lumbering towards the Sister of Silence with bolts. Multiple flashes lit up his interior, shining through corroded holes in his armour.

Voi inclined her head and was away, dancing through the combat, wielding the massive sword as lightly as if it were some tiny duelling blade.

Felix sighted another target, killing him with his boltstorm. Another died to a blow from behind. He switched from blade work, trusting instead to the power field surrounding his gauntlet. It was a slower weapon, but the greater destructive power it possessed put down the unnaturally resilient foe more reliably.

The counter for the device ticked down. He plunged his fist, still firing the underslung pistols, into the chest of a traitor, yanking out the creature's defiled hearts in a rush of thick blood and pus.

Dozens of the enemy were now pouring into the reactor control centre, and the building itself was reacting to the Imperial presence. A rush of stinking matter poured out of the corridor, forming a new, living floor to cover over the rotted grille. The slime river flooded after it. The combined weight of the Death Guard upon the deck would have destroyed the original floor, but the flesh held them up. As it spread it sprouted bizarre plant growths that blackened and died as soon as they bloomed. Spores choked the stinking air. Felix's atmospheric filtration unit peeped. Particulate filth was eating through his void seals.

Another Death Guard died. The flesh mat glowed, bathing the reactor centre with a sickening green light. The slime river, now falling as a wide, dribbling cataract as the flesh spread, carried the light with it, illuminating the floors below. Beneath, Death Guard that had fallen through the deck were picking themselves up.

Felix swore. Could nothing kill these abominations?

Three of them were on him, forcing him to fight with all

his skill. They were older than even him, but whereas he had spent the last ten millennia in and out of suspended animation, they had fought all the while. They knew his techniques. Heroes greater than he had fallen to them.

He was forced back. They jabbed at him with rusting blades. From the notched edges, a black poison dripped that boiled away before it hit the ground, causing the air to shimmer.

The counter hit zero. Felix held his breath. Nothing happened.

He had time to fear the worst. His back was against the wall. Euphain was down, Daler hard pressed. Kaspian had vanished from sight, though no mortis rune had rung out to mark his demise.

Failure beckoned.

An immense pressure built behind him, pushing through his body. This was not the overpressure of a mundane explosion, but a psychic assault of unparalleled power.

The heart in the reactor shrieked with a human voice, and died.

A strange skin of light engulfed Felix. Where light raced over the flesh mat, it died, disintegrating into a thin gruel that slopped down through the rusted floor.

Like the torpedoes, the device contained the powdered remnants of pariahs. Felix had heard dark whispers about them. It was said that they had no soul. Not only were they inimical to the denizens of the warp, but they affected every scintilla of otherworldly energy, including the souls of living beings.

That was why the likes of Voi were so uncomfortable to be around. This was that same sensation, multiplied a thousand times. The wash of the detonation physically pulled at something within Felix, lifting his psyche, plucking etheric energy from its balanced synthesis with his body and threatening to extinguish it forever.

It was excruciating, like nothing he had ever felt. His soul was on fire.

He screamed.

Steeped in the power of their diabolical god, the effect on the Plague Marines was far greater. They moaned and fell down, some stone dead. Others shrieked as if the horror of their condition had suddenly become plain to them.

Time seemed out of joint. There was nothing but shouting all around him.

Felix was among the first to recover, dragging up his body from the ground. He felt like he might vomit. His muscles ached. His head rang. He attempted to summon his retinal display, but the device was unresponsive.

The voice of Guilliman's Master Augurum spoke in his vox-bead. *'Tetrarch, we have detected the detonation of the psyk-out device. The shield is down. Confirm mission success.'*

'Mission success,' he croaked. The veins were shrivelled black threads on the ground. The pulse of the heart was silent. 'Reactor obliterated. We shall withdraw. Commence bombardment. Make sure what dwelt here does not return to life.'

'We are targeting the cathedra. As soon as you are clear, my lord, we shall level the power generatorium,' voxed the Master Augurum. The ship-feed crackled out.

Felix staggered on, oblivious to the danger posed to him by the floor, and put a round through the head of a groaning Plague Marine. Several lived, sprawled on the decking. Kaspian was up on his feet, putting down the fallen with his knife. Voi aided him, seemingly unaffected by the detonation of the psyk-out device.

'My suit systems are out. Report in,' croaked Felix.

Kaspian, Daler and Baskvo lived. The rest were dead. A final few bolt rounds blasted out, finishing off their enemy. They had no mercy for the traitors.

'Move out. The quicker we get to the surface, the sooner Lord Guilliman can level this place,' ordered Felix.

'I've got movement!' said Kaspian. The Reivers swivelled, training their guns on the entrance.

A group of Space Marines thundered down the corridor, all in Ultramarines blue.

Captain Sicarius of the Victrix Guard hailed Felix from the chamber's edge.

'Follow me, my lord,' he called. 'We have a cordon running back to the exterior. This is the quickest way out.'

'You join us in a hellish place, captain,' said Felix.

'I have seen far worse,' Sicarius replied.

CHAPTER THIRTEEN

SAINTS AND SINNERS

The quiet noises of diligent men at work on the wallwalk relaxed Devorus. His command staff went about their duties with focus. Low conversations and the occasional squawk of incoming vox messages were reassuringly human noises, clear and vital in the greyed-out day of Parmenio. The breach sheared through the wall not twenty metres from Devorus' position, but the defence lines set below to guard the gap were laid out with pleasing geometry, and appeared at that moment proof against the enemy's attentions. Peace held on the far side of the channel. No work was done on the mole that day. The enemy were waiting, as were Devorus and his men. The war had changed in a moment.

The Imperial Regent had come to Parmenio.

Shellfire rumbled over the distant mountains as enemy positions around Hecaton were obliterated from orbit. The blanket fogs that covered the plains were perturbed. No longer a solid mass, they broke into rolling banks whose motion over the wasted land revealed ruined towns and farms reduced to shell-pocked mud. The haze in the higher reaches of the air had dispersed, allowing him to see all the way to Hecaton for the first time since the enemy came.

Before the war, the view had been fine. The air was clean and clear most days, and Hecaton easy to see. The city spread lacily down the slopes of the mountains, a filigreed ornament upon nature's art, white peaks above, green lands below. People had come to Tyros' walls to see it, that view of Ultramar's perfection, where man and planet lived in tolerable balance.

What the blowing mists revealed horrified him. The peaks of the mountains were still white. All else had changed. Agricolae turned to toxic bog. Ruined towns white as bones in liquefied flesh. Worst of all was the fate of Hecaton. It was seventy kilo-metres from there to the island, a distance that reduced a city from a place to a detail. Devorus did not need to get any closer to know it was lost.

The fine towers were twisted and black, as if they had been partially melted by mistake and inexpertly mended by a fool who had no wit to see how poor a restoration he provided. The great dome of the Administratum Officio – a wonder in the days before, three thousand metres across and an eggshell blue that outmatched the sky – was gone. The suburbs were black smears on the mountainsides. When he used his magnoculars, Devorus saw rivers of filth pouring down steep streets.

War drummed its beat in the heavens, and lit them with sporadic bursts of power. Ships waged silent battle in orbit out of sight above the clouds, but debris falling from the fight and stray weapon strikes filled the sky over the plains with booms and whooping discharges.

From the far side of the River Sea where Keleton stood firm, stripes of linear light stabbed – the glaring blasts of the defence lasers of inland Edimos. A peculiar thunder was called from the sky with each blaze of collimated light. The clouds bunched in and swirled around their track, leaving bald slashes where the sky showed blue, a sight Devorus never thought to see again, before the clouds swirled back in to plug the gap with fitful washes of rain.

The lasers fired only when the Death Guard fleet strayed into their arc of fire. The curve of the planet limited their contribution to the battle. Devorus was pleased to see them used. Too long the defence laser battery had been a threat rather than an active participant in the war.

He held up his magnoculars again. Victory would be an act of defiance rather than something to be measured as a successful defence. The Ultramarines could take Hecatone back, but it was too late. Whole swathes of Parmenio would have to burn to clear away the Death Guard's taint.

Morbid though the thoughts were, he did not submit to despair. He could not.

The crunch of boots on rubble had him turn to face Sister Superior Iolanth. Behind her, the outer door of the airlock leading into the tall Shoreward Bastion was open, shedding bright lumen light into the grey of the infected day. Iolanth had her helmet off, and for perhaps only the third or fourth time since Devorus had made her acquaintance, he saw her face. He looked forward to seeing her face.

It was strange, he thought, how beautiful all the Battle

Sisters were. Service to the Emperor, especially in battle, should not require such aesthetic perfection. He suspected the hand of lesser, impure men in their selection.

Iolanth wore her white hair in braids down the left side of her skull, drawn so tight and close to the head they exposed the scalp between. The right side was shaved down to the skin, leaving an expanse free for a large aquila tattoo.

Two scars marred her face, one thick enough to crook the line of her lips where it crossed them, the other fine, pale as a moon, running almost level from one side of her forehead to the other. On the left, it turned down a little, and grew fatter, like a large tick, as if she had been approved by some cosmic, sanguinary power.

Devorus wondered where she had got those scars. He did not ask her. He did not dare. Iolanth was imperious and fierce, with piercing yellow eyes. Devorus had the impression that if he praised her beauty in any way, she would mutilate herself on the spot to prove her devotion to the Emperor was of more importance.

'The primarch comes,' said Devorus. His eyes lingered on Iolanth's face a moment too long, and he blushed. 'I have confirmation of it from the highest channels. We are to await relief.' He stared out over the harbour, wishing the orders were different, that they were to sally out and take the fight to the enemy. He was tired of hiding.

'Indeed it is so. The son of the Emperor Himself arrives to punish the traitors,' said Iolanth. 'Wondrous news, but not the most wondrous.'

Devorus slotted his magnoculars back into their case. The magnetic catch clicked.

'The girl is awake?'

'She is,' said Iolanth. 'Come into the bastion with me. I grant you the honour of seeing her.'

Devorus followed her inside.

The girl peeked at Devorus over her blanket, her large, brown eyes expressing a mix of shyness and confidence. He hadn't seen what colour they were before; the terrible light had obscured them.

He looked away. The light should surely have burned out her eyes. He couldn't shake the image of empty, blackened sockets.

'As you see, she is well,' said Iolanth. She nodded at the two Battle Sisters standing guard. They departed wordlessly.

The guards were within the chamber, Devorus noted, not outside.

'Doesn't she have a name?' Devorus said.

Iolanth shrugged. The detail was unimportant to her. The girl didn't offer one.

He went to the bedside of the girl.

'This is Major Devorus. He is the commander of the Auxilia Garrison of Tyros, and the master of this city. You owe him your respect,' Iolanth said portentously.

'Hello,' said Devorus. 'You really don't. Owe me any respect,' he said. He didn't much care for Iolanth's introduction. 'I'm just a soldier. Can I sit down?' He gestured at the chair by the bed. When the girl did not reply, he sat anyway. She followed him with her huge brown eyes. He leaned forward and looked at her encouragingly.

'They said I had to speak to you, but I thought Colonel Anselm was commander,' she said. It was not surprising a child of Ultramar should know who the military commander was. Once the war had begun and Macragge moved from civilian to military law codes, Anselm's word had become law.

'He died,' said Devorus. And Colonel Borodino, and Majors Vascus, Gled and Hawmanc. He didn't dwell on that.

'When did you take charge?' she asked.

'A few weeks ago,' he said.

Borodino's death had occurred six weeks past, and it had been a messy one. There was fighting in the transit tunnel beneath the harbour channel before they blew it up and washed the enemy back over to the other side. The colonel had been caught by one of the enemy's bio weapons after they'd lain the demolition charges. Devorus resisted the advance of memory, tried to stop its replay before he got there and saw the way Borodino's skin had melted off him, the way he gargled as he drowned in the soup of his own lungs, the way...

Not now, he thought.

He smiled. 'We don't tend to announce these things to the civilians unless there's a good reason.' Devorus leaned back in the chair. Sitting down allowed his tiredness to steal up on him and squat on his shoulders. A physical force wrestled with his eyelids, trying to force them shut. He yawned and pulled his hand down over his face, stretching it. Grit scraped against his skin. His last wash was... When had he last washed?

'I'm sorry,' he said. 'I'm tired.' He laughed as if this were amusing.

'I'm tired too,' the girl said. She pulled her knees up under her chin. Devorus reassessed her age at maybe fourteen standard. She'd seemed older on the line. He supposed his own daughters would be around her age by now, one slightly older, one younger. If they were still alive. He had no idea if they were.

'It's very tiring when He comes.'

'Who?' said Devorus.

'Him,' she said.

'Who's "he"?' he asked.

She stared at him silently.

'Do you remember coming to the front?' he asked.

She shook her head. 'I remember the blessed Sisters asking for me. They came into our basement and said they heard what I did with the well, and that I had to come with them and see you.'

'Do you remember purifying the well?'

'A little. I remember light. And something moving through me.'

'After that?' asked Devorus.

'Just like normal.'

'Until today. When you came to the front. You don't remember anything?'

She shook her head again. 'Nothing, until I woke up here.'

'Right,' he said. 'How are things in the city? I have not had chance to go within the walls recently.'

She shrugged.

'What will happen to me?' she asked. Only now did she look a little afraid.

Devorus leaned over and patted her knee. It should have been a natural gesture, but it felt awkward, and he regretted doing it as soon as he had. He was out of practice, and had never had the paternal knack. His girls had their mother for that. He had seen them so rarely.

'You'll be fine,' he said. The hollowness of his promise

ashamed him. He couldn't guarantee that. 'You get some rest,' he said.

He looked at Iolanth. She nodded. They went outside the room. Devorus strode, grim-faced, down the dusty corridor. He stopped beneath a broken light panel.

'What exactly are you going to do with her?' he asked. 'I understand this showing her to me is a courtesy.'

Sister Superior Iolanth's yellow eyes stared at him hard. She didn't blink much.

'It is. Although you are the interim governor of this city, in these matters of the sacred and the unholy the Adeptus Ministorum hold preeminence. I brought you here to tell you that, as commander of the chamber militant, I will oversee the girl's assessment.'

'What are you going to do with her?' he repeated.

Iolanth looked away, complex emotions seething beneath the surface of her beautiful, scarred face. 'There are two possibilities. The first is that the girl is possessed by a holy power. Her actions in the city suggest so, when she cleansed the well and made the unwholesome pure again. She remembers that, but there were more. Strange lights, predictions of missile strikes, and the annihilation of a daemon imp that had come within our defences.'

'When did that happen?' said Devorus with concern. The girl's actions at the well had been reported to him a few days since. He'd been too busy to chase it up. This other news was fresh, and alarmed him. There were strange creatures the Death Guard had brought with them, vicious insects and the tittering fat things like malevolent children that infested the land they took. If only one of them got onto the island…

'Eight days ago,' she said.

'Why didn't you tell me?' he said.

'Do not be angry. I found this out myself yesterday, when I went to bring the girl out of the city. Her people kept it a secret until we came. I had no time to pass on this information. You will remember the attack, and her turning back the engines of the enemy from the defence line.'

Was that a joke? thought Devorus. He doubted Iolanth capable of humour. 'How could I forget?'

'These phenomena are concordant with a holy influence.'

They looked at each other for a long moment, the man in his dirty uniform, the woman in her pristine crimson armour.

'The other option is that she is a witch,' Devorus said. 'That's the only other one, isn't it? A rogue psyker, or worse, a pawn of the enemy.'

Iolanth nodded. 'Regrettably so.'

'If not, she's what, a saint?' He couldn't believe that. Not on Parmenio.

'I do not think so. I have seen with my own eyes the blessed Saint Celestine. I have read the chronicles of the lives of the holy saints who have arisen at times of peril in the name of our most divine lord, the God-Emperor of Terra. This is something else. At the worst, it could be our undoing. Many times there have been beings who claimed to be saints, but who were not. The enemies of the Emperor are devious. This could be one of their tricks. It pleases the false gods to conjure hope in despairing hearts and to use our faith against us. We must be wary.'

Devorus narrowed his eyes. 'You spoke of something wondrous.'

'I did. If she is not a witch, and this is not a trick...' She paused.

'Then what?'

She would not say. 'Hope overthrows reason. Fact must be determined.' Iolanth's face hardened. 'She must be put to the test. She must pass the Probos Mallefica.'

'The witch testing? She's just a child. Does she deserve this?'

'Does anybody deserve any of this?' retorted Iolanth. 'Some of the worst monsters in history have been born of children. Innocence is no protection against evil. Be thankful I have told you. You cannot stop me. I do not require your blessing or your permission. That I inform you is another courtesy. You should be grateful.'

'You could at least ask her,' he said.

'Who said I have not?' said Iolanth.

'You did?'

'She agreed.'

'She's frightened,' said Devorus. 'She'd probably agree to anything.'

'With good reason. Tell me, major. If you were in her position, would you rather not know if you were a source of corruption? Would you rather die cleanly or become the means of destruction of all you care for? If she is pure, if what I pray for is happening, she could save us all. If it is not, then the least we can do is save her soul. A little pain and the death of one's mortal shell is a trifling price to pay to avoid eternal damnation.'

Devorus felt uneasy. The ruthlessness of the Adeptus Ministorum's excrutiators was well known.

'It's easy to say that when it's not your pain,' he said, surprising himself. He couldn't quite grasp why the suffering of this one child was so important to him.

Iolanth stared at him in contempt. 'I shall inform you of what we discover. Do not interfere.'

Devorus was very tired. He didn't want to argue, but his morals had him rebel against lassitude. 'Sister,' he began. It was as far as he got.

The bastion shook. Dust sifted from the ceiling.

'What was that?' he asked.

Iolanth was already moving faster than he could hope to match. He chased her down the corridor. She was out through the open fortification airlock before him. The door hissed shut behind her, and he hammered fruitlessly at its control panel while it went through its cycle. Another tremor shook the tower, and another.

The airlock door opened, and he hurried in. 'Come on, come on!' he muttered as the machines burbled to themselves, checking and rechecking for contaminants. A fourth tremor, stronger than the last, rattled both him and the devices in the airlock. Their operating lights shivered from green to red and back again at the shock.

'Purity maintained,' said the machines. A chime. The outer door slid back into its housing. Devorus shoved his way around it before it was fully open.

Iolanth stood on the battlements with a crowd of people. They had abandoned their tasks and were looking towards Hecaton.

Devorus arrived in time to see the fifth and final lance strike stab down from orbit. Multiple beams at various angles, probably coming in from different vessels. They were well placed, and struck so close in time they may as well have been simultaneous. He flinched at the searing light. Clouds raced away where the beams crashed through the air, heavy as hammers, flattening Hecaton's corrupted spires. An instant was all the measure of time they required to deliver Guilliman's judgement. They snapped off before the noise of impact had time to reach Devorus' ears. Rings of plasmic discharge rolled out from the impact site, the luminous gasses expanding and dissipating into the yellow fog. Finally sound caught up with light, and the false thunder of impact drummed its way over the plains.

Hecaton was an orange splash on the mountains. Brief flows of lava had replaced the rivers of filth.

All along the wall and in the defence lines below, weary men ripped off their respirators and cheered.

'And lo! The Emperor did judge His enemies unworthy of redemption, and smote them from the void and the ground and the warp,' said Iolanth, quoting text Devorus was unfamiliar with. 'Full wrathful did His anger wax, so that all who beheld Him trembled at His righteousness, and fell upon those who may be traitor, and the slaughter did grow by His will and His action.' Several men nearby got to their knees, whispering prayers over hands spread wide in the sign of the aquila. Several of the most devout called to the holy warrior, asking for her blessing.

'Back to your feet,' said Devorus, blinking after-images away. 'It's not over yet. Back to your duties.'

Iolanth looked at him triumphantly. 'The primarch has spoken, and before he comes here, I will be ready to offer him the head of a witch, or the means of salvation.'

She left the battlements, calling loudly into the vox pick-up mounted in her collar for her excrutiators.

CHAPTER FOURTEEN

THE PATH OF FLESH

Sludgy rain drizzled from green skies. The belches of war rumbled around the world, rolling from one side of the horizon. The servants of the Corpse-God were close at hand. Time was running out for the invaders.

The Death Guard had their camp in a shallow valley in the mountains to the north of Hecaton. It was a miserable, dreary place. At its centre a rusting platform of three interlocked circles had been raised high over the ground. Upon it were gathered three hundred and forty mortal wretches under the dull white eyes of Mortarion. They were the Cult of Endless Proliferation, a seercult dedicated to the service of Nurgle. Every one of them was a psyker, and some were of no mean talent. Their blighted lives lived out for the glory of the Plague God, they were meek, and keen to please their immortal lord. Though they had power of their own it was nothing to that of Mortarion. Beside the might of the lord of the Death Guard, their gifts were feeble corpselights next to the sun.

Mortarion sat upon a high-backed throne fashioned from stacked, greening bones. His armoured hands gripped armrests made of columns of inverted skulls. Around him were seven Deathshroud Terminators, their enormous, armoured bodies dwarfish near to the immensity of their daemonic lord. Their giant scythes were miniature compared to the great weapon Silence, hung on rusting brackets above Mortarion's head. The power of Chaos had swelled Mortarion well beyond his original dimensions. Made twice the size of a mortal man by the Emperor, Nurgle had stretched him further, so that he was thirty feet tall, a stature befitting his exalted status in the Plague God's court.

Up a long rug made of rotting man skins stitched together, the High Thaumaturge of the seercult made his wheezing way to Mortarion's feet. He was blessed with Nurgle's abundance of flesh. A tall, pointed hood decorated with a dull brass fly pin covered all but his scabby mouth. A long kilt covered his lower portions, but his chest was bare, and his distended stomach swung ponderously over his belt.

A skinny being, covered head to foot in dull green robes, accompanied the thaumaturge. He bore a dirty dry flag roughly daubed with Nurgle's fly.

The High Thaumaturge stopped before Mortarion's throne and kneeled with obvious effort. His faceless minion stood behind him, the standard of the cult flapping in the moist plague wind.

'We are ready, my lord,' said the man. Among his own ranks he was feared. Hundreds plotted against each other in order to please him the most. He was arrogant, cruel, well versed in the dark arts, and blessed by his god. Kneeling at the feet of the daemon primarch, he shook like a beast before slaughter.

Mortarion's breathing mask hissed plumes of toxic vapour. The lord of death's lungs rattled in a deep draught.

'Then proceed,' he said. Mortarion stared over the supplicant's head at the storm on the horizon. Lance beams stabbed at the surface. Munitions plummeted like meteors. His hated brother was going to destroy Hecaton. Explosions thudded from positions around the city in persistent beat. There was not much time. *'Bring forth Ku'gath and his Plague Guard before the fane and its clock is lost, or you shall suffer such torments that even the most sincere faith in the Plague God cannot blunt.'*

The man's hood quivered, amplifying his fearful shaking.

'My lord!' he said. For a man so fat and ill, he positively sprang to his feet. He bowed and scraped back down the rug of flayed skins, turning only when he had reached a respectful distance.

'In the name of Nurgle, all powerful god of life and death, let the ritual commence!'

A brass gong boomed dully. A chant began. The sorcerers made a hollow circle around the point where the three platforms intersected, leaving but one break in their wall of scrofulous flesh so that Mortarion, sitting at the extreme edge of the northernmost circle, could look into the centre with his view uninterrupted.

Seven of the three hundred and forty walked forward to the centre of this circle, their paces set to match the solemn time of the chant. They took up equidistant station, forming a smaller ring within the larger. At once, they reached up and cast down their hoods, then unpinned their cloaks and let them fall to the floor, leaving them naked in the rain.

Seven of the most blessed of Nurgle's followers had been chosen. Their range of deformities was impressive. Not one part of them was free of blemish or disease. This one had feet swollen to gargantuan size by elephantiasis, that one limbs withered and fingers missing to leprosy. Another's face had collapsed in on itself, its skull eaten by bone disease, leaving a puckered, whistling hole to serve as mouth and nose. All had sores, pocks, buboes and patches of garish lividity. Their skin was uniformly discoloured and slack. Parasites, revealed by their disrobing, scuttled for armpits and groins to get out of the rain. Their ailments exceeded the worst morbidities a man should bear without death. Nurgle had worked his flesh change on most. A wide maw lined with black teeth gaped in a woman's belly. A man cradled a thrashing tentacle that had replaced his right arm, and a third was surrounded by a swarm of flies that sang out the names of lost diseases at the edge of hearing and crawled in and out of delicate cavities in the man's skin.

'O great Nurgle!' intoned the thaumaturge over the droning of his coven. 'In generosity you have blessed these fortunates. We thank you for their afflictions, we give praise to your munificence, we grovel in worship at your kindnesses! We offer them back to you, to take into your garden, where you may admire your work and take satisfaction in your artfulness!'

His warbling voice rose. 'Take back your worthy sons and daughters into the heavens of your endless garths, take up their love and their worship to your rotting breast, so that they might forever live, and be reborn in all the multiplicities of decay's form!'

Lightning burst overhead, a thrashing, seven-pointed trident of virulent green electricity that flicked and cracked back and forth in the sky.

The seven held up ritual athames in fists and coiled tentacles, presenting the metal to the sky.

'Take us, O Grandfather, cherish us!' they sang.

The lightning burst again, earthing itself into their daggers. Shaking with the power dancing over their skin, the seven rammed the tips of their blades into their bellies, and with quick, agonised, upright jerks, eviscerated themselves.

They cried in pain and ecstasy as their entrails tumbled out. Already their god had accepted the offering, and their offal greened as the coven chanted, bursting with the squirming life of maggots.

To death's embrace the seven rushed, falling into the slime of their own decaying innards as life bled out of them into the pound of the downpour.

'Open the way!' cried the thaumaturge. 'By the three times three times three greater names of the Plague God, I command it to be so! Open the way!'

The corpses jerked. Lightning slashed down into them again. Their ribcages burst open with sickening cracks, wrenching themselves free of the dead flesh, tearing whipping spines behind them. Aglow with pestilential foxfire, the bones rose up, circling each other, growing in size. Black matter poured from nowhere to coat them. Tendrils grew from rib cage to rib cage, epidemic-fast, in twisting bursts. The tendrils flailed, hissed and wailed with inhuman voices, before touching and pulling at each other, linking the bones into a lopsided, elliptical archway twenty-five metres high.

'Nurgle! Nurgle! Nurgle!' chanted the crowd in feverish rhapsody.

A sickening light kindled at the centre of the gate, growing swiftly in brightness so that it glared dangerously into the eyes of all upon the platform. Reality rippled, warping glass caught in the heat of magic, bowing outwards in violent convexities that sang a tortured physics.

'Nurgle! Nurgle! Nurgle!'

Lance beams slashed the sky to the south. Hecaton's end had come. Nurgle had his answer to that.

Fire burst from the gap, rooting itself in the eye sockets of the seercult. Green energies shot from their mouths and their clothes, cooking off a ripe steam from their sodden gowns. A stuttering thunder that could have been a godly laugh rolled through the boiling sky. To a terrific boom, the gate burst wide, ripping open a sore on the skin of reality.

The seercult fell dead in one instant, leaving the High Thaumaturge and his banner bearer the sole survivors of their number. Their bodies thumped down to the brown metal like sacks tumbling from the tailgate of a cart.

Another world, more diseased and blighted than Parmenio, could be glimpsed through the sucking warp rift. Iax, the garden world, the planet Mortarion would remake and rename as Pestiliax, the heart and keystone of his plans to drag Ultramar entire into the warp.

The view through was suddenly obscured by a mountain of loathsome flesh, borne upon a giant palanquin carried by a horde of tittering plague mites.

Scowling miserably, the daemon Ku'gath pushed his way

through the warp, stepping from one world to another in a beat of his rotten heart.

Rain drizzled from green clouds, putting Ku'gath uncomfortably in mind of his rival Rotigus. Manifestation upon Parmenio had none of the joy of their ravaging of Tartella or the taking by plague of Iax. Septicus kept his horns hidden away under a cowl and his face sombre. His other lieutenants were equally morbid. The nurglings mewled and complained under Ku'gath's bulk. He rocked his platform spitefully, giving them something real to moan about.

The seven Great Unclean Ones of the Plague Guard legion approached Mortarion. The daemon primarch hunched on his throne, his wings folded against the driving rain. Parmenio was dark and miserable, but not in the right kind of way. Fresh winds probed at the edges of the stinking mists, threatening to tease them apart and blow away glorious foetor. Nearby, the weapons of mortals cut the atmosphere. This was not a propitious manifestation.

Ku'gath looked at aurorae in the sky visible only to daemon eyes.

'Nurgle's power is slipping away,' said Ku'gath. Iax had a shroud of warp current about it that he could draw strength from and force his existence upon the truculent cosmos. On Iax he felt vigorous. On Parmenio he could feel mealy mundanity under the flow of the warp, a grit under the sheets of a comfortable bed. He felt if he drew too hard on it to fuel his sorcery, it would give out. He would unravel, and the laws of the mortal realm would expel him. *'The perfumed air of the garden wafts but fitfully over this place.'* He turned his mighty head to look beyond the platforms over the Death Guard camp beyond.

'Your clock is in place. Does it not work?' He shuddered. There was a wholesomeness emanating from somewhere uncomfortably close. Ku'gath had the sensation of being watched by unfriendly eyes. All the daemons felt it. They trudged out of the rift quietly. The nurglings had lost their mirth, becoming as miserable as the plaguebearers habitually were, whereas the plaguebearers themselves had become withdrawn, and whispered their counts. Beasts of Nurgle slumped by on acidic slime trails, whimpering, too cowed to play. The Plaguefather looked back at his stony-faced lieutenants – Septicus, Famine, the Gangrel, Pestus Throon, Squatumous and Bubondubon, who of them all was the only one to keep his good humour.

'What have you tricked me into?' Ku'gath demanded. He leaned forward, eliciting squeals of alarm from his palanquin bearers.

'The plan has hit a further complication,' said Mortarion. *'The warp withdraws. The power that aided my brother through the othersea is at play here on the surface, working against our lord. I have hit a barrier at the western extremity of this continent, a city that will not fall. There is a protection over it.'*

'Which power stops you? Have you determined whether it is our ever-changing rival or… Him,' said Ku'gath. Misgiving filled his miserable heart and spilled out between his rotting teeth. So potent was the feeling that Mortarion sank lower into his throne, like a cur fearful of his master's whip.

'Beyond the city the lands remain unblessed by Nurgle's fecund gifts. All is slow stability, free of rot and rebirth.'

'I asked which power, O lord of death,' said Ku'gath. The muscles twitched around his loose eye, and he put up a fat hand to prevent its dropping out.

'It matters not,' said Mortarion. *'The result is the same whoever challenges us. Our goals are unchanged. Parmenio is a stage for the second act of Guilliman's fall. I have sent prayers to our Grandfather asking for his help. The portents are good. I am heeded.'*

'You need more aid?' asked Ku'gath incredulously. *'At your request I have brought the greater part of the daemonic host of Iax-that-will-be-Pestiliax.'* He shuddered. The flesh of his mountainous flanks quivered. *'No more can be brought here. The legions of Nurgle are septets of infinity, seven times seven times seven and on, forevermore, but there is not warp current enough to support more at this place.'*

'We shall see,' said Mortarion. *'Nurgle will provide. The great battle for the soul of Ultramar is at hand. I will not rest until I have claimed this realm for Grandfather. He will support my aim. We will conquer this world and bring my brother to his doom on Pestiliax.'*

On the horizon, the false lightnings of void war flashed ever brighter. The final stabs of light hammered down from orbit to obliterate Hecaton. The fires of its destruction lit up the louring skies with cleansing orange. At the destruction of the city the warp gate shrivelled behind Ku'gath, narrowing the way between the worlds. The daemon legion wailed in consternation, and picked up its pace to get through before the path was shut.

'Hurry!' shouted Pestus Throon. *'Hurry!'*

Ku'gath gasped. *'And now the power lessens more. Our kind cannot tarry long here.'*

'My brother has identified and neutralised my warp clock more swiftly than I anticipated,' said Mortarion. *'But the portents are good. All is going to plan.'*

Ku'gath was unconvinced. *'No more lies, Mortarion,'* he

said, and turned his attentions to holding open the gate long enough for his legion to pass through.

CHAPTER FIFTEEN

RELIEF

Another day closer to death. Devorus was in the forward observation post, right by the water. He had expected help after he had seen Hecaton burn. A week later none had come, and the enemy were closer to Tyros than ever.

A shell detonated in the harbour. Water spouted high, splattering Devorus with seawater already turning foul. The enemy were close. The guns of the city wall were depressed to their lowest elevations. The enemy were coming within their minimum range, and so the guns pounded the harbour more than the foe. The air around Devorus' position was mixed with seawater; moist and salty.

'Fire!' he shouted hoarsely. He had said the word so many times it had become meaningless. Lascannons shot, their beams persisting long enough to register as a burning, phantom flicker upon the retina. Molten metal ran from the dozer blades of the Death Guard siege tanks, mingling with the rubble they pushed into the water.

Devorus' hope that the enemy would abandon the mole and retreat from Tyros had gone unfulfilled. The arrival of the fleet spurred the enemy to a frenzy of activity. Work on the mole went into overdrive. Sickness sprang up in the streets of Tyros. Strange machine ailments compromised the city's defences.

Look to the mole, he thought. There is the threat. Concentrate. Thousands of the walking dead shambled alongside the tanks. They lacked the will to be useful as workers, so the Death Guard chained rocks about their necks and sent them forth. Driven on by their need to savage living flesh, the dead reached the end of the causeway and tumbled right into the water, the stones dragging them down to wet graves in the foundations of the siege works. Devorus ordered his men not to shoot them. It took too many hits to put them down, and they could not spare the ammunition. Arms flew away from bodies, and they did not slow. Shots punched through torsos, so all the guts fell out and clear air could be seen behind, but they came on. Even those whose legs were blasted away doggedly dragged themselves, hand over hand, towards the shore. There were more pressing targets to gun for. He would worry about the dead when they reached the island.

'Target the heretics! Kill the traitors!' he shouted, brandishing his laspistol over the broken docks.

Conveyors rumbled behind the tanks, pouring gravel into the narrowing sea. The hulking figures of Traitor Space Marines walked beside them, whipping the hundreds of mortal slaves they brought to work for them, and lending a hand directly themselves, using their enhanced strength to toss boulders the weight of Devorus into the ocean.

Devorus had not seen the Plague Marines so close for a while. There had been times, on other worlds, when he had faced them. Their appearance curdled his stomach nonetheless. His memories seemed too awful to be real; they had the enormity of lies. But the truth of the enemy was before him again. They were immense, hideous things warped beyond sanity's capacity to understand. Devorus looked at them through his magnoculars, and felt his fragile grip on reality slipping away from him. With the machine's aid he could see the Death Guards' malformities in gruesome detail. The skin sloughing from flabby, exposed torsos, the fringes of luridly coloured tentacles poking out around armour plates, the limbs turned to whipping worms. Their stench was worse than the sight. They stank so much he could smell them over the frothing water, even through his rebreather. He thought if they came nearer, he might die simply by being in proximity to them. They smelled of disease, of the most hopeless hospitals in the worst of warzones, and the deepest, darkest plague pits.

They should have been dead. Their wounds were severe and rotting, and their ailments obvious. Rather than weaken them and bring them to death, their afflictions made them strong. Their resilience was astounding. Their armour was close to scrap, but they shrugged off direct hits from lascannons and heavy bolters. Some of them waved cheerily when they were hit, or made juvenile noises. Their puerile behaviour only made them more terrifying.

Devorus avoided looking at them through his magnoculars if he could help it. Not that he would need them for long to see the enemy in detail. They were close. The mole was only a hundred metres from the shore, and every minute saw it creep a little bit closer. By his estimation he had only an hour until they crossed the harbour and made it onto the island. Then the warped Space Marines would set foot upon Tyros' land, and there would be plague walkers in horrific multitude. What would take him, he wondered, the living or the dead?

Dark clouds bunched over the siege tanks. Cold wind, rank with damp and mould, blew from the shore.

'Fire!' he shouted again. Once more, the beams of lascannons slammed into the blades pushing rock, soil and bone into the churning ocean. Rotary cannons on the fronts of the tanks replied. Bullets whined, furious and insectile, past the defenders of the shore. Devorus' engineers had strengthened the forward defences, making as good a redoubt as they could. A new wall constructed of shipping containers filled with rockcrete fronted the harbour, making a layered defence of three lines. Behind these barriers, the men were safer, but the volume of bullets was great, chance shots were common, and many died.

'Fire!' he ordered again. Heavy bolter rounds raked across pox walkers and Death Guard, hammering the former down, tearing chunks from the latter. The dead kept on coming, and the diseased Heretic Space Marines stood on open ground, inviting further tests of their fortitude with arms thrown wide. Worst of all, when the humans working alongside the traitors fell dead they were not long in getting back up, their faces fixed with the rictus of the pox walkers. They shambled forward, joining the mass.

'Fire...' Devorus said. His voice faltered. Over the mole a vortex of black smoke and sickly light formed. Mighty beings came to the front in the number of seven – Space Marine witches, draped in rotting man-skins and bearing staffs of gnarled green wood.

They pointed their fetishes at the sea, and chanted words that ripped at the air in twisting streamers, polluting the very fabric of reality itself.

Men shouted in alarm.

'Witchery! Witchery! Sorcerers!'

The sea boiled. White foam on grey water turned to black scum on stinking slime. The water jellied from liquid to solid. Squirming things pushed up through the thickening ocean, and a mat of pulsing veins formed, leaking ichor into the sea from dribbling nexuses. Flesh grew and spread between. Devorus recognised the shapes and form of Parmenio's native marine flora and fauna in the growing mat, but hideously twisted and enlarged, before all semblance to natural things collapsed into the morass of flesh. This abomination wriggled its way across the ocean, grasping with elongating pseudopods at the pilings of the water front, and wrapping themselves fast around them with wet, suckering sounds. As the fringed vanguard of the flesh-way reached the shore, the back end solidified, going from disparate, filmy patches of matter to a solid causeway of pulsing, diseased life.

A briny, rotten stink came from it, perceptible through his environmental gear. Vapours rose and stole ashore, switching this way and that with a life of their own. They appeared like shreds of ordinary ocean mist, but they were predatory, and aware.

'Fire!' shouted Devorus. He was close to panicking. He couldn't show it, or his men would flee. 'Shoot the bridge! Shoot the bridge!'

At once, the heavy weapons emplaced along the shore fired, pummelling the surface of the living causeway. Their efforts were fruitless. Many shots rebounded from rubbery skin, deflected away from the unnatural organism by warp-craft. The surface throbbed and boomed, a linear drum, sending out sprays of water with each impact. Where hits did catch on the flesh and penetrate, black fluids bubbled forth, and poured as killing slicks into the sea.

All around the causeway, things were dying. Sea life bobbed to the surface, crawling already with decay.

'Sir! Sir!' a sergeant called. His frantic pointing directed Devorus' attention to the far side. The tanks, thankfully, did not proceed; there was an apparent limit to the bridge's carrying capacity. But the infantry were coming, proceeded by huge drifts of droning, evil-looking flies. The Death Guard were shrouded by them, their massive shapes hidden amid the swirling mass. With comical lopes they bounded across, using the give and bounce of the mat to propel them, proving their invulnerability to the firepower of the Astra Militarum. Heavy weapons fire and lasgun fusillade alike were swallowed up by the flies, whose shifting clumps made false figures while obscuring those that were real.

The thumping of the enemy's self-propelled mortars started up afresh. This time, no viral bombs were cast but simple explosives instead. Shells slammed hard into the makeshift defences, blasting out the sides of the containers with wrenching bangs. The mist was worse, creeping up to soldiers silently, and worming its way through the smallest of gaps. Those chosen by the vapour died horribly. They shook so hard their limbs broke. Vomited blood coloured the lenses of their masks red.

Wounded men breathed their last in screaming agony. The lucky were annihilated instantly.

Death reigned over the harbourside, and still the Death Guard were yet to open fire.

'Sound the retreat,' Devorus told his bugler, gripped by the certainty of defeat. 'Now.'

The bugler clicked his heels and bravely ventured out of the bunker door with his face uncovered; his instrument demanded it. The clear music of the horn cut through the racket of war. As Devorus' officers and squad leaders caught the sound, it was joined by the far less melodious honking of air horns and the shrill of digital whistles passing on the command. Men shouted and began to fall back, all while shrieking shells rained down, and the diseased mist claimed more victims by touch alone.

Devorus waited a moment. Unable to see much beyond the embrasure of the post, he judged the progress of the retreat by ear. When he guessed most of his men had begun to fall back, he turned to his new voxman. 'Send a message, now. Bring down full bombardment on these coordinates.'

'What coordinates?' the soldier asked dumbly.

'On our position! Tell the wall guns to shell this position!'

The soldier stared back at him. Devorus swore, and snatched the vox-horn from his hand.

'This is Major Devorus. Watch-code Ultima Phi. The enemy are breaking through. Prepare second line defences. Commence bombardment of my sector immediately.'

A crackle told him he had been heard, though the words were lost. The buzzing of the flies reached beyond human hearing, infesting the vox waves.

The Death Guard were nearly over the water. A mob of disease-twisted Parmenians went before them, absorbing many shots that would otherwise have found their mark in the bodies of the traitors.

'We're leaving. Now,' he said. His command staff

scrambled out. Devorus, as suited his temperament, left last.

For the second time that week, Devorus found himself running away.

The daemon engines had been bad. This was far worse, a full-frontal assault by some of the deadliest warriors in the galaxy. He ran through the port, dodging explosions, all thoughts of command gone from his head. He did not think at all. Instinct took over. His body demanded survival and wrested control from his conscious mind. A crane took a direct hit and fell sideways, clanging down not far from him. He was dodging its fall before he even noticed it toppling. A unit of men was obliterated only twenty metres away, turned from running, shouting, thinking beings to smoking char in an eye blink.

All the city was firing now, obliterating its own port with its heavy wall guns. Devorus glanced back as he fled. The bombardment punched towers of yellow fire into the swirling mass of insects. There were, finally, dead Heretic Space Marines lying upon the damp rockcrete wharfs. But they were few and far between, and even if every one were felled by a lucky shot, the walking dead were too numerous to slay. They walked onwards, slow as a spill of tar towards the breach in the wall.

Behind him, bolters fired. The bang of release, the hissing of their rocket motors, the wet thumps as they exploded inside living flesh, made a roaring din. Terror had him. More than a fear of death. An invisible pall of fear was draped over the enemy, filling Devorus with cold, unthinking dread. He almost collapsed into a ball behind a stack of rusting barrels, there to await his end, but his body forced him on.

The second defence line lay ahead, built atop the rubble of the broken wall and guarding the breach from attack. It was there Devorus had witnessed the child's gift. From inside, the defences seemed respectable. From outside, looking at the mighty edifice of the broken wall behind, they appeared inadequate. Enemy artillery was pounding the breach. Where it hit unblemished sections, the walls held, but those shots that found their target knocked chunks away, bringing down boulders of rockcrete and widening the gap. In the port, already medium-range fire from the Death Guard was pounding at the prefabricated line sections closing the way into the city. They cruelly targeted the shore guard's lines of escape, filling trenches with plasma and storms of whirling shrapnel, daring the fleeing men to take their chance between volleys. Devorus made for one of these deadly alleyways, hoping that he would be one of the few to make it through the buckled plasteel sally ports while the enemy were looking to slay some other unfortunate.

The pounding of the city's batteries deafened him. Giant towers of spray lofted high where they hit the sea, columns of broken rockcrete mingling with shattered corpses where they hit the land. Devorus did not hear the returning fire of the enemy creeping towards him. It all mingled into a raw wall of furious noise.

Next he knew, he was flying, knocked skywards by the ruthless slap of overpressure. The air was driven from his lungs so hard his vocal chords involuntarily sang. He glimpsed the ground rushing at him, and then that hit him too, and less gently.

His ears rang. His vision lost colour. He felt displaced from himself.

Even so, he staggered up, the drive to live too powerful to overcome, and limped towards the second line. The ringing in his ears shut out all external sound.

He lost himself for a while into a foretaste of death. He came to, his environment suit and uniform shredded down the left-hand side and his arm bleeding. He was leaning against the smoking wreck of a bunker, whose plascrete, liquefied by plasma strikes, dripped dangerously near to him. He expected to die, but a curious sight greeted him as his consciousness regathered itself.

The flies had banked up, as if running into an invisible window. They battered at the obstacle, droning in annoyance. The dead passed this barrier, but as they walked through they became enfeebled, and when shot they fell easily and did not rise. Only the Plague Marines were unimpeded, but they felt something. Those of a jocular nature ceased their jokes and laughing. Those who were grim became grimmer still. Of most note were the sorcerers, whose power raced away from them as soon as they crossed the invisible line. Their enraged cries penetrated the battle noise. Devorus was amazed as they raised their rusted gauntlets and their warp-born power fizzled and dribbled away.

The enemy continued to advance. Their arcane might was diminished, but their guns still had teeth. A deadly crossfire hatched the kill zone between defence line and harbour. The Death Guard advanced through it carelessly. And although a handful more of them fell, it was far fewer than should have. Energy beams and bullets whined overhead, blasting apart the mob of living dead. Without the flies to choke off las-beams and obscure targets, it made a little difference, but not enough. The Heretic

Astartes were still moving in. Lines of men formed a desperate rearguard, firing and retreating by ranks, blasting the approaching monstrosities at close range, then point-blank range. One more fell, then two, three. Only three. Hundreds of shots fired, enough to shatter an army, for three dead enemies.

The Death Guard worked themselves up to a lumbering jog to close the distance. It could not be called a run. They were too obese and diseased for that, but their speed was deceptive. The men of Calth admirably held their nerve and received the charge with fixed bayonets. The Death Guard swatted them aside. Men screamed as their bones were pulverised by heavy blows, and unnatural disease rooted itself in their organs.

Even without their shrouds of flies and their sorcerers, the Death Guard were massacring the Astra Militarum.

Dazed, Devorus prepared to die. He sank to his knees, grasped his aquila pendant in his rubber gloved right hand, and prayed.

Roaring jet engines started him from his misery. A two-hulled gunship blasted overhead, guns barking, missiles streaking from its wings, and came to a hovering stop. Space Marines leapt from its open doors, guiding their grav chutes into the heart of the enemy. They were of the Primaris type, skull-faced warriors with long knives. More wearing flight packs rocketed in after the giant assault craft, guns blazing.

Further craft flew in, roaring to a stop, and putting down. Adeptus Astartes in heavier armour deployed.

The Death Guard abandoned their persecution of the Astra Militarum, turning their wrath on their hated brethren. Seeing the traitors face down Imperial Space Marines was terrifying. The energy released by the fighting shook the world.

Clean-armoured Primaris Ultramarines battled rotting hulks. Now they were set against one another, Devorus could appreciate more how far the Plague Marines had fallen. The ferocity with which they fought the newcomers was telling. The Primaris Marines reminded the Death Guard of what they had been.

The two sides were evenly matched. The Primaris Marines were durable, albeit in a different way to their damned cousins. They took hits that would obliterate a mortal man and fought on, though blows to the head or the chest seemed to kill them, whereas the Plague Marines absorbed all manner of pain before dying.

The first line of Primaris Marines to attack were gunned down by a hail of shot. As the first ranks of the Plague Marine band fired, their brothers behind pulled free mummified heads with wax-stoppered mouths and stitched eyes. Some of these were mounted on short poles in the manner of stick grenades, and they threw them in a similar manner, all of them at once, pelting the Primaris. The grenades slapped against them like rancid fruit, spilling diseased matter over their pristine armour. Paint bubbled and blackened. Ceramite, made brittle, shattered from movement alone. Space Marines, who no mortal disease could kill, spasmed, bloody foam spurting from their breathing grilles. Bolts hammered into the Death Guard, killing a few here and a few there. They dwindled, but still not quickly enough. The Primaris Marines lost many in return.

But the Death Guard's time on the shores of Tyros was short. Still more aircraft were flying in from the east.

Despite their foul appearance, the Death Guard had

lost none of their tactical acumen. Seeing reinforcements inbound, they formed up into a phalanx, and began to retreat. The fire from the far side of the sea intensified. Shells rained down on the wharfs while lascannon barrages forced the gunships away. The Death Guard fell back under fire from the walls, defence line and the Ultramarines. They passed over the tongue of the bridge, their flies enveloping them again, and vanished into a foetid mist.

Bigger guns were firing on the far side of the harbour channel. The Death Guard bombardment ceased shortly after, leaving Devorus reeling. It was not truly quiet; gunships were dropping down and delivering Space Marines of old and new kinds, and their voxmitted shouts were blaring and harsh. But without the shelling, without the constant crack of lasguns and cough of bolters, it seemed almost peaceful.

The mist was creeping back. Gunfire flashed in the docks over the water.

Devorus wrenched his mask off and vomited. Adrenaline left him a palsied wreck. With difficulty, he pushed away from the ruined bunker.

By then grav-tanks were pushing across the ocean, their impellers forcing deep valleys into the sea and sending the displaced water up high. When they hit solid ground, the water crashed back down and cascaded from their sides. Their grav fields flattened everything, and their engines made a tremendous, growling pounding.

Their ramps opened as soon as they crossed onto dry land, and more Space Marines jumped out. Medicae personnel followed, dispersing towards the casualties. Devorus thought they would find few alive.

Smaller lighters and unarmed shuttlecraft followed soon

after. Many bore the helical badge of the medicae. These roared overhead, heading towards the city.

Devorus limped through all the tumult. He had no clear idea of where he was going.

A heavily decorated Space Marine was asking questions of a soldier on a casualty bier. The man raised a weak arm and pointed in the direction of Devorus. The warrior immediately made for him and announced himself.

'I am Captain Sicarius, of the Ultramarines Victrix Guard,' he said. 'You are the ranking officer here?'

'You took your damn time,' said Devorus, all sense of deference battered from him by the fight.

'We are here now,' he said. 'You are Major Devorus?'

Devorus managed to straighten his back and nod. 'I am.'

'My orders are to secure this city for the primarch. Tell me quickly, what is the manner of protection about this place?'

'I don't know what you mean.'

'The enemy's magic was halted before the city perimeter. What caused this? Tell me now, and do not lie. Tyros must be secured.'

Devorus was puzzled. 'That wasn't you?'

'It was not,' said Sicarius.

Devorus' mind was a blank. The answer came to him unexpectedly, and with it his wits returned. He looked up at Sicarius wonderingly.

'The child. There is a child here, a wondrous child, not far from adulthood, but a child still. It must be her!'

'A psyker? Is she sanctioned?' Sicarius took a step closer. The tone of his voice frightened Devorus.

'She is not a psyker,' said Devorus with absolute certainty, though he knew as he spoke he had no claim to any knowledge that could back this statement. He just felt it.

'What then?' said the Space Marine.

'She is a miracle,' said Devorus.

Sicarius' vox equipment clicked as he switched channels. He did not enable privacy settings and spoke openly through his helm grille. 'Inform the tetrarch there is something strange here. I request his counsel. Tell the primarch that I advise he wait before he puts down. This could be a trap.'

'The primarch?' said Devorus. An entirely different kind of terror afflicted him. Ridiculously, he reflected later, his first thought was for the battered state of his uniform. 'The primarch is coming here?' Guilliman had returned in the time of Devorus' great-grandfather, but he never thought to actually see him, even when the news came he was retaking the planet. Devorus thought he would fight in the same war as the lord of Ultramar, but to actually see him... Guilliman was as much a myth to Devorus as he had been to earlier generations, when he still languished in stasis.

'Not yet,' said Sicarius. 'Not until I have had chance to vet this child for deviancy.'

'I shall–'

Sicarius held up his hand for silence while he listened to a private message.

The Space Marine growled and looked skywards. More ships were racing down. 'Damn all priests,' he said. He looked at Devorus, who saw accusation flashing in his ruby eye lenses. 'Do you know what is happening in the city?' he demanded.

'What?' Devorus said, afraid again. Having given in once to fear, it took him for its plaything.

'This procession,' barked Sicarius. 'This child of yours at

its head. I have reports from my scouts. The whole damn population is on the streets. You're in charge here, correct?'

Devorus shook his head numbly, though he was in charge. 'My voxman is...' he looked about, helpless. The giants in blue were so arresting he couldn't see anything else, his eyes wouldn't let him. 'I don't know where he is. My equipment's ruined. I've been down here since dawn. No contact. I told them to stay indoors. I ordered it!'

Sicarius gave him a conciliatory grunt. 'You lead from the front. Hard fight.' He switched vox-channels. 'Captain Sicarius to Strike Force Tyros Relief. Secure the harbour areas on the mainland and the island.' He responded tersely to replies Devorus could not hear.

On the far side of the water, fire flash and explosion skipped across the docks. The ongoing fight drew away from the River Sea grudgingly, pulling its pall of mist after it. The revealed shore was a skeleton yard of tumbled structures.

Three Space Marines in armour that exceeded in beauty all artwork Devorus had ever seen jogged up to the captain and wordlessly walled him in. Sicarius became a blue keep in a cobalt fortress encrusted with gold.

'You are coming with me,' Sicarius said to Devorus. 'Now.'

CHAPTER SIXTEEN

THE EMPEROR PROTECTS

Mathieu made his way through the streets of Tyros. Tall, steep-sided towers were favoured by the Parmenians, and made up the bulk of the city's architecture. They were all the same height and design, so tightly packed the city looked like a bed of nails from the air.

Open spaces made by the enemy broke the pattern. Around bomb sites and lance strikes, destruction ordered itself in concentric rings of graduated severity. At the middle nothing stood. Fractured ground was broken through to sub levels, pipes and transit ways peeking shyly from the rubble. Next was a flattened area carpeted with pulverised rockcrete fused into brittle glass. Ringing the flatness was a maze of shattered structures where the angles of walls and structural members bent by force defied navigation. A step up led to the next circle of taller walls leaning in disarray, and lastly around the damage were towers hollowed out by fire, their exteriors livid with heat bloom.

The city's grid of streets was interrupted. Broken facades slumped into the roads in unstable fans of ferrocrete. To allow foot traffic, narrow pathways snaked through the rubble, carved haphazardly, debris kept off by sheets of corrugated plasteel bolted into place and constricting nets sprayed from industrial webbers. The damage was worst around the breach of the Hecatone portwall. There the skyline was sculpted ragged for half a mile within the city. Artillery carved straight lanes through tower after tower, opening up queer passages and strange, vitrified alleyways that led nowhere.

Navigating Tyros was no longer easy. Flat, straight roads had been turned into paths as tricky as any mountain way. Mathieu could have had his pilot land in the centre of town, but he had instead ordered to be set upon one of the Keleton-ward towers, furthest from the arriving Imperial troops.

Despite Mathieu's sly departure from the fleet, news of his mission would get to the regent. Mathieu had a limited time to work. He expected Guilliman to be furious. He would bear whatever punishment was given him. His duty trumped all other concerns.

He had to find the girl from his vision.

There were many people on the streets, drawn out by the roar of craft coming in from orbit. News travelled fast through the cramped underground shelters. The siege was broken, the word said. The primarch was coming. The Tyreans came from their hiding places in the cellars and transit network to greet their saviours, slowly, slowly, and then in a flood.

Mathieu's ears were alive for news of the girl. He was not disappointed. Knots of excited people pushed past him, swapping rumours. They were jubilant, happy. Deliverance was theirs.

'She stopped the sickness!' said a chattering woman. Like many of those abroad, she had painted a skull mask on her face in powdered rockcrete and soot. Mathieu had seen this before, on other worlds. It was a token of faith with the Emperor, that the wearer would not accept the diseased unlife of the enemy, but stated their intention to seek a clean end in service to the Master of Mankind. Mathieu approved of the display. In other cities and on other worlds, loyal men and women had lost their senses to the psychic diseases of Mortarion's warp network and cast their lot in with the traitors, even on Macragge. But not so, it seemed, in Tyros. Surely, that was a sign.

Mathieu slowed to match the woman's pace, listening unobtrusively.

Under the scowl of the death's head, the woman's expression was rapt, and her eyes sparkled. 'Elody was on the Imperial Way,' she said, 'I told her not to go out while the curfew was on, but she did, and she saw the Sisters bring out the saint on a golden throne, and take her nigh to the wall. There, light shone around her, and the enemy stopped, ran away, Elody said. They went! Then the Space Marines arrived, called down by her grace!' She was elated, and gabbling. 'I told Elody off for being out, I was going to punish her, but she saw the miracle. She brought the news to me. When she told me...' the woman was swallowed up by the gathering throng. Mathieu caught one last glimpse of her, still talking.

Rubble spilled into the road ahead, and the street pulled into a narrow. The growing crowd slowed and swirled, caught in a bottleneck. Mathieu was drawn slowly into the alleyway through the debris. It was dark in there, close with the smell of people who had been trapped without proper sanitation for weeks. Mathieu had spent a lot of time with humanity's common herd. Mankind's scent was a holy odour to him, and did not offend. No one noticed him, no one knew who he was. He revelled in his anonymity. There was enjoyment in being a part of the mass, faceless among the painted skull masks.

The man in front was talking to a woman, perhaps his wife.

'She's a saint. A real saint. Come with the blessing of the Emperor!'

'Jarrold saw it,' said another. 'He was there when she cleansed the well. And they say He has abandoned us. People should be burned for that talk. The Emperor protects. He came, He came!'

And again, 'The Emperor protects.' And again and again, 'The Emperor protects.'

All around him Mathieu heard the warding phrase, and the repetition of, 'Saint, saint, saint,' so that the words laminated themselves, building a palpable aura of faith from sound and belief.

'The Emperor protects, the Emperor protects, the Emperor protects.'

He felt their joy, secure in the knowledge that the eye of their god had come to rest upon their world, and, seeing their plight, He had sent His saints and His son to bring them out of the dark.

Past the alleyway the crowd filled the street side to side. Candles appeared in hands. People were singing as the Angels of Death blazed their way in on wings of metal, their craft shaking broken windows with supersonic bangs.

Blessed Guilliman was merciful. He would already be landing aid for the populace. There would be food, water, and medical supplies hard behind the missiles and the grim warriors of the God-Emperor. Guilliman was so holy without knowing what he was. His mercy was but one proof of that.

Mathieu's resolve to save him grew.

Up ahead the drifting throng took on the appearance of an official procession, something from Ascension Day, or the feasts of the holy primarchs. To the fore Ecclesiarchical banners swayed. A swarm of servo-skulls buzzed overhead. He smelled incense over the sharp itch of rockcrete dust and the round, musky stink of unwashed bodies.

All these matters were physical, and that was the lesser part of Mathieu's world. But there was something else up there, something spiritual. Compulsion had him by the heart, dragging him forwards to whatever glory headed the procession. He shoved his way through, trying to reach the front. He craned his neck as he knifed his way between bodies sealed in embrace by the joy of deliverance. There! He saw. There was a throne of gold at the front. The high back obscured what sat within, but he knew it contained a living body and not some withered relic.

The girl from his vision was near!

He pushed and pushed, but so many people were emerging into the battered city that Mathieu found himself unable to proceed further. He was jammed in place by those around him, and his progress was slowed to the collective crawl of the Tyreans. Music came from the front of the procession, and the cries of priests like himself. He could not get any closer. Frustration tainted his piety, but just as he thought he might burst with it, the road came to a tattered end. Bombed-out buildings framed the soaring facade of Tyros' cathedral, an immense building, fronted by a brazen aquila as tall as the sky. The jam was unstopped, and the crowd poured into a square.

There was a mound of rubble in front of the eagle. The procession made its way to it, and the throne ascended. It was carried, Mathieu saw now, by Battle Sisters in armour the colour of red wine. He took advantage of the spreading of the crowd to push further to the front, well aware of the mass of people coming from behind. They would soon pack the square as tightly as they did the streets.

Banners ranked up around the pile. A band played devotional music. The display was threadbare compared to the grand shows Mathieu had seen put on for the primarch, but it was all the more powerful for its sincerity. He caught a glimpse of the girl, soon lost. Grunting with annoyance, he forced himself to a better position. She was too distant to make out clearly, a pale smear surrounded by gold, but it was her. He was sure of it.

One of the Battle Sisters stood up to the front, and she spoke.

'People of Tyros!' she said.

The chattering of the crowd dropped to a murmur, then silence. Even the continued roar of Space Marine attack craft and relief ships seemed muted.

'We bear witness to a miracle!' she said. The girl sat unmoving in her throne as the Sister spoke. 'In this city, at its greatest hour of need, has arisen a holy child, a pure girl, a noble girl, a girl of such perfection she is worthy to be a vehicle for the will of His divine majesty, the God-Emperor. Praise be!' she said. The crowd was quiet still, but from every heart Mathieu felt a holy ecstasy. 'Through this girl, this war shall be won, and the monstrous traitors, those vile idolators of false and evil gods shall be cast forth from Parmenio, and it shall be made wholesome again! We shall live again! And our lives, though interrupted by hardship and sorrow, shall be all the richer, for we have seen with our own eyes that the Lord of All Humanity, the Master of Mankind, He who dwells in permanent suffering upon Holy Terra for the continuation of the human race, He watches over us, one and all! I have seen this girl turn back the daemonic engines of the enemy. I have seen her change filth into pure water. I have seen her undergo the pains and the questions of my order's excrutiators without complaint, for she is pure! Within her burns the light of the holy God-Emperor. Within her is contained our salvation!

'Be thankful,' she said, her voice breaking with the joy of her pronouncement. 'Be vigilant. Give up your prayers to Him for His mercy. That is His due. Your love, and your service. Give it to Him. Give Him your–'

And then the girl gave a tiny cry, and raised her arm to point at Mathieu.

The crowd parted, opening a lane between him and the throne.

Ten thousand pairs of eyes looked at him expectantly.

Sicarius set a punishing pace through the city. The Space Marines jogged so fast that Devorus was almost sprinting to keep up. After they passed through the makeshift gate plugging the breach, Devorus began to flag. Without breaking stride, two of Sicarius' guard locked their weapons to their armour with magnetic clunks and picked Devorus up under the armpits. Complaining would get him nowhere, he saw that before the first protest left his mouth, so he hung limply between them. In shameful silence he allowed the demigods to carry him like the inconvenient human baggage that he was.

'Higher ground,' said Sicarius to his warriors. Everything he said was to the point. 'The populace is gathering around the cathedral.'

Armoured feet pounded chunks of rubble to powder. The Space Marines bounded up along the angle of a hab tower drunkenly leaning on its neighbour. Steep and treacherous was the path, but it made no difference to their stride, and they ran up it at a pace no mortal human could sustain. From their armour sounded the silky purrs and machine growls of hidden effort. Their power units radiated a benign heat. Warm gusts hushed from slatted vents to caress Devorus.

Angel's breath, he thought foolishly.

This was not Devorus' first time in the presence of the Adeptus Astartes; he was a soldier of Ultramar, and the bond between the realm's ruling Chapter and its subjects was strong. But he had never been so near that he might touch them, and indeed the act would have been a minor sacrilege to him. He could not have imagined this climb heavenward towards the sky, carried in the arms of angels.

They reached the top of the leaning block. Sicarius, tireless, leapt from the broken pinnacle, hurtling to the roof terrace of the next building. His men followed, and for a moment Devorus was flying. He looked down into the shadowed canyon yawning under his feet.

They landed with the hiss of shock absorbers, and ran on smoothly, their leap but another step in their jog.

Sicarius stopped by the shattered balustrade of the tower.

There had been gardens on the terrace, well-mannered shrubs and dignified trees confined in squares of grass, surrounded by the sober beauty of Ultramarian architecture. Chunks of rockcrete were scattered over the paving. The grass was brown, the pools empty, the trees gone to brittle lifelessness, and yet against all odds, good persisted. On one tree a soli-tary green leaf clung, turning back and forth in the breeze. It held Devorus' attention entirely. The tree was alive. While it was alive, he thought, Tyros might live again. He prayed it would.

'Major,' said Sicarius. He pointed his metal-clad finger downwards.

Devorus blinked. The leaf lost its significance. He had been set down without noticing it. He followed the captain's gesture.

They were overlooking the city's heart. The cathedral dominated the plaza, the twin-headed eagle of battered metal that formed its facade defiant over the rubble. The nave's roof was collapsed along two thirds of its length, and one of the transept towers had gone into a sandcastle slump. But the eagle stood, noble, hawkish and indomitable, beaks jutting skywards, wings folded around the sides of the cathedral in protective embrace.

Devorus had watched the plaza die. When he first arrived on Parmenio, it was the epitome of order. It too had its trees and shaded spots where scholam children gathered on sunnier days for their instruction. He had seen the plaza shake under the first of the bombs as explosion unmade artifice. He had seen it lit by defence laser bursts chasing the enemy back. He had watched the bombs crash through the cathedral roof and fill it with fire.

It looked like another place now, surrounded by eyeless

windows and gaping, hag-faced buildings. War scraped away the glory of man's work, showing beauty for a trick. Marble facings torn, and underneath, the ugly, tedious truth. In a city pounded by war, everything is revealed for what it is: compressed dirt and dust, hidden under paint.

The plaza had changed again. People thronged it in the tens of thousands. Emaciated humanity gathered again without fear under the open sky. It was cloudy, but the clouds were of the normal sort that brought rain, and not downpours of filth. The people stood on the new hillocks of shattered rockcrete and tumbled brick, lanterns and candles burning in their hands so they looked like a field of stars guarded by sentinel gods. Upon a throne before the aquila facade was the girl, surrounded by an honour guard of Battle Sisters. The crowd watched her in silence. The war showed its deference to her as much as the people. Explosions and gunfire from Hecatone whispered their destruction. Aircraft sighed apologetically in to land.

The girl sat, appearing weak. One of the Sisters was speaking. Iolanth? he thought. They were far below, but her voice carried, fine as a hawk's cry hurried over moorland on the wind.

Iolanth was talking about salvation.

'This is the girl?' said Sicarius. His growling voice made Devorus start.

Devorus could not speak. He was held enraptured. He nodded.

The Battle Sister had not finished when the girl pointed and spoke. She interrupted as if she had not heard anything the Sister said, but had been waiting in silence while she searched for something.

Iolanth stopped abruptly. The girl stood and pointed.

'There is one among us here,' the girl said, her words more felt than heard. 'There is one among us who comes from the stars and who brings hope.' Devorus fought the desire to kneel. Doing so would be dangerous in front of his companions, he realised.

'He is there,' said the girl.

The crowd parted around a man, leaving him conspicuous. To Devorus he was another speck dressed in tired clothes. He seemed to glance up at the Space Marines.

Sicarius tensed. His armour amplified his reaction to aggression.

The crowd parted and the man walked to the mound of stone and the throne atop it. He kneeled before the girl, who reached out and rested a hand atop his head.

Some feeling emanated out from the girl and the man into the crowd. In rustling quiet, the guardians of the candle stars knelt.

'The Emperor protects,' she said.

'The Emperor protects,' they repeated. A moan of devotion more than words, rich with piety and yearning.

The man stood. He faced the crowd.

'My name is Frater Mathieu,' he said, his voice as clear as Iolanth's. 'I am militant-apostolic to the Primarch Roboute Guilliman, last son of the Emperor, the Avenging Son, the Lord Commander of the Imperium and Imperial Regent.' He took a deep breath. Devorus could feel his ecstasy. He wanted to share it.

'I have witnessed a miracle,' he said. He pointed at the girl. 'The Emperor is here.'

Sicarius laughed a bleak laugh, breaking the spell. Devorus blinked unnoticed tears from his eyes.

'The primarch's going to love this,' said Sicarius.

CHAPTER SEVENTEEN

MUSTERING AT PARMENIO

There were grand arrivals and there was awe. There were speeches, orders and announcements. Tyros, bowed by war, ecstatic at salvation, reeled with the arrival of the primarch. Two miracles in a single day is more than most human hearts can endure.

Once the attempts at pomp were done and the ragged finery of Tyros put away, evening rushed its cool cloth over Parmenio's fevered skin. Then Guilliman found time to speak with his chief officers: the newly minted Primaris Tetrarch Felix of Vespator, and Captain Sicarius of the Victrix Guard, hero of the Ultramarines. Present also were Maldovar Colquan of the Adeptus Custodes, and Sister-Commander Bellas of the Sisters of Silence. There were others who could have been there. Many others. Generals of the Astra Militarum, senior princeps of the Collegia Titanica, magos domini of the Adeptus Mechanicus, and myriad high officers of multiple Imperial Adepta.

Most had had their turn at the council called within Tyros' walls; those that had not could wait. Guilliman needed level heads. Moreover, he needed minds whose sensibilities were uncoloured by religion. Of those upon the wall only Bellas was devout, but the primarch trusted her to leave her beliefs to one side.

There were too few believers he could call into his confidence.

For his platform Guilliman chose the flat roof of a bastion tower looking out over the narrow channel between Tyros island and the Hecatone coast that formed the city port. The land on both sides had been shorn of natural shape, forced into geometric patterns of squares and rectangles that months of battle could not erase. But the buildings on the altered coastlines were rubble and twists of metal dropped half in and half out of the water.

Damage like that was costly to put right. Months would come and go before the docks might be rebuilt.

Before then Guilliman had another purpose for them. Hecatone's spaceport was deep in enemy territory. The docklands of Tyros, with their large, flat spaces made for the storage of shipping containers, provided a viable alternative.

Work commenced to make Tyros docks ready for the muster. Sea port was remade into spaceport.

Guilliman's reclamation crews worked around the clock, clearing the far side of the channel. The land was divided into neat quadrants by winking beacon poles. Cleansing teams and chanting priests walked back and forth over these areas, venting steam and prayer into the warm summer night. They wended their way in and out of sight, disappearing behind bomb-shattered warehouses, reemerging from crumpled containers, not straying outside the beacons of delineation until the whole of each box was done.

The quadrants declared pure were set upon by building-sized construction vehicles, beneath whose dozer blades the land screeched with the protests of metal and the grumbling of ferrocrete rubble being shunted aside. The giant dozers moved slowly, pushing up the detritus of war into embankments around the mustering point. In the quadrants nearest the shore, the rockcrete was planed down entirely, outlines of lost buildings the sole reminders of what had been a thriving port. They were laid bare for minutes only; each one cleansed and bulldozed soon played host to voidships landing and unloading more construction equipment, prefabricated fortifi-cations, and hardened warriors to set vanguard garrisons.

Over the narrows of the harbour the collective shouts of veteran regiments running from their dropships piped under the grinding of the port's reshaping. The voices came and went, subsumed into the greater noise of vehicles. At perfectly separated intervals all sound was drowned out by roaring ships' plasma drives boiling the atmosphere. Amid the haulers, troop landers and heavy landers, coffin ships made their teetering descent, always on the verge of toppling, it seemed – like dowagers alighting from unsteady carriages – until, setting tentative pneumatic feet upon the earth, they stopped their wobbling and became giants' fortresses, opened up their gates, and prepared to usher out their titanic cargoes. Already a pair of Warhounds strutted back and forth at the edge of the docklands.

Guilliman observed the scene with a critical eye. The air was growing purer by the minute. Jetwash, plasma burn and promethium fumes wafted across the narrows, but the stench of sickness lifted. The harsh smell of man's technology drove it out. He and his officers removed their helms, breathed cautiously of the tainted air, and found Parmenio's breath to be sweetening.

All would have been well, were it not for bad tidings that had reached them hours before.

'We have had further astropathic messages from the Macragge System,' said Felix. 'Heavy Death Guard Legion presence confirmed. Ardium has been reinvaded. Macragge is under attack. The Fortress of Hera is besieged.'

'Master Calgar will deal with it,' said the primarch. His noble face looked more like a carved thing than ever. Only his lips moved. His expression was stern as stone, his eyes fixed on the progress of the muster as surely as if they were made of glass. 'It is a distraction. I have reviewed the messages. The forces landed there may seem numerous but the balance is of poor quality. My brother is alarmed at our gains. He wishes to divert me from this place.'

'Perhaps we should split our army, and send a relief force to Macragge,' said Felix.

'I cannot favour your practical,' said the primarch. 'We are aware of my brother's plan, this corruption of our realm with his daemon clocks and the webs that bind them. Macragge is free of their perniciousness, as you ensured yourself, Felix. We spoil his game, that is all. He makes a goading move.' Guilliman let his gaze rove over the horizon where fleeing mists were giving up the mountain foothills. 'Mortarion is here,' said the primarch firmly. 'I will destroy him and the invasion will fall apart. Marneus Calgar will hold Macragge. Those are the practicals we shall work to.'

The daemon primarch's presence is all over the psychosphere of this world, signed Bellas. *His soul infects it.*

'He will attack us,' said Sicarius. 'Soon.'

Guilliman's eyes narrowed, shifting his face from one sculpted expression to another. 'He withdraws his armies from their assaults on the cities of Parmenio. He will gather his men, march on our position, and throw himself at us. He has not changed. His preference was always for grand manoeuvre and the contest of resilience that open battle brings.'

'Let him come. I'll happily show him my skill with a blade,' said Colquan.

'It may not come to close quarters,' said Felix. 'Our Titans and armour will decide this fight. Mortarion's numbers are greater than ours, but his troops are inferior. His warp nexus has been destroyed. The fume of madness is lifting from the minds of the people. Our outer pickets report deserters who have come to their senses and abandoned him. His armadas of tanks are impressive, and I admit the large number of Death Guard here is a cause for concern. Their sum of Adeptus Astartes far outmatches our own, but three demi-legios of the Collegia Titanica are the Lord Regent's to command. Mortarion has one demi-Legio. Our knights outnumber his two to one. I have word today that Galatan has arrived in system. Once it reaches orbit, the enemy's fate is sealed. The final pieces are set. We will surely sweep him before us.'

'You Primaris Marines are over-confident,' said Sicarius. He didn't look at either primarch or tetrarch as he spoke, but stared out at the sickened plains. 'Theoreticals of certain victory preclude the formulation of practicals that will counter defeat.'

'I simply state what any man can see. We have the more powerful army. We will beat him,' said Felix.

'My own experience has taught me that certainties cannot be relied on,' said Sicarius.

The servants of the warp are unpredictable. Do not judge them by normal standards, signed Bellas. *Sorcery poisons this world.*

'Then we are lucky to have you on our side,' said Colquan.

'Our victory would be my assessment,' said Guilliman. 'But the theoretical here begs a simple practical, and that makes me suspicious. According to our information, Mortarion cannot win this battle, but though his plays in the theatre of open war remain the same as they ever were, he has become devious. He never had any subtlety before he fell, but his strategies in this war, the subversion of the populace, and this reliance on pandemic to circumvent the cleanliness of honest battle, are tricks learned from his new master. I expect surprises. We must be ready for them, and be able to counter. The casualties we will take from his unclean weaponry will be high whether he folds at the first blow or fights on to the bitter end. Listen to Sicarius. This will not be an easy fight, Tetrarch Felix.'

'It will not,' agreed Felix. 'I do not think it will be. But I have no doubt that we will win.' He rested his hand on the parapet. The wind switched round to the west, bringing with it the smell of more wholesome lands, and driving out the last of the noxious stink of the plains. The hills on the Keleton side of the sea were a mottling of green and brown and early evening shadow, clean of disease.

'The swamp is retreating,' said Felix.

'Without the warp nexus to sustain it, it will not last

long,' said Guilliman. 'Some taints are more persistent than others, but this Plague God's sickness waxes and wanes as surely as any normal disease, and will die back now its nourishment is cut off. A fact I am thankful for.'

Felix looked out over the seas of sucking mud beyond the port boundary. Though the pools were drying to curdled slime, and the fogs had gone, clinging on only over the most noxious hollows, venturing onto the plains would be a sure death sentence to an unprotected mortal, perhaps even to a Space Marine.

'The traitor has done a lot of damage,' said Sicarius. 'Never did I think to see worse harm inflicted upon Ultramar than that done by Hive Fleet Behemoth. I am sorry to have been proven wrong.'

'The Emperor made us to be good at breaking worlds. Some of my weaker brothers never rose above this purpose,' said Guilliman. His bitterness left Felix uneasy. 'If we dwell on what has been lost here, we will lose for despair. This evil can be reversed, you will see. We shall face Mortarion, and I will kill him for what he has done to Ultramar. Then we shall begin the long work of repair.' Guilliman's mouth set. 'What was undone in minutes will take decades to put right, but put right it shall be. Now,' he said, 'time runs onwards. We must turn to this other matter. That of the girl.'

'You should kill her,' said Colquan bluntly. 'She is a risk.'

'I cannot do that, and well you know it,' said Guilliman. 'Imagine if I slew the girl that saved a city. These people are in shock. There are those even here who believe my intentions to be impure. Killing a purported saint would prove to them all that my aim is to usurp my father's throne.'

'Mathieu's involvement makes this much more difficult,' said Sicarius.

'It is unfortunate, yes,' said Guilliman. The measured way Guilliman said this made his anger clear to all. 'He and I shall be discussing this matter closely.'

'I'll drag him out of the cathedral myself, if you want,' said Colquan.

'Let him preach,' said Guilliman. 'His sermons are good for the city's morale. It is too late to stop him, and I will not make any move that suggests an opinion either way on the veracity of this girl's claims.'

'She is quietly under guard in the fortress,' said Felix. 'I have assigned a security detail. All Primaris Marines, all Mars born.' He looked sidelong at Sicarius, realising his tactlessness. The older Space Marine looked pointedly away. 'None with any roots in Ultramar. None whose local connections might sway them.'

'It is for the best,' said Guilliman. 'If this girl is not what she purports to be, she will twist any chink in a warrior's soul into a grievous wound.'

Oblivion Knight Asheera Voi waits with her, signed Bellas. *The girl shall be safe while the attack on Mortarion's army is underway.* Bellas paused. Above the peak of her respirator grille her eyes flicked down then up. *Afterwards we must decide what should be done with her.*

'We must,' said Guilliman.

She might be what she says she is, signed Bellas.

'You might be biased by your faith,' said Sicarius.

Guilliman glanced at her. He still found the Sisters of Silence's conversion hard to grasp.

My duty is to the Emperor, signed Bellas.

'Many a bad choice has been made in deciding how to

perform one's duty,' said Sicarius. 'Many practicals stem from one theoretical, they are not all equally valid.'

'Do not squabble,' warned Guilliman.

As you command, I obey, signed Bellas. *Your word is more dear to me than any other, except that of the Emperor Himself. You are His living son.*

'Do not put your faith in me in that manner,' said Guilliman. 'Your belief in my divinity is misplaced. I am not a god, Sister, and you will not treat me as one.'

Bellas bowed her head.

'Felix, what is your opinion of our young guest?' said Guilliman.

'Theoretical, she is as she says she is, a saint of the Emperor.' Felix rapped his knuckles on the wall, as if testing the solidity of his own arguments.

'True saints are rare,' said Guilliman. 'As far as my researches inform me, there have been a handful of genuine saints in a legion of pretenders. History is littered with false claimants. And I am not convinced those deemed real are vessels for the Emperor's will.'

'Then what are they?' asked Colquan.

'My brother Magnus could have answered that, before he erred,' said Guilliman. 'Although I accept what I once regarded as superstitions as occulted fact, my grasp of the esoteric is limited. My guess is that they are a type of psyker, whose empowerment is stabilised by their faith in the Emperor. I have heard the Sisters of Battle manifest odd psychic effects when sorely pressed, and these are brought on by their faith. It may be a saint is merely an extreme example of this phenomenon.'

Bellas, the only one who might have disagreed with this reductionism, signed nothing.

'One day perhaps I will have time to turn my mind to the matter,' continued Guilliman. 'Some of these saints are at least sincere, whatever the provenance of their ability. They can be powerful allies.'

'Saint Celestine,' said Sicarius. 'She proved her worth.'

'She is an asset to the Imperium,' agreed Guilliman. 'Many psykers are, but the numbers of those who are a risk dwarf those that are not.'

'Further theoreticals,' said Felix. 'She is, as my lord suggests, a psyker of noble spirit. Or, she is a deception, a tool of the Change God, perhaps, set up to foil your brother Mortarion's aims here. Magnus and Mortarion's so-called deities are opposed. In either case, she is dangerous.'

'She is dangerous under every circumstance,' said Guilliman. 'If not physically, then politically.' He paused. 'Could Magnus' hand be in this? Scheming was more his preference than Mortarion's, but he was rarely this obtuse. He enjoyed displaying his intellect, although the god he follows is another matter.'

'Do we care? If they are at odds, we should be pleased. It is so much better when the foes kill each other,' said Colquan.

'It does not make them our allies, even if Mortarion and Magnus fight to the death,' said Guilliman. 'What is the current status of the girl, Bellas?'

The girl's abilities are subdued by hexagrammatic chains. She is blanked by Oblivion Knight Voi. If she were a vessel of the Emperor's will, neither of these things would affect her.

'Magnus could defy those things,' said Guilliman. 'If she is the instrument of my brother or some other agency she may be shamming. You must be careful. You cannot rely on your arts to block his power.'

So the legends suggest, her fingers flickered.

'They are not legends. Magnus is more powerful than ever he was in the days of enlightenment,' said Guilliman. 'I have witnessed his ability. Beware of this girl.'

At the first sign of impurity, I will see her dead, signed Bellas.

'See that you do,' said Guilliman. 'Until then, tread warily. Tyros loves its so-called saint. I cannot afford to have my people turn against me through rash decisions. Both my brothers know this. I will move soon, before Mortarion is ready.'

He lapsed into silence. A giant coffin came growling overhead, its grav-impellers thumping in preparation to take the load from the void engines. They watched it land, and the doors open. Sirens wailed as the loading bed extended, the hunched form of the Reaver upon it shaking as it was pushed out into the world.

When the noise had died, the primarch looked to the sky, where the first stars blinked in competition with the lights of the fleet, and spoke again.

'We await Galatan's approach. When it is near, then we attack.'

CHAPTER EIGHTEEN

ASSAULT ON GALATAN

Tocsins blared out angry warnings all over Galatan. The star fortress' real space engines remained constant in pitch, but the noise from the reactors changed substantially, ramping up to full power output. The noise was so distinctive that Justinian had come to recognise it quickly during his time aboard.

'Prepare, prepare,' said a machine-generated voice. 'Enemy fleet inbound. Enemy fleet inbound. Prepare for engagement in twenty-two minutes, three seconds. Initial munitions launched. Stand by for impact in twenty-two minutes.'

The alarms had been going for an hour. Shortly after they began, Justinian's squad had been pulled from the muster intended to land upon Parmenio, and reassigned station defence duties at a crossway fort some distance away. They eschewed transport, leaving the deck trains free for less mighty warriors, and jogged along a corridor fifteen kilometres long towards their destination. The corridor was so long it lost itself to perspective before it curved around the station's heart. It would take a mortal lifetime to get to know the whole of Galatan, but though massive, the corridor was thronged with people and crew trains rushing personnel to their stations.

Justinian followed a cartolith projected by his helm. A faint directional rune indicated the way he should go. His squad was a pulsing green dot. If he zoomed in on the dot, it broke apart to show his troopers individually, with tags revealing their names: Drusus, Pimento, Achilleos, Brucellus, Kadrian, Dascene, Donasto, Michaelus, and his second, Maxentius-Drontio. On the cartolith his own icon was decorated by a skull, Maxentius-Drontio by a white dot in the centre of the green.

Ten warriors, all until recently blue-clad members of the Unnumbered Sons of Guilliman. Now they were Novamarines, in name if not yet in heart.

A double-decker crew train rushed past on the monorail. The last half was made up of freight cars bearing tonnes of ammunition boxes, and, on flatbeds behind that, Astra Militarum tanks. The larger halls of Galatan were large enough to accommodate armour war.

The station was tense. They had been preparing for a landing action until this unforeseen fleet approached them halfway in system. The main plan was in disarray, supplanted by back-up strategies.

Chapter Master Bardan Dovaro had reacted quickly. Galatan had never been taken in all the Imperial portion of its history. The warriors aboard were confident that it would not fall now. The question was not if they would lose, but how long they would be delayed in reaching

Guilliman to play a decisive role in the battle of Parmenio, and what risks should be taken to shorten that time.

Justinian pushed these thoughts away. He was a sergeant, not a captain. These concerns were not his. He was being presumptuous thinking on them.

Mortal crewmen and Astra Militarum moved aside and cheered as the squad thumped past.

They came to their destination, a crossway fort built around a junction where a radial corridor intersected the ringway. Although thousands of years of additions had distorted Galatan's shape, it had originally been circular, and the interior was laid out as a series of concentric ring corridors pierced every three kilometres by routes leading to the periphery. Each intersection was defended by similar void-hardened fortifications.

The junction expanded the crossroad into a large hexagon half a mile across. Four round towers stood free of the walls in a hollow square so that fire could be directed on all sides. Their positioning gave the illusion that the corridors formed a simple cross. Reinforcing the impression were the monotracks for the ship-trains that crossed in the middle of the courtyard. The ceiling was a thirty metres high at the centre. Two armoured murder corridors joined opposite towers to each other diagonally, crossing in the middle to make a large X over the rails. Four others joined the corners of the square together. Four more armoured bridges led from the towers into the main body of the station.

As the Primaris Marines entered the courtyard the rune pulsed. Fresh info screed directed Justinian through the crossway fort's square towards its command nexus.

The squad moved in perfect formation with Justinian. Their double file curled round and came to a halt at the base of one of the towers. Remote weapons systems tracked the Primaris, while their machine-spirits requested the Space Marines' full ident codings from their battleplate.

Justinian halted his squad. 'Wait here,' he told them.

The door read his genetic coding. It opened grudgingly, shutting as soon as he was inside.

He found his way up to the fifth floor, whose entirety was occupied by a command station. Green-tinted armourglass windows angled down allowing views of the base of the tower. Firing slits pierced the metre-thick walls. Murder holes opened in the floor over the tower's banked base.

A Novamarine lieutenant was busy at the room's hololithic table, which displayed the immensity of Galatan and the enemy fleet tens of thousands of kilometres out, coming in like an army of mosquitoes advancing on a carnosaur. A couple of Novamarines and a host of mortals gathered around the desk. Most of the humans were unmodified Astra Militarum officers. There were a few who looked to be station crew, servitors of the usual recording subtypes, and a sole Adeptus Mechanicus adept with four spindly metal arms.

Justinian marched up to the gathering. They had evidently just concluded whatever business they had, and were dispersing when he presented himself.

'Lieutenant Edermo! Sergeant Justinian Parris, sixth auxiliary squad reporting.' He saluted, arm across his chest the Ultramarian way. It occurred to him then he had not seen the Novamarines formally saluting each other, and he had no idea how they did, or even if they did.

The lieutenant gave him a long, calculating look. He wore his helmet, and so his expression was hidden, but his body language betrayed his suspicion.

'I have been expecting you. You are attached to the Fifth Company?'

'For the last three weeks, yes. You requested reinforcements, so we were sent here.'

'I did,' said Edermo. 'You will not be aware, but the fleet that is bearing down on us is sizeable.' He gestured at the icons inching towards the three-dimensional graphic of Galatan. 'They are a match for the fleet in orbit around Parmenio. A new player has entered the fray. The lead ship is the *Terminus Est*. Do you recognise that name?'

'Yes, my lord, it is the flagship of the Plague Lord Typhus.'

'He is coming at us with all his followers. His involvement in this battle is unexpected, for he has been operating away from his fallen primarch. He will attempt to board us, and destroy Galatan. That is why you have been split from the landing parties and sent here.'

'I understand, brother-lieutenant,' said Justinian.

'Do you have experience of battle?' asked the lieutenant.

The question irritated Justinian. The lieutenant looked formidable, but Justinian was sure if they sparred, he would win. This was not the first time he had encountered a cool welcome.

'We have been fighting with the primarch on the Indomitus Crusade for the last century. My cohort was awoken shortly after he arrived on Terra. We have plenty of combat experience, lieutenant.'

The lieutenant relaxed. 'Good. There are stories about you Primaris Marines coming into battle straight out of stasis, and that has not always been successful. Even now, I hear of it happening. There appears to be a nearly endless supply of your type.'

'I do not think that is so, sir,' said Justinian. He hid his irritation at the man. It was easy to do. He had plenty of experience of that as well.

'It seems that way,' said the lieutenant. The rank was a new one to the Chapters, introduced in Guilliman's *Nova Codex Astartes*. 'I do not care how much training and hypnomat time you have had, nor for how long. In blood and fury is a warrior forged.'

'We have seen plenty of both,' said Justinian.

'All right, all right. Forgive me. I have not yet fought by the Primaris Marines' side. We are a Chapter with deep roots and an aversion to change.' He pointed at Justinian's bolt rifle. 'But change can be good. I hear these things have a range advantage over boltguns.'

'An additional effective sixty metres,' said Justinian. He offered his bolt rifle up. The lieutenant took it, and looked it over. For a second the weapon appeared awkward in Edermo's hands. A moment later he handled it like he had been using it for decades. He sighted down the combined block and barrel, which was substantially longer than that of the boltgun maglocked to his thigh.

'It is heavy. I do not know if I would prefer it over my bolter. Is the stopping power greater?'

'Not by much. Its greatest advantage over the boltgun is in its range, as you mentioned.'

The lieutenant handed the weapon back.

'Range is good, but this fight will be decided at close quarters.' He turned back to the hololith. It flickered, and displayed a floating roster. 'I have five hundred Astra Militarum here, and four squads of our Chapter.' He paused.

Justinian felt his cheeks colour. For an insane moment, he felt the lieutenant could sense his discomfort with his new brotherhood, and his words 'our Chapter' were a question, and not a statement.

I am being paranoid, he thought.

The lieutenant continued.

'Two full Tactical, a Devastator, and a demi-squad of Assault. I want you to shadow Devastator Squad Amarillo. Keep the enemy off them. They have Astra Militarum support, but you are superior guardians. If the enemy get in close...' He looked out of the window. From his vantage point he could see a good distance either way down both the radial and the circular corridors. They were long and plain with all buttressing plated over, designed to offer minimal shelter to boarding parties, but the nature of battle aboard spacecraft meant close-quarter engagements were inevitable. 'If they get in close, do whatever you can to stop them from taking out my heavy weapons. These plague warriors are resilient. We will need the heavy bolters.'

'Yes, my lord.'

Edermo did not mention how Justinian's squad was supposed to work with the mortal soldiers. Justinian inferred a contempt for their abilities from that omission. If he was right, that was another difference in culture he would have to assimilate.

'You are dismissed, sergeant,' said Edermo. 'I have a lot to do.'

The lieutenant turned to speak with a human aide. Justinian bowed his head and left the command post.

Outside, his Primaris brothers were busy checking their weapons. Talk between them was minimal.

Maxentius-Drontio gave a crisp, one-handed aquila salute over his chest-plate. 'Where to, brother?' he asked.

'We are to guard a fire support unit, tower tertio.'

Maxentius-Drontio snorted. 'Shooting things at a distance. I would prefer to get in close. I do not like to hang back.'

Justinian felt the same. Marching about the corridors of Galatan could not match the exhilaration of dropping from the edge of space onto the battlefield as an Inceptor, his prior posting. Here he was to be employed by his new brothers on escort duty, war of a far less glorious order. Kept out of the way, untrusted.

He could say none of this, even though Maxentius-Drontio knew they both felt the same.

'We have our orders. We will fulfil them,' said Justinian.

'Yes, sir,' said Maxentius-Drontio. He waved the others into action. 'Squad, you heard the brother-sergeant. Move out.'

The silhouette of the *Terminus Est* was known the galaxy over as a harbinger of terror, death and decay. Nurgle was bountiful to the flagship of his mortal herald. Ten millennia of his kind attentions had transformed it from a leviathan of plasteel into a decaying, prowling warpbeast of a thing, more dripping flesh than technology. The *Terminus Est* seethed with plague magic. It shimmered across the mortal realm in a haze of disease and frenzied fecundity. A part of Nurgle's realm had been cut free and turned loose to roam the stars.

In the *Terminus Est*'s company was an armada of craft from every part of history. Though vessels of the Heresy years predominated, human ships of all types and even xenos vessels flew together in putrid comradeship, prizes taken in war by Typhus' dread First Company.

Despite the ships' diversity of origin, they had more in common rather than less, for all were part transmogrified by Nurgle's power. Their crews were warped into hideous, disease ridden similarity. United in monstrousness, they were like nothing else in the galaxy but each other. There was comfort in their shared suffering.

Millions of tonnes of ordnance came ahead of the fleet. Aged cannon shells preceded torpedoes whose metal skins were knotted with arthritic bone. The slime covering them was defiantly unfrozen in the killing voidchill. Green fire guttered in drive units, forever on the edge of burning out, but they flew true enough, coming in a broad spread at the port side of Galatan. Fired half a day before the torpedoes, the shells had been hundreds of thousands of kilometres ahead, but the steady acceleration of the missiles had them arriving not far behind.

The ships followed their munitions at full burn, moving in a broad interception crescent to envelop the fort. In the prows of every ship, slavering, rotten-toothed maws concealed the emission vanes of ancient lance batteries. For the time being, these held their silence.

In void war, timing was everything.

The ships at the fore of the fleet were the least corrupted, still recognisable as built things. Strings of matter clogged gothic spires. Their hulls sprouted fleshy blisters from the metal, and their surfaces were unnaturally pitted with corrosive chemical reactions that should have ceased in the changeless void. But they were the least altered. Tormented ident-signifiers bleated out from them. If their appearance was insufficient proof, the cries of damned machine-spirits revealed the truth – recently captured Imperial ships ran ahead of Typhus' deadly armada. Their datacasts sent the machines of Galatan into twitches of fear. When they neared and the moans of their warp-cursed crew were vox-cast on all frequencies, the effect on the human defenders was the same. A bow wake of dread preceded the plague fleet.

The pieces were set. On one side, the corrupt and corrupting fleet of Typhus, the Herald of Nurgle. On the other, the mighty star fortress Galatan and its small escort. One side was bound by physics, the other was not. This was Typhus' advantage. Swarms of daemonic flies surrounded his vessel, conjured from the non-stuff of the immaterium to serve as a living shield. His vessels lived in a way machines should not, and they were resilient because of it. Their ammunition was possessed of many strange and deadly properties.

Galatan had a few advantages of its own. At the permission of the Mechanicus battle-conclaves who dwelt aboard, ancient weapons slid free of their housings and charged, drawing hard on Galatan's quad reactors which, by the activation of pledge oaths dating back thousands of years, ran near full capacity.

Before the torpedoes were eighteen thousand kilometres away, Galatan's primary weapons were unleashed. The science of the guns was long lost. They were plasma cannons of incredible might. Thousands of tech-priests were detailed to forestall burnout with constant prayer. But though misunderstood, the guns functioned still. Bright energies left lines burning upon the dark of space as they slashed out at the plague fleet. Void shields collapsed in toppled series, and one craft burned to nothing from the first salvo alone.

In silence this occurred. The plague ships glided nearer. Galatan coasted on, Parmenio growing slowly in the cosmic distance. To an outside observer, Galatan was an indomitable, sunlit mass, a single titanic creature, fighting off a predatory swarm of lesser things. The furious activity of its component cells was invisible; the prayers to the Emperor and Machine-God had no purchase in the void. From the strategium sealed deep in Galatan's heart to the least of its thousands of gun batteries, humans, cyborgs and tran-shumans engaged in the labour of war. All of this frenzy was concealed by austere exteriors and the flare of potent weapons.

Still the plague fleet sailed without returning fire, their spread of shells to the foremost, warped torpedoes following, then the captured ships running in close after.

Again the antique weaponry of Galatan conjured incandescent starfire. Again void shields flared, giving off colours unlike any Imperial energy barrier, sickly greens and bile yellows. A large ship was hit and disabled. Its reactor stayed whole – if that was indeed what powered it still – but it fell out of line, brief fires burning in the exposed, fleshy caverns of its interior, caping the vessel in the black smoke of singed flesh.

The astropaths within Galatan's relay winced at its screams.

The plague fleet came closer, ominous as a phantom flotilla from some backworld tale. Augurs and pict units caught clear images of what approached. It was a display of force, a promise of what was to come. Within his strategium, Chapter Master Dovaro was glad few of his mortal crewmen could see the horrors bearing down on the fortress.

The third time the ancient weapons opened fire, the lesser guns and devices of the station were within range. The third discharge signalled their unleashing, and the void was suddenly filled with a tumult of light and fire so intense that the calm of a moment before seemed impossible.

This time, the Imperial guns dared target the *Terminus Est*.

This time, the plague fleet returned fire.

Dancing streaks of green lightning leapt across the void, intermingled with the bright-line slash of lance fire.

Unleashed energies outpaced the torpedoes and shells in the blink of an eye, slamming into Galatan with devastating force. Flickering storms blazed all over its port side for twenty kilometres and more. Void shields flared bright, their light dropping through the spectrum as their ability to displace energy into the warp was reduced, until they became but purplish coronas creeping around jutting bastions and docking piers.

Galatan was blessed with dozens of shield banks. Deep within its armoured shell thousands of serfs laboured under the stern oversight of the tech-adepts. Choirs sang hosannas to the glory of the machine while labouring gangs ejected expended shield capacitors and replaced them with fresh ones brought on squealing rails from armoured storehouses. Each was the size of a small gunship, and required the muscle power of hundreds of men to switch. They heaved, rolling the devices from their transports and slamming them into cavernous sockets.

Weapons fire flew freely between the fleet and the battle-station. The moaning wails of the damned infiltrated the fortress' vox-net, until it overwhelmed communication, causing Dovaro to order it shut down, and all messaging to be moved to hardwires. It made no difference. An unholy meld of sorcery and science projected the screams. Simultaneously, the noosphere of Galatan was subjected to probing by sorcerous attack code. It came streaming in on pulse broadcasts of warp-infused EM-waves. Deep within the never-space of cogitator banks and serial-linked servitor minds, magi waged an informational war against daemonic attack. The machine-spirits of Galatan found themselves besieged before its human defenders had to raise their lasguns.

Again, the lightning batteries and warp-lances of the

plague fleet blazed. Again, their unclean magics raked at the void shields of one specific spot, stripping layers back until but one shielding matrix remained intact.

The shells hit a microsecond later. Titanic detonations turned the void into a boiling sea of fire that roiled and went out, taking down the last shield with it.

The torpedoes came next, burning the last of their fuel hard to increase their kinetic impact. They slammed into the hull of the fortress. With melta arrays and chomping ranks of daemon teeth, they chewed through layered ceramite and plasteel like maggots burrowing through the hides of livestock. They detonated deep within, bringing bursts of flaming atmosphere gouting into the void.

Galatan was unconcerned by such a petty wound, and continued to fire, bringing down two, three, then five smaller vessels in the main fleet. All but one of the enslaved Imperial ships were annihilated. Like all the masters of the Nova-marines before him, Dovaro was a master of void warfare. He could see what Typhus intended. The Herald of Nurgle had been responsible for the loss of three star fortresses already. His tactics were well known by now.

'Concentrate fire upon that captured ship!' Dovaro commanded. 'Do not let it through!'

Blazing fire all along its flanks, the final captured Imperial craft sliced through the gap in the shield arrays, and slammed hard into the weakened section of Galatan. The corroded prow rammed into the upper surface, smashing aside spires and gun towers, and ripped up the underlying hull skin like a divine plough turning a field of iron. Explosions blasted upwards from the impact. Clouds of gas roared outwards in white plumes, thousands of cubic metres of atmosphere vented in a moment. The diseased ship juddered, its underside trailing debris from the hit. Its rear rose up, its ram snagged in the star fortress, threatening to break its spine. The moans of tortured metal vibrated through the halls of Galatan. Dorsal manoeuvring engines fired. Jets of incongruous purity blasted from rusted slots and nozzles, and the ship came to a halt, hovering over the star fortress starboard side down, prow pressed in a dead kiss against the station's fabric. At point-blank range the remaining guns of its starboard batteries opened fire, turning the scar in the space station into a glowing chasm.

Behind it flew an armada of smaller craft. Ancient Dreadclaw assault pods and boarding torpedoes of every size raced around attack rams and Invader-class landing frigates. Anti-fighter fire made the void around Galatan a deadly weave of light, but there were so many ships. The *Terminus Est* came with them, fulfilling its ancient role of assault ship. Weapons fire of every conceivable sort burned against its void shields. They flickered sickening colours as they failed. The weapons' blasts hit the hull, tearing up flesh-steel. Pus wept into the void. Fires burned along its noisome hull, but it could not be stopped.

In the breach the captured Imperial ship was quickly reduced to a hulk. Pushed away by Galatan's fire, it drifted, burning, into space, the crew aboard sacrificed. It had performed its role. A wound had opened Galatan's thick hide to the void.

The forked prow of the *Terminus Est* opened its hangars. Hundreds of gunships blasted out between gargantuan teeth.

As numerous as flies in a swarm, the followers of Typhus, First Captain of the Death Guard, poured aboard Galatan.

CHAPTER NINETEEN

JUSTINIAN'S WAR

Noise. Chaos. Smoke. Justinian's head rang. He was lying on his back, pinned by a fallen stanchion. Warning runes blinked in his retinal display. Chimes bleated, mingling with the sounds of disorder that filled the crossway fort.

The pressure on his chest eased. A figure in scratched bone-and-blue armour threw aside the jagged metal, and reached a hand down.

'Brother-sergeant!' said the warrior.

Justinian shook the fog from his mind. He grasped the offered hand and was hauled to his feet, his stabilisation jets firing to aid his recovery.

'Brother Brucellus,' said Justinian. Already he was checking over his armour systems and silencing its alarms. 'My thanks.' Sound from outside his armour was becoming faint. His sensorium alerted him to low oxygen levels. The floor was canted at a sharp angle. The room had been badly deformed by impact. The tower was bent and their strongpoint had crumpled. The firing slits were crushed shut, obscuring the view of the corridors outside. Large slabs of the ceiling had come down, killing many of the unmodified humans. Their broken bodies lay about, leaking vitae. Severed limbs collected in drifts in the deformed corners of the room. Broken cabling spat sparks. Pipes hissed a mixture of gasses. Alarms blared from the unseen outside, growing quieter with every second.

'Atmosphere's failing out there,' Donasto said.

Sergeant Amarillo looked up from the corpse of one of his warriors. His armour was battered, and the signum array atop his backpack had snapped, hanging from its mount on a twist of metal and a braid of wire.

'A hit like that made a hole too big to plug. They will be sealing the station kilometres back from here. This whole section will vent itself into the void soon. We are probably trapped.' Amarillo gave his warrior one last check. He lifted the end of the shattered heavy bolter the Novamarine had been carrying. The trooper's modified backpack was cracked open. Boltshells glinted amid the mess of the ammo feed. He dropped the weapon. 'All of you, log his position,' he said to the surviving three men of his squad. 'Whoever lives through this is to ensure the Apothecaries are aware of where he lies, so they may retrieve his gene-seed.'

Dying Astra Militarum soldiers moaned around Justinian. He ignored them; there was nothing he could do for them. He brought up his tactical overlay, activating the status screeds for his warriors. The retinal display jumped a bit, settling down as his cogitator reconfigured itself. His men had been lucky. Most bore marks on their armour and some had to be dragged out of the wreckage, but the damage to their weapons and battleplate was minimal.

Green dominated their systems statuses, touched with amber. Only Achilleos was harmed. He sat examining his crushed left arm as dispassionately as if it were a broken gun. His vambrace was breached in several places, spattered with blood and dribbling sealant foam. Justinian went to his side.

Achilleos looked up. 'It is not making a seal,' he said. He peered at his injured limb critically. 'The plate's too badly compromised.'

'Then fall back,' Justinian told him. 'Go to the apothecarion on deck theta 19.'

'He will not make it,' Amarillo called over. 'There is no clear way through. He would be better remaining here.'

'I am not staying here,' said Achilleos. He got to his feet. 'If this will not seal, I will cut off my arm at the elbow, let it seal there. The work of a minute.' He half drew his combat knife.

'Very well,' said Justinian. 'That will be an awkward cut. Pimento, aid him.'

The rest of the Space Marines gathered around the two sergeants. Justinian's squad intermingled with the Devastators they had been assigned to protect, the Primaris Marines standing tall over their older comrades.

'We have been hit hard,' voxed Maxentius-Drontio. 'The mortals are shaken.' He looked over to the seven Astra Militarum survivors in the room. They wore void helms and heavy combat suits, but they were far more vulnerable than the Space Marines. Sweaty faces looked out through yellow plastek faceplates. A dozen more had been killed by the room's collapse. Those that were not already dead would be soon. The unharmed were brave, but Justinian did not rate their chances in the coming fight.

'Where is your squad leader?' Justinian asked.

One of them nodded at a corpse with its head crushed beneath a fallen ventilator.

'Who is in charge then?'

The man shrugged.

'Well volunteered. Approach me,' he said.

The man came over.

'Give me your name,' asked Justinian.

'I am Tesseran,' he said.

'You are responsible for the others,' said Justinian. It was not a question.

Tesseran nodded, reluctantly accepting the role. 'If you say so, my lord. What are we going to do?'

The Space Marines ignored him.

'Has anyone heard from the lieutenant?' asked Amarillo. 'All but my squad vox is out.' He looked over his shoulder at the shattered lenses of his sighting unit. 'This Throne-forsaken thing is just weight. What about you, sergeant? Let's see if this much praised Mark ten armour of yours is as good as they say.'

Justinian tried, scanning over every vox frequency. 'Squad Parris, Fifth Company, reporting. Heavy damage in our section. Awaiting orders.' Ghastly moans and the constant humming of flies were his only response. 'Nothing,' he said, shutting off the vox-link. 'The crossway fort is compromised. We are no use to anyone in this box. I propose we get out. First order of business. Orders can wait.'

'First order of business?' repeated Amarillo. 'Odd turn of phrase.'

'My father was a merchant, what of it?' said Justinian. 'Do you concur or not, brother-sergeant?' He put too much emphasis on 'brother' for it to be sincere.

'Of course I agree,' said Amarillo. He unclamped a melta-flask from his waist. 'I was hoping to use this on the enemy. It will get us out of here instead.' He examined the room for a moment, looking for the best place to site the device. 'Here,' he said, running his hand over part of the wall that now faced downwards. 'We will have to jump.' He slapped the charge to the wall and stepped back. 'You. Soldiers,' he said to the remaining Astra Militarum. 'Do not look at the light.'

The melta bomb went off with a roar, the one-use fusion reactor inside turning a man-sized portion of the wall into steam and slag.

Molten metal dripped away into darkness. As soon as the gap was made, the air rushed out. The glowing, ragged hole was an appropriate frame for the devastation outside.

The fort was a ruin. The pair of towers on the far side of the square had vanished into a chasm of shattered metal. The footings of their own remained firm, but only ten metres away the deck shelved steeply away into a mess of scrap. The other tower in their pair had been crushed as flat as a stamped-on ration tin, Galatan's roof pushed down onto it and sealing the circular corridor in that direction. Emergency lumens provided a modicum of light, but many of them were broken. The majority of the illumination came from strobing flashes down the radial corridor. Justinian's suit lights snapped on. Cones of light projected from around his eye lenses pushed back the dark.

'The station's open to the void,' Justinian voxed the others. The station shook with fresh impacts.

'Those are too gentle for explosions,' said Maxentius-Drontio.

'Boarders,' said Amarillo. 'If we are caught here, we are dead.'

The tower shuddered. The Space Marines swayed as its weight shifted. Metal ground on metal, conveying its pain through the soles of their boots.

'We have to get down. Now,' said Amarillo.

The climb was arduous for the soldiers, and the Novamarines were forced to help them down. When they finally gained the wrecked square, they discovered the radial corridor in the direction of the rim was also impassable.

'Two choices,' said Amarillo as they skirted the chasm cutting through the crossway. 'Head inwards, or head around.'

They reached safer ground without incident, and there Justinian reestablished patchy vox contact. Requests for aid were coming from the central hub of the station, fighting their way past buzzing interference patterning and the cacophony of moans. Though not directly commanded, Justinian and Amarillo agreed to take these as their orders, and the Novamarines set out without delay away from the rim towards the centre of the star fort.

The damage to that part of Galatan was massive. Though the coreward radial corridor could be travelled, it was open to the freezing void in many places, and airless throughout. The rain of constant impacts on their part of the station eased, being replaced by the distant quakes of explosions and the more measured reports of Galatan's own weapons batteries.

They were safe from unheralded death cast out by a distant voidship, but that was small comfort. The enemy was targeting other parts of Galatan because their troops had landed close by.

They moved at a cautious pace, their weapons ready. Amarillo's Devastators went first, their bulky heavy bolters primed for fully automatic fire. The Astra Militarum marched among them.

It was not long before they encountered their enemy.

Kadrian was scouting ahead. Without atmosphere they could not hear battle before they came upon it. Eyes were needed to see when ears could not hear, but the corridor was buckled in several places, obscuring clean lines of sight. The first notice they had were new tremors in the deck plating.

'Combat,' said Amarillo, glancing at his feet.

'Advance cautiously,' said Justinian.

They sent the Astra Militarum to the rear. Justinian's squad advanced in a fan ahead of Squad Amarillo, screening the heavy bolters. As they approached a crumpled hill of decking the tremors grew in intensity.

Kadrian ran up the hill, bounding effortlessly over its tortured floor. As he neared the top he slowed and ducked low. He stopped.

'Sergeant,' he voxed. Justinian patched into Kadrian's battle-plate autosenses.

The hillock ended in a low cliff of sheared metal. A crevasse at its foot led down into darkness lit by actinic discharge. Beyond it, the corridor was untouched. There a minor wayspace opened up off the radial way, though minor only on Galatan's terms.

In the ceiling over the foot of the cliff the blunt mouth of an assault ram came in at an angle. A group of around a dozen Plague Marines were dug into the debris on the near side of the chasm. On the other side, Astra Militarum tanks formed a barrier across the way leading deeper into the station. Most of the vehicles were dead, their hatches blown and weapons hanging loose in their mountings, but a hundred men in armoured void suits still blasted away at the enemy. A number of dead traitors were heaped in the centre of the corridor, but those that remained were more than a match for that number of mortals.

'They will not last long,' voxed Kadrian. He hid himself carefully while he watched.

'What do you see?' asked Amarillo.

'A dozen traitors attacking Astra Militarum,' said Justinian. 'We are behind them. We can take them by surprise.'

'Then we engage,' said Amarillo. Without asking for further intelligence, he summoned his men to him, and they marched up the incline. Justinian's men followed.

At the brow of the new-born hill the way was crushed down to a few dozen metres across. The broken bedding of the station monorail had been wrenched from its bed, and thrown widthways across the corridor. It made a serviceable barricade. Amarillo had the decency to hold fire until Justinian's men were in place. Their Astra Militarum followers hunkered down by the heavy bolters.

'We shall take up position forward of you, to keep them off your men. Cover our advance,' said Justinian.

Amarillo considered. 'The swiftest route to victory, but it will be costly. It would be better to establish a firing line where Brother Kadrian waits.'

'We cannot afford to become involved in protracted firefight,' said Justinian. 'We must get through to the centre. The enemy are occupied. We can be among them before they know we are here. If we advance your gunners too close, the chances are they will spot us. Wait until we are upon them before opening fire.'

'Then go. May Lucretius Corvo guide your hand.'

The blessing was unfamiliar to Justinian, but he was grateful for the sentiment.

'Squad, advance,' he said.

His nine Space Marines fell in after him as he scrambled down the cliff. The traitors were intent on the guardsmen, and they were not noticed until they opened fire.

The Plague Marines were well sheltered by debris and the corridor mouths. Only one died to Squad Parris' opening fusillade. The moment they took to react to being outflanked allowed Justinian's squad to advance a further ten metres.

Boltgun fire was quickly retrained from the Astra Militarum onto the Space Marines. Kadrian went down, blood spraying from his wrecked chest. Pimento followed quickly after, his faceplate smashed in. Then the flash burn of heavy bolt propellant speckled Justinian's vision as Amarillo's squad opened fire and drove the Plague Marines back into cover, and Squad Parris advanced without further losses.

The enemy were caught, and they knew it. Ignoring the Astra Militarum at their back, they lumbered from their hiding places. Las-bolts flashed on their mouldering ceramite, doing nothing but heating the plate, and they moved in to engage.

There were more than Justinian had counted. Twenty or so. They drew rusted knives and fired their boltguns one-handed. Three of the enemy were riddled with heavy bolts as they charged, yellow fluids bursting out of their decaying armour. Brother Drusus went down in return.

An ugly brute who was managing not to suffocate in the airless passage, despite the fact his helm was corroded through and his breathing grille missing, raised a dripping axe in open challenge to Justinian. Another Space Marine from a more choleric lineage might have charged to accept. Justinian placed pragmatism over honour.

Justinian switched his target to his challenger, placing half a dozen well-aimed shots into the Plague Marine. Only three penetrated, so far as he could see, but that should have been enough. However, the traitor did not go down but slogged on, even though his flesh and battleplate were cratered by the bolts' explosions. Amarillo's heavy bolters had a more noticeable effect, mowing down several of the Plague Marines, but they were targeted in response, and one of them was felled by concentrated bolter fire, and the aim of the remainder spoiled as they sought better cover.

The Death Guard heaved themselves over the rucks in the decking. Two more died before they could connect, then they hit the Primaris Marines with the weight of an avalanche.

The battle fragmented. Synthetic hormones flooded Justinian's system, speeding his reactions and slowing time a little, but these foes were sprung from the same roots as he. They possessed those same abilities, and more were given them by their Dark Gods. Melee became a grunted, bludgeoning whirl of blade and fist. A tentacle slapped across Justinian's face, acidic secretion etching the armourglass of his eye lenses. He rammed his shoulder into the mutated owner, throwing him down. A pig-faced helm stared up at him. Justinian stamped it flat with two strikes of his boot.

There was a clang, and he was knocked sideways. The traitor without the breathing grille flashed across his vision, and Justinian recovered to face him. The creature's rusted sword hurtled at his face.

Bolts slammed into the Plague Marine, blowing out its distended stomach and showering Justinian with its filth.

Amarillo was coming down the hill, the surviving Astra Militarum from the tower and his two remaining troopers with him. The fight was over. The last Plague Marine fell silently.

Slowly, Justinian's biochemical balances returned to normal.

'Costly,' voxed Amarillo.

Nearly half Justinian's squad were down. Dascene joined Drusus, Kadrian and Pimento in death. The survivors went about their tasks without emotion. Maxentius-Drontio was helping take Dascene's vambrace to replace Achilleos' broken armour component and protect his wound. From behind the wrecked tanks the Astra Militarum waved their guns in victory.

'Come on,' said Amarillo. 'We have a long walk ahead.'

CHAPTER TWENTY

LEGIO OBERON WALKS

Princeps Caleb Dunkel sat back in the command throne in an attempt to find the best position for the coming battle. The angular chair granted great honour, but little comfort. Steel input cables dragged at his head. The manual throttles were a little too far from his hands, the torso pedals a little too close to the seat. These controls were backups, crude mechanical devices intended for use should the mind impulse interface be broken, but they were necessary, and should be firmly grasped at all times. Keeping his limbs in place was uncomfortable. Soon, he would link with *God's Wrath* and the sensations of his human body would shrink into insignificance. Until then he focused on what was going on around him to keep cramp at bay.

Behind him, his moderati primus and steersman guided the weapons crew through their final calibrations. Query and response check cants went back and forth from the cockpit head to the gunnery command chamber. The half-sung phrases of the moderati were punctuated by the gentle click of buttons and the notification chimes of good function.

'By the grace of the Omnissiah, power feeds to chainfist at full capacity. Let the motive force flow,' said the primus.

'Unto the glory of the machine, do the missile tubes work smoothly. Send shell and explosion to rend the foe,' replied the weapons moderati by hardline vox.

'Let the mid-range fusion of your melta-cannon slag the unrighteous with blistering heat,' said the primus.

'So it shall be,' replied Arrin, the third of his weapons moderati.

Dunkel let their preparations lull him further into his altered state. The great metal body of his Reaver throbbed momentarily with increased reactor output as machinery was powered up, tested and powered down. Occasional reports from the enginarium buzzed into the cockpit, but nothing could disturb the soothing cant of his crew.

He shut his eyes, letting the senses of the Titan take the place of human sight and hearing. The discomfort of the manifold hardlines plugged into the back of his skull melted away. Hard seats and awkward physical controls no longer troubled him. All human sensation was as nothing when his mind spread to fill the metal giant. The sense of his own body dwindled, becoming little more than a remembered irritation.

Dunkel was becoming *God's Wrath*.

His giant feet were planted wide upon the hard standing of the marshalling yards. He felt the electric thrill of gyroscopes keeping him balanced, the minute adjustments the Reaver's hip pistons made to its posture. All systems operated perfectly. There were none of the catches in movement or stiffness in the machine's joints he had experienced last time. The overhaul given *God's Wrath* on the way to Tuesen had been total. The results were remarkable. The Titan's machine personality was equally pleased at its rejuvenation, and its bloody soul eager for the fight. Dunkel was apart from it yet. He saw his own mind as a series of layers, each function of his intellect isolated by the manifold so it might be more easily integrated with the greater being of *God's Wrath*. The engine's primitive soul moved beneath the electric ways of the interface, a leviathan mount that waited for Dunkel to grasp its reins. The echoes of its former princeps' psyches were ghostly priests in attendance to this metal demigod.

The princeps sank deeper into the mind of the machine, blending his consciousness with mechanical and electronic systems. His awareness brushed on each of the Titan's hundreds of devices, before they faded away from his somatic control, and their operation became as automatic and unnoticed as the beating of his human heart. The spirit of each mechanism leapt a little at his touch before they quietened, but the machine's interface smoothed out these interactions, and *God's Wrath* remained as unmoving as an idol.

From its electrical heaven, *God's Wrath* reached for Dunkel and his six moderati. Before Dunkel merged with his machine, the crew's minds bled together at the edges, networking through the glorious technologies of the manifold. Six became one, a sacred number, two times the trinity of the Machine-God. Dunkel exulted in his deepest being, for his was a holy and honourable calling.

God's Wrath's soul was a crimson ocean of violent need waiting for them. Dunkel plunged into it gladly.

A tremor shook the machine's war frame.

'Manifold interface finalised. All praise the Machine God,' Dunkel whispered to himself. But he was no longer Dunkel, he was *God's Wrath*. As his mortal body spoke, the words also emerged as a short, rising burst from the Reaver's warhorn. Somewhere, deep within the mass of plasteel, a scrap of flesh smiled, and was forgotten.

Like a sleeper rising, *God's Wrath* came to life.

The noosphere drew itself over the conjoined beings of the princeps, moderati and Titan, completing the fusion of man and machine. If he concentrated on his human being, Dunkel was still aware of himself and the individuality of his moderati, but it was a sensation at one removed, akin to looking at a cold-numbed limb, knowing it was part of himself, but being unable to feel it. *God's Wrath* was fully awake. With the whine of enormous gears and servos, it moved, swinging its coleopteran head from the left to the right.

Machine vision painted a world in miniature within Dunkel's vision centres. His human eyes had opened at some point, and a phantom image of the cockpit and the view through the Titan's yard-thick occuli imposed itself over what *God's Wrath* saw. It was easy to ignore.

Titans of the Legios Oberon, Atarus and Fortis stood in a chessboard formation, each in front of their coffin ships. Behind them washed the waters of Parmenio's ribbon-thin River Sea. The island city of Tyros stood battered sentry over the narrow channel separating it from the Hecatone shore. The mainland docking grounds had been cleared, bulldozed down to rockcrete, and dozens of coffin ships stood like starscrapers in a temporary city. The rails for the Titans' maintenance gantries had been laid, allowing the cranes and ammo lifts that tended to the metal giants to roll forth from the coffin ships into the open air, where they might more easily perform their duties. Guilliman's plan of attack had been kind to the legios; there was no perilous drop into combat, no desperate fight free from their conveyances. The Collegia Titanica would march in good order.

The ultimate line of Guilliman's new defence network ringed the Titans about. Three demi-legios amounted to one hundred and two of the towering war machines, of all classes, and so required a wide bailey of their own. The Titan grounds were the Adeptus Mechanicus' headquarters on Parmenio, and the full might of the Machine-God was on display. There were thirty-six of Legio Oberon's white and sable engines present alone, a great gathering. Many were heroes upon the field, engines that had fought for dozens of centuries, princeps and crew whose reputations were won in the desperate fighting following the opening of the Great Rift. Scores of Knights of the Questor Mechanicus and Questor Imperialis lined a road wide enough to allow the passage of the great engines out of the fort, their banners stirring in the breeze.

Around the Titans' feet waited tens of thousands of skitarii in robes of several forge worlds; red, ochre, white, black and grey. Next to them three thousand war robots of the Legio Cybernetica waited in neat ranks. Beyond the line of the freshly cast curtain wall were other fortifications, other centres of martial power; the regimental headquarters of the Astra Militarum and the drop-castella of the Ultramarines and the White Scars. There were flags of other worlds, forces representing might drawn from across the sector, but the majority were of Ultramar and its affiliated forge worlds. This war was an affair of the Ultramarines and the Adeptus Mechanicus.

Hundreds of thousands of warriors. Wherever they were from, they were waiting, waiting for the Emperor's steel gods to walk.

The primarch made a speech. Dunkel heard it and didn't hear it. The words he understood, he forgot the moment they were said. He was in thrall to the sluggish belligerence of *God's Wrath*, and *God's Wrath* cared nothing for talk.

Orders were given, passed on from the primarch's high command through to the various heads of the divisions on Parmenio. Dunkel's commands came from Princeps Seniores Urskein, the maniple commander, aboard the Warlord Titan *Retribution*.

The words were simple, more felt than heard.

'Death Bolts,' he said, using the legion's Low Gothic name, 'walk.'

The Warhounds were off first, warhorns howling, beetled backs swaying side to side with their excitement at the hunt. When the last of the Scout Titans loped beyond the perimeter, the remainder set out.

God's Wrath chafed while his brothers *God Sworn*, *God's Doom* and *Mercy of Fire* stomped out. His rising frustration threatened to drown Princeps Dunkel, and he had to assert his will strenuously to tame the machine's heart. Finally, his turn came. Dunkel responded to the need of his engine to walk rather than Urskein's spoken command.

With ponderous majesty, the Reaver's splay-toed foot took its first step on the road to battle. Unable and unwilling to blunt the engine's excitement, Dunkel shouted a wordless war cry in time with *God's Wrath*'s hooting wail.

God's Wrath's iron brothers joined their voices to the choir of slaughter, venting machine-made wrath and their earnest intent to wipe the traitors from the surface of Parmenio.

Legs swung, ponderous as wrecking balls, mighty as towers. The shattered lands of Hecatone swept by *God's Wrath*'s feet in a blur of mustard yellows and drab greens. Shell holes from the Death Guard's initial attack made the land a moonscape. In the sucking wilderness stood shattered trees and stepped triangles of bricks, broken free from their service as the corners of buildings. Fertile lands had become slurried bogs, a marshland born of bombardment breeding sicknesses of all types. Shreds of mist steamed from metal-skinned mires. No road remained whole, no building without damage. Death's silence crushed all life away. Parmenio's creatures had perished or fled, and the Plague God's daemonic offspring had yet to replace them. Guilliman's army came, the squelching of a hundred thousand feet and the frustrated roar of tank engines fighting through mud filling Hecatone with life again.

Tanks by the hundred beat a path for the infantry. They carried walkways of wire and wood in rolled bales, unspooling them from spindles welded to their rear facings. The wood had been taken from elsewhere upon the planet, manufactured from trees felled in those untainted lands where the Death Guard had yet to tread, leaving wastes of stumps where forests had grown. The taint of Nurgle spread far by diverse means. Oftentimes, the cure was as bad as the disease.

The legios walked at quarter speed at the fore of the hordes of men and machines. They were the warlords of the armies of ants scurrying at their feet. For all their size and heft, the Titans moved quietly, each step far spaced, their reactor hum and gear noise modest components of the advance. Only when each step terminated and met the ground with heavy impact tread, shaking ripples in water smeared with rainbows of pollution, did the Titans' might make itself known. Each footfall was the compression of thunder into the earth, pounding out the slow drumroll of armageddon.

They pushed on into the wasted lands, and Dunkel's view – *God's Wrath*'s view – became of a sea of curling fog. The further they advanced, the denser it became, rallying itself after its earlier breaking. As surely as an army regroups after a minor defeat, Mortarion's poisonous airs thickened. *God's Wrath* ploughed through it. With no comparator for scale, the machine seemed a man wading a vaporous sea. The hunching Warhounds carved impermanent paths ahead like the backs of large fish cutting the water. The greater Titans, the various marks of Warlord and others, were larger men, perhaps fishermen pushing into the shallows to cast their nets, their vast carapaces like coracles balanced upon their backs. Space Marine attack craft roaring overhead were seabirds. The horde of men beneath the roof of mists were an army of stealthy crabs.

Augur readings poured into Dunkel's mind as readily as the sights of his own eyes. Radar pulses sketched out contours in fleeting washes of light. Dark light and heat sight gave their own, different views, all mingled with Dunkel's native vision, and the sharp, high resolution machine sight of *God's Wrath*. For one unaccustomed to the blending of sensory input, the experience would have been nauseating; to Dunkel it was as if he was ordinarily blind, and only when he sat in the command throne of his engine were his eyes suddenly, gloriously opened.

Vox chatter and data squirt intruded into the serenity of walking. He made himself pay attention, lest he forget his duty was war, and not solely to exult in the piloting of his engine.

Huge numbers of voices competed for attention. *God's Wrath*'s cogitators helped order them according to importance. His own superiors in the Legio were given priority, those of high command next. The rest, all the generals, colonels and clade leaders, hung about at the edge of his awareness, waiting for him to think of them and bring their chatter into mental focus.

'Death Bolts Maniple Quintus, come to a halt,' commanded Princeps Seniores Urskein. His order was an echo of one delivered a second before from Legio command, direct from the primarch's liaison. *'Battle formation. Three-line defence in depth. Execute.'*

God's Wrath obeyed before Dunkel could. A mighty foot planted itself firmly in the ground, pushing up a rim of mud around its square toes. The back leg adjusted. *God's Wrath* sank into a firing stance, braced against the recoil of its gargantuan weapons. *Mercy of Fire* came to a halt five hundred metres away to the left, *God's Doom* and *God Sworn* off to the right, making part of a line that curved off in the direction of the shores of the River Sea fifty kilometres away, where its narrow gulf was widened briefly by a series of bights. The Titans of other maniples were looming shapes cut off at the waist by the fogs. Beyond them, the other Legios were smears of shadow in mustard vapour.

The entire Legio arrayed itself similarly to Urskein's

maniple. Princes escorted by their royal guards, the Warlords took up their positions three hundred metres back from the gaps between the smaller Reavers, forming a deep regicide board pattern.

Order chatter decreased, became more localised as each part of the Imperial war machine looked to its own business. Tension grew.

The entity that was Dunkel and brutal machine soul combined swept its gaze across a sea of mist. There was no sign of the enemy, but they were close. *God's Wrath* felt it. Always before combat the meshing of men with machine was at its most heightened. At those times, the princeps came close to forgetting their individuality. Dunkel fought to save himself from dissipating into *God's Wrath*'s soul. It happened, sometimes, princeps immersed so far in their engine's being they were lost, and disconnecting them broke their minds. In the hard places of his eternal being, all that was separate from *God's Wrath*, he knew this, but it was hard to resist. He wanted to go deeper, to taste power at its source, join with the spirits of those who had come before and become one with the machine. One day, perhaps, he would be placed into an amniotic tank and enjoy the pleasure of the annihilated self. But not yet.

The Warhounds moved further off. They strutted through the fog silently, eager hunters capable of ambush and surprise despite their enormous size.

More orders pulsed out, spreading down informational pathways with the flicker jump of electronic projection. Dunkel supposed if he could see it, it would resemble the tree of life, described by the sacred flow of the motive force.

Fifteen Knights of House Konor loped past to support their larger cousins. They were slower than the Warhounds, and their shorter legs put them at risk in the difficult terrain. They wove complex courses to stay upon the firmest ground. One misstep would see them mired. They made not one.

Along down the line, the Warhound packs of the other legios were advancing, supported by their own allied Knightly houses. In the shadow of the walking engines the men and lesser machines of the army drew themselves up into battle lines, refusing to let the heaved up earth of Hecatone break the strict tenets of the Tactica Imperialis. No man would want that in view of the primarch, whose own writings had done so much to inform the sacred text.

Tanks drew up in a shallow delta formation. Infantry sheltered in their lee. At the centre of the army, behind the line of Titans, a large cohort of Ultramarian super-heavy tanks deployed in a formation dictated directly by the primarch. By sheer weight and engine power they forced their way through the mire, massive dozer blades levelling ground that would not submit. Such a number in that configuration had been seen only rarely since the days of the Heresy, so it was said. Moving steadily but at a safe distance behind them came Roboute Guilliman's command crawler.

The Imperial army waited as the skirmish line of giant machines scouted ahead.

Urskein sent out a number of alternative deployment patterns across the datanet codified by single words chosen specifically for that engagement. Dunkel knew them all by heart. The fog was rising up in a wall as tall as the god-machines to the west. The mountains slipped back into invisibility. Soupy murk obscured the plains. The sunlight at his back reflected off the mist brightly.

Detonations flashed in the fog. The bright glare of plasma discharge silhouetted one of Legio Oberon's war hounds and a supporting pair of Knights a mile out in the murk. A squall of vox-communications burst out from the advance.

'Engine contact! Engine contact!'

A volley of three giant rockets whooshed overhead, narrowly missing the Titan *Ultimate Fortitude*. One was interdicted and brought down by the fire of the army's rearward air defences. The others plunged down through the ceiling of the mist, blasting up towering cones of debris where they impacted; mud, men and machines intermixed. The explosion rocked *God's Wrath*.

'No atomics. No chemical. No plasma. Standard warhead configuration,' voxed Urskein. Harsh garbles of higher-level vox traffic overlaid his voice. *'Stand easy.'*

Datasquirts pulsed between the Titans, carrying the rapid binary talk of machines. Picter feed flashed through Dunkel's head. Shadowy shapes snatched by the scout Titans. Enemy engines shrouded in mist.

The flashing of high energy weapons was joined by the delicate tremble of shell detonation some way ahead.

'Prepare for immediate engagement. Seventeen engine contacts and rising. Attack pattern escutcheon,' said Urskein. He was calm and measured, no sign of the machine's soul he shared at that moment impinging upon his words. *'Prepare to receive retreating scouts. Cover and protect.'*

A dozen of the Legio's scout engines loped back behind the stacked line of Titans, coming about in a wide arc to shelter at the heels of the Warlords. From there, they could strike out again to outflank the enemy when the heavier engines were engaged. Fires guttered along molten scores on their backs. The Knights remained embattled. Their combat chatter distracted Dunkel, and he shunted their terse exchange to the back of his awareness.

An orange flare smeared the thickening fog, then another. Knight reactor death. The small, one-man engines were in trouble.

God's Wrath shifted under him. 'Steady, steady,' said Dunkel, as if he were soothing a flesh and blood mount. At the same time, he exerted control via the mind impulse link over the machine's processing centres, damping down its atavistic need to kill.

More Warhounds came back in ones and twos between the spread line of the Legio Oberon. One of Urskein's maniple, *World Pain*, was missing. Dunkel spared a moment for the strategic cartolith displaying the state of the rest of the line; the same was happening up and down the front.

The racket of war grew closer. The enemy harassed the retreating skirmish line, but were too battle wise to come into optimum engagement range. Only a few shots blazed through the air towards the engine line.

'Adept Sine, keep shields to maximum replenish rate in case those strays catch us,' Dunkel spoke into the hardline vox. Using his mouth felt strange. *God's Wrath*'s urge to hoot along with his speech was a bubbling need in his heart. 'Take us into combat at maximum aegis.'

'*As you command, princeps,*' Sine voxed back from his station in the reactor room. The hum of the engine deepened.

As the fight became closer and more intense, the Knights broke off and followed the Warhounds. They moved past Dunkel at a run, their stooped backs hiding their heads from his view. The lesser machines came only up to *God's Wrath*'s chest. Dunkel read thirty per cent losses for their support household. The Knights always paid to keep the larger engines safe. Fast and small compared to their larger cousins, their role was to divert fire away from the Titans, relying on their speed to stay safe. But agility saved nothing from a direct hit of a god-weapon.

'Where are the enemy's support?' voxed Princeps Gugglhem of *Mercy of Fire*.

'Contacts made,' voxed Urskein. *'Forty-seven enemy engines majoris, circa two hundred engines minoris in support.'*

The flash of weapons cut out as the last of the House Konor Knights straggled back behind Oberon's lines. The steady tread of advancing war machines took the place of the armament roar.

'They're coming. Visual contact,' voxed Gugglhem.

'Prepare for engagement. All weapons charge. Hold formation, break on my command,' responded Urskein.

Dunkel saw them then, looming out of the mist. They were the same in many respects as Oberon's engines, but the character of their souls altered their appearance, making them crookbacked and ominous where the Imperial Titans seemed stooped with the weight of duty. A crowd of them advanced in right-hand echelon, a pair of Warlords on the leading edge bristling with close combat fittings. Linebreakers.

The badges of a Legio were unique, and every Titan's markings were as individual to it as a man's fingerprints. Not even the traitors were cowardly enough to hide their sins. They proclaimed their allegiance and identity proudly.

'The Legio Mortis,' said Fantorp, princeps of *God Sworn*. *'Death's Heads.'*

'Pride. They still have that, when all other virtues of honour have deserted them, they remain proud,' said Moscov of *God's Doom*.

'Confirm. Confirm,' voxed Urskein. *'Legio Mortis traitoris. Transmitting enemy idents now.'*

Names and numerical designations for the Titans entered the noospheric datanet. Dunkel's mind filled with a litany of atrocity stretching back through history in the starkness of Lingua Technis.

Where the Death Bolts' defensive grid was grouped maniple by maniple, the Death's Heads attacked in a demi-Legio strength formation, all its heaviest machines at the leading edge. There was no cover for either force, and the weight of the enemy was coming right at Dunkel's position.

'They're seeking a way through. Do not let them break the line,' said Urskein.

The enemy line let out wails of challenge from their warhorns.

Oberon responded, as did Fortis and Atarus.

Mortis opened fire. The loyalists returned the favour.

Instantly, the space between the two lines was a kill zone inimical to life. Titan weapons were awesome in their destructive capabilities, outmatching all but the greatest voidship armaments. The air ignited around energy spikes. Supersonic shockwaves of hauler-sized shells ripped up sprays of water from the ground. Linear thunder cracked off las discharge, shaking cones of mist into rainbursts. Fog was boiled into multicolour plasmas.

In support of the two melee Warlords was a monster fitted for long-range fighting designated *Poison Master*. Bearing a plasma annihilator on the right arm, a volcano cannon on the left, and its carapace mounting two huge laser blasters, its role was to smash a hole through the defences for Legio Mortis' close combat specialists to barge through. All its weapons spoke together, slamming hard into *God's Doom*. Its voids took the impact, shutting off with deafening bangs as they were overwhelmed. The Reaver was moving aside, trailing smoke, when *Poison Master* opened fire again, scoring bright lines across *God's Doom*'s composite plating. It rocked on its feet. Its motivators locked in the left leg, and it limped on.

'Forward!' ordered Urskein. 'Take the fight to them.'

Other princeps seniores followed suit. The Legio Oberon's game-board line broke up, each maniple locking onto a section of the enemy echelon. Strategically, their bunched formation allowed them to concentrate their weapons on individual targets. The opposing echelon of the foe gave all their Titans clear lanes of fire. To break this advantage and maximise their own, Legio Oberon moved forward in staggered, unpredictable lines of advance, the maniples obscuring one another, thus preventing any one Titan bearing the brunt of too much fire for too long.

Three missiles streaked out of *God's Wrath*'s carapace-mounted array, the engine's only long-ranged weapon. Twenty rounds were all he had. Dunkel wanted every one to count. His position as princeps of *God's Wrath* had been hard in the earning. He wished to live up to the honour.

The missiles slammed into *Poison Master*'s shields. Fires washed over crackling purple energy fields, spoiling its aim. *God's Doom* limped out of its sight line, fire dripping down its left leg.

More missiles raced away from *God's Wrath*. Blazing

pillars of las light slammed into the void shields in reply, the flare they brought dazzling Dunkel.

'Void shield one at twenty per cent. We cannot take too many more hits of that intensity,' warned Sine.

'Push the reactor. More power to locomotors. Ready the meltacannon,' ordered Dunkel. He itched to get close enough to use the weapon.

Mercy of Fire opened up with its gatling laser, belting burning lines at the enemy. *Poison Master*'s void shields thrummed and snapped in the mist, sectioning it with a skin of light where illuminated water droplets swirled in mesmerising patterns. The Warlord retaliated with a full blast from all its guns. A firestorm erupted from both weapons arms, engulfing *Mercy of Fire* in a boiling shawl of flames. The Reaver's initial void shield gave out, the secondary collapsing moments later, then the third and the fourth. A laser blaster shot slammed directly into *Mercy of Fire*'s chest armour. Urskein's *Retribution* was advancing past the damaged Titan, bringing its weapons to bear on *Poison Master*, but power spikes were showing across Dunkel's senses as the *Poison Master* prepared to fire and finish off its target. Two of the three Reavers were out of the fight for the moment, one perhaps permanently. The next maniple moved up closer, drawing fire from *Poison Master*'s combat partner, and blocking out the fire lane from the enemy echelon. They suffered for it, their void shields blazing with dangerous light.

A blast from *Poison Master* slammed into *Mercy of Fire*, smashing its shoulder armour free and mangling the joint. The arm locked in position, gun drooping uselessly towards the ground.

God's Wrath wailed a polyphony of anger at the

wounding of its comrade. It lurched forward suddenly, taking Dunkel and *Poison Master* by surprise, intercepting the next hits intended for *Mercy of Fire*. Sparks rained over Dunkel's helm. A servitor jerked in its alcove, smoke pouring from its input ports.

The engine's discordant challenge was met by an inhuman screaming from the Warlord.

'Keep back! Dunkel, keep your engine back!' ordered Urskein.

Dunkel's engine was spoiling a clear shot from the princeps seniores' Titan, but *God's Wrath* would not be restrained. Its ersatz animal soul slipped momentarily free from Dunkel's command. It leaned forwards, accelerating into a lumbering run. The Titan's belligerence was well known in the Legio, its name deliberately chosen to match, as was its armament. Dunkel was supposed to be the match of its wrath. He was failing.

'Tame it!' Urskein yelled.

'Activate perceptual dampers,' commanded Dunkel. He wrestled with the unresponsive manual controls.

'Logic engines are locked out, princeps,' responded Sine. *'It will not be dissuaded. This is the will of the Machine-God.'*

'Then we go in hard. Open fire, left arm, now!' Dunkel wrenched himself free of the machine's mental embrace, summoning enough individuality to target the enemy and order his moderati to engage the meltacannon. *God's Wrath* was running. Its systems were bent on the intimate murder of hand to hand combat. The aim was poor. Dunkel selected a point at the centre of *Poison Master*'s mass and prayed to the Machine-God that it was a hit. Moderati Obersten struggled to bring the arm up. *God's Wrath* was fighting against Dunkel, attempting to bring up its close combat weapon to strike, but Dunkel kept it down to stop it from obscuring the shot, and Obersten managed to engage and release the meltacannon fusion beam before *God's Wrath* slammed hard into its foe.

Hitting an enemy engine directly with the meltacannon was the best outcome, for the power of it could vaporise plasteel. *God's Wrath* could cripple a larger Titan, even kill it, with a single shot. Active void shields scattered the weapon's high gain microwaves into the warp, so the next best solution was to take down the shields with the cannon and leave the foe open to blade work.

The charging of the cannon was sloppily executed, the weapon fired before the fusion focus was properly sighted, and yet somehow, *God's Wrath* vented its fiery breath on target.

The beam focal point fell just inside the void shield. Optimum siting on a shielded engine would have been exactly on the field boundary, but the hit was close enough, allowing a near full fusion reaction to take place outside before wave scattering disrupted the hit. Beams of high lethality microwaves intersected upon the target point. Now the meltacannon was in full discharge, *God's Wrath*'s vast array of weapons cogitators keeping the focus constant as the engine moved in to attack.

Water in the air reacted first, heated to explosive temperatures by the cannon, then the air itself turned into an expanding ball of hot plasma.

The explosion burst across *Poison Master*'s void field. Lightning raced all over the energy envelope, earthing itself along crooked lines of energised ions generated by the blast. The explosion, the discharge and the random conduction patterns generated by the agitated atoms of the atmosphere combined to bring *Poison Master*'s void shields crashing down one after the other.

God's Wrath smashed through dispersing aegis and into the body of *Poison Master*.

The Warlord had several metres of height on the Reaver, and was massier, but such was *God's Wrath*'s impetus that the impact knocked *Poison Master* sideways. Dunkel relented from his attempts to restrain the machine's soul, gasping at the pain the effort caused him. He shared the machine's eager joy as he gave the Reaver its freedom. It roared a haunting wail. Without his or his moderatis' input the chainfist was rising, the flexible chain of teeth blurring into action. The chain was wider than a tank's tracks, each tooth as big as man. It scythed down, taking *Poison Master*'s left weapon arm at the elbow while it was still staggering. Molten chips of metal blasted all over *God's Wrath*'s cockpit. Dunkel's vision shook with the skip and bite of the teeth, the sawing through the metal vibrating the entire machine. The enemy Titan was covered in some kind of organic matter that wept corrosive slime. Patches of rust marred its plates. Its sallow, skull-faced helm cockpit seemed alive in some unnatural way.

'Harder!' Dunkel roared. He was by now entirely in thrall to the Reaver's battle fervour. 'Harder!'

His mind worked with Moderati Kren and the Titan's machine-made soul, guiding the huge, lopsided weapon through the Warlord's arm. The Reaver leaned in, putting its entire weight onto its left arm, carving its way through its larger cousin's limb. A void shield reengaged, enveloping them both.

Poison Master wailed in pain and outrage, calling to its brothers to aid it. Dunkel had lost sight of the linebreaker

Warlords; their melee weaponry would make short work of *God's Wrath*, but it was too late now to worry about them. He had to finish the enemy or he would die. *Poison Master*'s ranged weapons were useless at such close quarters. It discharged them anyway, sending off fountains of plasma. Its missile racks emptied. The munitions roared off almost vertically, disappearing into the sky.

Dunkel grinned. The enemy Titan was in machine shock, the mind rebelling against its pilots. Vulnerable.

A flight of naval Marauders roared overhead. Missiles hammered into the Warlord, bringing its void shields down again. A handful detonated on the carapace. Its knees sagged with the blow.

Point defence lascannons needled *God's Wrath*'s side as the Reaver continued its butchery.

Poison Master's weapons arm fell, sheets of oil and unwholesome fluid spraying down the smaller Titan's front. The Warlord was suddenly freed by the loss of its limb and staggered backwards, carapace weapons swivelling to get a lock.

'Dunkel, rein the machine's spirit in. Get clear of my shot!' Urskein ordered.

'All power to locomotors!' Dunkel's order was half a scream. He seized the mind of his engine again. It fought him every step of the way, wanting nothing but to rend and slash at the rival who had hurt its comrade. Dunkel heaved at the motive levers, using them in conjunction with the manifold to force *God's Wrath* forward past the Warlord.

The enemy machine paced back and swung around, plasma coils on its remaining primary weapon arm lighting up ring by ring as it charged to fire. Pintle lascannons and point defence guns mounted all over it continued to lash out at the Reaver, tracking it as it ran on by, but they could not hurt *God's Wrath* through its void shields.

The plasma cannon could.

Poison Master locked on to *God's Wrath*, targeting the vulnerable rear where the armour was thin. A full power shot would punch through the shields, armour and into the reactor. Dunkel pushed his machine around in a long arc, trying to outpace the turn of *Poison Master*. Metal gods performed a ponderous, clumsy waltz.

'We are going to be hit,' he said. 'Brace for impact!'

A sudden surge from *God's Wrath* saw *Poison Master*'s shot go wide and glance off the Reaver's void shields with a harsh thrum. Cabling flashed and caught fire near to Dunkel, burned out by feedback from the overwhelmed shield.

But they were still standing.

Battered by the hit, *God's Wrath* became pliant again. Dunkel brought about the machine to weather a second strike upon his forward arc.

Poison Master was dying. Dozens of lesser engines crept up in *Retribution*'s shadow, joining their fire to the Warlord's. Three Knights joined forces to scythe off *Poison Master*'s leg at the knee with combined shots from their melta cannons. *Retribution* punched through its armour with volleyed shots of its twin volcano cannon.

Alarms sounded in Dunkel's cockpit.

'*Reactor critical!*' yelled Sine. '*Get clear!*'

Poison Master's reactor burst free of its casing in a hemisphere of blinding plasma. Somehow, the power source had remained pure when the engine itself had been corrupted, and its cleansing light burned away all trace of its fall from grace. After all this time, the soul of the engine escaped to be received to the mercy of the Machine-God.

A Knight fell down bonelessly, systems knocked out by the electromagnetic pulse. It was luckier than its fellow, which was consumed by atomic fire as it turned to run.

Dunkel had a moment to take stock. He had broken through the enemy line. His was the sole Titan on the far side of it. Mortis' echelon held, and was bowing back. Oberon's initial disposition had been teased apart. Though the loyalists were wreaking a great deal of damage, their engine line had been disrupted. Mortis were retreating engine by engine, the halves of each pair taking it in turns to cover their brother machines, peeling back and drawing the engines in. One of the line breakers burned, still upright, a mile and a half to *God's Wrath*'s left. They had been a ruse, expensive sacrifices to pull the loyal Legios into the echelon's full storm of fire. The second line breaker was rampaging through the army, under fire from thousands of tanks. Atarus had been funnelled towards the left-hand side of the echelon. Fortis had been less easy to trick, and was advancing to attempt to outflank far to Dunkel's right.

Sprung trap revealed, orders came from high command, demanding the engines halt. Reluctantly, *God's Wrath* walked backwards, joining the line of machines opposing Mortis, and commenced firing again until its rockets ran out. It was then restricted to engaging targets that came close enough for its oversized fusion cannon.

The Legios remained like that for some time, trading blows with their wicked brothers throughout the night and into dawn.

* * *

Guilliman's command Leviathan ground inexorably across the sodden plain. The weight of the giant machine pushed it deep into the mud, not so much moving across the landscape as sailing it.

Upon a chart desk, the primarch surveyed the disposition of his brother's forces.

Sheltered by the engines of Legio Mortis was a huge and malevolent fly, fat and as dominating of the landscape as a geoglyph. A centre made of three interlocking masses of elite troops, each supporting the other, formed a geometric, angular abdomen. The flanks swept back as stylised wings. Skirmishers ranged ahead in long formations, making up the legs and mandibles to the fore and flanks, the rearguard mirroring them. In total there were twenty-one blocks of troops, the pointed ends of each formation fitted together in such a way that they gathered close by the body. The angles of these corners formed a pattern that Guilliman suspected had some meaningless, arcane significance to his deluded brother.

In the strategium, the lights were dim. Reactive armourglass glazed the slit oculus looking out over Hecatone's ruined land. Mist blanketed everything and was still growing thicker. Moisture leached sound from the air, and spread the light in a painful, flat glare. To dim this light and the constant strobing of Titan weapons in its swirling depths, the oculus had turned itself to a smoky brown. The interior was consequently gloomy. Pale holo-shine lit attentive faces scrutinising tacticaria; Space Marine, Primaris Marine and unmodified human.

'Why are you waiting, my lord?' Maldovar Colquan growled.

Guilliman refrained from rebuking him for his tone.

Colquan had been one of his most vocal critics on Terra, which was why Guilliman had ordered him to join his Indomitus Crusade. Keep your enemies close, King Konor had always said, a tenet Guilliman had not always adhered to, to his eternal regret.

'Something,' said Guilliman. 'Something less expected.' He gestured at the line of Legio Mortis' god-machines, now curled back so far that the right flank almost touched the advancing fly formation. 'He entices me into a trap. It is a stratagem so obvious it can only be part of a greater play. Mortarion is a fine general, even when he is seeking to prove how indomitable he is. He is there, right in the middle of his army. It is a taunt. He wishes to draw me out.'

'He has not been sighted,' said Colquan. He paced, rarely still, angry as he always was.

'He is there.' Guilliman waved his gauntleted hand over the hololith. 'In this nonsensical formation we have renegades, Traitor Space Marines, enemy Titans, mutants, aberrant abhumans, sellsword Knights, heavy artillery, tracked armour and all the rest. The usual parade of Mortarion's diseased, deluded followers. What we do not see…'

'…is daemons,' said Colquan. He leant his heavy, golden gauntlets on the chart. The image broke up around his fists. 'Where are the Neverborn?'

'It is that which troubles me,' said Guilliman. 'Where indeed? Until we know, I cannot act. Mortarion may be holding them back, waiting for me to commit. Where they are, he will be. What is Galatan's status?' the primarch called over to a vox monitor.

A pale-faced man in a smart uniform turned from his bank of blinking machines.

'The fleet reports the station draws nigh but remains under assault by Death Guard assets. Our own vessels have moved to engage.'

'Distance?'

'Five hundred thousand kilometres and closing, my lord commander.'

'Status?'

'We have lost contact, lord commander. Our signals are being jammed, but the station continues to fire on the enemy.'

'Then it has not fallen,' said Guilliman.

'It might yet,' said Colquan.

'It might,' agreed Guilliman, his attention on the flare and crash of simulated weapons fire emanating from the hololith.

'Then allow me to take my warriors there, my lord, and force the issue in our favour,' said Colquan. He stopped all of a sudden, tensed, hoping for release.

'No,' said Guilliman. 'Galatan is well garrisoned. We must trust to its defenders. We cannot afford to become distracted from the struggle on the ground.'

Colquan ground his fist into the table in annoyance. 'Then what is your command?'

'We pound the enemy, hold the line,' said Guilliman. 'And we wait.'

CHAPTER TWENTY-ONE

THE DEFENCE OF CRUCIUS PORTIS II

The fighting on Galatan continued for hours, time measured in short engagements followed by periods of walking. No more of Justinian's men fell, though Amarillo lost one of his remaining warriors to injuries. They left him as his body spun its mucranoid sheath and promised him later retrieval. Once the Space Marines crossed the chasm, the Astra Militarum there insisted on accompanying Justinian and the rest. They said they wanted the honour, but Justinian suspected they thought their chances of survival higher. If so, they were wrong. They died one by one, until only Tesseran and a score of others remained. When they came across a half regiment of Ultramarian auxiliaries holding a major transit hub, Justinian ordered the unmodified to join with them, his justification being they might fight better. More probable, Justinian thought privately, they can at least die in the company of their own kind.

Not slowed by lesser men, the Space Marines picked

up speed, following vox directions when they could and the tremors of battle ringing through the decks when they could not. Twice they made tense detours around enemy groups too large to tackle, negotiating service tunnels or creeping along companionways over the heads of the foe.

Others they fell upon without mercy, slaughtering boarders yet to join with their parent formations.

In this way they eventually came to bulkhead doors sealed against further atmospheric loss, guarded by machine-spirits and hyper-vigilant weapons. Novamarines passcodes gained them entry, and they emerged through armoured airlocks into stale ship's air.

From there, they went on for further hours. All the while they came closer to the central hub, until, weary and battle sore, they arrived at the Crucius Portis II.

Great gatehouses guarded the four principal radial corridors leading into Galatan's hub. The other roads stopped at the walls. There were no ways in to the centre except through the Crucius Portis redoubts. The core was almost a battlestation unto itself.

A pair of towers projected from the station's adamantium-clad inner wall. Wide battlements looked down onto a killing field two kilometres across. Weaponry more commonly employed on the exterior of a void structure filled their outward faces and gathered around their bases: giant macro-cannon turrets, missile batteries, and direct energy weapons so large that if they were emplaced within a smaller construct and fired, they would risk punching clean through the hull.

Galatan was large enough to take such punishment.

The final of the station's concentric ringways went

around the central core, broadening out gently around the killing fields, and narrowing to half a mile across once away from them. The inner station curtain wall was studded all around its circumference with weapons points and shooting balconies. Every mile smaller castles projected out into the road.

The hub of Galatan had been forged in the Dark Age with technologies inconceivable to the tech-priests of the present day. The armour around the heart was one hundred metres thick, and made of pure adamantium cooled in such a way that the crystals of its structure were all of uniform size, and interlocked perfectly. It was a single-piece construction that could only have been made upon a forge built from a star. Teleport baffles laced its structure, and upon its outer faces were inscribed, also by ancient art, warding symbols that were proof against any warp entity. The technoarchaeologists who probed Galatan's secrets theorised that these were much later additions, dating from the fall of Old Night.

Justinian led Brucellus, Achilleos, Donasto, Michaelus and Maxentius-Drontio across the vast metal plain before the closed gates. Automated turrets tracked them, their crossfires designed to inflict maximum casualties on the enemy.

There was no challenge to their approach. A postern in the main gates opened a crack, spilling yellow light across the field. Their identities were discerned from afar. If they had been found wanting, they would already have been obliterated.

From behind the gate a line of Terminators cast giants' shadows down the long tunnel of the postern. Behind them were the tanks of the Novamarines.

'Enter, brothers,' a voice boomed out. 'And be quick. The enemy is coming.'

There was little time for rest. Justinian and his men were resupplied. Sourcing the rare ammunition for their bolt rifles sent a tattooed human quartermaster of the gate off with a scowl on his face. He returned an hour later with three plasteel crates.

'That's all there is, my lords,' he said, his annoyance at having to find the unusual bolts fighting with the shame that he could find no more.

'Thank you,' said Justinian. The man made troubled apologies, his tattooed face contorted with embarrassment.

Justinian and Maxentius-Drontio handed out the ammunition.

'There is more than enough here for the six of us,' said Maxentius-Drontio.

'Were it there were ten of us still,' said Justinian, 'and we were shorter of bullets.'

Shortly afterwards, Sergeant Amarillo was sent elsewhere. He and his surviving squad members left the group with the curtest of farewells. Neither he nor Justinian had much heart for words. Both had lost many brothers. Neither understood the other.

'The Novamarines are quiet in their grief,' said Achilleos.

Justinian nodded absently. He was still confounded by the Chapter's dour character.

The reduced Squad Parris was ordered to take station in a room in the right-hand gatehouse tower overlooking the prime quadrant killing field. From their vantage point four storeys up, the metal kill zone looked starker than it had at ground level. Turrets constantly roved back and forth in endless cycles of target acquisition, though for the time being the radial way they covered remained free of the enemy.

A switchback corridor from their bunker led through the metres-thick walls of the inner station. This was blocked in the centre by a quintuple-layered door, opening up onto more corridor, at the end of which was a mirror of the outer bunker overlooking the fortress' inner bailey. The radial corridor was significantly narrower on the inside of the gates. A line of four Land Raiders barred the way into the fortress' heart. The forces arrayed against a potential gate breach were impressive, for a Chapter. Sixty Terminators formed a living barrier in front of the tanks. Three tactical companies close to full strength manned the gatehouse. Nine Assault Squads waited in reserve behind the Land Raiders. Many of the Nova-marines high command were deployed around the area. Six thousand mortal troopers of various regiments reinforced them. Here was concentrated the greater part of Galatan's might. Chapter Master Dovaro had commanded it to be so. The enemy showed all signs of massing for single, concentrated assault on the Crucius Portis II.

The remainder of the fort's defenders had been pulled back to defend the three other gates and wall. Dovaro abandoned large swathes of the outer station to protect the core where the fort's main drives, reactors, command centres and – most importantly – the banks of ancient weaponry were housed. Justinian knew then that Tesseran and his ilk would most certainly die.

Justinian and Maxentius-Drontio took themselves away from their brothers for a moment to confer in the inner bunker. They removed their helmets, glad of a respite from their own rebreathed air.

'Hold them, push through their fleet, aid Guilliman at Parmenio whether we have forced the enemy back or not,' said Maxentius-Drontio, observing the assembled Novamarines. 'It was a risky strategy that should have taken into account the possibility of Typhus' attack.'

'Needs must,' said Justinian. He had no access to the command datasphere – the systems were overwhelmed – but he could imagine the casualty counts among Galatan's population if the Chaos forces decided to attack its lesser weapons batteries and ring engines instead of driving for the core. 'If we do not hold the centre, we will be dead in the void. Our course is set. The traitor fleet cannot stop us moving unless they wrest control of the hub. Nor can they disable our primary weapons. We can arrive swarming with heretics, and still tip the battle in the primarch's favour.'

'We have a grave duty ahead of us.'

'We have powerful allies.' Justinian pointed out of the firing slit into the bailey, where silver-armoured warriors waited in the shadows. 'What do you know about these grey brothers?'

'Not much,' said Maxentius-Drontio. 'They call them the Grey Knights. They are specialists, daemon hunters. Psykers. They keep themselves to themselves. It is best not to ask questions about them.'

'That is all you know?'

Maxentius-Drontio nodded.

Justinian looked out again. 'Disappointing. That is all I know also. I have fought in fourteen separate engagements alongside their Chapter before. I have never spoken with one of them. Do you know what else?'

'Edify me,' said Maxentius-Drontio.

'I have never seen a single Primaris Marine among their formations. Why do you think that is?'

'As intriguing as these questions are, we are not the ones to answer them,' said Maxentius-Drontio.

Justinian looked at his second. 'You will be wanting my sergeant's skull-mark soon, with talk like that.'

'It is my duty to help you do yours,' said Maxentius-Drontio humourlessly.

'Then I thank you,' said Justinian.

'See,' said Maxentius-Drontio, pointing over his shoulder. 'Lord Dovaro comes.'

Neither Justinian or Maxentius-Drontio had met the Chapter Master, and they watched his arrival with interest. Dovaro came out from the darkness behind the Land Raider line and went among his men. He was taller than the average Space Marine, and the bone-and-dark-blue quartering of his Terminator armour was heavy with adornment celebrating his many accomplishments. His left pauldron bore the spiked nova-burst and skull of their Chapter, the right an ornate shield decorated with his personal heraldry halved with a crux terminatus. A servo-skull linked to his armour by ribbed cabling bobbed over his head, single red augur lens glaring. A pair of mortal serfs carried a wooden sled bearing Dovaro's massive two-handed power sword resting on a velvet cushion.

Dovaro went to the centre of the inner bailey, and began his speech. It was what one would expect before a battle. Justinian had heard many before, and given several himself. He remained unmoved despite its passion.

'His words appeal again and again to brotherhood,' said

Justinian to Maxentius-Drontio. 'I confess I do not yet feel it for these warriors.'

'It will come,' said Maxentius-Drontio. His tone gave no indication of whether he suffered feelings of alienation like Justinian. 'This is a noble Chapter.'

'Here is a third of its strength, at this one redoubt,' said Justinian, aware he was straying into dangerous territory. 'How small it looks when compared to the Unnumbered Sons.'

'Those days are gone, brother,' said Maxentius-Drontio. 'The Lord Guilliman obeys his own law, as set down in his Codex, that no man shall command more than one thousand Space Marines.'

'He does,' said Justinian. 'But at what cost?'

'That is his concern, not ours,' said Maxentius-Drontio, the warning clear in his voice.

'How long have you been with the Novamarines?' asked Justinian.

'Four years, standard,' said Maxentius-Drontio. 'Around twenty relative. The Chapter travels a lot.'

'And do you feel brotherhood for them?'

There was a pause. 'I understand what you are asking me, Brother-Sergeant Parris,' said Maxentius-Drontio carefully. 'Leaving the brotherhoods we had in the Unnumbered Sons, being seconded to Chapters whose history we do not share, and who rightly look upon us as their replacements, it is hard for some.'

'Is it hard for you?' asked Justinian, hoping for some reflection of his own sorrow.

Maxentius-Drontio turned to face Justinian. 'In truth, I do not care. I have my duty. It was what I was made for. Where I do my duty is irrelevant to me.'

Justinian, abashed, changed the subject. 'Dovaro is a great warrior, by all accounts.'

'Many of them are,' said Maxentius-Drontio. 'You will see, in time.'

In the bailey, Dovaro finished his speech and the Novamarines cheered.

Maxentius-Drontio fastened his helmet in place.

'Speech is over,' his vox-grille growled. 'It is nearly time.'

'Leave the bunker door open, the wall divider too,' Justinian said, glancing around the inner bunker as they left. 'We will have need of this place soon enough. Every fraction of a second will help us.'

The first sign that the enemy approached was that the turrets upon the killing field ceased their roving, stopped and aimed at the same point of the radial corridor.

Seconds later, the chants of Nurgle's followers reached their ears as a distant, irritating buzzing.

Justinian strained his eyes down the way. The perfectly straight corridor sides seemed to touch in the distance. Then he saw that the end appeared to be getting nearer.

'They are coming,' he said to his squad. His words prompted the clatter of bolt shells racked into firing chambers.

'All units prepare for engagement,' voxed Dovaro to his Chapter. *'The enemy is upon us.'*

The great guns of the bastions opened up, roaring destruction down the length of the corridor. Galatan shook to the punishment it meted out to itself. The growing war-drone of the foe was drowned out.

Shortly after, the smaller weapons of the field turrets began to fire. Long-range las weaponry and macro cannons at first. The many autocannons and heavy bolters waited for range confirmation and clear target locks.

Through the explosions boiling down the corridor, the end still appeared to be getting closer and closer. The hordes of Nurgle advanced behind a wall of slowly moving siege mantlets. They were so tall that their tops scraped away the tubes and pipes that festooned the station ceiling, and so thick the shots that got through to them were turned aside. Most never reached the metal, exploding well ahead of the mantlets on a shimmering energy shield.

'Terra's dust,' said Maxentius-Drontio. 'Look at the size of those things.'

'The Emperor alone knows what powers them,' said Achilleos.

They awaited revelation, fingers tense on the triggers of their weapons.

The mantlets ground onwards on squealing iron wheels. They were nine in number, smooth, black with recent forging, showing few of the signs of decay that afflicted all things used by the Plague God's minions. The bombardment from the walls increased its tempo, targeting the intersections of the energy fields where their waveforms would be most spread and weakest.

The two-mile killing zone glared with reflected fire. Ruby las beams cut through the air. In the enclosed space the harsh smell of fyceline and promethium discharge built quickly, filling the air with thick battle smoke.

A defence laser blasted the energy shield at what was point-blank range for a weapon of that size. The field flickered for a brief moment, long enough for a slamming tattoo of shell and las-fire to drum into the leftmost mantlet, sawing it in half. It turned aside, and fell, revealing the semi-mechanical daemon thing pushing it. An opening made, the defences of the wall targeted the engine, obliterating the creature.

Smoking pieces of metal and meat rained down over the killing ground. An indistinct horde of things behind was revealed, a multitude of twisted bodies and horned heads and helms.

Locking on to the foe, the lesser turrets joined in the crash and roar of war. The whine of assault cannons cut through the smoke. Autocannons added their tuneless clatter to the chorus. The triple bangs of heavy bolters ripped out in quick series. Despite the thunder of the Imperial defences, the enemy continued to advance. Their voices rose up in praise of their dark god.

Still the mantlets pushed on, their impetus so great they crushed the outermost of the lesser defence turrets beneath their massive wheels. They were huge, easily a hundred metres tall. The enemy came within a kilometre of the gatehouse, then three quarters. Another mantlet, this one near the centre, was brought to molten ruin. The gap closed with leaden slowness as the remaining seven advanced. Imperial heavy weapons reaped a high tally from the monsters coming behind.

At half a mile, a baleful fanfare blared, and the enemy came out from behind their shields.

Masses of armour rumbled from the shelter of the mantlets, opening fire as they drew themselves up into formation. Ungainly siege tanks lobbed shells over the horde that crashed into the hub's outer walls, spraying superacids over the defences. A poisonous fume arose as metal dissolved and gun barrels crashed from their mountings. Land Raiders in numbers no loyal Chapter could field concentrated lascannon fire upon weapon after weapon, blasting them to pieces. Daemon engines loomed behind them, their warp cannons spitting lightning that rooted infection in the walls and gates.

The mantlets picked up speed towards the gates. The traitors blasted away at the defenders' guns, silencing many, though their rotting tanks paid a heavy price, and soon the field was cluttered with burning wrecks whose smoke smelled of charring flesh. A dismal, stinking mist was rising from the horde, occluding the killing field further.

The enemy were a few hundred metres away, within a bolt rifle's effective range.

'Open fire!' ordered Justinian. His squad aimed their bolt rifles carefully, ensuring every shot was a kill. From the walls came a rain of las and bolt. The enemy were riddled from above. Many fell.

The mantlets parted, pushed sideways to shelter the assault from enfilading fire. Thousands of Plague Marines angled up their rusting weapons and opened fire. Bolt shot raked the loops and slits of the Crucius Portis II, and the screams of dying men within the fortress added to the cacophony.

A device four hundred metres long was brought forward. It was as much flesh as machine, streaming with rot. The stench of it was unbearable. Its smoke-belching engines were inadequate to the task of pushing it, and thousands of diseased slaves laboured under the lashes of the Death Guard to turn its hundred wheels and help it on.

The front was a long snout, part organic, pointing upwards at an angle of twenty degrees. Jawbones showed through metal and necrotic flesh, dripping with filthy slime. Rows of teeth were visible through holed cheeks, but were fused, being nothing but a mounting for the array of melta cannons protruding from the throat. The rear was a mass of bulbous engines. Yellowed plastek tanks all along the spine sloshed with brightly coloured bile.

Grossly twisted figures worked all over haphazard platforms upon the flesh engine. A command went up. The engines belched more acrid smoke, clouding the field further. Bile tanks bubbled. The snout creaked down. The whole thing juddered, and the foreparts revolved as they dropped level with the gate, spinning faster and faster. With a roaring belch, meltacannons ignited. Volcanic heat washed into Justinian's position, forcing his men back a moment until their armour compensated for the sudden rise in temperature.

The remaining guns of the Crucius Portis II blatted loudly, but the daemon engine's green flesh took the hits without apparent harm. The engine gurgled with malevolent glee. Roaring with heat, the snout was pushed against the gateway.

The engine began to melt its way through. As it worked, lesser siege teams came forward to assault the foot of the wall with their own melta devices and sprays of stinking acid. Plague Marines climbed rickety ladders to lob grenades through firing slits. Leering daemons on giant flies the size of horses buzzed along the wall front. Justinian filled one with bolts. Thick fluid burst from the wounds, as if it were a sack full of pus, and it crashed into the seething mass at the base of the walls, but there were hundreds more, possibly thousands.

'They must have summoned these things aboard,' said

Maxentius-Drontio. 'There is no way they landed so many troops by conventional means.'

'Fire below!' Justinian ordered. His men repositioned themselves.

In a blur of fusion fire, the daemonic ram burned its way through the gate, opening a hole wide enough for a Dreadnought to pass through. The heat from the breach cooked the putrid flesh clothing its body, and it shrieked in pain through its fused-shut mouth, but its masters drove it on. Its snout plunged deeper, burying the full length in the gate. The platform upon the back passed under Justinian's position, exposing the adepts of the Dark Mechanicum working banks of toggle switches, or watching displays sunk directly into the diseased thing's hide. The tanks of bile around them gurgled empty, consumed by the unclean engines set in front of their control stations.

'Kill the operators!' voxed Justinian. Bullets, bolts, and las shot blasted at Squad Parris' position, eroding the smooth lips of metal to jagged, pockmarked wounds. A fly daemon flew by, lobbing a severed head into the room. It collapsed like a fungus, filling the space with toxic gases that ate at their softseals and corroded their breathing apparatus. The Primaris kept their aim on their targets throughout.

Justinian destroyed one of the traitorous tech-priests, his bolt exploding him to black scraps. His men killed another. Daemon-servitors turned arcane weaponry on the bunker, shearing off Donasto's head with a green sheet of fire. Justinian continued to riddle the adepts and their machinery with bolts, but his efforts did no good.

'The gate is breached. All defenders prepare for melee.' Dovaro's message was short.

On clanking treads, the daemon ram drew back and wheeled off to the side, reversing over hundreds of daemons and wailing cultists. It was under fire the whole time, and gushed reeking liquids. It squealed horribly in pain, like a farm's worth of swine burning alive, but its work was done. The horde parted, opening a path for a phalanx of Plague Marines to march towards the breach in the gate. The seven ranks at the front pushed wheeled shields, miniature versions of the great mantlets standing outside the beleaguered gate. The rest bore rusted axes and blades, and dribbling chem-sprayers. Covered by the thousand boltguns of their comrades, they marched in proud lockstep in a disgusting parody of Imperial discipline. Their armoured boots crushed the dead. Justinian and his men remained at their firing slits and joined their fire to others targeting the Death Guard, although their bunker rang to the hailstone rattle of endless rounds blowing on the exterior, and microshrapnel pinged ceaselessly around the room.

The Death Guard lost a handful of their number, no more, as they went through the gate into the steaming tunnel.

The wall was swarming with enemy. Cultists and daemons were shuffling through breaches along its length. Explosions blasted out from gun chambers. The last of the wall's weapons fell silent.

A bolt jetted past Justinian so closely its propellant burn flared in his eyes. It ricocheted off the roof and detonated.

'We can do no more good here,' shouted Justinian against the relentless firecracker snap of bolts exploding on the wall exterior. 'Michaelus, Achilleos, take the ammunition. Maxentius-Drontio, rig grenades on the door. Maybe that will kill a few of them when they break in here.' He ejected a smoking magazine from his bolt rifle and slammed another home. 'Retreat to the inner chamber.'

CHAPTER TWENTY-TWO

THE EMPEROR'S WILL

By evening battle moved away from Tyros. The coughing thunder of the defence lasers on Keleton troubled the twilight occasionally, but the time between their discharge was lengthening as the fleet battle drifted out of their lines of fire. The vast shape of Galatan grew, bleached out by the last moments of daylight's death. An airy painting of a castle, ramparts picked out in shades of ethereal blue and purple, glowing with ten million points of light. A phantom fortress whose destructive power was all too real. Armadas crowded it, fighting their own wars. Galatan's terraces of plasteel loomed behind the naval fight, a mountain range in space more backdrop to the struggle than a part of it, it seemed, as distant hills framed the combat of armies upon the ground. But these hills spoke with fire and thunder, targeting all and sundry around the fortress. The allegiances of the ships were unknown to the soldiers upon the walls of Tyros. Mathieu had learned enough of warfare at every scale to guess that Galatan was contested, and different banks of weapons fired on different targets depending on who held them.

The tread of armoured feet approached from behind. The machine whine of powered armour was well known to him now. Too light for a Space Marine. A Sister, he thought. He smiled to himself. Iolanth had come to him, as he had expected. All was as the Emperor ordained.

'Sister Superior Iolanth,' he said, without turning around.

'Frater Mathieu,' she said, and came to stand by him. She rested her red-armoured hands upon the parapet. The coming dark dulled the colour of her armour, casting it with a bloody tint. Such hands are steeped in the vitae of martyrs, thought Mathieu. Being near so pure a tool of the Emperor's will sent a shiver of delight through him that threatened to trip the castigator routines of his autoflagellator. He tapped the palm button with his index finger, considering setting it off manually anyway to punish his unseemly pleasure.

'It pleases me you use my humble title,' said Mathieu. 'Humility is a virtue in the eyes of the Lord of Terra.'

'A vain man cannot expect grace,' she agreed. 'Nevertheless, I respect you as militant-apostolic as much as I do a mere frater,' she said. 'You are bold, and fight with honour. Your reputation for valour has reached my ears.'

'Do not call me brave,' he corrected her. 'I do not acknowledge fear because I have nothing to fear. The Emperor is my comrade at arms, and protects me at all times.'

'Praise be,' she said.

'Praise be,' he responded.

'It is a hard battle,' she said, looking out at the flash

and roar of the plains, then up to the phantasmal castle. 'I wish I were away from here, in the fight.'

'You could be,' said Mathieu with a sly glance. 'Go down to the fields of worship, wield your holy tools in bloody praise, and I shall tell no one.'

She laughed at his conspiratorial tone. 'I have my duty here. We may be denied guardianship of the holy child, but we will stand ready to be called. The Emperor ordains it. The red sacrament must wait. What of you? Will you not go to the front?'

'I have been ordered to stay here also,' said Mathieu. This was something of a lie. He had requested to remain to be nearer to the girl.

'For the sake of the child?' she asked.

'Not entirely,' he laughed shamefacedly. 'It is because I annoy the most sainted primarch.' That much was true.

'Your personality, or your calling?' she asked neutrally.

'I am vain enough to believe he has a little time for me as a man, but he has very little respect for priests in general,' said Mathieu.

'Then what they say about him is true?' she asked. 'He does not believe in the divinity of the most holy God-Emperor?'

Mathieu nodded. 'Lamentably so. He witnesses all the wonders of his father around him, and yet he cannot see His power at work. Guilliman denies it.'

'How can he not believe?' asked Iolanth, troubled by the idea.

Mathieu spoke thoughtfully. 'It is as if he is willingly blind. He does not want to see it, so he does not. The Lord Guilliman rarely speaks of his father. When he does, he insists on His humanity. I see it as my holy purpose to open Lord Guilliman's eyes. To make him see, to help him *believe.*' He paused. 'I had a dream.'

'Good or bad?'

'A bad one, with a good message.'

'The Emperor speaks to the most faithful through dreams.'

'So it is said,' said Mathieu ambivalently. Let Iolanth draw her own conclusions.

'What did the dream tell you?'

'The grains of time slither by so eagerly,' said Mathieu. 'Battle goes on in the void and upon the plain. We teeter on the cusp of defeat. Soon that vessel, O mighty Galatan, will be close enough to accurately target the surface of this world, and the battle will be decided. If the traitors hold sway there, we will perish. Imagine how more likely a favourable outcome would be if the primarch were free to aid the defenders. He is detained here, and yet here on this world is the key to an easy victory. We should use what we have, aid him, and speed him on his way to orbit.'

'You are speaking of the child.'

'I am.'

'Lord Commander Guilliman ordered that she be held here,' said Iolanth.

Mathieu smiled serenely at the mist hanging over the plains, where Titans duelled with weapons of light and power, and a million men fought desperately beyond his sight. 'I would die to save the primarch. I would gladly suffer all the torments of the warp if he would see clearly for but one second the truth of his father's nature. I am sure if he did then mankind would prosper as never before.' He paused, then turned quickly to look the Sister Superior in the eye, and spoke fervently. 'Tell me, Sister Iolanth. Would you die to bring the son of the Emperor fully into His light, as I would?'

'I would,' she said. 'I desire nothing more than to serve the Master of Mankind with my life, and my death.'

'Then kneel,' he said.

She hesitated. He opened his hand and indicated the floor.

Iolanth dropped to one knee. Her braids swung over her face. Mathieu rested his hand lightly upon the crown of her head. 'I cannot tell you what is to come, for that is the Emperor's gift alone. But I shall tell that the child can save the primarch. By showing him he does not fight alone, but that his father is by his side, the primarch can be brought into the Emperor's light. She might save the whole Imperium, if she opens his eyes. Whosoever aids the girl will be called a saint.'

Iolanth looked up at him.

'Why do you not do it?'

'I cannot act. The primarch will be angry with the one who shows him the truth. I must be there to guide him once it has been presented to him. He will resist at first.'

'You are well placed to show him the way,' Iolanth said.

He nodded.

'Then I know what must be done,' she said.

'I will not command you,' said Mathieu. 'I cannot. If you decide to follow this course, it must be by your own decision.'

'I have made my choice.' Her voice dropped to a whisper. 'Bless me, militant-apostolic, so I might be forgiven whatever transgressions I must make to fulfil the Emperor's will.'

'Sometimes good intentions require bad deeds to realise them. The Emperor's grace already surrounds you. I can see it. The light of purity enfolds you.'

'I am a good servant. My faith is strong.'

'I see that. It is a pure faith, a powerful faith. That is why the primarch needs you when I cannot help him.' He gripped her head and closed his eyes. 'In the name of the Emperor of Terra, Lord and Master of all Mankind, I bless you and commend you to His protection.' He opened his eyes. 'Rise, Sister Superior Iolanth,' he whispered.

Iolanth stood. She gave Mathieu a fierce look.

'I am a warrior of the Emperor, and I shall serve Him unto death.'

Mathieu smiled. 'That is all He requires of us. Now go, and perform the Emperor's will.'

Iolanth's warriors were armoured from head to toe, but they could move silently when needed. Two of them ghosted along the corridor towards the part of the Shoreward Bastion where the girl was kept, the faint whine of their armour mechanisms hidden by the thump of weapons being fired a hundred kilometres away. They kept to the shadows, two at the rear, bolters up and ready to fire, a third out ahead, her knife in her hand. The lead Sister came to a soundless halt, her hand up. Her Sisters stopped a few metres up the corridor and covered her with their weapons.

The advantage of infiltrating your own facility was that you knew where all the blindspots were.

A sole member of Devorus' regiment stood guard at an intersection. There was only one; nobody expected an attack from within the Imperial ranks. The door was locked. All six of the indicator lights on the door's control panel were an unwavering red. Though Tyros was not currently under threat, the soldier took his duty seriously, neither too relaxed or too tense to do his job properly. He stood at wary ease, his lasgun ready across his chest, finger straight beside the trigger guard. His vigilant eyes flicked back and forth, covering all three approaches to the door, ahead, left and right. The Sisters shrank back when his gaze darted in their direction.

Iolanth approached him from ahead. He did not stand to attention or salute, but shifted his gun ever so slightly, ready-ing it to fire. He was a veteran killer. Ordinary men did not survive long in the Imperial Guard by taking things on trust.

'Sister Superior Iolanth,' Iolanth announced herself. 'I am here to see the child. Open the door.'

'I know who you are, Sister,' said the soldier. 'I can guess why you're here, and I'm not opening the door.'

Some soldiers were highly religious and held the Battle Sisterhood in awe. Some soldiers didn't give a damn. Devorus had chosen his sentry carefully.

'Very well,' said Iolanth. 'I shall frame my request as an order. Open the door.' She moved a few centimetres to her left. The soldier followed her enough to keep her fully in his sight, but he didn't turn his back on the corridor to his left where the three Sisters hid in the shadows.

The soldier brought up his gun and sighted down the barrel. 'Back away from the door, Sister,' he said. 'I can't let you through.'

'That is regrettable,' said Sister Iolanth.

The soldier was skilled, but she was better, moving to the side and grabbing the end of his lasgun with her open right hand. It discharged once, a lonely crack of superheated air. By the time Iolanth had crushed the barrel, the other Sisters had moved up.

The knife of the lead Sister parted the man's neck, destroying his vocal cords and opening his veins before he could call out. He fell with a helpless gurgle.

It did them no good.

A sensor blinked on the man's breast, noting his stilled heart. An alarm went off. Now the game was up, other Sisters came jogging down the corridors, and took up firing positions.

'Throne,' said Iolanth. The mission was turning regrettably bloody. The lights on the door blinked and turned blue. 'Lockdown. Squad Evangelis, remain here to repel reinforcements. Sister Rhapsody, krak the door. All of you, ready to follow me as soon as the way is open.' She readied her gun. 'The Emperor has decreed we face a challenge. In His praise, we shall rise to the test.'

Sister Rhapsody took an oval implosion charge from her belt and clapped it to the door. 'Stand clear!' she said, and withdrew.

The grenade banged. The door burst inwards. Rhapsody kicked it back into its housing and stood to the side, making way for Iolanth to step over the soldier. As he was twitching his last, she was moving down the corridor.

War blinked over the plains of Hecatone, casting coloured light upon the ceiling. Night was well entrenched, but battle raged. It will proceed for days, thought Devorus. He had welcomed the orders to remain behind, but now he was getting bored, and his companions made him uneasy. He itched to join the rest of the army in the simpler work of fighting.

There were four people in the room: Devorus, the child, the Sister of Silence and a giant Primaris Space Marine that Tetrarch Felix had set to watch over them. All Space Marines were strange to a baseline human, and most were emotionally stunted, with little interest in conversing with other men. But the Primaris type seemed even less talkative than their predecessors. This one stood in the corner, his blue armour blending with the shadows, still as a mountain.

The Sister was worse. She kneeled on the other side of the room, the point of her drawn sword against the floor and her eyes closed in meditation. She had a name, Voi, he thought. He had been told several times, but it wouldn't stick in his memory, and every time he reminded himself of it he doubted his mind. Her presence made him queasy. Despite the revulsion she engendered his eyes kept sliding back to her. When she had come near to him he had felt a terrifying, sucking nothingness, as if death stood at his side. He probed the sensation repeatedly, eliciting shudders every time, as if it was a sore tooth he could not leave alone.

He needed distraction.

'Why don't you tell me your name?' Devorus asked the child for the fourth time that day. By now, he had no expectation of an answer whatsoever. She'd not spoken to him since their first meeting. Both her physical and mental condition had deteriorated.

The girl pulled her knees tighter into her chin, her face buried in her arms, presenting a greasy head of hair at him. She had looked healthier when Iolanth had first brought her in. He half feared she was ill with one of the enemy's diseases. She had been given a long nightdress woven out of vegetable fibres brushed until soft, a fine gown of a sort worn only by the wealthy. It was kind to the skin, but the sleeves and high collar couldn't hide the scars of excruciation on her flesh, and there were stiff patches, especially across her back, where leakage from her wounds had hardened. The hexagrammatic bonds she wore pulled at her wrists and ankles. Across the back of her neck smaller chains snaked in and out of her hair.

'I'm sorry to keep asking,' said Devorus, putting a smile into his voice he didn't entirely feel. 'It seems like a reasonable question. We're going to be in here together for a while, until the fighting is done.'

Devorus liked being useless only marginally more than he liked being bored, in other words not at all. He'd had his fill of staring at the battle on the plain and the battle in the void. There had been precious little he could see during the day, even with his magnoculars, and now both conflicts had been reduced to glaring light shows that hurt his eyes.

He gave up and sat down on the room's only chair. Without realising, he had put his chair as far away from the Sister of Silence as it was possible to get, on the far side of the bed. This brought it closer to the Space Marine, but anything was better than being near to her. A moment's impulse had him kicking out his feet. Ordinarily he watched the way he behaved. He was a high-ranking officer, with standards to uphold, but he was so tired he was past caring. Resting himself for a few moments he felt the weight of months of exhaustion pile on top of him again. He grunted in surprise, a strange, breathy explosion of air he hadn't meant to make at all, and sat forward.

'Fine. Sitting is bad.'

'You're tired,' said the girl in a small voice. 'I can feel it.'

Devorus clamped down hard on his amazement at her speaking. He had to handle this carefully, or she'd fall silent for good, he was sure. 'Can you now,' he said with forced nonchalance. He pulled his hands across his face and yawned. His eyes did not want to stay open. 'You know, since the primarch arrived I've had some time to sleep. It's only made me more tired.'

'Why aren't you fighting?' she said. She still didn't lift up her head to look at him.

'The primarch, Emperor bless him, deemed my men and I worthy of respite from our long labours.' He leaned over and held up his hand to his mouth, comically shielding it from the Primaris Marine. 'He told me to stay here and look after you. He thought I was a good man for the job.'

'Tetrarch Felix gave the order,' said the Primaris Marine robotically.

'My, my, you can talk too,' said Devorus, turning to the blue giant. 'Well, yes, I suppose he did.' He remembered the words, and spoke them aloud, deepening his voice. '"Lord Guilliman will test her," the tetrarch said, he's got a very deep voice,' he explained to the girl. '"Until then, she remains here. Do not allow her to depart this facility. Do not allow anyone but yourself to have contact with her, Devorus. Consider these orders as coming from the primarch himself." Very serious stuff.'

The Primaris Space Marine still had not moved.

'Is that it? You're going to wake up for a spot of pedantry then fall back asleep?'

'I am not asleep,' said the Primaris Marine. 'I do not need to sleep for another thirty-six hours.'

'Fine,' he said. The Primaris Marine put him on guard almost as much as the Sister. His fear came out as irritation.

'I correct you because incorrect information compromises efficiency,' offered the Primaris Marine.

'He's a charming one, this fellow,' said Devorus. The girl peeked out from under her fringe. Devorus leaned in a little closer. 'Charm's probably not needed when you're that big. Isn't that so?' he said to the Primaris Marine.

The Primaris Marine said nothing.

'So,' he said. Clapping his hands on his knees and doing his best not to glance at the Sister again, he returned his attention to the girl. 'We're in here together. I thought asking your name wasn't an unreasonable question.'

'Kaylia,' she whispered. 'My name is Kaylia.'

Devorus smiled. That felt like a triumph. 'Thank you.'

'I didn't say before because it's not important any more,' she whispered. 'Only He is.'

'Why don't we talk about Him?' Devorus said. 'I'm getting a little bored you see, Kaylia, and he's not much of a conversationalist.' He nodded over at the Primaris Marine. He didn't refer to the Sister.

Don't look at her, Devorus thought. Just don't.

'He doesn't have much to talk about,' Kaylia said. 'He doesn't think like you. He doesn't care about the same things you do. Not food, or sleep, or love or peace. He wants to serve, like you, but that is all he wants. He wants to fight.'

'Really?' said Devorus. His eyes strayed to the hexagrammatic chains. They were proof against psychic ability. And then there was the Sister... Kaylia couldn't be reading the warrior's mind. He glanced at the Primaris Marine. He looked resolutely ahead.

'I can sense it,' she said. 'Ever since He came to me, I've known things about people without being told.'

'When did this begin?' asked Devorus.

'A week ago,' she said.

'Were your powers fully fledged?' he asked.

Ordinarily he kept what little he did know about psykers quiet. Talking about such matters brought unwelcome attention on a man, and he didn't know much anyway. What he did know was that it wasn't unusual for psychic tendencies to manifest during the teens. He wasn't convinced that was the case here. He looked Kaylia over carefully. Such times as he had been exposed to the abilities of nascent witches had been very different. Minor poltergeist activity, or uncanny readings of the Emperor's Tarot. People like that didn't tend to last long. Devorus had helped round up more than a few himself. The devices used to contain psykers had a devastating effect on them. Their minds dulled to the point of stupidity, they suffered pain. Devorus had seen chains like Kaylia's only once before, when a powerful witch resisted detention and the Black Ship crews had come down from on high like the vengeance of the Emperor Himself. The effect they had on the psyker had been terrible. When Devorus had touched them, they'd made him vomit, and he was as psychic as a ferrocrete block. So it was disturbing the girl wore them like they were jewellery. Even so, he felt no danger from her.

'They're not my powers,' she said. 'They're His.' She looked up at him defiantly. 'You want to serve, He wants to serve. So do I. I let them hurt me. I let them to show them that what I say is true. The Emperor. It is Him. He tells me to fight. Why am I being kept here? He doesn't want it. He wants to help the primarch.'

A witchfire glow glinted in her eyes. Phantom tastes

filled Devorus' mouth. Her flesh should be burning under the chains.

He swallowed. He glanced up at the Sister. She was staring at the girl with unfriendly eyes.

'You're afraid of me,' Kaylia said. 'You shouldn't be. I won't hurt you, but I must leave.'

'I think it's for the best if you stay here,' said Devorus. He looked again to the Primaris Space Marine, hoping for some indication of support. The warrior stared ahead, expressive as an empty suit of armour.

'Please,' she said. 'She'll kill you if you don't let me go.'

Devorus' spine went icy. He looked again at the Sister. She was standing, hefting her sword. Kaylia might be referring to Voi.

He stood again and straightened his tunic. 'We'll see what the primarch says.'

'He needs my help,' the girl said.

'We'll see what the primarch–'

The wail of the alarm cut Devorus dead. He stiffened. His hand went instantly to his holstered laspistol. The shouts of his men in the guardroom next door spilled out into the corridor.

An explosion followed, short and hollow. The Sister of Silence went to the girl's side, her massive sword held ready. Her proximity to Devorus made him nauseous, but again the girl seemed unaffected.

'Krak bomb,' said Devorus. More explosions followed. 'Bolters?' he said incredulously, but he already knew who was coming.

'Wait here,' said the Primaris Marine.

The Space Marine stepped sideways through the door without even looking to see what awaited him, his gun levelled and firing as soon as it was clear of the room. Devorus didn't heed him, and followed, peeking through the gap between transhuman warrior and door jamb.

Men were shouting. The air was thick with fyceline and the ozone smell of ionised air. The body of one his men lay on the ground. Devorus couldn't see much past the Primaris Marine. The Space Marine had his bolt rifle up tight into his shoulder, and was switching targets with alarming surety, squeezing off staccato bursts. The roar of a melta-gun changed that. The Primaris Marine staggered backwards. A wash of air hot with vaporised ceramite and burned flesh singed Devorus' nostrils. He was almost too slow in stepping back. His eyes swam with the heat. The Primaris Marine crashed down hard, a neat hole in his torso. Greasy meat smoke rose from the wound. Incredibly, he was still alive, attempting to get up with half his organs cooked.

A hail of bolts slammed into him, breaking his armour and detonating in his flesh. Fragments of metal peppered Devorus' leg. It hurt, but he had been injured worse than that before, and he drew his laspistol on the women advancing down the corridor. He didn't waver even when they paused to finish off his men.

Iolanth emerged from the gun smoke.

'Put the gun down,' she said. Her voxmitter granted her voice an extra layer of authority. He almost obeyed.

'I don't think I will,' he said. 'You better surrender, before this situation gets worse.'

'You can't hurt me with that pistol, not in this armour.'

'I could,' he said.

'You'd have to be lucky, and the Emperor is with me today, Devorus. You know what she is. The Emperor has a plan for her. You are a faithful man, a true warrior of the Emperor. Heed His call. He needs your help.'

'I would prefer it if the primarch were a judge of that. She's a psyker. She could be dangerous.'

'The primarch cannot see what is in front of him. She's no psyker.'

'Know him well, do you?' said Devorus. 'I'll take your surrender. Drop your weapons. Come on, do it now. This can finish, if you choose.'

Iolanth's warriors spread out across the narrow corridor, taking positions in doorways, covering the way they had come.

'You've seen the miracle she performed, Devorus,' said Iolanth. 'Those chains don't stop her. She is not warp-touched, but something else, something glorious.'

'I've seen a lot of things,' said Devorus. 'Some of them have been like this. Some of them have been performed by good people, others by people bad through and through. All of them have ended badly. She might save this world, but she'll damn it in doing so.'

'There are many powers at work in the galaxy. Not all of them are evil.'

He smiled sadly. 'I can't agree with that. It is always, always better to assume the worst.' He pushed his thumb along the power slide of his laspistol, bringing it up to maximum.

'Major Devorus, you are a good man. But good men must suffer so that all may live. They are blessed who are martyrs, for they shall be with Him at His side for eternity. Drop your gun to the floor, and you may continue to serve Him in this life.'

'You can't do this. These are the primarch's orders. The child is to remain here.'

'My guidance comes from a higher power. The highest of all.'

Devorus' finger twitched over the trigger.

'I can't let you. I'm sorry.'

Laslight flashed. The beam duration was too short to register on human vision. The noise of its passage and impact were too closely spaced to tell apart, blended into one loud bang.

Smoke curled over Iolanth's heart. Devorus was a good shot. Iolanth was only a metre away, but her armour was amongst the best in all the Imperium, and though her undersuit was visible through the hole, she was unharmed and unmoved. Devorus was mildly surprised to see he had broken the surface of the armour at all.

'I am sorry, Devorus,' said Iolanth. 'The Emperor's will cannot be obstructed by any man, especially one as inconsequential as you. May you live forever in the Emperor's light.'

Iolanth's gun barked.

Iolanth advanced into the room over Devorus' body, her weapon roaring.

CHAPTER TWENTY-THREE

THE PLAGUE GUARD COMETH

Morning broke most unwell, the whey-faced sun crawling into the sky. Light filtered through depthless mists, reducing everything to a silhouette, and making all appear unreal.

God's Wrath waded through noisome fog that had banked higher and higher through the night, until it overtopped the Reaver's head. The engine was as blind as everyone else, reliant on disrupted data pulses from its brother engines and machine senses crowded with false positives. The bigger picture of the battle slipped from Dunkel's grasp. His tactical overlays jumped with interference, pushing awful pictures over the manifold link that displaced his mission cartograph. The snatches that got through showed the fly-like formation of Mortarion's army from orbit, never disrupted no matter how many of its soldiers were slaughtered. The Legio Mortis continued to resist, its blighted god-machines doggedly holding their line to the east, though several had been brought low in the night. It angered Dunkel how effective the traitor machines were; their engine kill ratio was point five above that of the Imperials.

The larger fight was beyond him for now. Early morning saw the Legio Mortis forced back. Their line was finally losing its coherency. *God's Wrath* and *God's Will* were ordered forward into a gap that presented itself nearby. With Warhound support and a dozen of the Knights of Konor they plunged into the seething hordes of lesser foes on a mission of extermination, commanded to scorch them from Parmenio. The tactic was sound if a common one: penetrate the enemy, destroy the flow of reinforcements, and allow the lesser men and mechanisms of the Imperial war machine to break the attack at the front. But the enemy did not break. They came on without pause: tanks, daemonical engines, and thousands and thousands of infantry. The Titans vaporised them by the hundred. Tanks that dared raise their gun barrels towards the Titans' towering shapes were smashed to atoms. Misguided human cultists took terminal lessons in the Emperor's disapproval.

Did they repent of their sins? thought Dunkel. Did they apprehend the light of the Emperor-Omnissiah one final time before life was stolen from them?

Kill counters rattled upwards in cockpit displays. The sums were nominal only, for the weapons of the Titans were too destructive to allow accurate tallies to be taken of such small targets. Thousands and thousands dead, and hundreds added to the score with every frame-shaking discharge of the Titans' weaponry. All *God's Wrath*'s rockets had been expended. The lowly infantry were too far beneath the engine's reach to suffer the attentions of its chainfist. But feet did as good work in the slaughter as any arcane weapon, while the melta-cannon changed the living to steaming vapours.

Void shields throbbed under a heavy rain of shells. The fusion roar of the main armament was as repetitive as the pounding of surf. The reactor cycled up and down with each firing, its sound so much a part of Dunkel's being he had ceased to notice it. The Titan's feet raised steady quakes from the ground. Dunkel lost the sense of his own body. He and his men and their machine were one by the holy will of the Omnissiah, united in the dealing of death.

Some sense broke Dunkel from blessed unity, a ripple across the surface of reality as silky as a ring of waves upon a still cavern pool.

God's Wrath looked to the west, where Legio Mortis still held its ground, trading blows with Fortis and Atarus. Danger signifiers leapt up on his cartograph, and he turned his attention eastwards again. Three full households of pestilent traitor Knights were moving up around the comma tail formed by Mortis' staged retreat of yesterday, seeking to outflank Oberon and get to Fortis' rear.

A sure sign of a fresh push.

'I have enemy engine minoris activity, coordinates three-three-nine, seven-six-eight. Enemy Knights, moving in fast.'

'You are heard, and understood,' Urskein voxed back.

The Knights were but the vanguard. Blocky shapes vaster than Titans were emerging from the fog, or perhaps they came from some other dimension, materialising from nowhere into that place, that time, to oppose the Titans of the Machine-God. Where there had been nothing, now there was definitely something.

Dunkel squinted. Neither his eyes nor *God's Wrath*'s were giving him a clear view.

'Cleanse auspex, give me a view on those engines,' he ordered. *God's Wrath*'s horn array burbled along with him.

The shapes looked more like buildings than engines. They were tall rectangles, like bastions. But they weren't buildings. They were moving.

'Stabilised picter feed available,' voxed Adept Sine from the reactor room. *'Maximum magnification.'*

A grainy vision imposed itself over Dunkel's mind's eye, fed to him by the Reaver's glassy stare.

Seven enormous wheeled towers rolled out of the fog towards the Imperial line, surrounded by hordes of beast-headed humanoids.

'Cog and teeth. Where did they come from?' Urskein demanded over the vox. Communications were suddenly clear, like the foe had a sense of humour and wished to savour their dismay.

'Provide engine identification,' voxed Runstein, princeps of *God's Will*. He was back a few hundred metres, too far to see himself.

'They are towers, wheeled towers.' Datascreed scrolled through his MIU link display that had him pause in disbelief. 'They are made of... wood,' reported Dunkel.

'How can such things be a threat?' asked Runstein. He did not scoff. Dunkel felt his unease over the manifold. The laws of the universe were upended. They fought things woven from bad dreams. Why could a wooden tower not be as deadly?

'Be cautious,' ordered Urskein. *'Legio Oberon forward. Form up on* God's Wrath *and* God's Will.*'*

Titans of Atarus and Fortis adjusted to make way for

the change, pinning the Titans of Mortis in place with concentrated volleys while Oberon walked out from the line. Orders pulsed back and forth between numerous layers of command, exploiting this moment of clear communication.

Dunkel upped the magnification of *God's Wrath*'s augurs. Yellow fog scudded across the battlefield, obscuring the towers anew, and allowed no further detail to be discerned.

Concern sped the Titans into position. *Retribution* set itself behind *God's Wrath*. Its weapons were in range, and they spoke with one voice, targeted upon the lead tower. *God's Will* joined its fire. The ruby bands of laser destroyers, violent pink in the middle, lashed at the structure. The mists danced around the light, obscuring the target.

'*I see nothing. Maniple Five, report. Is the tower still standing?*' asked Urskein.

Dunkel had his mind's eye riveted to *God's Wrath*'s external feeds. The tower reappeared in the forward picter view through a billow of mist, undamaged, fires guttering on its front. 'No change to the tower. They are shielded.'

'*Then prepare to engage, close melee. Dunkel, you first. We shall topple them onto the masses with the force of our contempt. Maniple One, I request you divert and engage traitor Knight engines.*'

'*As you wish, Urskein, but you owe me a good kill,*' voxed Opisa Elias, princeps seniores of Maniple One.

'*Keep them from the superheavy tanks. Baron Konor, do we have your support?*'

'*It is an honour to march by your god-machines. We pledge to you our service.*'

'*God's Wrath, God's Will, forward, maximum power. Retribution will follow. Princeps Elias, advance your maniple and anchor position at point four-nine-two, six-six-four, engage with full weapons fire at distance. Cover our advance.'*

In a shallow arrowhead, *Retribution* and its guardians marched forward. Nothing could stand before them. They were the Emperor's vengeance manifest.

A green discharge flashed at the top of the leading shape. A smoky light arced skywards, like phosphor bombs thrown from a monstrous catapult.

Dunkel watched the missile resolve itself into a flaring comet. Anti-aircraft weapons opened fire all along the Imperial lines. Tracer shot flickered their belligerent dashes. Missiles slammed into the falling mass, but nothing stopped it. When it landed the earth convulsed, a retching shudder that shook the world. A hemisphere of green fire burst amid the Imperial lines. Pulsing energies filled the vox-net with otherworldly screams, and shortly thereafter came a physical push that lit foxfire along *God's Will*'s arms. As the force passed through the god-machine, its spirit shivered like a dog in the presence of ghosts.

'What by the Throne was that?' voxed Urskein.

No report came to them of the casualties the weapon inflicted. There was no one alive to communicate the damage. Then the data came pouring in, and did not stop. Thousands had died in an instant.

'*Increase speed!*' ordered Urskein. '*Death Bolts Maniple Five advance with fire. We must destroy the towers! I am requesting immediate reinforcement from Legio command. All princeps, pass on targeting details to allied forces.*'

From behind *God's Wrath* rivers of light flew straight as javelins. Super-heated fog danced madly around lines shocked clear by the las-beam's passage. House Konor's Knights swept aside enemy troops and armour, but without the support of heavier engines they would not advance far. Dunkel pushed *God's Wrath* to up its pace.

Now all seven towers flickered. Green balls of lightning hissed through the mist, discharge and passage near silent.

'*Void shields to maximum. Brace for impact,*' voxed Urskein. '*Trajectory–*'

His last words. The green comets fell soft as rain, four targeted on *Retribution*, three upon *God's Will*.

The howling static of annihilated void shields blared over the voxnet. *God's Wrath* was running before the noise ceased, aware before Dunkel was what the sound betokened.

Engine death.

Retribution's reactor exploded first, giving out in a maelstrom of heat that punched a hollow into the ground a hundred metres deep. *God's Will* died a microsecond after, falling down ablaze into the stinking mud. Its plasma core deactivated harmlessly, but the machine was dead, too broken to ever walk again.

God's Wrath weathered the electromagnetic storm of *Retribution*'s reactor failure, stumbling in its run but not falling. Burning liquid from *God's Will* sloshed onto its leg and scorched at its warframe. It wailed for its dead brothers, and picked up speed, pushing deep into the quagmire the enemy had made of the plains of Hecatone.

'The pleasure of this kill shall be mine, the pleasure of vengeance shall be mine!' shouted Dunkel, but if they were his words or the engine's escaping from his throat he could not tell.

The lead tower ploughed on through the muck, giant wheels caked in filth. It ran over the beast creatures thronging its base without care, lubricating itself with their blood.

The tower was not worthy of the name of engine. It was akin to the siege towers of backward peoples, nothing at all like the holy war constructs of the Machine-God. Iron plates streaked with orange armoured it foot to top, but the main material was of unfinished wood. Wedge-split planks layered the sides. Whole trunks were incorporated into its body. No sensible being would wish to see the forests that grew the timber, for the trees were convoluted and repulsive to look upon. The tower was covered over in their gnarled protrusions. Branches raked at their surroundings with the viciousness of claws. Slimy ropes held the tower together. Nails as large as men stuck bent from the lumber. Enormous leering faces adorned the three forward facings, their brass and bronze green, the nozzles of primitive guns protruding like tongues from their open mouths. Matter dribbled from every gap, coating the thing all over. Sheer-sided at the front, the tower sloped down at the back to a base housing a huge engine that belched noxious smoke. Pistons the size of *God's Wrath*'s cannon bullied the larger middle wheels into motion to move the thing forward. It was wholly primitive, wholly impure.

'Burn it!' roared Dunkel.

His order was superfluous. Already *God's Wrath* had made that decision. A cone of superheated air shimmered before the meltacannon, striking the tower in the middle. Strange energies rallied to hold back the fury of the god-machine. They failed.

Dunkel felt his crew and engine's savage glee as metal ran and mouldering wood caught fire. He would have fired again, but Dunkel's command of the engine's bellicose spirit slipped further, and *God's Wrath* took control. Surging forwards, injured leg still steaming with chemical burns, it built up to a lumbering run, drawing back its giant chain fist to strike.

God's Wrath slammed hard into the side of the tower. The siege engine was twice its height, but narrow based. It rocked upon its wheels, turning slightly from its path at the impact. With frenzied abandon, *God's Wrath* punched into the rotting side of the tower, chain blade pulling out vast, dripping splinters of wood. *God's Wrath* howled. Knights came stalking behind him, sensing a kill. Battle-cannons fired triple shell bursts into the wheels. Thermal cannons cut the middle axle in two.

The tower stopped, locked wheels smoking. The upper reaches were ablaze.

'If it can be wounded, it can be killed!' howled Dunkel, and prepared to deliver the final blow.

The tower had one final surprise.

Broad fans of putrid liquid vomited from the carven mouths set upon the tower, shooting out in vast arcs from the pipes. Filth rained to the tower's forward arc, showering onto *God's Wrath* and the knights prowling about his feet.

Void shields stuttered and sparked. The slop ran too slow to trip the displacement reaction of the aegis, but the liquid interacted with the field in some strange way, running down it in places like it was solid matter. In others, it washed past and slapped hard against the Titan's plating. Ceramite composite fizzed, plasteel burned. Armour melted as readily as plastek before a plasma torch. Dunkel screeched with the machine's pain. *God's Wrath* blared an angry fanfare, half in agony, half in defiance.

The tower gurgled. The pipes jutting from its scabrous back whistled out green-tinged steam, and the gargoyles vomited again.

This time, the Reaver's protective void shields did nothing, and the whole of the liquid burst over its torso. Hyperacid flooded down the front. The loin banner rotted to threads. Paint blistered and ran free, tinting the slop with stolen colour. Insulation was eaten from cabling. Hydraulic tubes perished and burst. The solution ate into the metal almost as fast as it did the softer parts, corroding the Reaver's angled plates to a spongy, sagging mass.

Death allowed the Reaver a final swing. The chain fist slammed into the face of the machine, chewing its way through, rupturing internal tanks. A wall of noxious fluid spilled over the tower, stripping it of its ugly garden of twigs and mould, its own structure melting as readily as that of the Reaver's.

The Titan came apart and slipped down the front of the tower, arms clasping it in belligerent embrace, as its legs disarticulated.

God's Wrath fell into the bubbling earth, sinking as it dissolved. Three Knights flopped around it, melting away. Their household blared a hymn of hate, machine born and machine voiced, and let fly into the holes in the wood carved by *God's Wrath*'s final blow with battlecannon and fusion lance. The ferment within burst aflame, then exploded with violence. The Knights hooted their revenge.

The first tower had been stopped.

Dunkel screamed as his machine died around him. Then, as the fluid ate through the carapace of the cockpit and spilled upon his human flesh, he screamed again. *God's Wrath* howled for both of them as they died, its final shout halfway between thunder and a leonine growl, then acid ate through the final connections, and the Reaver fell silent forever.

The remaining Blight Towers rolled relentlessly towards the Imperial Titans' line. In their wake daemon legions strode. They arrived by no mortal means, but drew themselves together from the mist. Vapours thickened into daemon form, and there marched thousands where before there were none. At the fore came uncountable nurglings, though that did not stop the plaguebearers following them from trying. Swarms of giant daemon flies descended from foul skies. Lolloping packs of beasts giggled with excitement at all the fun. Great Unclean Ones towered over their servants – vast, bloated hillocks of flesh who wobbled their way towards the enemy. Every form of horrific disease and disfiguration was displayed proudly upon their bodies. Wounds gaped, spilling entrails upon the ground. Streams of maggots tumbled from holes in their skin. The stink of putrescence clung to every one. But set in pox-scarred faces were eyes full of intelligent malice. Decay and blight made Nurgle's children strong. Sharp minds dwelled in their soft flesh. They set aside their japing for the day, and looked upon the foe with calculation.

Drums boomed, horns wheezed. The insane music of nightmares infected living minds. In the mortal contingents of Mortarion's army men dropped dead at the legions' arrival. They fell covered in sores, vomiting pus, clawing open their stomachs to pull out their guts. Those so favoured were regarded with envy by their comrades for receiving Nurgle's boons. The Death Guard saluted their daemon allies and looked to their own tasks.

As the daemons manifested, the formation of the fly's head grew enormous eyes and a long proboscis. By the Neverborn's might, Mortarion intended to break his enemy.

At the centre of daemonic host was the Plague Guard, Ku'gath's cavalcade, among the strongest of all Nurgle's legions. Seven of his greatest daemons ruled the Plague Guard, which was three times bigger than other legions, and seven times mightier.

They marched through the sucking marsh, pipes squalling, counts droning. Repetitive songs both silly and sombre belched from rancid throats.

Ku'gath's palanquin proceeded at the fore of this squealing mass. Around him were his six lieutenants: Septicus, the Gangrel, Pestus Throon, the enormously obese Famine, Bubondubon and Squatumous.

Beholding the legions would damn a man to madness, but though they had power beyond mortal knowledge, all was not well with the children of Nurgle. The warp's grip slipped from Parmenio. The refreshing breezes blowing from the garden of their master dropped. There was barely enough of its influence to sustain them, and every exertion, every sorcery incanted, shortened the measure. The soul furnaces aboard the towers helped, feeding the daemons with stolen essences and funnelling the winds of change through their beings. But one tower had fallen already. Should the others be laid low, then so would the daemons.

'Quickly! Quickly!' shouted Septicus. *'This war keeps the Plaguefather from his business! Back to Iax Ku'gath must go, to craft the greatest plague ever conceived. Quickly! Quickly!'*

The other lieutenants plied the lash over the backs of the rest, laughing with every switch.

Septicus' witchsight perceived the candles of men's souls wavering in the mist. They made a pretty display in their multitude, fit for any dreary fane, though their number shrank by the hundred, flashing brightly when they were taken into the warp. Fine as the sight was, flavoursome as they might be to savour, these lesser essences were not Septicus' quarry. The soul he sought was brighter than those of mortal men, a bonfire almost as bright as the one in himself, for the being he hunted was as much of the warp as it was of the materium.

Mortarion swooped low on moth's wings and wheeled about Ku'gath's tottering palanquin.

'Find my brother, and bring him out,' said Mortarion, his voice a phlegmy whisper. His wings beat soft vortices into the mist. *'Do not kill him. Not here. Wound him, infect him, smash his armies. But let him live! The seeds must be planted in the soils of despair. Let them flower, and take him towards desolation before we finish him on Iax.'*

Ku'gath scowled. Septicus, who had abandoned pipes in favour of plague flail and plague sword, interrupted his cheerful humming to reply.

'Lure him in, trap him, then away to Iax we shall go, there to complete the primarch's plan and ruin all this tedious sterility!'

The others snickered. Bubondubon laughed uproariously.

Mortarion's humour was not like theirs. He was more like Ku'gath in his solemnity. *'Find him!'* he hissed. The Great Unclean Ones laughed at his graveness as he flew away.

Tanks were lambent outlines like paper lanterns, illuminated by the souls within. Titans were huge, wicker men afire in pagan ritual, their own strange machine beings bright with half-realised life. The mass of infantry coming behind was an ocean of bobbing dots, luminous creatures in nighttime surf, secret, yet exposed.

The soul light on Septicus' side of the battlefield was of a different quality: red as old scabs, yellow as pustules about to burst. A simmering, fever-hot field of diseased light. Corrupted war engines flickered with the rage of the daemons enslaved within. Mortals who had pledged themselves to Grandfather were blisters, already fading. The giant Blight Towers shone a virulent green, lit by the souls burning on the furnaces inside. Where the two lines met, the lights blended, motes of blue white and morbid red aswirl.

'He is there!' It was the Gangrel who wheezed, lifting a skinny arm to point. His black talon shook with palsy.

Septicus looked. A huge shape, entirely material, lumbered behind three-score giant tanks. At its top, mounted like a beacon upon a distant shore, burned a soul so pure and powerful it hurt Septicus to perceive it.

'Guilliman!' Septicus called. *'Guilliman is there! He comes, he comes to find his doom! Forward, my pretties, forward!'*

Corroded bells rang loudly. The daemon legions shambled forward. The Plague Guard led the way.

Above, Mortarion shrilled a triumphant cry, and swooped low over the ground.

'Come out, my brother!' he bellowed. *'Come to me!'*

Mortarion banked around the Plague Guard. From above the noisome phalanx, he shouted once again.

'Roboute Guilliman! Come out! Come out!'

His challenge was answered. The Leviathan stopped. Its forward ramp opened.

Guilliman emerged, and Mortarion leapt into the sky.

CHAPTER TWENTY-FOUR

A HERO VANQUISHED

The Crucius Portis II shook with explosions as Squad Parris ran to the inner firing room and took up position overlooking the breached gate. From his station Justinian could see only a little way into the hole bored through the gates. The metal glowed still with its melting. There was a moment of quiet where his suit sang soft alarms. Several systems were damaged, and its hermetic sealing compromised. He could no longer trust it to protect him from the enemy's diseases.

He shut the tocsins off. There was nothing that could be done for the damage now. He sighted his bolt rifle into the bailey.

A bowed line of Terminators awaited the enemy. A thousand guns were trained on the entrance.

A moment of silence. Every warrior was still, gun pointed at the breach. Breath stilled in throats.

Through the tunnel, phlegmy battle cries echoed.

The enemy emerged into a wall of death.

Mortarion's sons came in fighting. They pushed heavy shields in front of them, lobbing their poison grenades over the top and shooting with admirable discipline through firing slits. No protection mundane or divine could shield them from the blaze the Novamarines pumped into that breach. Dozens fell, their shields burned through by lascannons and melta beams. But there were so many, driven on by a boundless hatred for the Space Marines, and they kept coming, those behind forcing the bloated dead forwards. Bit by bit, death by death, the Death Guard gained the bailey. Behind interlocked breaching shields and wheeled mantels they spread out, then the shields opened, and they poured outwards. At that point many more fell, tumbling like the petals of a rotten flower, but every wave felled allowed those behind to advance further, coming closer to the First Company's guns. The noise was tremendous, deafening to autosenses. Justinian's systems damped out the din, leaving him with the muffled crackle of innumerable gunshots and a hiss of white noise.

Squad Parris fired down on the inside of the gateway. The Death Guard were so tightly packed they could not miss. Ancient helmets were cracked wide. Beings that should have perished three hundred generations ago were finally ended.

Perhaps all would have been well if the battle had continued in this way. But on the outside, on the killing fields, the enemy were coring their way through the wall unopposed. The defenders of the outer line were dead from disease and poisons or withdrawn to the inner surface. Death Guard Plague Marines were not the only warriors in the enemy's army.

'The wall is breached at holdfast rho-seven, requesting aid!'

Justinian ignored it. Rho-7 was half a mile away, too far away to help. His battle was there by the gate. More pressing were vox-net reports of a breach closer to hand.

'Get to the door,' he ordered Maxentius-Drontio. 'Cover the ingress.'

No sooner had his second reached the portal than he shouted back into the room. 'They are coming up the inner corridor!'

Justinian swore and snapped off three more shots with his bolt rifle. He joined Maxentius-Drontio. A lateral corridor ran along the inside of the wall, linking the inner defences together. A set of reinforced doors was broken a hundred metres away, and Plague Marines were making their way along towards Squad Parris' position, the last on the line. Men attacked them from the bunkers to the side, but they were swatted down as the enemy cleared the fighting galleries and redoubts one by one.

Justinian opened fire, Maxentius-Drontio joined him. Their bolts peppered the lead warrior, a giant in putrid green whose armour ran with black juices. He danced a jig to the bolts' impact, absorbing enough explosive force to kill a platoon of normal men, until he finally collapsed. His comrades took stock of the armoured, inset doorway Justinian and Maxentius-Drontio sheltered in, and withdrew.

'Fourteen times we hit him before he had the manners to die,' said Maxentius-Drontio, taking cover from the enemy.

'Krak grenades,' said Justinian.

They tossed a handful up the way. The strangled bangs of implosions drove the foe further back.

'Seal the bunker door. Michaelus, cover it.'

The blast door slammed into position, its piston lock engaging with a solid thump.

'We shall kill as many of those outside as we can, before those within the wall get in to our position,' said Justinian.

'Aye,' said Maxentius-Drontio. 'Because they will get in.'

Justinian returned his attention to the outside. The situation in the bailey had taken a turn for the worse. The many breaches in the wall forced Dovaro to divert men holding back the foe at the gate. Alarms blared everywhere, barely loud enough to be heard over the endless roar of guns. Enemy were emerging from the wall corridors inside the defences. They were few at first, a mere distraction, but they kept on coming. Outflanked, the Novamarines took significant casualties. The Terminators stood firm, their weapons smoking as they fired and fired, but warriors in power armour around them were not so lucky. Many fell to plasma beam and bolt, while the serfs rushing to reload their masters' weapons were annihilated, and guns starved for want of bullets. Justinian and his men fired from on high into the press of Heretic Astartes, but their weapons had little effect.

For a few minutes, battle wavered on a knife edge. The Novamarines held back the Death Guard. Then a critical point was passed. No fresh ammunition was forthcoming for the First Company. Guns fell silent as they ran dry or their owners were shot down. Ground was gained by the sons of Mortarion. Without the sustained fire of the First Company, more Death Guard made it into the bailey. Soon the space was packed with a hundred. Howling madly, the enemy launched themselves into ferocious hand-to-hand fighting with the Terminators.

'They are through!' snarled Justinian, snapping off shots into the heaving mass of broken armour and diseased flesh beneath the bunker.

Brucellus was rummaging through the crates upon the floor.

'Brother-sergeant, we are running low on ammunition,' he said.

'Numbers,' said Justinian, still firing.

'Fifteen magazines,' Brucellus said.

'Divide them out. Now. No more pauses. We fire until all rounds are spent.'

A banging started at the door, then the loud click of magnets locking into place. A fusion roar followed moments later.

'Meltas,' said Michaelus. He shifted his gun, though it was perfectly aimed before. Metal creaked. The door held.

'Ceramite laced. They will be a while getting through that. They shall have to bring up something better to crack our shell,' said Maxentius-Drontio, the grin audible in his voice.

'They shall and they will.' Justinian looked around at his men. 'Until they do, we fight on.'

An awful buzzing sound, loud as a hundred chainswords, imposed itself over the battle's noise.

'By the Throne, what now?' said Achilleos. His wounded arm hung loose at his side, but his bolt pistol smoked in his right hand.

Justinian turned back to the firing slit to see a fresh horror emerge. From the hole in the gate burst a roaring cloud of flies. They were winged, and had composite eyes, six legs and all the other characteristics and form of Terran insects, but the similarity was superficial. They were daemon-kind, a pestilence from the Plague God's realm, and they carried death on their wings. They boiled past the bunker firing slit, obscuring the view for a moment, then swirled down and dived upon the defenders in the bailey.

The daemon-flies swarmed the defenders. Where they touched, they killed. Armour corroded into flakes of nothing, the Space Marines within reduced to disease-riddled cripples. Out the swarm fanned, corrupting everything it touched, clogging the workings of those machines it did not outright destroy.

Into the heart of this came a massive, one-horned figure, clad in ancient Terminator plate, an enormous scythe in his hands. From his back sprouted bony chimneys, and from them issued the flies in unending streams.

'By the Golden Throne of Terra, that is Typhus, First Captain of the Death Guard,' said Maxentius-Drontio. 'If I had but the chance at him myself...'

'Pray he does not hear you,' said Justinian. 'He will end us all.'

The Herald of Nurgle and vector of the Destroyer Hive had arrived on the field.

A Terminator moved to stop him. Typhus held out one hand, and the veteran sank to his knees, coughing up black blood through his breathing grille.

Swinging his scythe, Typhus pushed through the line holding the breach, cutting Space Marines in half like they were armoured in paper. Behind Typhus were his personal guard of Terminators, all as bloated and unstoppable as he. They followed, engaging their estranged white and blue clad kin in duels, continuing a battle begun long, long ago. Justinian's remaining men blazed away at the traitor captain's honour guard. Their bolts flashed to nothing on ancient aegis shields, or exploded harmlessly on gnarled armour.

Typhus strode brazenly for the Land Raiders behind the Terminators. The amount of fire coming down from the wall's inner surface slackened. Justinian continued to aim and fire methodically, his shots screaming off the cowlings of the enemy Terminators below. But he was unable to see far through the swarm of the hive, and the flies were spreading, killing every-thing. Shouts blasted across the main vox-channel. Pleas for help, panicked reports, all delivered to a background of weapons fire and the awful chants of the traitors.

Behind the Terminators came more plague warriors, and daemons, and now they flooded in, pulling down the veterans of the Novamarines First Company, widening the gaps and letting yet more filth through. The disciplined volleys of fire from the back of the Novamarines line degenerated into local firefights as the enemy engaged them at close quarters. The Land Raiders' engines growled, and they rolled backwards, putting distance between themselves and the attack, continually firing on the Death Guard as they formed a second line deeper down the main transit way. Typhus walked into their fire fearlessly. Lascannon blasts caromed off his energy shielding. He held up his hand again. Air rippled about his fist. Energy crackled around his fingers and he swung his arm violently aside. A Land Raider slammed into the wall, tracks squealing. Typhus squeezed closed his fist and the tank crumpled, shattered plates of armour banging off the walls and knocking loyal men down.

There was a roaring of fire from the back of the Imperial line. Billows of violet-tinged flame burned through the daemon flies from left and right, clearing them from the air.

A squad of the grey brothers armed with long-hafted force weapons and armoured in gleaming blue-silver Terminator plate moved to block Typhus' path. With them came Chapter Master Dovaro of the Novamarines, and his honour guard.

'Drive them back!' called Dovaro. 'Cast them out! We march for Macragge!'

In wordless challenge, Typhus raised his scythe. Warp lightning cracked upon its blade.

Justinian drew a bead on the first captain. He had rarely had a finer shot. He pulled the trigger, and the gun clicked empty. Cursing, he slammed home another magazine, but could by now find no easy target. The swirl of melee was too intense down there at the centre. Typhus moved with horrible grace, his enormous, diseased body no hindrance to his skill. His giant scythe was a weapon unsuited to combat. Typhus wielded it as if it were as carefully balanced as a rapier. Sickly light glowed around his hands and the blade of his manreaper. The warriors of the grey brotherhood jabbed and slashed at him with skill almost the equal of his, and their helms shone with a nimbus of pure warp power, but Typhus had been fighting for ten thousand years. He had been steeped in magic since he was a child. His mastery of blade and the warp were complete. One of the grey brothers fell to a spear of black light. A second was bisected by Typhus' scythe. The halberds of the grey brothers could find no way through to the First Captain of the Death Guard. The slippery wood of his scythe blocked them when it should have broken. The corroded head foiled every thrust and cut. Three remained.

Typhus forced them back, cutting the arm from one with a blurring sweep of rusty steel. The Grey Knight fell with a cry, black veins of corruption spreading from his wound and already marring the blue-silver of his battleplate.

A cry went out.

'Typhus! Traitor, lord of disease and filth! I challenge you! I defy you!'

Bardan Dovaro, master of the Novamarines, stepped forward to fight.

With a warlock's might, Typhus swatted aside the last two Grey Knights. His bodyguard fell on them, their own scythes rising and falling through arcs of blood. Dovaro's men moved to intercept the bodyguard, squaring off with the three warriors as their lords duelled.

There was no posturing, no talk. The two attacked each other furiously. Both were armoured in Terminator plate. Dovaro's was of the nimbler Indomitus type, Typhus' of the Cataphractii mark, slower but equipped with powerful field generators. Dovaro committed to a series of punishingly fast attacks, his double-handed power sword crackling. Typhus stepped back, twirling his scythe about in both hands, deflecting blows that would have deceived and ended any other foe.

'Dovaro is pressing the traitor!' Brucellus shouted. 'Victory is in sight!'

It seemed it was. The Chapter Master fought with such skill that Justinian thought Typhus would fall and the day would be won. He watched, spellbound at the skill on display.

Typhus retreated a few more steps, patient as time, until he saw an opening Justinian did not. His scythe moved with ruthless certainty, cleaving armour. Dovaro stopped with a jerk, his battleplate's supplementary musculature twitched by confused sensory inputs. His sword fell. He reached up to grasp the scythe's head buried up to the haft in his chest.

Wet laughter boomed from Typhus' white helm. He ripped the scythe back. The length of the blade burst through Dovaro's ribcage, its disruption field annihilating ceramite, bone and flesh. What was left of Dovaro's innards were hooked from their seat and scattered across the floor.

The Chapter Master died immediately.

'All is lost,' said Brucellus.

'Do not speak so!' snarled Justinian. His reaction to the Chapter Master's death was surprisingly personal. Dovaro was a man he could have followed.

In their dismay, the Novamarines stood firm, but the lesser men were losing heart. Such fear they had endured, such terror, that Justinian was surprised they had lasted this long. The loyalist line began to waver.

'Target the traitor's bodyguard! Rip away his protection!' Justinian opened fire again, tapping into the coldness of his anger to keep his aim straight. His bolts blazed true, but every shot was turned aside by the traitors' energy fields and heavy plate. Bolts exploded all around Typhus' men as the remaining Space Marines within the wall and ranged between the tanks of the Land Raider line fired at them. A single warrior fell, an eyeless, carcharodon-toothed horror whose Terminator plate was held together by twists of rusting wire. The rest laughed, shrugging off impacts that would have blown apart a Dreadnought, and continued with their slaughter. They reaped a bountiful harvest of flesh for their lord. The floor of the bailey ran with blood and they pressed forward hard. The fire from the inner surface of the wall dropped to nothing. The enemy were coming through in several positions. Soon, the Death Guard would be in among the tanks, and the final line would fall.

Justinian ran through his magazine rapidly. When he reached to his belt for a replacement, there was none.

'Ammunition!' he called.

'We have none!' said Brucellus.

'Brother, something occurs outside!' Michaelus jerked his head at the door.

Hammers clanged. A brief silence was followed by the sound of a large object being dragged into place. Drill bits screeched into the metal. A series of ominous clunks sounded through the door.

'They are coming through!' shouted Maxentius-Drontio. He cast aside his bolter and drew his bolt pistol and combat knife. 'Grenades when they breach. Knives and pistols after!'

Justinian dropped his empty gun. Outside, a new challenger approached Typhus. One of the Grey Knights, a psyker lord. His armour was a startling silver. Light of uncanny source shone from the angles of his plate. Badges of complex heraldry decorated his pauldrons and aillettes. A nimbus of warp energy played about his head, and his great halberd gleamed with arcane power.

The noises outside the bunker reached their culmination.

'Stand ready!' said Maxentius-Drontio.

In the bailey, the psyker lord and Typhus fought, much as Dovaro had fought before. The psyker lord matched Typhus in sorcery, and the air was rent with daemonic screams and wails as they contested for their souls.

A loud tolling sounded outside the door, distracting Justinian from the duel in the bailey. When he glanced through the firing slit again, he saw the Librarian thrust hard.

With an unearthly cry, Typhus staggered, the glittering spear of his foe run through his armour. Thin red blood leaked from the wound. Psychic power burst from the weapon, and the traitor reeled.

He had time to contemplate victory before the door to the bunker exploded inward. The last he saw was red hot fragments of metal ripping Michaelus apart, then a blinding light as the explosion engulfed him, then nothing.

CHAPTER TWENTY-FIVE

THE FATE OF THE WORLD

Iolanth took the girl out by Arvus lighter while her sisters sacrificed themselves to hold back the Astra Militarum.

They were away before the men broke through, flying through the evening over the harbour narrows and down the coast to where a crimson Rhino waited.

Iolanth cut off her vox and disabled her suit signum so she would not be tracked. The girl was catatonic, staring ahead with unblinking eyes. The lighter rushed away from Tyros, hugging the water surface. Out past the shelter of the island, the River Sea became choppy, and ocean spray slapped at the machine's hull.

The girl did not move once, but sagged against her restraints. Iolanth's eyes returned over and over again to the melted remains of the hexagrammatic chains. The girl's nightdress was scorched with heat. Long rips were scored through the cloth, lined with black. But her flesh was pure, no new scar on it.

'I'm sorry.' Those were the only words she had heard the girl say. 'I'm sorry.'

It happened like this.

Devorus' murder done, Iolanth had come in through the door, her bolter trained on the Oblivion Knight. To fight one of the Emperor's own handmaidens filled her with the thrill of blasphemy.

'I come to take the girl in the name of the Emperor. She is needed to win this war,' Iolanth had said, knowing she would not be heeded.

The Sister of Silence was ready and waiting. Iolanth had her gun up and was shooting as she came into the room, but the woman was so fast her bolts did little but blow chunks out of the walls. The girl screamed. Then the Oblivion Knight attacked.

Iolanth's skill as a warrior was feted in her convent. She regarded herself as living proof that women were every bit as capable as men under arms. She was a champion in her order. Xenos, daemon and heretic had fallen to her sword.

She had never fought someone like Asheera Voi before.

The Oblivion Knight came for her with the long talon of her blade extended in a forward guard. Iolanth cast aside her bolter, drew and activated her power sword with one movement, turning the sweep of her weapon into an interception that smashed Voi's weapon aside. Power fields crackled as the blades ran down one another. Voi was fast, disengaging and going for her opponent's leg. Iolanth swung her sword around in a move that saw her opponent's blade slide within centimetres of her thigh. Iolanth was quick, precise. Her moves were perfect, but Voi was better.

'Stop!' said Iolanth. 'It does not have to be this way. Let me take the girl. I do the Emperor's work.'

Voi's eyes blazed with hatred over her deep bevoir. *You betray your vows*, they seemed to say. *You betray yourself*. She struck again, turning and lifting and sending her sword buzzing towards Iolanth's throat.

Iolanth threw herself aside, her power armour's strength helping her leap clear. She landed badly, her power pack clanging on the rockcrete. Voi was on her immediately, driving her long sword at the Battle Sister like a spear. Iolanth rolled aside along the wall, her own weapon clashing uselessly along the floor. She rolled again. Voi's blade punched deep into the rockcrete, its disruption field carving a smoking crater. She renewed her attack so swiftly that Iolanth felt the beginnings of fear.

Iolanth parried three times, overhead, left and right, a swing of the wrist downwards to block a blow to her torso. Voi was so very quick that she had no opportunity to return threat either by riposte or direct attack. The noises of fighting outside were getting louder, many more lasgun reports adding to the bang and propellant whoosh of bolt weaponry. Devorus' regiment was moving in. She had to finish this quickly.

The only end she could foresee was her own. Voi outmatched her.

The Oblivion Knight battered mercilessly at Iolanth's defence and forced her away from the girl. The sickening presence of Voi's blank soul swamped Iolanth, numbing her nervous system. Her stomach rebelled. She was losing strength more quickly than she ever had before in a fight. Her mind was unfocused. Against the non-presence of Voi's being, she could taste the flavour of her own thoughts, and they disgusted her. Her yearning for glory, her fetishisation of duty, her abandonment of individuality, her pride. Voi was a pitiless mirror. Iolanth felt dirty and small in comparison to the woman's greater devotion to the Emperor.

'Stop!' she shouted again, taking a blow in a two-handed block that threw her back. 'You know Him as I do. We are both His servants! I do His will, as do you!'

Voi's eyes bored into hers. Her sword rose. Iolanth barely caught the strike. It cut across her side, opening the armour on her flank. The edge drew a burning line through her skin.

Already the sword was returning.

'*Stop!*' A voice. That voice. *His* voice. Iolanth moaned at its speaking. The word was a nail driven into her eardrums. She tasted blood in her mouth.

'*Stop now,*' the voice said again. '*I command it.*'

She and Voi staggered; the words had a pressure that hurt. The girl rose up from her bed where she hovered, floating into the air. Golden light boiled from her skin. The hexagrammatic chains glowed red hot, then white, and then with a vaporous rush evaporated into scalding steam.

The girl drifted upwards unharmed and turned upright, so that her dirty feet were hanging three feet from the floor. The light burned most brightly in her eyes. A divine light. The light of the Emperor.

Voi paused. Iolanth treacherously took her chance, hating herself for the blow, but Voi saw it coming, and caught Iolanth's sword upon the quillions of her weapon. They pressed into one another until they were face to face, armour clashing, noses almost touching as the golden light flared brighter.

Voi shook her head. With a savage twist she wrenched Iolanth's weapon from her hand. It bounced off the floor, its power field cut out, and it skittered into the corner.

Voi moved in to finish her.

'No,' said the divine voice. Voi flew sideways, bent at the middle as if caught hard by the swipe of a giant's lash. She crashed into the wall, and fell down.

Iolanth looked up at the floating girl surrounded by the nimbus of energy. The girl stared back, mighty, imperious, all powerful.

'Oh, my lord,' Iolanth said. She fell to her knees, her head bowed and eyes shut tight, waiting for judgment. 'Oh, my Emperor.'

'I'm sorry,' said the girl, in her own voice. 'I'm sorry.'

The light fled. A soft thump of a body hitting the floor had Iolanth open her eyes. The girl was on the ground, breathing shallowly and staring at the ceiling. The skin round her eyes was blistered. The whites were red. Tears coursed down her cheeks. Outside, the bang and crack of fratricide continued.

Wincing at the pain of her wound, Iolanth retrieved her weapons then scooped up the girl. She spared a glance for the unconscious Sister of Silence. Iolanth judged that her back was broken. She thought for the briefest instant of killing her, and knew for that consideration she damned herself.

She left the Knight behind and gave a silent prayer she would be found and treated.

Sheltering the girl's limp body with her armour, Iolanth burst from the door. Lasgun fire smacked into her back, setting her cloak on fire as she fled to the stairwell. On the roof she boarded the Arvus lighter.

The vox-link to the cabin crackled harshly, shaking Iolanth from her recollection.

'Sister Superior, we will be landing in two minutes.'

Iolanth readied herself. The road to perdition awaited.

The Arvus flew towards a bank of shingle glowing orange in the rising sun. Water spray arced high behind the ship as it came in to land. Through the pilot's canopy Iolanth had a glimpse of a tideline of dead creatures slain by the Plague God's sickness. The ship banked over furze-cloaked sand dunes, then slowed, and set down near a Rhino covered with camo netting.

'Disembark. Leave no trace of us on this craft,' she told the two Sisters in the cockpit. 'Then burn it.'

She went back to the passenger bay. The girl had flopped back into her seat at the landing, but still stared off into nowhere with the same expression. Iolanth unbuckled her and lifted her up. The passenger ramp hissed down. There were three more Sisters of Battle waiting to help outside. Iolanth handed the girl off.

'Where are the others?' asked one of the Sisters.

'Gone to the Emperor's light, Sister Verity,' Iolanth said.

'And the girl, will she wake?' Sister Verity followed Iolanth as she strode across the night grass towards the Rhino. Other Sisters were pulling back the camouflage. Lumens blinked on. The engine turned over. The side door opened, spilling red combat lighting into the dawn, and the girl was taken aboard.

'The Emperor willing,' Iolanth said.

'Then it will happen,' said Verity passionately.

'I have faith it will,' said Iolanth. 'He came again to me. When I was retrieving her. He cast down one of the Sisters of Silence, a Knight no less, to allow the girl to be taken.'

'Then we are blessed.'

Iolanth paused in the circular hatch of the Rhino. The two Sisters who had piloted the Arvus lighter ran from it.

It exploded behind them. Iolanth watched it burn.

'We are either blessed, or we run pell-mell into the arms of damnation. Let us pray we are doing the right thing,' she said, and clambered aboard.

The Rhino drove through crowds of soldiers into a storm of iron. Downpours of shells cratered ground already cratered a hundred times. Beams of coherent light tore up the sky. Violence came their way unheralded, always shocking. Bombs cast from distant guns murdered indiscriminately, culling those who expected to die in that moment along with those who thought death waited a few hours down the line.

War is chaos. Information flows sporadically whatever technology an army may possess. Iolanth's group passed through the rear lines of the army without incident, just another boxy troop transport struggling its way to the front line. If news of Iolanth's crimes had left the walls of Tyros, they had not reached anyone who might have stopped her. Would any have cared to, she wondered. Long columns of troops strung themselves out across the shattered plains, scattering under bombardment, then drawing back together when the shells ceased. The soldiers at the rear were without the blessings of gene-seed or the strength of her faith to shield them. They were normal men and women with only the basest training, flimsy equipment, and a vague, half-believed hope that the Emperor might save them from a fate worse than death as protection.

She and her warriors were a symbol of their distant god. The crimson Rhino, decked in symbols of devotion, brought cheers and tired waves from many of the soldiers as it drove by. Some fell to their knees and prayed. Priests pointed them out, shouting blessings and encouragement. Entire regiments made way, stepping into stinking ooze to yield the road to the Sisters.

And they did not even know what travelled with her. Oh, Iolanth thought, if they could see *her*.

The army was strung out between waystations, depots and medicae camps. Guilliman had drawn a grid of neatness over the wastes of Hecatone, sectioning Mortarion's vandalism with comms lines, link roads, exactly spaced resupply points and all the rest, as if he could turn back the tide of chaos by overlaying it with order. The primarch's hand was everywhere in the organised nature of retreat, reinforcement and resupply. A lesser commander would have been defeated by the terrain alone.

Regiments passed each other in opposite directions either side of Iolanth's tank, heads down. One column comprised battered units returning to base immersed in the horrors of what they had witnessed, their skin burned, limbs bloodied, their blinded comrades in long columns with hands rested upon the shoulders of the men in front. Reinforcements passed the opposite way, occupied with the fear of what they might see. Iolanth entertained the notion of throwing open the large firing hatch over the Rhino's passenger compartment, and showing the girl to them all so that they might draw strength from the saint.

If only everyone could be made safe, but she had known almost from birth that it was impossible to save everyone. They said the Emperor protects, but most of the laity misunderstood the saying. They assumed the Emperor would protect them personally, but the Emperor's role was to safeguard the species. A single man meant nothing at all. Though every event of every miserable human life howled out this truth, people still hoped, still prayed to their embattled god that He watch over them against all evidence.

It was sad, hopeless. The knowledge would crush the spirit of every human being, even her, were it not for miracles like the saint.

'The Emperor protects,' she said into the rumbling, jerking progress of the Rhino. She looked at the girl.

The saint sat mute, her eyes staring straight forwards.

When they became stuck awhile in a shell hole she did nothing to help. Sister Verity gunned the engine and uttered words not fit to pass the lips of the Emperor's warrior maidens. Only prayer from the Sisters caused the tracks to snag and haul them from the quagmire. After that, the ground became ever rougher. The lands of Hecatone had been well drained, with good soil suited to all manner of food crops. The marsh that had overwhelmed it was drying, but was still so sodden that the grains of dirt and sand that made up the earth had become a thick suspension, deadlier than free flowing water, for what it caught it would not let go, and where quicksand did not hold sway, the ground had been heaved up into soft hillocks by repeated shelling. The temporary roads laid over the top drew together, becoming fewer in number the closer they came to the front. More often they were blocked, bombed, or clogged with the wounded. In those cases Iolanth ordered her driver to follow the original roads between the region's towns, but these too were jammed with vehicles and soldiers trying to find their way, and often they were forced to detour across treacherous ground. They prayed for clearer routes.

Still the girl said nothing.

They passed the army's fighting rearguard, where command centres were set up, staffed, filled with frenzied activity then taken down again to be moved half a mile further on as the battle shifted. Batteries of long-range artillery occupied the brows of low hills, where the mud held its shape. The guns spoke without pause, their barrels glowing hot. Missiles screamed from racks while officers shouted pointlessly at servitors to bring reloads from haulers. The mist strobed with the firing of guns. Distant gunfire crackled from afar, sharp as dry leaves or ration packets trampled underfoot. They ground slowly past six Deathstrike launchers primed to fire, their missiles tilted. They looked benign, blunt, harmless. When the first crawled off its launch ramp, so deceptively slowly, it looked like it could not fly, but would belly-flop into the mud not far ahead. But it rose, and rose, disappearing to become a moving sun in the fog. The others followed like fledgling avians leaving their roost for the first time, rising uncertainly into the morning.

Three minutes later white light sheeted the world, and the ground shook. The Rhino was passing an entire regiment of men and women waiting to be ordered into battle, all of them huddled into approved brace positions. The burst of atomics turned them into solid pieces of darkness. When the initial flash dispersed, whistles rang, and the soldiers sprang up and began jogging. Hot winds scoured the mud, dissipating the mist at first, but great volumes of steam rose from the drying earth, and it quickly thickened again. The troops vanished, swallowed by fresh effusions of vapour.

They passed more regiments attending to the task of war. As they moved nearer to the front the roads quieted a while. They moved aside to allow a Space Marine Scout biker laden with message pouches to slew off down the muddy road. Then the rearguard was left behind, and they came to the start of the killing fields.

The situation behind the leading front gave a false impression. Shifting battlelines broke off pieces of themselves and strewed small wars across the plains as the Imperial army pushed forwards. Between the rearguard and the principal combat zone was a collection of desperate struggles dying off like neglected fires. All manner of forces faced off against each other. A fierce firefight raged around a ruined agricola where light infantry and sentinel walkers fought renegade Space Marines. Elsewhere, squadrons of tanks duelled. Ahead, a pair of Titans, isolated from their battlegroups, traded salvoes of raging energy while Adeptus Mechanicus cyborg troops battled a horde of pestilent, goat-headed mutants around their feet. There were signs of trench networks and the like, laid down in the earlier battles when Parmenio fell, but neither side made much attempt to occupy them. Only nearer the front did these isolated skirmishes clump together into grand battles, where entire Chapters of Space Marines made war in the mud with their damned brothers, and Astra Militarum soldiers fought bayonet to claw with tides of shrieking abominations.

These things too they passed. Iolanth expected trouble as they joined the raging interface of traitor and loyalist, but the Rhino passed them all without detection. They were simply not seen. Holes opened in the front to let them through. Iolanth gave a thankful prayer, for she knew this was the Emperor's doing.

The state of grace would not last. To achieve her goal,

Iolanth had to go to the one man in the army who would certainly kill her for what she had done. She had to reach Roboute Guilliman. She felt it as an ache in her bones, her heart and her head. Her body was urging her to the primarch's side; He was telling her where to go.

They reached the place where god-machines made war in number. Their torsos and heads were lost in the murk. Their disembodied feet trailed streams of water and blood as they lifted and planted themselves in the churned earth. Actinic flashes blazed high above. Rattling cracks and weird moans sounded from the heavens where the engines fought. Seeing these mighty avatars of her Emperor so near dazed Iolanth's mind. There were so many of them, arrayed in long lines and phalanxes. War had progressed so far it had come full circle, back to the tribal wars of ancient man, the first wars, conducted by a handful of champions standing in a field, smiting each other at close range until one side gave way. Only their size had changed.

'Sister Superior, I have located the Lord Guilliman's Leviathan.' Sister Verity's voice broke the spell. Iolanth turned from the view slit.

'Take us towards it, fast as you can,' she said. The vehicle jerked around on one track as soon as the words were said, slipping slightly, then driving true. Iolanth looked at the girl. 'The fate of the Imperium is in our hands.'

CHAPTER TWENTY-SIX

NEVERBORN

Roboute Guilliman disembarked first, against the wishes of his guards.

'I will lead the way, as it must be,' he insisted.

Maldovar Colquan and his Adeptus Custodes begrudgingly obeyed, and followed the primarch in a shallow crescent. Flanking them were a dozen champions of the Sisters of Silence. The Victrix Guard came next, moving quietly down the ramp, their guns high and steady as they scanned the blank fog. They spread out on the polluted mud. Their colours were radiant spots for a moment, but then, like paint dissolving into water, their vividness faded into the murk. The fog was thick as wadding. It could be prodded and shaped. An intimidating malice camouflaged itself within the swirling droplets, watching the champions of humanity with greedy eyes.

Guilliman surveyed the wall of fog. Moisture beaded on his armour. Droplets ran down the plates. The primarch was a knightly champion from a distant age at the castle gates of his enemy, the conclusion of his quest ahead, where death was as likely an outcome as success. Or so it should have been. What he saw was... Nothing.

For hundreds of kilometres across the plains guns rumbled steady thunders. Titans trod monster heartbeats. Out to the left and the right of the Leviathan, Baneblades and Stormhammers in the heraldry of Ultramar forced a path through the cloying mud. An Astraeus superheavy tank grunted by, its grav field pounding the earth into a seeping pancake. But all their noise was stolen by the fog. Their colours were drained away, their forms eroded and consumed as they moved into position. They dissolved. The primarch and his entourage might have been lost on some desolate highland alone. Though they were close to the crawler, close enough to touch its open ramp and bathe in the clean blue light shining from inside, even that seemed far. Nurgle's mists forced forbidding distance in between. War raged everywhere but where the primarch was. In front of Guilliman there was a moist void. No foes, no brother, only blankness, cold and soul-sapping damp.

Unimpressed at Mortarion's ploy, Guilliman made a dismissive noise, and spoke a quick order into his vox pickup.

Several hundred Space Marine infantry in many colours emerged around the crawler and formed up, bolters ready, quiet, tense, eye lenses glowing like phantoms in yellows, greens, blues and reds.

'My brother is a coward,' Guilliman said. He then drew the Emperor's sword, and held it aloft. Fire burst from the edges and guttered in the small winds of distant detonations. The mist moved against the breezes' direction, shrinking from the fire.

'Mortarion!' Guilliman shouted, his godly voice amplified a thousandfold by his armour. 'I am here. Come and face me!'

Silence.

'Mortarion! I am your brother, the last loyal son of the Emperor. If you have any shred of courage, you will face me!'

Guilliman's clarion voice was swallowed up without a trace.

Guilliman lowered his sword. 'Face me,' he said. 'He calls me out, but does not come.'

'He will not, my lord. He wants to goad you,' said Sicarius uneasily. His voice, so much lesser than the primarch's, was strangled to a whisper.

'Then consider me goaded,' said Guilliman. 'He wants to draw me out, I want to draw him out. We have the same aim in this war. It is inevitable we fight. I have a trap for him, he has the same for me. I want him here, now, so we can conclude this affair.'

The earth shook. Colquan glanced to the hidden skies.

'We do not have long to wait for the end,' he said. 'Galatan arrives. Its mass perturbs the world. We do not know who holds it, and soon it will open fire. This place is not safe. We should get you away from here.'

'I agree with the tribune. You must have the upper hand,' said Sicarius. 'I urge you to withdraw. The Blight Towers–'

'I will not withdraw until my brother faces me,' Guilliman said firmly.

'Where are the Neverborn?' asked Colquan. 'The Titans saw them. The psykers within the crawler say a horde of thousands should be here.' He and his warriors waited around the primarch, vying subtly with the larger Victrix Guard to protect him.

'They are here,' said Guilliman. 'This god of disease has a sense of theatre, that is all.'

In answer to Guilliman's statement, a bell tolled with a note of such misery all who heard it were touched by a sublime melancholy.

'They come!' said Sicarius.

'I will slaughter them in such number, Mortarion will come at me in wrath,' said Guilliman. 'Stand ready!'

A second toll rolled out, billowing the mist into dragon's breath. Roils grew faces that gibbered to nothing on a growing, putrid wind.

Colquan and his men presented the blades of their guardian spears. Sicarius murmured the names of his lost Second Company to himself in private litany as his men fanned out further. The taskforce of Space Marines split, squad by squad, maximising the efficacy of their firing positions.

'I am Roboute Guilliman!' shouted the primarch. 'I will not stand for your presence upon this world!' Stoked by his anger, the flames of the Emperor's sword flared higher.

A third toll, close now and loud. The fog twisted in agony. Misty figures danced in painful ecstasies, teased apart, reformed, howled and dissipated.

The belligerent song of Titan warhorns lowed back. The ground quivered to their tread. Guilliman stood at the head of an army of metal gods.

Music played, doleful and mischievous tunes at playful war. From the fog a carnival of decay appeared. A carpet of titter-ing, squat imps scurried out first, rolling over each other in their hurry to find fresh meat. A droning set up over the sound of pipe and bell. Lazy shapes flitted overhead. Huge horned beasts towered behind. Giant swarms of buzzing flies switched back and forth over the horde. Shortly after the sight, came the stench.

Guilliman gripped his sword. 'Open fire,' he said.

The tanks to the rear spoke as one.

Announced by thunderous cannonade, the primarch charged.

Iolanth's Rhino moved towards the Leviathan. The crawler swam through the mist, disappearing and reappearing with uncanny inconstancy. Though its tracks were not engaged, its position was in flux. One moment it was four hundred metres, the next two hundred, the next a thousand, to the left and the right and then almost behind.

'I cannot keep a fix on the command crawler,' Verity said, her frustration plain. 'It keeps moving!' The Rhino jiggled as Verity tried to maintain the correct heading.

The girl stirred, and looked up. Her hair was greasy and lank, and her skin had become pale. Sweat sheathed her face. Her lips were cracked and white, but from her eyes shone a glimmer of the golden light that made her seem purer than ever before.

'We are nearly there,' she said. She looked at Iolanth. 'You must guide me to the son of the Emperor.'

'I shall,' said Iolanth. 'But first you must guide us.'

After this brief exchange the girl hung her head again. But now the Leviathan stayed where it was supposed to be. The Rhino finished the rest of its journey fast, coming so close it drove under the aegis of the crawler's void shields.

'Stop here,' said the girl weakly. 'We must walk. Please, Sister, help me. My strength is gone.'

Her pleading face stirred Iolanth's heart. She was so young, and the power in her was draining her soul away. But it had to be, when the loss of one soul was set against the loss of billions.

Iolanth bent down to help the girl up, wincing at the pain the movement brought to her wounded side. She allowed her to drape one weak and boneless arm over her shoulder. 'Are you ready?'

The girl nodded.

'Then we shall go.' Iolanth hauled her up. She weighed next to nothing.

The rear ramp opened onto soft ground. Dankness blew in along with a cacophony of gunfire, moans and terrible shrieks.

Iolanth's Sisters ran out ahead. Iolanth followed, her bolter held one-handed, the other supporting the girl.

Tank fire boomed all around them. The giant cannon at the front of the Leviathan pealed thunder and belched flame. The girl looked up at it fearfully.

'Pay it no attention, we will get you there,' said Iolanth.

Six Sisters fanned out either side of her, bolters panning across the racing mist. The battle had moved on. The bubbling remains of Neverborn were strewn liberally in the mud, intermingled with the occasional corpses of the Adeptus Astartes whose bright livery broke the slick of residue with colourful islands.

'Follow the thickest part of the corpse trail,' said Iolanth. 'It is there we shall find the primarch.'

The mist deadened sound. The battle seemed distant, right until the moment they came upon it.

A slobbering thing bounded out of the mist without warning, cannoning into one of Iolanth's Sisters. The beast licked her effusively, picked her up in its mouth and tossed her into the air. Acid burned through her battleplate. By the time the beast lolloped over to play some more, she was dead. All this happened before the rest of Iolanth's group could react.

The daemon beast nuzzled the corpse in whining disappointment. The first gunshot made it spin around with fresh excitement, sending its mop of tentacular hair flopping wildly. Here were some new friends, its moronic face said. It let out a happy yipping, then ran at them.

It was an ugly thing, part mollusc, part canid, part man, a collection of body parts that should never have been made into one being, gone rapidly into death and decay. But it was alive, in its way, and enthusiastic. It bubbled and giggled and barked.

Bolts slammed into its slimy hide. Chunks blew off it. Slime wept from the craters in its flesh. On it ran.

'Bring it down!' Iolanth shouted. 'Now!'

Verity tracked its movements, her boltgun steady in her grasp. She waited for the last moment. She waited so long, Iolanth thought the opportunity gone.

Yelping playfully, the beast of Nurgle ran at them.

Verity's gun shot once. The creature skidded to a halt, frowned, and looked up at the hole drilled into its squamous forehead. Blood leaked out. It made a curious noise.

The bolt exploded. The beast keeled over with a disappointed whimper and dissolved into the soil.

'Their faith is not so strong as ours,' said Iolanth with satis-faction. 'See how quickly they decay. The lords of the warp have no sway here.'

'Their power here is limited and they are growing weak,' the girl said wearily. 'But there is worse ahead.'

* * *

Roboute Guilliman plunged into a crowd of malodorous beings. Plaguebearers was their common name, though they had many others. They pawed at him with slippery hands whose skin split over puffy flesh. They snapped black teeth and moaned his name. Swords of crystallised death, deep green and black, swung at him, and while they fought they counted on and on, a relentless murmur of meaningless numbers.

Shells ploughed into the horde, blasting daemons to scraps, limbs wheeling high on pillars of fire, dissolving into black sludge as they flew. Titan weapons ploughed up flesh and earth, mixing them together, adding them to the fog as superheated vapours.

'You are weak!' Guilliman shouted into the face of a rotting horror. 'Your souls have little purchase on my realm! You are not welcome! Begone back to the filth whence you came! Begone!'

The Emperor's sword blurred around him in fiery orange arcs. All the daemons that it touched shrieked piteously as their essences burned in the Emperor's wrath. The sword was a potent tool of war against any foe, but there was no greater weapon against the Neverborn. Suffused with the power of the Emperor, it burned them to nothing, cleaving their unnatural souls to tatty streaks of psychic energy. Slowly, realisation dawned upon the tallymen of Nurgle that Guilliman was a threat to their immortal existence. They wavered, and fell back in terror, their count warbling. Guilliman pushed forward hard, exploiting their fear of him to drive deep into their ranks.

'I bring you the end, the true death, the destruction of your wicked souls! In my right hand is the glory of the Master of Mankind. You have no place here!'

The sword cleaved. The sword hacked. The sword roared fire. Its touch was death to any daemon, and they fell in staggering number before Guilliman. Tribune Colquan and his warriors kept close by Guilliman's side. They fought apart from one another, each golden warrior surrounded by a mass of diseased bodies. Their guardian spears hummed through the air in blurs, lopping off limbs and splitting torsos. They were individual warriors following unique paths. Their techniques were their own, irreproducible by any but themselves.

In an arc around the blue-clad primarch and his golden bodyguard fought the Sisters of Silence. Where they went the Neverborn shrieked and died, their essences unwoven by the null fields of the Sisters' abyssal souls.

Captain Sicarius and the Victrix Guard expressed another form of martial mastery. Where the Sisters and Custodians fought loosely grouped, the Space Marines were a single unit, each one a component in a machine of destruction. Their bolters banged in unison, blowing apart daemons by the score. Further out, other Space Marines, less exalted, pushed the wings of the wedge as Guilliman headed deeper into the horde, widening the gap. And behind them rolled the superheavy tanks of Ultramar, their guns smashing down the daemons at point-blank range, so that their heraldry was covered in curdled blood and the slime of disincorporating warp things.

Silence became maelstrom, Guilliman at its eye.

Giant flies burred overhead, their riders tossing putrescent heads into the infantry following the tanks. Guilliman kept his mortal warriors back from this push, but even Space Marines fell as the heads exploded in clouds of ravenous spores, even Space Marines found their bodies ravaged by disease. White Scars bikes roared past, a blizzard of white and snapping pennants. Leaping beasts licked affectionately at tanks, their acid saliva melting through armour and exposing the crew to the poisonous air. Warp energy targeted fighting vehicles. Nurglings poured into broken armour. Space Marines wrestled with daemons whose strength belied their feeble appearance.

The daemonic horde pushed back against the Imperial advance. The lines ground to a halt, but not where Guilliman strode. He pressed on while his tanks were mired by the sheer weight of bodies and his Space Marines brought to a standstill. At his side were the Victrix Guard and the Talons of the Emperor.

The fields of Hecatone were pandemonium. The brother-on-brother battles of the Heresy had once seemed the height of madness to Guilliman. That was before he had fought directly against the powers who had manipulated his brothers, poisoned their hearts and brought mankind close to apocalypse. To fight daemons was to fight nightmares. They were the fever-sick imaginings of the mad and perverted, the lonely and the afraid. Every whim, every dark desire, every wayward thought was a seed that grew in the churning of the warp. Legions of daemons trod the soils of Terra during the siege. For a long time, Guilliman questioned why his father had kept the secrets of the warp to Himself. He had fought daemons so many times that their impossi-bility became normalised. But it was only after his awakening and his exposure to the Cicatrix Maledictum that he truly understood what the Emperor had been trying to do, that these things were not his father's true enemies, but rather their source was. Revealing the truth of daemonkind would have strengthened them enormously, for men would never have been able to put them from their thoughts.

The Emperor had been trying to save mankind from the horror of its own mind.

The universe hung on the brink of destruction. The balance tipped so far in the favour of evil that Guilliman could not see a way to alter the weights. Off the field of battle, fate's caprice weighed on him heavily.

At times like this, it did not matter. Guilliman let free all his pretensions to order and to progress. He unleashed his skills of destruction. Fighting for mortal man was what he had been made for, freeing the Emperor to wage a higher war.

Roboute Guilliman was a living weapon.

Explosions burst as orders fought their way through the daemon voices crowding the vox-waves. Artillery zeroed in. Strike craft roared by, dropping incendiary bombs with pinpoint accuracy.

The daemons played their infernal music all the louder. Guilliman was cleaving his way through their mightier soldiers now, tall champions, rot-gutted warlords, giant things with maws of tentacles. He smote a many-eyed, elephantine beast down, and was through to a macabre marching band of flautists playing perforated shinbones, and bagpipers wheezing into living stomachs. Drums with screaming faces, bells that wept, all manner of madness flashed before his eyes before the fires of the sword consumed them and rendered them into ash.

Guilliman cut down a wailing plaguebearer and found himself in an open space. Six gigantic beings shambled to encircle him. Diverse in type, they were fat and they were thin, they were miserable and they were jolly. But all were rotted. All stank. All bore gigantic weapons of rusted iron and greening bronze.

'Well, well, well, if it isn't the Anathema's most tedious son,' said one, waddling forward to take position as their spokesman. He unhitched a flail of rusting chains and mossy stone skulls from his shoulder. *'I've been looking for you. I am Septicus Seven, Seventh Lord of the Seventh Manse, as I'll tell you freely. No mortal can name and keep me in his power, and certainly not you.'*

Colquan burst into the ring in a welter of green blood as Guilliman roared and swung back his flaming sword. Septicus Seven chortled and whirled his flail around his head.

'Let's have at it then, Roboute Guilliman,' he said. *'I've been looking forward to this.'*

Daemonic iron met divine fire. The shockwave battered at the giants, forced the lesser beings back. Septicus held up the smoking remnants of his weapon. Colquan called his Custodes to his side. The Sisters emerged alongside them, then the Victrix Guard, reduced by half in number. The shouted orders of Guilliman's warriors seemed unimportant in that ring of flesh. The confrontation between the primarch and Ku'gath's lieutenant arrested the attention of all the universe.

'That was interesting,' Septicus said. He drew an immense sword from across his back. His dripping, sore-covered tongue licked poison from the blade's edge. *'Let's try this one more time, eh?'*

From then on, battle was joined in earnest.

CHAPTER TWENTY-SEVEN

THE EMPEROR'S PLAN

Ku'gath held back from the melee. He was content to hurl jars of cultured disease that he plucked from the racks on his palanquin into the foe. From his slimy fingers shot spears of warp energy, laying low warriors in flashes of sorcerous power. His mouth billowed stinking winds that caused ceramite to crumble and flesh to slough off.

The rest of the Plague Guard lords fought claw and sword amid the mortals' ranks. The Gangrel knuckled through groups of Space Marines, bowling them over with his wildly swinging crippled legs, smashing them aside with emaciated arms as their bolts buried themselves harmlessly in his body. Pestus Throon toyed with a half company of brightly garbed warriors. Famine smothered men under his ample folds of flesh. The mortals fought too well and too hard for Ku'gath to feel completely safe. Their tanks pushed into the daemonic horde, close to encircling his position. Large groups of their war engines had broken through the line of Titans loyal to Nurgle, wrought havoc on his warriors, and moved off to engage the Blight Towers. Artillery fire stirred the mist into agitation. Clouds of flies and buzzing plague drones kept the sky free of machines, but that was a passing advantage. The multitudes of mortal warriors on Ku'gath's side lacked resilience, and were being slaughtered. Only Mortarion's decaying sons, the Death Guard, held up the enemy and, in rare places, pushed them back.

'Curse and blast,' grumbled Ku'gath. *'This is no activity for a creature such as I.'* He lofted a dirty flask into the advancing tanks. The glass shattered upon a track guard, and a gluey mess spread across it. The tank ground onwards a few paces, before rust spread wildfire quick, eating through its plating and locking up its tracks. The guns continued to fire, until they too were corroded fast. A shell, stuck in the breach, exploded, lifting off the turret with a little pop of fire. Another Great Unclean One would have delighted at the effect of this metal-eating phage, but Ku'gath just sighed, and lethargically speared an Ultramarine through the head with a splinter of wood he conjured from the air. *'I should be on Iax, brewing a greater curse,'* he moaned. *'Or never shall I smile, not once, I swear. Why can I not get anything done?'*

Septicus, on the other hand, was enjoying himself. Not far from his master he gigglingly battled the primarch. His giant's sword thrummed through the air, catching Guilliman's weapon in a series of ringing clashes that flung out gobbets of fire and poison. Where the poison spattered the Armour of Fate, it blistered. Where fire splashed Septicus, his flesh streamed black smoke, but never did the mirth leave him.

'Why can I not take such pleasure in war?' grumbled Ku'gath. *'Why?'*

Squadrons of plague drones drifted by, ragged wings a blur, death's heads raining among the Corpse-Emperor's servants.

'I wish you would all just stop. You do not see,' announced Ku'gath to the Emperor's warriors, *'how misguided you all are.'* He leaned forward, forcing the nurglings to carry him onwards, closer to his audience. *'Your god is a liar, and a quiet one at that. He does not even speak! He offers nothing but his cadaver's smile for all your efforts on His behalf. Death is yours, and then to follow, extinguishment of your being in the wild, wild warp. But!'* he declaimed. *'If you were to come into Nurgle's garden, a different fate would await you. The Garden is a paradise for all, where nothing ever dies. Every soul, every life force, from that of the littlest virus to the greatest of beasts can rise again from the muck. There is no death, there is no pain, and suffering is a sweet and constant joy! Your lord offers no rebirth, no hope! Why do you fight for Him?'*

His preaching had no effect. The Space Marines were deaf to it.

'Very well,' he sulked, *'suit yourselves,'* and continued to kill them instead.

Squatumous was the first to be cast back into the warp. He was surrounded on three sides by the Custodian Guard and Guilliman's soldier sons. Riddled so thoroughly with bolt shot that there were more of his guts outside his body than within, he became weak. The Sisters of Silence moved in for the kill.

Alarmed at their approach, for their killing him would bring the true death, Squatumous let out a mighty fart, and decapitated himself with his own sword. Ku'gath snuffled as Squatumous' soul shrieked out of the mortal realm. That was not good, not good at all. He died too easily. Parmenio's warp current was thin gruel to the daemons, too weak to sustain them without the nexus of Mortarion's clock. They were running out of time.

'Oh, Lord Mortarion, where are you?' Ku'gath asked the sky. He nervously watched as the Gangrel engaged in a duel with the Custodian leader.

Another blast of soul force quaked the flesh of creation. Invisible to the mortal combatants, it was a painful light to daemon eyes, for it illuminated defeat. It shone upon disaster. Ku'gath hunted for the source, and found Bubondubon lying upon his back, arms outflung, his laughing mouth silenced as his corpse dissolved into clotted ooze and piles of squirming maggots.

'Oh dear, oh no!' Ku'gath said. *'Bubondubon smiles no more!'*

The banishment of two of the Great Unclean Ones was bought at great cost to the mortals, but Guilliman's army was cheered nonetheless, and pressed their advantage. The Custodians sent hundreds of plaguebearers back to the Grandfather's wards to await the indulgence of their god. They were the lucky ones. The Sisters of Silence slew them by the dozen, cutting their souls to shreds and ending them for good.

Ku'gath licked his lips nervously. Upon Septicus' shoulders the day rested. He might require some aid, thought Ku'gath. He looked about. The Gangrel fought on against the lord in gold. Pestus Throon wailed and swiped at his assailants with a madly tolling handbell whose peals sent the daemons nearby into exuberant jigs. Famine continued to roll about like a demented fleshy barrel in a storm-tossed ship's hold. Guilliman was isolated, but ever so mighty. Things looked bad.

Ku'gath wrung his hands. *'I cannot help myself, of course,'* he muttered. *'Much too important.'* He feared the primarch's blade. *'If I attack, I could die, permanently! Come on, Septicus, a drop of blood, a single drop, that is all we require for the binding to be done.'*

His nose twitched. His dismay abated. He nearly smiled. The blood was forthcoming. He could smell it trickling down time's twisting ways.

Guilliman fought with terrifying skill. He was, thought Ku'gath, a god in his own way, though one fermented in a jar, a most ungodly means of creation even compared to his own undignified birth in Nurgle's cauldron. But like a god he fought, relentless, powerful, with speed no mortal could match and few daemons either, though he was not infallible. Ku'gath was closely associated with the divine. He knew no god could avoid mistakes entirely.

Guilliman carved a flaming trough through Septicus' gut. The greater daemon's cackles rose up towards a higher note, where laughter stopped and screams began, but he wrestled back his pain, and while the primarch prepared his next attack, reached out his hand.

A tiny opening presented itself to Septicus. A long black claw caressed the primarch's arm. Though it blistered in the unholy aura surrounding the Anathema's son, it did its work, snagging on the softseal in the hollow of Guilliman's elbow and opening up the space between vambrace and rerebrace.

The primarch's body closed itself. His immune system

condemned Septicus' best diseases to swift extinction. The suit bled sealing gels that closed up the ribbed hyperplastek, but not before a single drop of demigod's blood slid out of the wound, and fell glistening to the ground.

Septicus shrieked with triumph.

'Now, dear Ku'gath, now!'

'Oh ho!' said Ku'gath, approaching something close to happiness. He held aloft his left arm and snapped his fingers once.

The noise produced was no fleshly click, but a thunderclap roar. Mouldering horns hallooed, and then so did the towers, hidden in the fogs. They turned their soul furnaces to a new purpose. Dirty lenses atop them turned upon squeaking mounts.

The mist blinked green. Writhing beams of energy squirmed their way out of the murk, one cast from each of the unseen towers. The first caught Guilliman about the wrist as he raised his blade to strike down Septicus. The second wrapped itself about his neck. The third about his waist. Each snare caught him, held him, until he was immobile.

Septicus grinned wickedly. Ku'gath wailed in triumph.

'We have him! We have the primarch!'

At Ku'gath's call, cool downdrafts stirred the mist. Dropping from the sky came the Lord of Death, Mortarion, primarch of the Death Guard. He landed, wings extended, Silence in his grasp. The earth shook.

Mortarion drew in a rattling breath through his respirator. Cumuli of mustard yellow fumes jetted from its underside.

'Hello, brother,' he said.

* * *

Guilliman struggled against his bonds. The daemon who had fought him stepped back and gloated. Battle continued in all quarters. Imperial armour pushed into the enemy. Colquan and the rest continued their fights, barred from aiding their master by the remainder of the Plague Guard lords. He could not move. The energy lash around his sword arm was the weakest, its warp energies sapped by the power of the Emperor's sword. Perhaps, given time, he might wrest his limb free. But he had no time.

Guilliman stared up into the face of his brother. Like Fulgrim, like Magnus, Mortarion was no longer a being crafted by ancient science, but something more, and something less: a half-man warped by Chaos.

Mortarion had always been taller than his brother, but as a daemon he was so much bigger that comparisons of height lost meaning. Mortarion was of another order of creature to Guilliman, a demigod remade as a monster from a child's story. Beneath his cowl, his stern face had decayed on the bone. The eyes were white, the skin grey, and ropes of mucus ran from the fleshless hole of his nose visible over his respirator. All that was human about him was inflated to preposterous degree, and gilded with insanity.

From his back two giant moth's wings spread. Nor had his wargear escaped alteration. The Barbaran plate had turned from its original white to a pondwater green, pockmarked with glistening sores and grown to suit its wearer's new stature. Chains hung reeking censers and trinkets that displayed Mortarion's allegiance to the god of plagues. His warscythe had grown to the size of a communications mast, and sprouted osseous frills. His xenos pistol, the Shenlongi Lantern, had changed the least, only growing to fit his size.

Falls of corposant welled up from within Mortarion's robes and rolled to the ground, filling the mist with ghostly faces. Daemon flies and mites flew around him in solemn circles, bearing symbols of false religion.

'I face you at last, my brother,' said Guilliman.

Mortarion chuckled. *'You make it sound as if you have brought me to heel, and will beat me in combat! After ten thousand years, you remain pompous. Look about you. I have you. I have won.'*

'You have not won yet.'

'If this is not a victory,' said Mortarion, *'then I should probably consult one of your tedious manuals to better acquaint myself with the meaning of the term.'*

'It's not over.'

Guilliman continued his efforts to free his arm while he spoke. Mortarion glanced down at the Emperor's sword.

'Father gave you His blade, I see. Or did you take it off His dead knee? I suppose it matters not. You will not wield it against me.'

'Fight me, you coward,' growled Guilliman. The flames on the Emperor's Sword flared.

Mortarion laughed.

'Do you think I would stoop so low as to fight you, my brother? Look at me!' He spread the shrouds of his wings wide, fanning Guilliman with plague winds. *'You are so far beneath me. I am mightier than you could ever be. Why would I waste my strength on crushing an insect like you?'*

'Instead you save your wickedness for my people, who cannot fight back at all,' said Guilliman. 'How noble of you.'

'Wickedness?' said Mortarion. *'Is that what you see? I bring them salvation from the hell our father created. I bring them the joy of endless rebirth. I bring them life.'*

'You cast yourself as a warlord-prophet. But you are a slave. I pity you brother, you have deceived yourself.'

'It is you who is the slave!' hissed Mortarion. *'The slave of our uncaring father, who made us to do His bidding! You who trod the path He laid out for you without question, sure that the lies He told were the truth, too stupid and trusting to question them for yourself. You never saw what He did to me. The first time I met Him He stole from me my life's struggle. It was nothing to Him, a bump in His smooth road to godhood. He took what I had worked and suffered for and He did not care! He called Himself the Emperor! What kind of being has the presumption to claim such a title? Who takes and takes the affections of His sons and gives so little in return? He would not even deign to tell us His name! You swallowed it all, poison milk from our machine mother, machines He created, things like we are. I tried His way. I should never have compromised my own principles. But I did. I was a champion of common people. I abandoned them for a galactic despot. Now I serve the people again.'*

Mortarion glared at Guilliman with milky eyes, defying him to challenge his pronouncements.

'If I am a puppet of an uncaring master, then what are you?' said Guilliman. 'A being who wallows in warp power while crying hatred for the witch? A plaything for corruption and disease? You blustered long and hard against psychic power, and claimed total fearlessness and indomitability none could match, yet when faced with death, the ultimate challenge, you failed.'

Mortarion flinched and rose up in the air, his insect wings beating quickly.

'You do not know what you speak of! You do not know

what it was like! I was shown the depths of suffering of a kind you could never understand, and as death beckoned I was given the power to withstand it.'

'I know no suffering?' Guilliman laughed bleakly. 'I saw my brothers, many of whom I loved, all of whom I respected, turn their backs upon our creator and plunge the galaxy into war. I saw humanity reach for one golden moment of peace, brush it with its fingers, and then I saw you and the others spit upon it and tear it away. I died at the hands of my kin. I awoke to a galaxy so far from the glorious enlightenment of the Emperor it resembles the Catheric hell. You turned your back on all you claimed to stand for, cravenly, without a second thought. Where was my brother who could weather any storm, whose body shrugged off poison, who would never, ever give in? What happened to him? The Mortarion of old would never have allowed this. He would have died with honour. You must have seen, as your warriors were transformed into these hulking monsters, what awaited you should you say yes to salvation. You who called yourself the strongest of us, the redoubtable, the master of any pain or sorrow! How hollow those words seem to me now. I at least know what I am. I look at myself, and though I perceive many failures I know with unshakeable certainty that I perform the duty I was created for. That I fight for the preservation of mankind.'

'Then you do not fight for the Emperor?' asked Mortarion, his voice an insinuating rattle.

'I fight for what He believed in.'

'An advocate's quibbling. You fight for yourself.'

'I remain a champion of humanity, whereas you are the lackey of evil.'

'Am I?' said Mortarion. His wings beat softly. *'Then tell me, Roboute, if our father were so good, look me in the eye and tell me that He loved us all as any father should love his sons.'*

Guilliman stared at him, his jaw clenched in anger.

Mortarion laughed. It began as a wheezing in his lungs, thick with phlegm, rattled up his dry throat, and clacked his teeth together behind his breathing mask before hissing out in puffs of yellow gas. *'You know, don't you, Roboute? You've seen it.'* He wagged one long, skeletal finger at his kin. *'I knew something was different about you.'* He leaned close. *'You spoke with Him on Terra. Tell me, what did He say? Did He plead to be released? Did He beg you to be set free from His Golden Throne?'*

Guilliman said nothing.

'Oh, my brother, it cannot be,' Mortarion said in mock horror. *'Did He say nothing? Is our father dead?'* He stood back and shook his cadaver's head. *'Of course He isn't, is He? Not in any real sense. Beings like Him are beyond mortality. You are so misguided. He sought godhood, and in a way He has what He wanted. He is a Corpse-God, a lord of death more terrible and vile than my adopted grandfather, who offers those who follow him the gift of endless renewal!'* Mortarion gestured with Silence. *'You look at this land and see only ruination. It is a shame for you that Nurgle's potential is invisible. Where you see destruction, I see but one phase in a cycle of death, rebirth, fecundity and decay. It is glorious, colourful, vital! So much more than our father's pale lies. All secrets might be known within the warp,'* said Mortarion. *'It is timeless and eternal. Everything that happens here is reflected there endlessly. Every moment can be accessed, every lie heard, every broken*

promise relived. I have been deep within, far from Nurgle's garden, into realms where secrets flock like corpse flies. I found many interesting things there. Do you know why He made us?' He drew back the scythe. *'Do you think it was for affection? I think, once I've crippled you, and you lie blind and useless in an iron cage, begging to die, I might tell you, and then your fine words here will burn in your mouth.'* Mortarion made a wet, clotted sound behind his mask. His white-eyed gaze moved over Guilliman's limbs. *'But that is yet to come. Legs first, I think,'* he said. *'You will not be needing those at all. Do not worry, my brother, my scythe is sharp, it will hurt only a little.'*

Silence descended.

A blinding light stopped it dead.

Maldovar Colquan, tribune of the Adeptus Custodes, was the first to see the girl arrive.

He was fighting the long-armed daemon with the useless legs who had cannoned through the Imperial side like a crippled ape until he stepped in its path, grasped one filthy, emaciated arm and pulled it towards him. They duelled still.

The bolter upon his spear flashed, sending explosive rounds into the thing at point blank range, blowing out craters in its flesh. Black blood poured from its hide. It would not fall. It blocked his thrusts with iron hard forearms, knocking away his blade. It carried no weapon. It was little more than a collection of bones wrapped in mouldering flesh, and its ribs were clearly visible through the meanness of its muscles, but it was monstrously strong, supporting itself upon one hand to swipe at him with the other. Filth leaked constantly from its paralysed hindquarters. Urine dribbled from between its knotted thighs. Faecal waste splattered against Colquan's golden armour as he dodged and swung. His plate could not withstand a blow from its grimy paws; only his speed kept him safe. In full armour, a Custodian Guard was immense, but he moved with angelic grace.

Colquan did not trust Guilliman's motives. He was among the few dissenting voices among the Ten Thousand who queried what the returned primarch's intentions to the Throne truly were. But he hated Chaos more. When Guilliman was snared and Mortarion landed in front of the primarch, he shouted out, urging his Custodians to Guilliman's side. Their way was blocked by a wall of daemonic flesh. Four of the greater daemons still rampaged about the battlefield, shrugging off attacks that would shatter cliffs. Innumerable lesser fiends attacked from all sides. Two of his warriors were down, their golden shapes pressed into the mud. The thing he kept away from the Emperor's last living loyal son growled and hiccupped its glee, and battered twice as hard at him with its long arms.

'To the primarch!' he shouted. 'To the primarch!'

The daemon's laugh clicked in a disease-ravaged throat. The damned thing seemed to have no voice of its own, expressing itself solely through violence and mirth. Colquan stabbed at it rapidly, driving it back. It shuffled around on its calloused lower limbs, evading every blow.

Then, at the height of desperation, she came: a young woman walking through the press of magic-born evils as if she negotiated a market crowd. A lone Battle Sister walked at her side, an escort who had become a herald. The girl was lit golden and walked lightly. Though the ground was churned to mud, her feet left no imprint where her companion slipped and struggled.

'The saint of Tyros,' he whispered to himself. He could not think of any other word. Time slowed. The sound of the battle retreated to celestial distances. His spear ceased moving. The fight went from him. The girl took a hold of something inside him that made him forget where he was.

Her eyes were hollows and her skin blotched. Atop her head her hair was coming out in hanks. The white shift she wore was marred by burns. She was falling apart, but around her was a soft lambency that grew as she neared the two primarchs, filtering between the combatants, setting the mist aglow, turning it from something foul to a net of glorious light. Colquan's gaze could not leave her. The conversation of the primarch brothers faded from his hearing. The creature fighting him ceased to be a concern. He could have died then, killed by the daemon, but the Neverborn too was enchanted. The fleshless septum of its nose quivered as she walked past. It raised a quivering finger, and spoke in a hissing bellows voice, creaking and choked with grave dust.

'An-ath-e-ma...'

One word. It swam across the air, wafting towards the girl as soft as silk carried off on the wind.

Time slid to a stop. Atoms stopped their motions. Light hung unmoving in the air. Sprays of blood made solid arches over the field, bolts hung midflight, the candles of their propulsive units stilled. An eternal cold gripped Colquan. Only he, for reasons he did not know, could look about him freely. All warriors were locked motionless in tableau vivant. Guilliman strained in bonds of living light. Mortarion had his scythe raised over his head.

But although all things had ceased their movement, so that the universe was trapped within a slice of a moment as insubstantial as a pict conjured from water, the girl still moved. She turned her head and looked at Colquan. In her face burned golden eyes as old as time, and from her mouth sprang the luminance of a star.

Within his ornate helm, Colquan's mouth fell open.

'My lord?' he whispered.

Dammed time broke through, crashing reality's clockworks back into motion. Once more, the progression of events proceeded upon its unstoppable course.

Everything, having been stopped, rushed to make up lost seconds, and occurred at once.

The gangly daemon rocked upon its ruined lower quarters, amazed at what it saw. Colquan came to his senses before it did, and swung his spear around. The blade whooped through the air, connecting Colquan to the Neverborn's neck by a bridge of arcing power. The daemon turned to strike back. As it did, its monstrous head fell from its shoulders. Its soul departed in a flurry of flies, and its body fizzed into nothing.

The girl stepped into the air above the melee. A dome of light sprang up from the ground. It expanded with light's speed, catching everything in its shining radius. Men and Space Marines staggered. The Neverborn screamed. Mortarion's weapon was caught the instant before it could descend.

A mighty wind blew up, blasting the fog away. Near the girl, the mist vanished. Further out, it flowed quickly back, revealing more and more of the battlefield, until only the farthest reaches were obscured. The sun broke through, and lit upon the broken plain. The lesser Neverborn evaporated like ice in a furnace, cast wailing back into the immaterium. The greater staggered, their bodies scourged by the girl's glow. Their skin blistered. Their eyes cooked in their heads. They howled and screamed. Mortarion, being more daemon now than human, was flung backwards, his wings bent around his body. The bonds holding Guilliman shattered to glowing motes, and the primarch surged free.

Guilliman did not pause to consider the strangeness of his liberation, but strode forth immediately, brandishing his father's sword.

'Mortarion, enough! Now you will face me, and collect the wages of treachery,' shouted Guilliman.

The Lord of Death staggered up to his feet and hefted his scythe, but he did not turn to attack his purer brother. He swung Silence backwards instead, its edge opening a slit in time and space. The daemon Ku'gath staggered through first. His palanquin was left in flaming ruins on the field, and his own back was afire.

'I will face you, Roboute Guilliman,' said Mortarion, *'upon Iax. Follow me there, where we shall do battle the final time. We shall finish this, you and I. Your life will be forfeit, and I will take your kingdom for my own. On Iax!'*

'Stop, damn you, you coward! Come here and fight me!' roared Guilliman.

Mortarion shook his head, and flung himself through the rift. It closed behind him.

'Mortarion!' shouted Guilliman. 'Mortarion, you treacherous bastard! Come back!'

The primarch let out a wordless roar. Frustration and rage boiled up through his body. He tore off the helm of the Armour of Fate and cried out up at the brightening sky. His face was red. The cords of his neck stood out. Colquan had never thought to see Roboute Guilliman wear such an expression.

'Mortarion!'

'To the primarch!' called Colquan again. 'Protect the primarch!'

This time, his warriors were able to obey.

Septicus Seven was trapped. Skin peeled in burned sheets from his back as he waddled for the warp rift, reaching it as it slammed closed behind Mortarion. He wheeled about, blinking dripping fat from his eyes. His grip on reality was weakening. His body was damaged and disincorporating around him. The earth shivered with subterranean fevers. The star fortress was coming.

The others fell, their links with their impermanent bodies cut, their souls flung out from the world back into the seething energy of the warp. Within its currents, their scattered essences would reform, and drag themselves sheepishly back to the Garden of Nurgle where they would be reborn in time from the pods of monumental gnarlmaws, should Grandfather forgive them their failure. The Gangrel joined Squatumous and Bubondubon on their journey back through the veil. The others would follow soon. Pestus Throon was completely flayed of his blubber, which lay as a discarded suit around him. The skin from his legs was wrinkled around his ankles like the trousers of man surprised while dressing. He was blind, his great plague weapons steaming in the mud. Reality pressed hard on all of them as the warp's energies raced from Parmenio.

Famine lay in his own half melted fat and could not rise. The lesser Plague Guard had been banished already, or were on their way. As Septicus watched, a flight of plague drones frittered to nothing in the air. Nurglings popped like sad balloons. The Imperial army was surging forward. Throon was surrounded by a ring of forty Space Marines, and blown apart by a thousand bolt rounds. Famine got to his feet with a chortle of triumph, only to find himself staring down the end of a Stormhammer's primary armament, and was duly blasted to pieces. Their souls passed, howling misery, yet confident in rebirth.

Septicus had undergone the process himself uncountable times, but he feared that this time was going to be the very last.

Roboute Guilliman came at him in a frenzy worthy of his brother Angron. His sword trailed a crescent of fire that singed Septicus without touching him, curling back the edges of his black soul with its furious heat.

'A truce! A parlay!' Septicus called, catching the Emperor's sword upon his blade. Deep strata of his being shook at the ring of metal on metal.

'Speak? With you? I will destroy you all!' roared Guilliman. 'All you daemons, you plague monsters, change bringers, blood worshippers, tempters. I will cast you into nothing. I will wipe your stain from existence. I shall not rest,' he shouted, bringing the Emperor's weapon down over his head one handed, Septicus turned aside the blow, 'until every one of your vile kind,' Guilliman drove at Septicus' belly, and again the Great Unclean One parried it aside, retreating further, 'is destroyed, and the galaxy is freed of your presence!'

'We cannot be destroyed!' said Septicus. *'We are of the warp!'* He swung his sword back at Guilliman. The primarch batted it away with the Gauntlet of Dominion.

Septicus could not beat the Avenging Son, not now. All he had to do was hold him off for long enough until his body disintegrated and his soul could escape. He could feel it going, feel the fetters of corporeality loosening around his spirit. By his will, he hastened the process, laughing in anticipation at the look on the primarch's face when he slipped from his reach. *'You cannot win. Galatan comes!'* He pointed a weeping hand up to the sky. As the fogs sped away, a vast shape loomed. *'Typhus is there. You may slaughter us all like swine, but you cannot bring that down! We are legion. We can never be destroyed.'*

'Maybe not,' said Roboute Guilliman. 'But I can make a start with you.'

The Emperor's sword burned bright. Septicus shrank back from its blowtorch roar. His eyes shrivelled in his head, their jelly running in thick tears down his face. He never saw the blow that ended him.

The fires of the sword doused themselves in his guts. Septicus looked down sightlessly at the weapon buried up to its hilt in his heart.

'And when you are driven from this universe,' said Guilliman, 'I shall purge yours also, until the warp is purified, and calm comes again to the minds and souls of humanity, though you shall never see it.'

No chronicle would mark Septicus' last words as worthy. *'But–'* was all he said.

Shouting, Guilliman ripped the Sword of the Emperor up through Septicus' disintegrating body, cutting through softening ribs, cooking rancid organs, slicing multiple chins and his bactridian skull, until it burst from the top of Septicus' head in a shower of gore.

Blackness exploded from the slain daemon. Guilliman's sword flared bright again, driving it into shadow, and out of existence.

The light of the Emperor burned Septicus away forever.

The sun's light was swallowed by eclipse. Galatan rolled across the sky, bringing false evening to the plains. Guilliman stood back from the stinking remains of Septicus Seven and looked about himself. He mastered his anger. The battle could still be lost.

The centre of the enemy army had been ripped out. Daemon corpses dissipated into rancid smears of black goo. The more of them that fell, the quicker the rest lost their hold on reality. The Legio Mortis were withdrawing from the field, guns to the enemy, but their battleline was hemmed in by tightening packs of Imperial Titans, and Guilliman thought their destruction inevitable. He squinted across the plain, his primarch's vision enabling him to see for kilometres, until battle haze and the remnants of the fog cloaked the distance from his view. The Blight Towers remained a problem, flimsy as they looked. They spat magic from their weapons that wreaked heavy casualties upon his army.

'Mortarion,' he said. 'Mortarion.'

Colquan came to his side. The remaining Custodians formed up about him. The earth quaked again, stronger now, as Galatan's immensity pulled at the planet's core.

'The enemy are retreating,' he said. 'Galatan is here.'

'Then we will soon know who has won, and who has lost,' said Guilliman. He looked for the source of the light that had freed him. All he saw were bodies lying before the bulk of the Leviathan. Its guns boomed. It seemed huge now the fog had gone. 'The girl,' said Guilliman. 'It was the girl who freed me.'

'Yes, my lord.'

'How did she come here?' he asked.

'Does it matter?' said Colquan. He motioned up to the star fort, black against the sky.

'Yes, it does, tribune. It matters very much. I must find her. Come.'

They located the girl a few minutes later. The Sister Superior Iolanth, pale-faced with blood loss, sat next to her. The girl's body was ruined by whatever had a hold of her, but it breathed. Her chest rose and fell very slowly. Death was coming for her. Her eyes had burned away. Her lips were scorched back around her teeth. Nothing mortal could contain that much power for long. She was out of place on the battlefield, but otherwise looked like the uncountable innocent dead Guilliman had seen on worlds the length and breadth of the Imperium. He knelt by her, and took her tiny hand in his massive gauntlet.

'Leave me,' said Guilliman.

Colquan turned away, motioning his men to stand back.

'She lives?' Guilliman asked the Battle Sister.

'For now,' answered Iolanth.

'How did she come here?'

'I brought her,' said Iolanth.

'My orders were that she remain in Tyros.'

'Sometimes the Emperor dictates unpalatable actions be taken.'

'And now she will die,' said Guilliman.

'You care for her death?'

'You do not?'

'Are you not concerned she might be an enemy trick

or a dangerous psyker now, my lord?' Iolanth was bitter, past caring about punishment.

'All I see is a dying girl,' Guilliman said. 'Whatever she is, or was, she was in the first instance a child of Terra.' He looked skywards at Galatan's underside filling the sky. Lights shone where fighter craft duelled one another, dodging, weaving, firing, exploding, in frantic dogfights. They were utterly insignificant next to the star fortress' mass. 'In a few moments, we will either be victorious or obliterated,' he said. 'Tell me, Sister, do you think this is the best mankind can hope for? Do you believe we can ever survive and know peace?'

Iolanth was surprised at his question.

He looked at her earnestly.

'I have faith, my lord.'

'Faith?'

'Yes, my lord. Faith in your father.'

Guilliman nodded. 'Sometimes, I wish I had faith.'

The girl groaned, and turned her eyeless face towards him.

'Are you the Emperor made flesh again?' the girl asked in a quiet, quiet voice. Her wounds seemed worse now she was conscious. The words were mangled, barely comprehensible.

'I am not He,' said Guilliman. 'He made me. I am His creation. I am His son, the thirteenth and only primarch, Roboute Guilliman of Ultramar.'

'You look like Him,' she said, though she was blind. She sighed, a smile spread over her face. 'I have seen such wondrous things.'

'Who are you?' Guilliman asked. 'Magnus?' He hesitated. 'Father?'

Her head lolled. A last breath sighed from her mouth.

'Who are you?' he demanded.

The girl could no longer answer.

Iolanth shuffled closer to him, her hand pressed against her injured side. 'Take heart,' she said. 'Those who die in the Emperor's grace are not lost, but shelter within His light in the everlasting empyrean. Oh, my lord, it is beautiful.' She moved a strand of hair from the dead girl's face and smiled a bloody smile. 'The Emperor protects,' Iolanth said. 'Never forget that the Emperor protects.'

Guilliman looked at the girl's mutilated body.

'I can never believe that,' he said.

The building whoop of powerful weapons charging rang out across the heavens. Guilliman looked to Galatan.

'But we shall see the truth of it in a second, Sister.'

Galatan's cannons spoke. Burning sheaths of air ignited around lances of plasma. New lights lit the primarch's face.

A plague tower was incinerated by a single blast, then a second. Secondary armaments followed in the sunfire's wake, crashing down on the retreating Titans. A traitor Warlord rocked under the bombardment, void shields stripped away, and collapsed into burning ruin. Bombs rained down further towards the mountains, engulfing enemy formations in expanding wavefronts of fire as wide and thick as the fog had been.

Guilliman watched Galatan deliver its judgement on Parmenio a while, then let the girl's hand drop, stood and walked away, ordering his generals to make their reports to him aboard the Leviathan.

CHAPTER TWENTY-EIGHT

FAMILY TIES

Needle pain pierced the blackness. A soft light illuminated the interior of Justinian's helmet. A chime sounded.

The glow came from a thumbnail back-up helmplate. All Justinian could see was a blur through the mucranoid crusting gumming up his eyes. He blinked it away.

The display was cracked. Luminous liquids trickled from the glass. Where the screen still worked, sigils announced a miserable tally of damage and injury. His armour had been running for days on minimal power consumption. He had gone deep into hibernation. Looking at the wounds starkly presented to him in beads of light, he was not surprised. If he survived he would be a while healing.

The Belisarian Furnace in his chest was working, sending his human-born healing systems into overdrive. The furnace pushed him along a dangerous path. It was keeping him alive, but it raised his temperature dangerously and consumed his body's resources. If he were not rescued soon it would kill him. How much longer he had remaining before that happened was beyond Justinian's ability to calculate.

But he was alive. The pain in his back was a good indicator of that. He tried to move, but all he managed was to shift his head. Metal scraped against his eye lenses. His body was cocooned by mucranoid excretions within his armour, and this hindered his movement further. Data runes blinked in warning. The reactor in his battleplate was running poorly and could not stand the extra power draw of his supplementary muscle fibres. He was weak. He could do nothing but wait.

He was terribly thirsty. He called upon his battleplate to provide him with sustenance. None came.

After a few moments, his armour sedated him and he drifted off back into dreamless sleep.

When he woke again he felt stronger. But he still couldn't move, and a gentle beeping in his left ear told him his air supply was close to exhaustion.

The grating whine of power saws sounded over his face. It stopped, replaced by the wrenching squeals of metal. More saw-noise followed, then the hiss of pneumatic shears and the soft yielding sound of plasteel being cut. Someone was digging down towards him. He wondered who. Did salvation await, or torment? He realised that the last time he had really thought about dying was that day in the scholam, when the stern-faced recruiters had come for him and changed his life forever.

For some reason that struck him as funny.

He was still laughing when the last great weight was pulled off his body. Not until it had gone did he realise how constrained he had been. His suit opened his breathing mask to replenish its stocks of air. He arched his back and he took in a great, rasping gasp, but he was not free yet. A length of plasteel across his chest held him firmly in place.

A slack-mouthed servitor looked down on him, its pasty grey head framed between a pair of massive lifting claws. It bent down, grippers opening, reaching for him. The thing's idiot brain perceived him as another piece of wreckage to be hoisted away. He had been saved to be crushed.

'Wait, stop!' said Justinian.

The servitor bent closer.

'Hold!' commanded a voice. The servitor stood upright and pivoted to one side. Running lights on the unit bolted to its skull blinked an idle sequence. Footsteps rasped over debris. A Novamarine in the rusty red livery of the Martian priesthood appeared over the hole. A brace of servo-skulls hovered behind him, playing scanning beams over the fallen Space Marine.

'I have one here!' shouted the Techmarine to someone Justinian could not see. 'Brother-Apothecary! Your aid please, this one is alive.' The Techmarine addressed him. 'Keep yourself still, brother. Aid is coming.'

'If you free me, I can pull myself out,' said Justinian. His voxmitter crackled. 'I want to get out of this hole.'

'You Primaris Marines are strong,' said the Techmarine admiringly. Another scan beam ran up and down Justinian's body. 'You are injured, but not mortally,' the Techmarine said. 'I will aid you.'

His servo arm unfolded itself from the side of his power plant, and moved forward and open. The plasma torch held beneath its grips ignited. The Techmarine started to cut away the plasteel bar.

'Did we win?' croaked Justinian.

'We won,' said the Techmarine. 'Typhus withdrew. Galatan arrived in orbit in time to turn the battle in the primarch's favour. The last of the enemy were driven off the station by armies redeployed from the surface.'

'Dovaro,' he swallowed. 'Did he survive?'

The plasma torch cut through the metal. It parted with a crisp ping. More pressure came off Justinian. Finally, he could move his arms.

'The Chapter Master is dead,' said the Techmarine sadly.

'What about my warriors? Am I the only survivor?'

'From this bunker, other Primaris Marines?' Delicately, the Techmarine moved his servoarm over to the other side of the wreckage. The plasma torch burned again. 'Two others live. They are in the apothecarion. They should survive.'

'That is good.' The metal came away. Justinian pulled it from his body. Unpowered, his armour dragged at him, and it took him two attempts to shift the metal.

He attempted to rise.

'Steady!' commanded the Techmarine. 'Your armour is non-functional, and you are half encysted.'

'I will stand,' said Justinian.

'Well, if you insist.' The Techmarine took a step down into Justinian's temporary tomb and extended his hand, exposing the blue and bone shoulder pad on his red armour. Justinian reached up and grasped the warrior's hand.

With care, the Techmarine pulled Justinian upright. He winced as pain shot through his legs. He leaned against the Techmarine for support.

'Take it slowly,' the red-clad brother said. 'Are you sure you do not wish to sit?'

'I am sure.' Justinian defied the pain to stand unaided. He allowed the Techmarine to steady him.

'Where is Brother Locko?' the Techmarine complained. 'Locko! Get over here, before our Primaris brother walks off on his own.'

There were servitors everywhere, digging through the wreckage of the Crucius Portis II under the direction of a dozen Techmarines. An Apothecary in white hurried over, wiping down his bloody reductor.

'I am coming. Unlike your charges, mine bleed to death if I go hurrying off to look at something new,' said Locko.

'There, you are free, and you have aid,' said the Techmarine.

'You have my thanks,' Justinian said to the Techmarine. He paused. 'Brother,' he added.

Upon Parmenio there was a silent vigil. Candles were carried through the dark streets of Tyros to the cathedral. The people wept to see the body of the saint upon her bier. Prayers were given. Thanks were lifted by singing voices to the primarch and the Emperor.

In orbit on the *Macragge's Honour* an atmosphere of a different sort prevailed. In closed conclave Guilliman and his highest officials sat in judgement of Iolanth, he upon his throne, they in chairs of black steel arrayed in a semi-circle around him. Iolanth wore a simple dress, not unlike the shift Kaylia had died in. Her hands and bare feet were manacled, but she held up her head proudly, and looked Guilliman unflinchingly in the eye.

'You admit that you disobeyed my orders?' said Guilliman. 'And that you did so to release from custody the girl Kaylia of Tyros?'

'I do, my lord,' said Iolanth. 'Though only to save you.'

'And your warriors murdered my servants in commission of this crime.'

'They did so at my order, my lord,' said Iolanth.

'Did anyone else encourage you upon this course of action?' said Guilliman.

'No, my lord.'

'Do you swear?'

'I do.'

'By the Emperor of Mankind?'

'I do, my lord,' she said. 'I swear by He who sits upon the Golden Throne.'

'Very well.' Guilliman swung his monumental head about to stare at Mathieu. His face was set with such stony hostility that Mathieu's soul crumpled.

'Lord Arbitrator, please tell this court what the penalty is for treason.' Guilliman continued to glare at the militant-apostolic.

Guilliman's Chief of Arbitrations stood from his seat. He was an old man retired from frontline duties for many years. His hawkish eye looked upon Iolanth without mercy.

'No one who defies the holy will of the Imperial Regent can be permitted to live. For defying you, she should be condemned to death.'

'And for the breaking of her vows, under Ministorum law?'

'Death by immolation.'

'Death by fire?'

'That is the penalty, my lord,' said the Chief of Arbitrations.

Mathieu could feel Guilliman's anger surging under his

calm exterior. He was a volcano ready to erupt, but all the primarch displayed was a tic in his upper lip. Mathieu was glad when the primarch returned his attention to Iolanth.

'Do you repent, Sister Iolanth?'

'I have nothing to repent, my lord,' said Iolanth proudly. 'I will not ask for your forgiveness. I defied you, but I would do it again without a second thought were the moment to come again, and even were that moment to present me many other choices that would save my life, for the sake of my soul and the Emperor's love, and for your sake, my lord, I would take the child to the battle.'

'So be it,' said Guilliman. 'Pronounce my judgement.'

'For the crime of breaking the order of the primarch, death,' the Chief Arbitrator said. The room was silent. 'For the crime of murder, death. For the crime of endangering the person of the Imperial Regent, death. For the crime of unleashing an unsanctioned psyker, death.'

Guilliman stood. His presence grew beyond his stature, smothering the breath from Mathieu's lungs.

'You shall be treated fairly, for your prior service,' he said. He motioned to a pair of his Victrix Guard. 'Take her away. Make her death quick and clean.'

The Space Marines led Iolanth from the room. She looked dead ahead, her head held high.

Guilliman stared about. 'Clear the room.'

The lords and generals of Guilliman's staff got up from their seats, bowed and departed. Mathieu made to leave with the rest.

'Not you, militant-apostolic,' said Guilliman.

'I will remain, by your command, Imperial Regent,' said Mathieu. He went to sit again.

'You will stand, priest,' said the giant, Maldovar Colquan.

The tribune had a savage look on his face that made his noble features ugly. Alone in the room, he was armoured, and he pointed a golden finger at the space vacated by Sister Iolanth. 'Here,' he said.

Tetrarch Felix glanced at Guilliman. They shared a look. Felix nodded the slightest amount. Mathieu had no idea what passed between them. Had they condemned him earlier, in private? Was he to be executed? He steeled himself against the possibility. There was no greater death than that in service. He would be brave.

'Tetrarch, ensure I am not disturbed,' said Guilliman, 'and that this chamber is shielded against all forms of surveillance. Shut off the vox and picters. This conversation will go no further. Colquan, you are to remain as sole witness. You will write a sworn account of what is said, which shall be duplicated, sealed and deposited with the Inquisition on Terra, the High Lords, and my own archive, in the event that the Adeptus Ministorum decides to elaborate upon this event for their own purposes.'

'My lord,' said Colquan.

Felix left. The doors hissed closed.

Guilliman waited for a signal from Felix. When a chime notified all present that privacy protocols were in place, he looked again upon his priest. Mathieu flinched at the force of his animosity.

'What have you got to say for yourself, militant-apostolic?'

'Sister Iolanth acted under her own recognisance, my lord. The true servants of the Emperor recognised the girl for what she was, and rushed to aid you.'

Guilliman took a step forward. He loomed over the priest.

'You will not ever lie to me again, militant-apostolic,'

he said plainly. 'You are lying to me now. You even convinced Sister Iolanth to lie under oath. By the Throne, man, what deviousness is present in you.'

'My lord, if I may–'

'You may not!' Guilliman's shout was sudden and terrifying. 'This was your doing,' he said calmly again. 'A good man lies dead. My warriors turn upon one another. A champion of the Emperor is grievously wounded, another is executed, and all this for no other reason than your arrogance. You believe yourself to be better informed than I. I want you to understand now that is not the case.'

'I swear, Iolanth did not act upon my orders,' said Mathieu.

Guilliman growled deep in his throat, an inhuman sound that should never have emanated from so perfect a being. It struck fear into Mathieu that he could not hide.

Guilliman snorted in contempt.

'You disobey my orders again. You lie. Confess. You were responsible.'

'My lord regent…' Mathieu began. He looked into Guilliman's eyes and saw the fury that would consume him if he dared deny again. 'You saw what happened,' he said instead.

'Confess, preacher,' said Guilliman. The heat of anger coming off him beat at Mathieu. 'Tell me that you did it. I want to hear you say it.'

Mathieu took a step backwards. 'Did you not see! Your father was on the field with us, working through the child,' said Mathieu. 'She was a vessel for your father's power, chosen by Him. His will worked through her!' He retreated further as Guilliman advanced on him. 'She threw back the daemons. No child could have done that! A golden light issued from her… The Emperor was there, He was with us, all around us. He helped you win! The Emperor is with you!' gabbled Mathieu.

'Was he now?' said Guilliman. 'I saw unbounded psychic ability let loose. It could have come from any source, not least the gods who are rival to my brother's patron.' Guilliman leaned forward. A vein pulsed in his broad forehead. 'You speak, you priests, as if you know my so-called father, as if you are privy to His will and His word, as if He would speak through you!' His fist clenched. Out of his armour he seemed more dangerous. 'You have never spoken with Him. Not one of you damnable fanatics has ever exchanged so much as a word with the Emperor. I lived with Him. I fought at His side for centuries. I studied with Him. I learned of His dreams for mankind from His own lips and I raised my sword and spilled my blood to make them a reality!'

'But there are visions–'

'There are lies!' shouted Guilliman. 'I am the only living being to have spoken with the Emperor for ten thousand years. Ten thousand years, Mathieu, and yet you dare to suppose you know His mind? You priests burn, maim and condemn on the basis of supposition. You practise your barbaric religion in the name of a man who despised and wanted to overthrow all of these things. The Emperor's purpose was to lead us out of the darkness. You, Frater Mathieu, you and your kind *are* the darkness!' He turned his head aside in disgust. 'These feats of faith can be explained by the workings of the empyrean. No god need be invoked, and if one is, it is rarely the thing that is called upon. There are beings in the warp that hearken to such entreaties. I assure you they are not gods, and the Emperor is not one of them. None of what you believe in can be trusted. None of it!' His voice rose to a condemning shout that echoed off the marble walls. Colquan looked shocked. Mathieu was battered to his knees. He bowed his head and cowered.

Guilliman reined his anger in, his voice fell to a harsh whisper. 'You cannot be trusted.' He swallowed and continued in more measured tones. 'The man that created me did His job well. The battle would have been won without any intervention from the powers of the warp. That girl was a psyker of rare ability, nothing more, whose presence on the field could have done a great deal of harm. By ordering Iolanth–'

'But, my lord, I ordered nothing!'

'Do not interrupt me!' Guilliman said. He held up his hands as if he were going to grab Mathieu by his homespun robes and haul him up into the air and crush his skull, but his fingers stopped short of the priest, where they trembled with rage. 'By ordering Iolanth,' Guilliman repeated, 'to bring her to the battle, you risked the annihilation of all our forces. If she had not mastered her ability, if she had become a conduit into the warp...' Guilliman bared his teeth.

Mathieu had never suspected the primarch might harbour such depths of rage. Guilliman had always been described as such a bland fellow, a competent genius untroubled by the miseries of unbounded humours. In the scriptures it was his brothers, and mostly the traitorous fiends at that, who had exhibited the unsaintly traits of anger. But the primarch was angry, and it was a primordial rage born in the hearts of tortured planets and fast-burning stars. In the brunt of his fury was the anger of the God-Emperor Himself.

Mathieu quailed, and yet he felt the beginnings of religious ecstasy creep into his gut. The thought of being destroyed by Guilliman, of falling to the Emperor's only living son, almost undid him.

Guilliman recoiled from the adoration shining from Mathieu's eyes. 'You disgust me. I will not kill you. I cannot. I miscalculated, choosing you. I should have appointed another parasite to your position, like Geesan and the rest. Instead I thought it best to have an inspiring man by my side, to make a virtue of your religion. And this is the repayment I get for giving weight to your faith? You could have killed us all! Chaos has tried to trick me several times – me! Do you think you are below its attentions? It will use anything to see our species fall. Be sure that your faith does not give it an open gate into your heart.'

'You saw, my lord. You saw your father's light!'

'He is not my father,' Guilliman said. 'He created me, but I assure you, priest, that He was no father. King Konor was my father.'

Mathieu blinked at him. 'My lord, please.'

'Listen to me. You live by my indulgence alone. You may have manipulated Tetrarch Felix. You may even have hoodwinked me. Enjoy your success, it shall never happen again.' Guilliman extended his fist. Again, Mathieu thought the primarch meant to strangle him, but he pointed a single, accusing finger. 'Disobey me again, Mathieu, either the letter of my orders or the spirit of my leadership, or if you so much as varnish a single one of my words, then I shall commit you to the cleansing flames your cult is so fond of, no matter what ramifications such an action might have. You might seek to gather more power to your religion by winning me over. I say it shall never, ever happen. I will never give myself over to worship of the Emperor. I will not put myself in thrall to you and all the other priests. I tolerate the Adeptus Ministorum as a necessary evil. Do not force me to reevaluate my position.'

Mathieu abased himself on the floor.

'I seek only to serve you, my lord.'

'We are done here.' The primarch's rage turned off. The heat left the room. He seemed smaller again.

'Watch your step, priest,' said Colquan. 'The Lord Guilliman might not move against you, but there is nothing stopping me.'

'Colquan,' said Guilliman. 'Enough.'

Colquan pointed at Mathieu.

'I am watching you.'

'Colquan!' Guilliman went to the door. 'Guard, I am finished.' His voice was hoarse with rage.

The doors opened. Mathieu got up off the floor and called after him.

'One day,' Mathieu said. 'One day you will see, my lord! You will see the truth! That day will be a glorious day, a thankful day. I shall not relent in my attempts to save you! I cannot! It is your father's purpose for me!'

Captain Sicarius stood to attention and saluted as Guilliman walked out, then he and his Victrix Guard fell into line behind Colquan. The balance of Primaris Marines to Space Marines had shifted in the guard. Those that had fallen in battle had been replaced by the newer breed.

'You will see!' Mathieu called. The doors slid closed, leaving him alone.

'The Emperor watches us all,' he said.

He clasped his hands and closed his eyes in prayer.

'Glory, glory,' he whispered. 'Guilliman sees! He begins to see! Glory, glory.'

Night and day aboard a vessel are arbitrary things. Turn down the lights, and lo! it is night. Flick a switch again, and so it is day. Power like that was once the province of gods.

Roboute Guilliman sat alone in a night of his choosing. The scriptorium was empty. The ship's life went on beyond the sealed doors, but within, in the silence, Guilliman could fool himself that he was alone in the small hours and the stars outside shone for him alone.

He was at his desk. Nothing much had seemed to change since the last time he had had a few minutes to sit and think. Datascreed continued its endless scrolling down his displays, but where usually he would take it in as he worked, and act upon the most urgent items in the middle of whatever else he was doing, this time the primarch spared none of his mind for it. Lines of data were born into green text, pushed down the display and died in the dark of the screen's bottom without him seeing them.

Guilliman's every thought was directed towards the stasis unit given to him by Yassilli Sulymanya and the book that it contained. For now, the container was closed, nothing more sinister than a wooden box decorated by a plain pattern on the lid. But it dominated his desk. He was reminded of the box of woes from an ancient legend no one in the current age remembered.

He debated opening it and reading the book inside.

'There will be no hope beneath it,' he warned himself.

Guilliman had never read the book in the box. He had refused at the time it was published. Having never made the same decision about any other book, he had made a public point of ignoring this one. Back in the Age of Enlightenment, Guilliman had always thought of himself as one of the more reasoned of the primarchs. He had been a man of learning, rationality was his first and last resort, and yet he had ostentatiously condemned this work. Why? He had done so to please the Emperor, as he did everything back then, but that was not the only reason. He should have made his own mind up. He should have read the arguments and addressed them, not dismissed them. The creed of the Imperial Truth he stuck to so hard was just that, a creed. It was flawed, and in large part based on a lie.

His refusal was a calculated insult. Lorgar and he had never seen eye to eye. Guilliman was a rationalist, Lorgar was a quester after metaphysical truths. Faith was his mode of thought, and Guilliman had disdained it. The Word Bearers' way of war had annoyed him. How petty of him. He knew by spurning his brother's beliefs so bluntly he had hastened the end of everything the Emperor believed in.

Professed to believe in, Guilliman corrected himself. He had never had chance to speak with the Emperor about the truth. The war prevented it, and when it was over, the Emperor was gone beyond communication. Only that one time upon his return to Terra had Guilliman been in His presence and received something more from his creator other than silence.

He thought back on the meeting, as he often did, still unable to reconcile what he thought he had seen with what should have been possible.

Maybe, he thought, I did not read it because I was afraid that Lorgar was right.

How can I know without reading it? He did not care that he had wronged Lorgar, but that he had abandoned his own intellectual rigour. He had been a fanatic as much as Lorgar was, after his own fashion.

Theoretical: I must set this right. Practical: I must read it.

Guilliman flipped open the lid of the box. The book was slender and rested inside a shallow compartment bathed in the still light of the stasis field. It was so old, almost as old as him. Together they were relics of another age, time-lost things.

In appearance the book had nothing that suggested the power it possessed. But it was powerful, and so disruptive that Guilliman himself had banned it after Horus' betrayal. Every copy that could be found was burned, its words deemed tainted with a traitor's lies. It was expunged from history, scraped out of the record. People had died to protect it. The faithful called them martyrs, but the Imperial Cult had been small and ridiculous and he had ignored it. By then, the damage had been done. The thoughts were out, a memetic virus spread from mind to mind. It had no cure. The writings in this book, the thoughts and beliefs of an arch-traitor, were the foundation of the Imperial Cult.

He speculated if the high priests of the Ecclesiarchy were aware of this fact.

Often the book was poorly printed, dashed out of underground presses in furtive acts of samizdat. This one was finely made, the property of a rich man or woman. That could have explained why it had survived. The lonely title was emblazoned on the cover in flaking golden leaf stamped into light brown leather. There was no author's credit. The skin oils of its owner stained the lower right-hand corner of the cover. The sole trace of a person ten millennia dead; the book had been read many times. Guilliman wondered what manner of person they had been. Imagining was a fruitless exercise that yielded an infinity of theoreticals with no resultant practicals. A waste of time. He cut dead the trains of thought.

Imperial Gothic had evolved since the book was written; even the highest, most ossified form had been dragged out of shape by the tides of change. The script on the book was of the oldest kind. Reading it brought a sudden flush of memories to the primarch. They intensified Guilliman's feelings of displacement, and he almost abandoned the idea in favour of destroying the book and its box.

He did not. His finger depressed the hidden stud, shutting off the stasis field. He stared at the book some more.

He picked it up. The leather was dry and flaking. The paper smelled as old paper does: a fusty sharpness, the smell of hidden wisdom and dying memories.

Ten thousand years after Lorgar Aurelian set pen to paper to create this tract, Guilliman began to read it.

Rejoice, for I bring you glorious news.

God walks among us.

So ran the first two lines of the *Lectitio Divinitatus*.

ABOUT THE AUTHOR

Guy Haley is the author of the Horus Heresy novels *Titandeath*, *Wolfsbane* and *Pharos*, the Primarchs novel *Perturabo: The Hammer of Olympia* and the Warhammer 40,000 novels *Dark Imperium*, *Dark Imperium: Plague War*, *The Devastation of Baal*, *Dante*, *Baneblade*, *Shadowsword*, *Valedor* and *Death of Integrity*. He has also written *Throneworld* and *The Beheading* for The Beast Arises series. His enthusiasm for all things greenskin has also led him to pen the eponymous Warhammer novel *Skarsnik*, as well as the End Times novel *The Rise of the Horned Rat*. He has also written stories set in the Age of Sigmar, included in *War Storm*, *Ghal Maraz* and *Call of Archaon*. He lives in Yorkshire with his wife and son.

YOUR NEXT READ

LORDS AND TYRANTS
by Various Authors

Many are the horrors of the 41st Millennium, from alien tyrants to dark lords in the grip of Chaos. But arrayed against them are champions of humanity, who fight to defend all that is good in the galaxy. These 16 short stories showcase some of these heroes and villains.

For these stories and more go to **blacklibrary.com**, **games-workshop.com**, Games Workshop and Warhammer stores, all good book stores or visit one of the thousands of independent retailers worldwide, which can be found at **games-workshop.com/storefinder**